LEPER ERRANT

FALLON O'NEILL

World Castle Publishing, LLC
Pensacola, Florida
Copyright © 2026 Fallon O'Neill
Hardback ISBN: 9798891264922
Paperback ISBN: 9798891264939
eBook ISBN: 9798891264731
First Edition World Castle Publishing, LLC, February 15, 2026
http://www.worldcastlepublishing.com
Licensing Notes
Cover: Nix Whittaker
Editor: Karen Fuller

PROLOGUE

Sunlight cast a sickly pall over the Cité du Vermillion, rippling in golden mists upon its salons and smokestacks. Under the elevated railways lay fissures into poverty, alleys segregated into densely packed slums in the shadow of the Grande Chateau — a baroque palace in a sea of steel. Such a site dominated the ringed districts, visible from every apartment and palace, its opulence smothered by smoke and steam. Approaching its facade, ornithopters and magnificent flying machines howled over labyrinthine streets, escorting the swollen balloon of the *Tarrasque*. The iron jaws of the palace hangar yawned open — sirens sounded. The dirigible was swallowed whole and docked upon an interior pier. Operating in single file, the Imperial Guard, with their rifles and thrice-cocked hats, made way at once for the fleet's passenger.

"So returns the Fool General," they sounded, trumpets at their lips.

The fanfare made him wince. Flanked by the bright red banners of the fleur-de-lis, Pierrot thrust open the silver doors without regard for formality or etiquette. He mimicked the goosesteps of accompanying soldiers, boots jingling with plodding thuds down the Hall of Mirrors. Dressed in a poorly tailored uniform, Pierrot was pale and thin, his face marked by a black mole on his right cheek. His garments were ill-fitting, ruffed at the elbow, trousers exposing his weak ankles, though not without bits of military finery — epaulets, ribbons, and dozens of medals. He was a rococo clown with a history of violence.

The operations in the colonies had been a mad success.

Upon reaching the Round Room, Pierrot was greeted by colonnades, marble tiles and oil paintings framed along the high walls. Even with open windows, the air was hot and humid, reeking of stale tobacco, perfume, and unwashed bodies.

He almost preferred the colonies to the capital city. At least the settlers could be pacified without a fuss. Here, he had to play nice with the esquires and courtesans flocking to the emperor like crabs on a crotch.

"Ah," cooed the chamberlain, "General Pierrot. His Imperial Majesty was not expecting you so soon." He was a louse of the aristocracy, crowned with a periwig and dressed in lavish pastels. "I trust your flight was a pleasant one?"

"You may dispense with the pleasantries," Pierrot snipped. "I'm here only at the behest of the powers that be. Where is he on today's schedule?"

"I assure you, while His Imperial Majesty is quite 'intrigued' by your reports—"

"Let me guess." Pierrot eyed the ticking clock. "He's entertaining our delegates, no?" He raised a thin eyebrow. "I assumed as much and prepared accordingly."

"I beg your pardon?"

"I've taken the liberty of bringing tribute for," he swallowed a mouthful of spit, as speaking that title always made him nauseous, "His Imperial Majesty." His lips curled into a faux smile, masking his bitter annoyance. "Are they gathered in the usual room?"

"Yes, they are. I'll see if he'll accept your audience."

"Excellent." Pierrot clapped his gloved hands, and a host of manservants emerged with cloche and dish at hand. Dwarfish in stature, his entourage was selected to make the Fool General seem taller than in truth. "Well then," he said. "Don't keep me waiting."

"May I ask what you've brought?"

"Let's not spoil the surprise," Pierrot winked, "but I think he'll enjoy it."

The chamberlain bowed and obeyed, turning to the inner apartments. Left to his own devices, Pierrot stared at the fresco on the far ceiling—depicting an allegory of the spheres with the sun at its heart, beaming upon the chamber as an icon of absolutism. It was sickeningly garish. A testament to the emperor's narcissism and obsession with painting himself as God's gift to the nation. Moments of silence passed. It wasn't long before Pierrot's impatience got the better of him. He ventured into the Banquet Hall on his own accord, minions trailing not far behind. He swung open the lacquered doors and marched on, smiling and waving at the peerage, who stifled smirks at his audacity. Pierrot carried on, all but prancing to the court's amusement.

Of course, such pretense quickly ran dry.

Emperor Louis glowered at the Fool General from across the table. "You have my permission to speak, Lord Pierrot." With silk stockings and a waistcoat, bouffant and bib, he was the spitting image of decadence. Great locks of auburn hair flowed down Louis's shoulders, and his face was white with powder. Slicing into a swan leg with a silver knife, he extracted a buttery morsel and sipped at a flute of bubbling wine. "What news in Othello?" he asked.

"Oh, just your usual massacres," Pierrot said. "For the enemy, of course." He was content to reach for a passing brandy. "Suffice to say, we have taken ample prisoners for interrogation and entertainment. My men are working most diligently on the matter." He raised the glass in a mocking toast. "Rest assured, our borders will expand soon enough."

The Fool General made his way down the table, eying the feast of succulent poultry before him, consisting of swans and herons, pineapples, pomegranates, and other delicacies from the colonies in Othello and Khand. Coffee was a popular treat served in cups and saucers of fine porcelain. He plucked a bit of brie en croute and popped it in his mouth.

"Is that all?" Louis asked.

"Not remotely," Pierrot said, his mouth full of molten delight. "They not only surrendered but also accepted terms of vassalage."

That caught Louis's interest. "Did they now?"

Pierrot sneered. "I didn't give them a choice."

The fires of war were fresh in the Fool General's mind, crackling, as memories of screams filled his ears. When he lounged on the deck of his dirigible in a satin robe, cognac at hand, conducting in tune to a cacophony of cannonfire. Under his orders, the *Tarrasque* made its descent to the city of Othello. Volley after volley, the guns fired into its sandstone battlements, reducing the walls to smoldering pyres, inching toward the sultan's palace.

"But, sir," a lieutenant objected, "the fire!"

"Consider it our dramatic entrance," Pierrot said, dismissing his protests with a wave. The dirigible had caught fire as burning debris fell in torrents upon its deck. He did not care. Even as the crew reached for extinguishers, he spun around and snapped. "Leave it! Now, then," he clapped, "lights!" Electric beacons shone upon the high stone balcony as the sultan winced in horror. "Ah, your lordly corpulence. I've been looking for you." Pierrot held a microphone to his lips, basking in the ambient flames. "How's the view from up there?"

"Pierrot," the sultan shouted, "I demand you cease your attack!"

"I'm sorry, you'll have to speak up." He twirled the cord around his finger. "Can't quite hear over your people's dying screams. Anyway." He shot his gunners a nod. "You've been a thorn in His Imperial Majesty's side for quite some time."

"That bastard is not my emperor, nor would I kneel to you even if he were."

"Oh, but I think you will," Pierrot said. "Judging by my legions alone versus your garrisons, your odds of surviving the siege are, frankly, pitiful." He sighed. "I understand the glory of being a martyr to your people, but part of my cunning plan is the lack of upstarts to revere your noble sacrifice. Tilting the scales, as it were. If you take my meaning."

"I know you'll butcher me the moment I leave my manor."

"Not necessarily," Pierrot said. "Your conspiring neighbors survived my little skirmishes when they 'took the knee.' What's to stop you from quitting while you're ahead?" There was a long pause, punctuated by the screams of innocents being butchered at the Fool General's command. He raised his glass, and a servant refilled his glass with the finest brandy.

"It's your choice," he said with a sigh. "Surrender or extermination. Life or death. Know that I honestly couldn't care less what you chose."

Silence stung the air. The sultan drew his ceremonial sword from the balcony, no doubt in an act of defiance, only to drop it several stories into the courtyard below.

"Sir," asked a sergeant, "are we really going to spare them?"

Pierrot grinned madly and cupped the microphone. "Of course not," he said softly. "Send in a firing squad. Start with the youngest and hang them where the people can see."

Within the hour, Othello was reduced to ash and smoke. Pierrot watched in giddy awe as his tactics paid off. The sultan had been dealt with, and the city silenced. He capered about the ruin as the sun rose, basking in the aftermath of summary executions. Pierrot was nothing if not thorough. Then he noticed something amidst the rubble—a passage beneath the Grand Mosque, perhaps the remnants of an undercroft. That much piqued his curiosity.

"I've heard you've also brought tribute from our new vassals?" asked a gourmand.

Pierrot snapped back to the present, surrounded by the Imperial Court once more. Fattened by politics and pretense, the emperor kept them pacified with hunting trips and contests of favor. It was how he maintained a centralized state. Those who saw through his facade were well aware of the issues plaguing the Empire—crippling poverty, overexpansion, the decline of feudalism, and the war with half of the world—and often sought to succeed.

That was when Pierrot was let off his leash.

"I've heard you've also brought tribute from our new

vassals?" asked a gourmand.

"Indeed, I have." Pierrot nodded and whistled for his little manservants to step forward, offering their silver trays with shaky knees. "I've brought quite the delicacy from our subjects. Please," he unsheathed a cloche with the enthusiasm of a child, admiring the grubs in all their girth, "by all means, enjoy. The seasoning makes them impeccably delicious."

The "seasoning" was, of course, tears—figuratively and literally.

The court didn't need to know how Pierrot had poisoned the wells, reducing the colonized to culinary desperation. He watched with callous intent as a taster took the bait, spearing a mouthful of worms with a fork. One by one, the others followed, taking in mouthfuls of pampered vermin with shut nostrils. Pierrot watched on in amusement.

"Quite…exotic," one choked.

"Indeed," said another, "the texture is reminiscent of pappardelle."

"But the flavor!" cried a third.

"Could use some salt, though," Pierrot admitted. "Never say that I don't care about the palette of my fellow courtiers. This wasn't cheap." That much was true. The price of imported spices was nothing compared to the overall expense of the war.

Louis took a bite and paused, eyes wide with surprise. "Delectable."

In this lay Pierrot's greatest strength—he was so honest in his buffoonery that no one suspected him. So effective in his strategies abroad that no one dared question him. He was the antithesis of these sycophants. He said exactly what he meant, yet toed the line between crass and candid flawlessly, letting him wield knives of intrigue better than most. The practical joke was nothing compared to his ruthlessness on the battlefield.

"Unrest in the colonies has been a thorn in our side for some time," Louis said, stifling a belch. "And you managed to pacify them in less than a month? How?"

"You have your manner of rulership, and I have my way of waging war."

"Fair enough," Louis said. "I care not so long as your claims are true." He dipped a bit of brioche into a pit of drawn butter. "As recognition, I have another assignment for you."

Pierrot bowed as low as he could. "Your Imperial Majesty," his tone was tinged with thinly veiled sarcasm, "I'm not worthy."

To his surprise, Louis stood and pushed his own chair aside. After wiping his face with a fine cloth, he bid the Fool General to follow him to the lower levels of the Grande Chateau. Perhaps this wouldn't be a waste of time after all. Beneath the palace lay the secret libraries and laboratories of Vermillion, with alchemical facilities and tall shelves of scriptures by candlelight. Huddled in the dimness, scholars pored over texts looted from occupied lands.

"You uncovered more than culinary delights in your exploits," Louis said.

"What of it?" Pierrot asked.

"What do you know of the Conqueror Worm?"

"Only bits from bedtime stories," he lied.

"Then you should know," Louis continued, "the flame of civilization was extinguished when it last stirred. Only with the advent of our dynasty have we ushered forth a brighter age and built our glorious empire." His eyes glimmered with hubris. "And yet, there are many secrets and wonders to be found in the dark corners of the earth."

"And you seek to weaponize them?"

"You understand better than your peers."

"With all due respect," Pierrot said, "I have no peers."

"That is why I trust you," Louis said. "Such 'authenticity' would be the death of you in any other court, however, I put stock in results first and foremost."

"Then what is your decree?"

Louis smirked as if amused by Pierrot's reluctant obedience. "The Kingdom of Mulgrave has uncovered something beneath their capital city. Something that could be quite useful in our conquests. An artifact of sorts. Intelligence has yet to discern exactly what, but if they've ceased excavation, that raises more than a few questions." He laid a hand on the Fool General's back. "This should be a trifling matter for you. Retrieve it for me."

"When do I start?"

"Immediately."

ACT ONE

CHAPTER ONE

Blood dripped into the clay bowl, billowing in water—a cloud of crimson. Hollow clanging echoed throughout the palace. Baldwin lay his arm, covered in nodules and open sores, upon the table. Even as the physician wrapped that limb with firm care, fluid seeped through the bandages. The leper's fist did not tighten.

"Are you sure of this?" asked the physician, his eyes glistening behind greasy spectacles. "There is no shame in rest, my liege. We may yet ease your suffering."

Baldwin stared at the leatherbound book on the table. The royal chambers had been converted to his own lazaretto, windows draped with emerald curtains, razors and saws dangling from hook-ended chains on the ceiling. A garrison of ceremonial guards stood by the door, halberds at hand. Beyond the heavy wooden doors, Baldwin heard the sobbing murmurs of his subjects. His crown lay on a cushion, tainted by disease.

"There is only shame in staying here," Baldwin said, voice raspy and wet. "I will not be a burden to my people. Nor will I waste my final days in misery." An attendant snipped a long strip of fetid skin—the leper felt no pain. "There is no place for me here."

"I see." The physician gave a solemn nod, handing Baldwin an ornate box. "Come what may, you will not live another year. Such a malady claims all who contract it."

Baldwin's mind was elsewhere, reminiscing over his adolescence. Every morning, he woke to cotton sheets and feather pillows, welcomed by the sound of bustling markets. He spent most of his days within the high palace walls, trying to capture the world in poetry.

To understand the human condition.

Despite the protests of his advisors, Baldwin would visit

the sick and dying, providing what comfort he could. Among the lanes of mud brick huts, clotheslines wove in webs above, and filth littered the slums. The air was thick with flies. Supplicants asked for alms with palms cupped, eyes milky with a fevered will to live. A crone uttered a pitiful wail, toothless words muffled by a shawl. Baldwin pushed past his councilors and embraced her warmly. Dry earth shifted underfoot as he knelt. Her flesh was cold and damp; fluids wept against his fine robes, and tears trickled onto his neck. One by one, he tended to the pariahs, passing out provisions from the palace, enough to sate their hunger for a day or two.

"However," the physician continued, ushering his liege's thoughts to the present, "this morning of spring is fair indeed. Even if to embark on a doomed journey."

Baldwin opened the chest, revealing a bronze mask to cover his face on the unforgiving road. A mask of eye-slits and stoic expression, suitable for a man of his affliction.

"Indeed." He stood and took the mask with a bow. "Thank you for your service. All of you. May you serve the regent just as well."

He gazed out the window upon the arid vistas sprawling across the Holy Land of Golgotha, rough on the feet, while gray shrubs sprouted from the uneven hills. Further still, old olive trees and cyclopean pillars loomed in the countryside, if one knew where to look—memories of antiquity. Baldwin smiled, watching the goatherds tend to their flocks.

"You will be honored and mourned," the physician said, "Good King Baldwin."

"I am not your king." The leper donned the mask with a form-fitting click. It covered his noseless face, stifling the flow of putrid bile. "Not anymore."

Taking the journal, he turned to the threshold—the royal guard stepped aside. Baldwin pushed open the doors, feeling a springtime breeze against his lips, where he could still sense it. He took a deep, ragged breath. It had been a long time since he felt such a thing. As he opened his eyes, the steeples seemed to loom inward, and death knells tolled across the Holy City. Petals rained upon his pauldrons. Step by step, Baldwin moved along the crowd. His people flanked either side of the street, heads bowed in grief and reverence. They offered him dried herbs, baskets of bread, and other tokens of goodwill. Baldwin took nothing for the mundane had long lost its meaning. Poem after poem, he had written on his deathbed, channeling hope into fevered stanzas, until he summoned what strength remained. He took up the Broken Blade, choosing to live the epics he so admired — to abdicate his throne. Baldwin carried on, tears hidden beneath the mask, until the Pilgrim's Gate closed behind him with a firm, final lock. Embarking on the road to nowhere, he opened the journal. Its pages were blank, just as he had requested.

———

When Baldwin awoke, muted sunlight shimmered through the dense forest canopies. His mask was moist with blood and hot breath. The campfire was a pile of dying embers, shimmering off logs and dead leaves, swallowed by black-barked trees. Silence stung the stagnant air. And yet, the leper was not alone. Not entirely.

"Sorry. Didn't mean to wake you," Gipi said, fiddling with the pegs of her lute. She was dressed in motley garb and a sagging cap and bells, lips carved into a scarred smile, dirk and sickle sheathed to her tight belt — a troubadour and court fool. "Sleep well?"

"As well as one can," Baldwin muttered.

The leper's bones seemed to crack as he stood, reaching for the Broken Blade by his bedroll, stabbed into the earth like a grave marker — hardly three-quarters of an executioner's blade.

He opened his book and scribbled a few more lines.

I cannot endure a life wasted in misery. Though my body is rotting, I shall do good wherever I can. Such is my will. My mission. My purpose.

Lost in worsening fever, he mulled over another canto for his epic. Until he saw a little blue thrush — a rare beauty in a cruel and unforgiving world. The bird was perched on a hollow trunk, pecking for grubs. Baldwin smiled, scribbling half a stanza in his journal, until a thunderous boom echoed in the distance — the thrush took startled flight.

"What was that?" Gipi asked, bells jingling as she jerked her head aside.

Baldwin did not reply. The smell of sulfur and gunpowder passed as quickly as it came.

The jester stood and brushed filth off her boots. "At any rate, shall we set out?"

"Indeed. We've lingered too long," Baldwin said, shutting the book.

The wayfarers resumed their trembling trek down the road. Black pools of water littered its muddy trails, as towering trees leered on either side, their skeletal branches clawing at the mists, conspiring to blot out the sun. The Old Road wound through wooded cemeteries, shallow graves flanked by headstones and statues of weeping saints, claimed by writhing roots.

The Holy City seems half a world away….

"With all due respect," Gipi said. "I don't think this 'detour' was a particularly good idea. Do you even know where the next stop is?"

"Detour implies a destination," Baldwin replied. "However, the hamlet of Gravesend is not far off. East through the Grünewald. Soon, we will have sanctity by the hearth."

"I should hope so," Gipi muttered. "Seems like a fortnight since we left the last inn."

Baldwin kept a hand over his sword's hilt, marching through the groves, unable to smell the lingering petrichor. Not a bird or beast was to be heard. The leaves were unnaturally large, falling to earth in a pall of sickly gamboge — never to grow again. Indeed, he couldn't feel the wraps sticking to his sores, even under cloak and cuirass.

And yet, he carried on through the gloom.

"Hang on." Gipi donned her gloves, drawing a pair of tongs and scraps of linen from her pouch. "Good lord, you need a fresh one. Can smell you from here." She lifted Baldwin's sleeve. "Don't know why I'm being dragged along. Then again, you'd be dead without me."

"I did not ask you to join," Baldwin growled. "You came of your own volition."

"Oh, I know." Gipi dipped a needle in a bottle of brandy. "Because I still see 'Good King Baldwin' beneath that mask. I did swear an oath in your service, after all." She peeled off the bandage and snipped at a bit of fetid flesh. "Still, what I wouldn't give for a pint or two. Maybe a room with a warm body." She chewed on a bit of tobacco. "This'll have to suffice."

"I never understood your sapphic tastes," Baldwin muttered. "God does not condone—"

"Oh, please." Gipi rolled her eyes. "I've been like this before we met. And I've 'performed' for quite a few ladies, you know. Of course, some were quite nobler than others."

"Ah," the leper said, looking away. "Yes, I often forget about that."

"I wish I could." Gipi gritted her teeth. "Before you, I'd learned to keep my blades sharp, and my wits even sharper."

"What happened, exactly?" Baldwin asked. "With your previous lord?"

Gipi laid a hand on a macabre trinket over her breast—a finger bone on a chain. "Oh, you know how 'grand' a vizier can be. But I had the last laugh. Let's leave it at that. You were one of the better lords. And I wouldn't go on this fool's errand for just anyone."

Baldwin couldn't help but smile, remembering her ballads on All Saints Day, banquets of roasted duck and lamprey pies, surrounded by concubines, and yet, such nostalgia was fleeting. Slowly, the leper's thoughts dragged him to the present, haunted by the life he had left behind.

Now, there is only the way forward....

Past the looming trees, Baldwin saw a lopsided shadow in the distance. He squinted into the mists and beheld a toppled stagecoach, its driver dead in the dirt, and horses lying in the middle of the open road — as if shot and cut down with violent efficiency.

"Brigands?" Baldwin stepped forward, shocked. "We should take a look."

"Great idea." Gipi's voice dripped with sarcasm. "Would never get sepsis from prodding a dead nag. For your sake and good health, my lord, let me do the work."

Baldwin rolled his eyes and moved aside. Pulling out her knife, Gipi examined the carcasses, while the leper noticed boot prints leading off the trail.

"Let's see here." Gipi prodded the steeds. "Dead for a solid two days."

"How can you tell?" Baldwin asked.

"Maggots." Gipi stuck her knife into a wound and dug out a grapeshot. There was a squirt of bad blood. She dodged, eyes wide with disgust. She gagged, brushing the dirt off her trousers.

Then, her eyes fell upon something — an unopened letter.

"Hello. What's this?" She picked it up. "Never seen this seal before...."

As Gipi rambled on, Baldwin approached the carriage. Its windows were shattered, and inside, he saw the corpses of a mother and child — throats slit. The leper's blood ran cold.

Who could have done this...?

A gunshot jolted him. Baldwin spun around. From the briars emerged a trio of brigands. They were clad in the shoddy leather uniform of some forgotten mercenary unit, armored with hauberks and scraps of chainmail — faces covered by high collars and hoods. One clutched a rusty blunderbuss, while the others drew snaphaunces and short swords.

"All right," one hissed. Give us your purses, and we'll be on our merry way."

Gipi slunk back towards the stagecoach. Baldwin grimaced, imagining himself as a hero of the epics, about to carve into the flesh of giants. Even as the brigands readied their blades and pistols, the leper glowered. He would not go gently. Another pointed a knife at Baldwin's throat.

"You deaf?"

Entranced by a fever of glory, Baldwin felt no pain, even as that blade dug into his blistered neck. The leper drew his sword with blind fury. His voice rose to a roar, drowning out the brigands' rallying shouts. Feeling steel against flesh, he cut down a bandit in a haze of gore, and yet, his mind was elsewhere, flooded with verses and stanzas—all yet to be written.

As the blood splashed him, Baldwin felt something whistle past his head.

....*Gipi?*

A knife flew into the bandit's throat, and the jester emerged from behind the stagecoach, clutching her dirk and dueling sickle. Gipi leapt over wreckage and debris to Baldwin's aid, quickly and quietly. Side by side, they drove their blades through sinew and leather until the leper slammed a boot into the last bandit's chest and pointed the Broken Blade at his heart.

"Who are you?" Baldwin snarled. "What are you doing here? Speak!"

The bandit had cracked his skull against a stray stone, neck tilted, and blood pooling onto the soil. There was no use interrogating the dead. The leper sighed deeply, the implications of a life taken dawning upon him. Gipi came to his side, fingers twitching over her knives.

"Who were they?" she asked.

"Scourge of roads less traveled." Baldwin wiped his blade clean, staring into his own reflection. "Still, I never thought they'd attack a king—"

"You gave up that privilege with your throne," Gipi chuckled. "Good King Baldwin is dead, as far as the world's concerned. Now, you're just another vagabond."

Baldwin turned to the stagecoach, shaking. He thought of the mother and child. What drove them from home? What terror did they feel as these men murdered them? Harrowed by the scene, he lay a torn sheet of canvas over the corpses, whispering a prayer over his rosary.

"Hey, you asked for this," Gipi rambled on. "You wanted the life of a 'hero.' Still," she picked up a stray pistol, "black powder isn't exactly cheap—"

"What does the letter say?" Baldwin interrupted.

Gipi cocked her head. "Huh? Oh, that...." She opened the envelope with a flick of her knife. "Dated a week ago," she read the hastily-scrawled script aloud.

Salutations, Men-At-Arms,

In the throes of the Great Peasants' War, our humble parish of Gravesend has fallen to occupying forces. Martial law is enforced by a mercenary garrison, the Undertakers, who are given free rein to pillage our lands and environs. My deputies and I are powerless to stop them. But if you are men of honor, seek out the Widow's Wake, our local house of ill repute. I await you there for discussion of prospects and payment.

Oscar Hitchcock, Mayor of Gravesend

"Well," Gipi folded the well-creased letter, "whatever happened, that carriage didn't make it far. And I bet you there's something else. How far is Gravesend?"

"Not a day's trek," Baldwin said. "We should arrive by nightfall."

CHAPTER TWO

With the weald behind them, Baldwin and Gipi traveled under a veil of eerie twilight. Crows pecked at eyeless sheep as flies buzzed about the carrion. Charred farms and granaries littered the fallow fields, punctuated by the odd scarecrow or tent amidst rows of crops. Low stone walls and wooden palisades surrounded the farms, as if erected by peasant militias to defend crude fortresses. Banners of local heraldry swayed in the wind, and few homesteads were left untouched by war. Most had been pounded apart, their sweet acres soured by black powder.

"Damn," Gipi said. "Is this the work of those bandits?"

Baldwin looked away. "I would not doubt it." He jotted down half of a stanza and saw a crossroads ahead, marking a handful of villages. "We are not far now."

A quarter-mile up the Old Road, their destination was already in sight—a parish composed only of a high street and a few intersecting roads, lined with tall lamps, until the damp cobblestones meandered to the modest yet gothic chapel atop the hill. Half-timbered houses flanked the open green, whitewashed and lacquered, their windows staring out from curtained pools of dim light. Vast acres of tightly packed gravestones and monuments sprawled north of the churchyard. Some bore the names of souls long passed. Others had been left blank. The soil was enveloped by a pall of pale mist. All seemed quiet.

"This place reeks of death," said the leper.

"With all due respect," the fool nudged him, "you're not one to talk."

Gravesend was a macabre town, for its trade was the crafting of headstones and coffins, and the burial of men-at-arms, and yet, it somehow had escaped the horrors of war. Baldwin watched the townsfolk go about their evening business; thin and pale, eyes narrow with suspicion, sweeping their porches and drawing water from the well in the town square. Merchants sported dark yet colorful vests, scarlet and purple, while the gravediggers wore beige tunics and solid boots, shovels at hand. Flat-topped hats were especially popular among the bourgeois, as were trinkets and baubles plucked from the battlefields. By a stone crypt, a simpleton stared at Baldwin, spitting on freshly shoveled earth.

"C'mon," Gipi kept her voice low. "Let's not loiter."

A church bell tolled. Baldwin raised his head, gazing upon a steeple against the setting sun, as Gipi returned to the high street, spying the coffin-shaped sign hung askew, which read, "Widow's Wake Inn." Gloomy as the town and its folk were, the inn seemed a lively place, as laughter and pipe smoke wafted from the two-story taphouse, illuminated by dim candlelight against lurid silhouettes. Baldwin knew they were being watched—a pair of unsavory characters pointed at him, armed with stunted pikes, glaring behind their rusty visors at the alley's end.

"Perhaps we should seek sanctuary at the church?" Baldwin asked.

"To hell with that," Gipi pushed open the doors, "I need a drink in me."

As the door shut behind them, the throng stared in bitter silence, but resumed their revelry on a moment's whim. Baldwin wove past the locals and patrons who gathered around the tables. The smell of roasted meats filled the tavern, as the barkeep polished the same clay mug over and over again, eying his regulars. Gamblers rolled bone dice on felted tables near the back, erupting into rambunctious laughter and raking in heaps of coin, while a one-eyed bouncer kept watch for cheats and foul play alike. Amidst the drunks, rogues, and sultry wenches was an open casket atop a table, occupied by a blue-faced corpse, perhaps a local author or favorite patron. No doubt the strangers had stumbled upon a lively funeral. Regardless, Gipi made herself comfortable at the bar, sampling local ales, while Baldwin watched the dancefloor's flow, as a minstrel played his accordion for tips onstage.

"Can I get you anything, love?" a woman cooed. She wore a scarlet corset and leaned forward, exposing her smooth, pale cleavage. "Got a spot upstairs."

"I—no, thank you," he managed.

Baldwin pulled that hood over his face, trying to avoid brushing arms and hands, and sat at a back table. He knew the truth. Lepers made poor lovers. The harlot was about to say something when Gipi brushed past her, holding a pair of frothing tankards.

"Pardon me, miss," the jester said.

As the woman left, Gipi slid into a seat, pushing a mug towards the leper. "Drink up." The jester chugged her ale, while Baldwin took a delicate sip.

"You're going to run us thin, again." The leper shook his head, returning the nervous stares of passersby. "What do these people want? Don't they know who we are?"

"They don't see nobles," Gipi said. "Just a pair of strangers."

Baldwin's eyes fell upon the woman again—her locks of auburn hair and emerald eyes. She laughed with the rabble, as if soliciting for a partner and payment, as one of her profession was prone to do. In days long past, Baldwin would've asked the woman for a dance. Or perhaps he would've courted her within the boundaries of chivalrous etiquette. Now, he knew better.

"You okay?" Gipi's tone was tender. "That can't be easy. I mean, never, right?"

"I took the vow of chastity for more than one reason," Baldwin said. "In part to ensure that no one else shares this fate. But no, it's not…easy."

The leper opened his journal, scribbling lyrics. He laid a hand to his clammy brow, muttering in disappointment—such verses were devoid of inspiration.

"Out of curiosity," Gipi asked, "why the book?"

"It is my legacy," Baldwin replied. "What I will leave

behind, once leprosy takes me. Of me, little is written, save in the annals of the most minor of kings."

Gipi nodded. "The fear of death is a strong one."

Baldwin continued to write and did not look up. "The fear of a life wasted. My pilgrimage is to walk the earth, and to do good, wherever I can."

"Well, if you need critique with your poems, let me know." Gipi propped her boots on a nearby stool. "I suppose you're still shaken by those brigands, too."

"Who wouldn't be?" Baldwin scowled. "I have never seen such cruelty before. Not in the open, like that." He looked up as a few patrons stood and left. "But something else is at work—"

The doors swung open, and the merriment came to a sudden halt. A squad of guards barged into the tavern, equipped with kettle helmets, pikes, and soiled gambesons—whatever they could scavenge on the field. At their head was a deputy whose slicked hair drooped low over his neck. His eyes were burdened with exhaustion, wielding a studded truncheon.

Try as he may to command authority, all Baldwin saw was a hound on a leash.

"Strangers," he called. "Lord Hitchcock wishes to have a word. Come without resistance, and perhaps we'll send you on your merry way."

By the light of the hearth, locals exchanged relieved glances.

"Under what charges?" Baldwin retorted. "Is it a crime to spend coin at the inn?"

"Charges?" the deputy scoffed. "I never said anything of the sort." His eyes narrowed. "But your kind are not welcome here. What brings you to Gravesend?"

"Just a letter." Gipi flopped the parchment across the table. "Recognize the writing?"

A fevered sense of justice had all but blinded the leper, as he was reminded of wicked constables who extorted their own people, though he knew nothing of this man.

The deputy examined the letter carefully, only for his lips to curl into a smirk.

"All the more reason to come without a fuss." He jerked his head to the barkeep and yelled. "Boil their mugs. The vagrants may be contagious."

Something snapped in Baldwin. He launched out of his seat and drew his sword, revealing his height in full, towering over the deputy. Though a cumbersome heavyweight, he was still of royal blood. And not a man to be trifled with.

"Imprudent thugs," he growled. "If you think yourselves men of justice—"

"Your pardon, gentlemen." Gipi lay a hand against his armored chest, all but telling him to shut up. "My friend here's got a bit of a fever. Sick in the head, he is. Can't hold his ale."

The guards chuckled at each other as the deputy pocketed the letter. Baldwin scowled, but slowly loosened his grip on the sword's hilt. If he didn't know better, he'd think Gipi was stabbing him in the back. In hindsight, discretion would've been wiser.

"Come," the deputy said. "The constable doesn't like to be kept waiting."

Down the darkening roads, the deputy took Baldwin and Gipi to the west edge of town, approaching a mansion upon the hill. Thorny vines crawled up the lopsided edifice, the finish on the walls was faded, and the windows cracked and grimy with dust, and yet, Hitchcock Manor clung to some vestige of prestige; its aviary piercing the sky as a beacon of authority.

A posh manservant in a ruff opened the front door. Once inside, the leper looked about the foyer, eying scarlet carpets and twin staircases. His footfalls were damp and dirty against the smooth marble tiles. The white plastered walls were adorned with coats of arms and portraits of ancestral barons, heavy oaken doors shut tight, while a chandelier swayed from the hall's rafters, dripping wax onto the floor. The deputy guided the guests up the stairs and to the east wing and slammed a door behind them.

Baldwin listened to a pair of voices behind thin walls.

"Enemies of the state, eh?"

"Troublemakers, by the look of them."

"Capable men?"

"We'll soon find out."

Baldwin and Gipi glanced at each other uncomfortably. Finally, the door opened, revealing the drawing room, complete with bookshelves, furred rugs, liquor cabinets, and a chess table. Wooden supports creaked by the brick fireplace, and behind the oaken desk sat Oscar Hitchcock, surrounded by piles of parchment and paperwork. He was a corpulent man with a balding, reddened scalp, dressed in the ill-fitting clothes of his younger years. His girth threatened to send brass buttons flying from his frilled vest, as if his rings and lambskin boots attempted to gild his greasiness. His eyes were glazed with indifference, tapping a quill against the rim of an ink jar, bound to his ledgers by reluctant duty. A set of yellowed dentures was visible as his lips curled into a false smile.

"Greetings," he said. "Indeed, it is not every day we see persons of your stock here. Please, have a seat. Both of you."

Reluctantly, Baldwin and Gipi did just that, as the deputy took his leave.

"Now then, isn't this a fine chance?" Hitchcock rambled on, but Baldwin's mind was elsewhere, staring at the landscape painting above the fireplace. How long could these introductions take? "Don't you think so," the constable finished, finally, "my dear vagrants?"

Baldwin snapped back to the present. Silence followed.

"So you weren't listening?" Hitchcock frowned and laid a bulging purse on the desk, spilling with silver shillings. "I suppose a matter of coin might lend me your ear?"

Gipi's eyes widened with greedy joy. "I'm listening—"

"Payment is of no concern to a dying man," Baldwin interrupted, sliding the purse aside. "If it is my ear you want, you may have it free of charge. My sword, however, is another matter entirely. It is one of righteousness. I trust you understand. However," his eyes fell upon the purse, "this is the reward of a desperate man. Something is very wrong here."

Gipi stared at the leper, absolutely disgusted, but Hitchcock managed a genuine smile as he stood. "Come with me." Hands clasped, the constable guided the wayward souls to the ornate balcony, overlooking the wold and weald, where monstrous trees loomed in the mist and sulfur stung the air. "I take it you've uncovered the letter I sent. One way or another."

"On a corpse, regrettably," Baldwin said.

"I see." Hitchcock looked away, feigning sorrow. "God rest their souls. I fear the nature of our predicament is nothing less than a renegade war band."

"You mean the brigands?" Baldwin asked.

"A year ago," Hitchcock's words oozed with self-pity, "I commissioned the Undertakers to quell a petty revolt. You see, what with the famine and all, many of the peasantry demanded better pay. At least softer taxes, to form committees and inquiries, and even to own plots of land." He shook his head.

"I couldn't stand for it, and the rabble was getting nasty."

"So you beat them into submission?" Gipi crossed her arms.

"No," Hitchcock retorted. "Dampe did the dirty work. I merely paid the brutes what we'd agreed upon. The warlord had the nerve to demand compensation for 'cost of equipment' and 'his men's lives,' and so, I called upon the lord's cavalry to drive them out."

"How quaint," the fool muttered.

Baldwin's gaze wandered to the night sky, his eyes settling upon the rustling trees. Sighing, he leaned on the wooden railing and indulged in the despot's tale.

"However," Hitchcock continued, "I may have, how do you say, underestimated Dampe. Since then, the Undertakers have taken to the back roads, lairing in the woods, waylaying any traveler unfortunate enough to cross paths with them. And when my lord was called to another province. Well, I was left to deal with Dampe with a garrison of less than two dozen men."

"And you sent out a call to arms," Baldwin said.

"Indeed. Of late, the brigands take to our farms, trying to bring famine and crisis to our province out of spite. And, thus far, they are succeeding." When the three came back inside, the constable glanced over a few documents and scratched his scaly scalp. "The town is isolated and, since all aid is silent, I ask you to help us."

Gipi propped her boots on a nearby stool. "Yeah. No offense, but this sounds — how do I put this, like you've dug your own grave? Coin or not, how is this our problem?"

"Would you have the blood of this parish on your hands?" Hitchcock shot Gipi an indignant glare. "And besides, what would a fool know about these matters?"

"More than you'd think," she said. "In my time in the court, I've seen things — "

"Enough, Gipi," Baldwin interrupted, calm yet stern. "I'm afraid you're not giving us much to go off of, constable. What would you propose we do about this?"

Gipi shot her companion a venomous glare.

"I say do what my men cannot." Hitchcock downed a shot of brandy. "I ask you to rid us of Dampe, once and for all." He reached for the carafe on the desk. "I shall pay for your lodging tonight and trust you'll intervene should anything happen."

"I will ensure your town survives and offer my sword in its defense," Baldwin said. "However, know that I am not a mercenary."

"Capital." Hitchcock clapped with glee. "Most capital. Bring me the warlord's head and I'm sure we can come to an agreeable arrangement for your troubles."

With a solemn nod, Baldwin saw himself downstairs and out the door. He took in a lungful of fresh air and raised his head to the rising moon, grand and gibbous with its craters and ridges. Fiddling with his baldric, the leper returned to the open street and began his stroll.

"Should we return to the inn?" Baldwin asked.

"Yeah, sure," the fool pushed past her liege, "whatever...."

The leper felt eyes upon him—cold and unrelenting. A lonesome figure stood in the mists, gaunt and gangly, draped in flowing black robes, leaning against a long scythe like a crone with her humble cane. Face shadowed by the wide brim of a straw hat, she stood motionless in the street, more like an eerie statue than any villager. No one seemed to bat an eye.

Not even Gipi.

CHAPTER THREE

Dampe lounged amongst his men in the mess hall, pouring himself a glass of port, eying the sanguine legs as he swirled his snifter. Between the raids across Mulgrave and the stockpile of resources they'd acquired, the Undertakers were ready to expand. He raised his glass and drummed his fingers against the arm of his "throne," salvaged from a carriage not long ago.

"Gentlemen," he spoke, voice slick as silk. "I propose a toast to yet another successful raid. May our coffers and goblets ever be full."

"Hear, hear," the men erupted.

Just then, the double doors swung open, and a scout sprinted down the hall. With a gray rag wrapped around his armor, he was one of Dampe's. The warlord stood and marched from his throne. The scout stunk of sweat and horseback, and must've come here in a hurry. He did not bother to kneel, hands on his knees, wheezing, catching his breath.

"What happened?" Dampe asked.

"The Manfred Boys," he managed. "They've been killed. On the Old Road."

Dampe raised a thin eyebrow. "A rival band?"

"No, two vagrants. One with a broadsword. The other, a sneak of sorts. They were on foot and stumbled upon the ambush site."

"Go on." Dampe kept a hand on his flintlock pistol, eying the open door for any sign of intrusion or betrayal. "Are you sure you weren't followed?"

"No, sir," the bandit stood. "They made for Gravesend."

Dampe sneered, imagining how Hitchcock would react to a pair of heavily armed strangers in his estate — a false promise of payment. He always had a way with sweet-talking muscle to his side. "Of course." He adjusted his ruffled collar, recalling a rumor of a king in exile. "So, the swordsman. Did he look particularly... rotten? As if he'd suffer from, say, leprosy?"

"Can't say," the bandit said. "I only found our boys."

Dampe softened the grip on his pistol. "I see." He imagined what titles and deeds the fledgling lord possessed. What profit could be reaped from such an opponent? He gestured to the long banquet table, preferring to ponder these matters alone. "Please, join your brothers."

"Aren't you —?"

"Going to send a party after them? I think not."

With a nod, Dampe bid his men to carry on without him, to fill their tankards and feast on roast mutton. He climbed up the stone steps to pay the war room a visit. He eyed the maps sprawled about the round table, anchored by paperweights — tactical plans. Gravesend had ample time to pay their fees, and Dampe was a patient, if callous, man. This was the last nail in the coffin. The time had come. With the shift of pawns to the front, they'd overwhelm the town in a matter of hours. Dampe admired himself in the mirror and rustled through his hats and codpieces for such an occasion. Announcing, let alone performing, a raid was not to be taken lightly. As a landsknecht, and a particularly seasoned one at that, dressing as garishly as possible was part of the job. With a skewed hat and mismatched pantaloons, his colors of crimson, royal purple, and pitch black would more than suffice. Calling him a "popinjay" was fine and dandy until they wound up on the wrong end of a pike.

"We rest easy tonight, men," Dampe announced, climbing down the steps, returning to his stolen throne. "There's quite a job ahead of us tomorrow. By the way," he turned to his lieutenant, "did the miller finally pay his protection fee?"

"No," the bandit replied. "Not yet."

"Very well," Dampe waved, "you know what to do. Give him extra attention."

His lips curled into a savage smirk, imagining the windmill

burning bright like dry tinder. Such wanton violence would no doubt lure the wayfarer. Deep down, the warlord knew it would be a waste to explain his motives, that he sought to bait and do battle with a king, however wretched. He was a soldier of fortune, but a soldier nonetheless. With that came a certain bloodlust. Besides, the novelty was undeniable.

Baldwin of the Holy Land....

Safe within the walls of the Widow's Wake, Baldwin and Gipi lounged at the bar, staring at the shelves of glistening green and brown bottles, ranging from whiskey to chartreuse from the neighboring abbey. Only the hollow clink of glasses broke the quiet. Cobwebs shifted against the dying hearth, and the tabletop corpse was beginning to smell, but the leper was grateful to have a moment's respite at last, now that the regulars had turned in for the night.

"Still can't believe you listened to that asshat," Gipi said.

"Listening and obeying are different things," Baldwin replied. "I was merely being courteous in the hall of our host. And you were not. Such is the etiquette of nobles."

"Well, you're not a noble anymore, are you?" The fool sighed. "Besides, men like Hitchcock will do anything to fill their coffers. Hiring adventurers or silencing opponents, it doesn't matter. Man's got a lot of blood on his hands."

"I do not deny that. But I also see a town in peril," Baldwin said. "Perhaps there is a purpose for me yet. God willing, I might accomplish something for these people."

Gipi rolled her eyes. "You can be a real idiot, you know that?"

Grueling silence followed. The leper's mind wandered to far corners of thought. The promise of a life worth dying, and the threat of being forgotten.

"Odd."

Gipi turned her head. "What?"

"This whole circumstance," Baldwin said. "Wandering

into a foreign land, only to uncover an affair such as this. It is almost too promising. I pray this amounts to greatness."

"Oh, for fuck's sake," Gipi groaned. "You're going after some bandits, not some 'giant of yore.' Besides, you don't really think it's that simple, do you?"

"Should I not?" Baldwin turned to the doorway. "At any rate, I bid you goodnight."

"Where're you going?"

Baldwin glanced over his shoulder. "To find shelter."

"Why?" Gipi asked. "There're more than a few vacancies."

Baldwin sighed deeply, not expecting her to understand his burden. "Those less noble would contaminate a bed for a night's rest. I am not among them. If something should wake us before morning, I suggest we take a look about."

"No harm in that, I guess," Gipi said.

With that, Baldwin set off for the outskirts, walking down the damp roads, watching the crows perched on thin branches, until the leper sat down on a bench among the gravestones. He stared at his bandaged palms, reflecting on his nearing death. It was hard to believe — a month ago, he was a bedridden husk of a king. Now, he was a penniless wanderer, searching for wrongs to right and evil to defeat. Such was the way of the righteous. Old verses and images drifted in his head, tantalizing him with the promise of remembrance.

And so, Baldwin set sail into dreamless sleep.

When the cock crowed, the leper raised his weary head. Dawn had crawled over Gravesend, rays of sunlight rippling through the swelling clouds, blanketing the land in a luminous haze. No fire had kept him warm. His only blankets were the tattered clothes on his back. Only a fool would have chosen to sleep in the cemetery, given a choice. Baldwin re-wrapped his limbs with care, watching the townsfolk pass by and quickly look away — a reminder of his loathsome affliction.

He was getting used to the stares.

A bell tolled in the distance, and Baldwin raised his head.

He smiled upon a familiar sight. On the north side of town was a slouching stone church with a bulging steeple in the back, walls lined with stained-glass windows depicting pious saints, as the Holy See's foothold in this land. Truth be told, Baldwin couldn't remember the last time he partook in communion, let alone prayed in mass. The leper pushed open the doors, welcomed by sacred silence. Past the pews and pillars, Baldwin gazed at the altar from afar, where a priest knelt by dim candlelight, reciting psalms for wayfarers. The leper's footsteps were heavy on the stone floor.

The priest glanced over his shoulder, eyes heavy and sleep-deprived.

He neither flinched nor gawked at Baldwin's deformities.

"Greetings, child," the priest said. "What brings you to the House of God?" The priest was a portly man, dressed in pale robes with crimson trim. However, he was of a different order than those Baldwin knew, as made clear by his flushed cheeks and the snifter in his hand. "I am Father Thelonious," he said, trying to hide a slur, "the pastor of this church."

Baldwin nodded in turn, mesmerized by the light behind the windows. "Hard to believe that peace can be even found here." He looked away. "Your pardon, father. I am simply —"

"No need," Thelonious replied. "But may I ask what brings you to Gravesend? A man of your, well, condition is clearly a long way from home."

The leper turned his head and saw a choir boy by the transept, staring at him with fearful eyes. "It is not a pleasant story," Baldwin admitted. "However, I am a soldier of righteousness who found himself along the Old Road. Circumstance and coincidence brought me here."

"I see." Thelonious reached for a bottle on the altar, almost tripping over his own feet. "Would you care to join me in morning prayer?"

Baldwin looked over his shoulder. "Should we wait for more to arrive?"

Thelonious shook his head. "They only come for evensong."

With that, Baldwin knelt before the altar, pressing his hands together as he clutched a rosary. He shut his eyes, clearing his mind. And so, whispering the prayers of the Holy Land, he sought the guidance of the divine. With the sign of the saltire, Baldwin rose to his feet. His mind was cleared of doubt, wondering what Gipi was doing right now.

She was either fast asleep or day drinking.

"Would you care for some of our ale?" Thelonious asked. "It was brewed in these very cellars. Blessed by the deacon of our most esteemed parish."

Baldwin shook his head. "I must temper my spirit for the road ahead."

"Ah." Thelonious cracked a wry smile, refilling his glass with syrupy brown ale. "Quite the oddity in this day and age. Men of your conviction are rare indeed."

"You need not compliment me out of pity, brother."

Thelonious finished the glass. "Peace be with you, good knight."

With the church behind him, Baldwin ventured tentatively down the alleys, as folk backed away. For those distracted by the morning market, he rang a tin bell to alert them to his presence. Though the bandages on his feet were already coming undone, Baldwin scarcely noticed the speckled trail of blood behind him. It wasn't long before the leper made way to the Widow's Wake, weaving past the masses. He was better off in the elements, in the shadows, lest he earn the ire of the less forgiving.

"Who is that?"

"No idea. Probably some sellsword."

"Wait, that bell. Is he...?"

"C-c'mon, let's get inside."

Baldwin pulled the hood over his face, not wanting any trouble. It was hard to tolerate this treatment, and sadly, he was getting used to it. Knowing full well the cruelty of men, Baldwin wouldn't blame them for anything short of violence.

"Gipi," he muttered to himself. "We must depart soon."

Come noon, Baldwin sat alone at the farthest table in the tavern. The floorboards creaked as he shifted on his stool. The leper stared at his pease pottage, munching on an overcooked turnip pie—a peasant's breakfast. Opening his purse, Baldwin shifted what shillings remained. When the leper stood to pay for his tab, footsteps clomped down the wooden stairs.

"Ready when you are," Gipi yawned.

Outside the tavern, Baldwin wrapped his beige cloak around his cuirass, watching his hot breath join the mists. Market Day was well underway. Wilting garlands and pitched tents lined the high street, as merchants and peddlers bartered over their wares.

Drawn to dried herbs, pottery, and rosemary breads, the bustle grew livelier with every passing hour. The smell of spices and roasted meats wafted through the air. One cart in particular sold pork sausages and pies. With pastry in hand, Gipi turned to her liege, who was busy gathering provisions. With a sackful of supplies, Baldwin left the marketplace, watching the townspeople go about their business. Children ran through the alleys, chasing a yapping pup, and the world seemed a little less unforgiving.

"Come," Baldwin said, "the day is young. Let us embark sooner rather than later."

"What about breakfast?" Gipi trailed after him. "I haven't eaten yet."

"It's well past noon. And you have your rations," Baldwin retorted. "Besides, unless you want pottage back there, I recommend you settle for the pie. Far more palatable—"

Suddenly, a wide-eyed miller shambled out of the crowd. His clothing was tattered and covered in crimson splatters, as if he'd been stabbed by long knives. The miller slumped to his knees. "P-please. The Undertakers, they…." Blood pooled on the cobblestones as the miller bowed his head. Before anyone else could help or speak, Baldwin bolted to the man's side.

"What happened? Who did this to you?"

"T-they took her." The miller's eyes glazed over. "My daughter. I couldn't pay the protection fee. So they razed my farm and slaughtered my livestock. When I tried to stop them," tears trickled down his cheeks, "they took her to their fort. Please, save—"

A gunshot silenced him. Bystanders screamed as the miller collapsed into Baldwin's arms. He breathed no more. A musket ball had found its way into the poor soul's back.

"Holy shit," Gipi gasped.

Without a word, Baldwin heaved his Broken Blade aloft and charged past the onlookers. A shadow fled on the edge of sight, down the alleys and towards the woods. Cobblestones shifted underfoot, and the leper's mind was ablaze in a fever of mad justice. Men would die for this. The pursuit took him to the church's threshold in the town square. Baldwin chopped into the musketeer's shoulder, not bothering to question or give quarter, only to howl with rage. Perhaps not the wisest decision. The leper grimaced as he carved into flesh and bone, severing tendons and splattering blood. Here and now, the world seemed as numb as his own nerves.

"Ah," Gipi slinked to his side, "that escalated quickly. Not up for questioning?"

"Justice has been served." Baldwin glowered like a bitter phantom, trying to soothe his shuddering breath. "And his accomplices shall suffer the same fate."

The fool stuck to the shadows. "Now you're just scaring me—"

An alarm bell rang through the dim streets, punctuated by the rallying footsteps of men-at-arms. Baldwin and Gipi glanced at each other, sheepishly. Neither of them wanted to explain to Hitchcock why a dismembered corpse lay on the church's doorstep. The leper scribbled a line in his journal, but did not smile. He departed in silence, and Gipi followed in kind. Trite as the mission was, there was much work to be done.

CHAPTER FOUR

The Old Road twisted around the ridges south of Gravesend. Baldwin carried on as twigs snapped underfoot. Murders of crows took flight, sounding in a dirge of caws. The smell of sulfur and gunpowder promised to lead him to the hidden fortress.

"Just follow the path, huh?" Gipi asked.

Baldwin nodded. "The Undertakers can't be far off."

"And what exactly are we looking for?"

"The miller's daughter," Baldwin said, "and this Dampe villain. Hitchcock requested the warlord's head, and I plan to bring him just that. Justice is reward enough."

"So you've mentioned. Do we have a plan? No, let me guess," Gipi sighed, "charge in, cut down everything in our path, and be back in time for happy hour?"

"Have you a better one?"

Gipi fiddled with her dirk and sickle. "We'll get there when we get there."

Side by side, they delved ever deeper into the Grünewald, as the road wound along sharp crags, filled with brambles and still water. Excursion took its toll, and the leper grew weary.

"Perhaps we should rest for a moment," Baldwin said.

"Yeah, I could use a rest."

Then came the rain, pattering on their cloaks in a haze of damp misery. Under cover of dusk, the wayfarers stopped to rest underneath an old, rickety bridge. As Gipi piled a few dead branches to make a meager fire, Baldwin felt eyes upon him again. Huddling against the flickering flames, the leper spread some sheep's cheese on stale bread. His muscles grew still more weary as he wrote in his journal, while Gipi struck a match, lighting her long pipe.

"Quiet, isn't it?" she said, puffing a smoke ring.

Baldwin did not reply, sketching an antlered skull in the mud.

"Talkative, aren't you?" Gipi stood, loosening her belt, as if to relieve herself.

As she stepped into the bushes, Baldwin noticed plumes of black smoke over the ridge.

"Gipi," he called. "I think we're close."

"Really?" She pulled up her trousers and stepped back to their fire. "Where to, then?"

Baldwin led the way off the trail. As they crouched behind rows of brambles, they spied a most suspicious sight. From atop the hill, Castle Mourne loomed like a broken molar embedded in the flesh of the earth, its walls, turrets, and rotund keep splintered by siege and skirmish, braced with wooden fortifications. The gates were left ajar, yet no guards patrolled the parapets.

"Do you think it's abandoned?" Baldwin asked.

"Hardly." Gipi began to climb the shallow ravine — she almost tripped, as stones slipped under her boots, rolling down the slope. "Shit!"

Baldwin offered his hand, but Gipi brushed it aside.

"I'm fine," she sighed.

As they descended, the leper fixed his eyes upon the sturdy gates, drawing his sword with care. He gritted his teeth, fully expecting an ambush, only to find a series of boot prints, single file, marching from Castle Mourne to the Old Road. Strangest of all were the wheel tracks in the mud, as if numerous wagons had been escorted from the courtyard, flanked by horsemen.

"I don't get it," Gipi said. "I'm no tactician, but that's a bad move. Leaving your keep unguarded like that." She gave a devious smile. "Bet you there's a ton of loot inside."

Baldwin gazed upon the central keep. "That I do not doubt."

Within the courtyard, they were welcomed by shoddy tents and sheds erected by cracks in the walls, as palisades and stacked barrels formed rows of barricades meant to funnel intruders like lambs to the slaughter. Black banners hung low from the walls, bearing the skulls and crossed shovels of the Undertakers. Judging by the dying torches perched upon the outer walls, the brigands had camped here recently. Baldwin advanced with caution, careful to avoid the overgrown patches of weeds, not daring to test what traps lay hidden. Atop the turrets, he spied a host of gun ports and cannons, facing out and into the woods, flanked by matchsticks and piles of shot, giving away the hold's purpose as an artillery fort; it had been erected recently, though its dilapidated state implied dire struggles. A few lights came from the keep itself, as sconces cast sharp shadows along the curving walls. Baldwin and Gipi came to the wooden vestibule and shoved open the double doors. The ground floor was composed of a dimly lit barracks with bunks and armories in most of the side rooms. Linking the dirty kitchen and larder to these quarters was a large common room, complete with tables, chairs, and no small amount of loot — mostly limited to stolen provisions. Rats scurried past the intruders, bits of raw flesh in their mouths. As the leper pressed on, he discovered a spiral staircase which linked the basement to the ground and first floors. A wet draft wafted from the passage below.

"Great place to hold captives for ransom," Gipi whispered.

"Indeed, I—"

Baldwin smacked his head on an archway with a thud, loud enough to carry throughout the hall. As the leper cradled his skull, Gipi lay a hand on his shoulder, if only to muffle his jingling mail. They took a moment to collect themselves. Against his better judgment, Baldwin lit a torch and ventured down the stairs. The lower halls encircled the fortress perimeter in a loop, leading to barred cells and storage rooms. Between the bloody manacles and piles of discarded clothes and shoes, it was clear that the dungeon was still in use. Cold sweat trickled down the leper's brow. He was uncertain as to who or what lurked down there until soft whimpering echoed from ahead. Slinking down the corridors, he came to a dingy cell with a straw mat and bucket, where a young woman, no older than sixteen, with mousy blonde hair, sat on a cot, so despondent that she didn't even raise her head. Bruises and cuts covered her body, though she didn't appear injured, as if the brigands saw her as "delicate merchandise."

The leper kept his distance, not wanting to frighten her further.

"Are you hurt?" he rasped.

She shook, but did not reply.

"Gipi. Get her out."

The jester knelt and fiddled with a slender lockpick. "Gimme a sec."

Slowly, the girl raised her head. "W-who are you?"

Baldwin was about to indulge in his full title, but given the circumstances, thought better of it; that a simple name would do. "I am Baldwin. And you are the miller's daughter?"

She nodded, haltingly.

"Your father sent us to save you."

Her face brightened for a moment. "Did he? Is he all right?"

Baldwin's silence spoke louder than any words. No comfort would change the truth. Nor was he a skilled liar. As tears trickled down the girl's cheek, Gipi unlocked the door.

"I'm," she managed, offering a gloved hand, "sorry for your loss."

Baldwin sighed and shook his head. Just then, dust trickled from the floorboards overhead, as muffled voices echoed from above — the brigands had returned. Once they'd crept up the steps, Baldwin peered around the corner to the ground floor. A troupe of drunken brigands had stumbled into the common room, as if returning from reconnaissance or a hunt. A muscular thug, sporting a bare, battle-scarred chest and rippling muscles, reached for his wineskin and belched, "Where did the boss go?"

"Who cares?" said an accomplice. "We've enough wine to last us a lifetime."

"Or at least until tomorrow," laughed a third.

"What about the girl?" asked the strongman. "Should we take her out?"

"Don't be an idiot. Dampe was very specific about what he'd cut off if we try anything."

"What the boss doesn't know won't hurt him—"

Without warning, Baldwin bellowed and barreled into the nearest cutthroat, slamming his skull against the wall with a gory crunch. The second fumbled for his rifle, while a third dove with shanks at hand. Gipi flung a knife into the rifleman's sternum with swift grace and plunged a dirk into another's chest, raking her sickle across his throat. As the last took aim, Gipi tackled him aside, straddled him, and pressed a knife into his groin.

"Sorry to disappoint, but we're tonight's entertainment." She twisted the blade, relishing his screams. "We've got a couple of questions for you. Answer or lose your manhood."

"G-get off me—!"

Gipi backhanded the brute without a second thought. "Firstly, where's Dampe?"

As Baldwin collected himself, he turned to the girl cowering behind the pillar. He tried to quell his violent flare, if only to put her at ease. The girl fixed her eyes upon the flagstone floor. The leper watched in disgust as Gipi's captive pleaded for his life, answering questions with half-truths and declarations of ignorance. Baldwin crossed his arms and let the fool do her dirty work. Amidst the cowardly babbling, a few bits of trivia were brought to light.

"W-we've got about thirty in our ranks," the brigand stuttered. "Boss's out on a...."

"Go on," the jester said.

"You'll kill me either way—"

Gipi inched the knife towards his testicles.

"S-shit!" he squealed. "Alright, alright. Gravesend. He's launching a raid on Gravesend. We've already bled the countryside dry. Says it's time we go after bigger game."

Gipi turned to Baldwin, eyes wide with shock. "A raid?"

The leper's heart sank. He imagined the town burnt to the ground, looted and pillaged, men and women dragged from their beds to be slaughtered or worse. All in the name of a warlord's greed. In his panic, the leper barreled into the courtyard and past the gates, deaf to Gipi's warnings. He was already sprinting to the Old Road as cannon fire and distant screams carried from Gravesend, highlighted by billowing smoke and the glow of a town ablaze.

The Undertakers were claiming their due.

———

Through smoke and moonlight, Baldwin sprinted for what seemed an eternity, only to find Gravesend engulfed in shadow and flame. Sulfur flooded his nostrils — a reek he recognized all too well, accompanied by shrieking whistles of artillery. Fire burned from behind every window, reducing the tall houses to blackened ghosts in the night. The sweltering air was singed with cries and shouts, as mobs of shadowed soldiers fought in the streets.

A thunderous boom echoed from afar.

"Cannonfire!" someone cried.

Baldwin turned to the high street — the church's steeple collapsed, blasted by an unseen mortar, reduced to splinters and shrapnel in the smoky air, as its bell clanged to earth.

The leper reached for his sword.

"You can't be serious," Gipi shouted. "There's at least thirty of them and one of — "

"Two of us, should you have honor," Baldwin retorted.

Gipi flipped her lucky knife. "I'll look after the townsfolk."

Screams filled the air. Gangs of bandits flooded the town, armed with torches, flintlocks, and swords, chasing the denizens of Gravesend, cutting them down in the open street. They roared in a rough choir of rage as the leper advanced alone.

"Slaughter them all," a brute yelled. "It's been a long time coming!"

The brigands made their way, tossing grenades and torches into the townhouses, howling like rabid dogs. Hollow iron balls rolled across the dry earth, only to erupt in a barrage of shrapnel. Baldwin charged into the flaming chaos without hesitation. Blood splattered his mask. He would give them no quarter. Corpses lay at his feet. Even the local guards looked upon him with shock and terror. A cacophony of panic erupted from the Widow's Wake; a burning silhouette against the carnage.

Without a second thought, Baldwin cleaved through the collapsed doorway, hacking his way through a barricade of toppled tables and chairs, enduring the choking smoke and sweltering heat. Before he could intervene, the bartender was hurled from the balcony by a brigand, only to land in a pile of smoldering debris, dead on impact. Baldwin charged up the stairs and ran the bandit through, not bothering to so much as look him in the eye. He kicked in door after door, ushering the trapped townsfolk outside without a word. The world seemed to swirl in a miasma of suffering as the leper wheezed in the raw heat. On a whim, he leapt out of an open window and onto a tiled rooftop, where musketeers took potshots at the scrambling peasantry below.

Maybe it was the fever, but there was a certain malice in their eyes — foul and barely human. As if a lifetime of murder and thievery had corrupted them into mockeries of men. Whether it was a keen observation or a symptom of madness, Baldwin did not know. Nor did he care. Steel clashed against steel as he cut the bandits down. Leaving a trail of blood behind him, the leper imagined himself as a skald of the north, carving his way through these unworthy reavers. And yet, the fire raged on, and the screams of innocents filled his ears. Out of the corner of his eye, Baldwin watched Gipi attempt to help an old woman to her feet amidst the fleeing townsfolk, only to be cut off by a burst of shrapnel. Dirt and dismembered cadavers were sent flying by detonating explosives. Slowly, the bandits backed away to the east. Hearing the pounds of machinery, Baldwin came to the town square and glanced over his shoulder. A host of gunners and fusemen wheeled forth a weapon of gunpowder and tempered steel, forged in the smithies of honorless men. It was a massive mortar, flanked by tower shields, the skulls of knights, and trophies from uncounted skirmishes.

"Fire!" shouted a fusilier.

With the strike of a matchstick, the cannon erupted with a deafening quake, sending a sixteen-pound shot careening through the houses, reducing them to rubble. Baldwin dared not step forward as it clanked nearer. By its side, atop a black stallion, he beheld the captain, crowned with a skewed beret with a peacock's feather. Clutching a mighty zweihänder, the captain's eyes pierced through the leper, and his lips curled into a cruel smile.

Even in his frenzy, Baldwin knew a duel was nearing.

"You there," he roared, readying his sword. "Dismount and fight!"

To his surprise, the warlord obeyed and marched towards him, brandishing his two-handed sword. With a crimson tunic and striped trousers, the mercenary prince was the spitting image of grim flamboyance, letting his powdered wig flow, revealing a scarred, stubbled face with a waxed mustache. His eyes were feral, yet his voice was slick and calm.

"You must be the 'wayfarer' I've heard so much about," he said, a hint of respect in his tone. "I compliment your skill and swordsmanship. You've done nicely as a thorn in my side."

"And you must be Dampe," Baldwin spat.

The brigand bowed low. "At your service. Tell me, where do you hail from?"

"Nowhere of consequence," Baldwin lied.

"Very well." Dampe's entourage readied their guns and knives, but the warlord raised a hand, ordering them to stand down. "I simply like to know my opponents a tad before I cleave them in two." His facade dropped, revealing a bestial cruelty. "Come at me!"

Baldwin rushed forward, swinging his sword wide.

Dampe dodged the blow with ease.

"Well then," he sneered, "I should've expected it, but you're rather sluggish, aren't you?" With the flip of a dagger, the captain plunged his blade into Baldwin's side. He twisted deep into his sinew. "For one of your condition, I'm surprised you can even lift a sword —"

In a surge of wrath, Baldwin slammed his bronze mask against the warlord's nose, relishing the crunch of cartilage. With a shift of stance, he engaged in a deadly dance with his foe, one of sweeping motions and clashing blades.

"You will pay for your crimes," the leper roared.

"Oh?" Dampe sneered past the blood. "And where should we start? There aren't enough hours in the day to count them." He parried Baldwin's blows with ease. "And what a waste it would be to try, I assure you. Out of curiosity, though," he slid about the cobblestones, "I've heard a rumor of a king incognito. One suffering from a nasty little skin condition. Spotted along the Old Road. It's not every day that such a rumor is founded."

Baldwin shoved him back. "What of it?"

"It's nothing, really. Dueling the King of the Holy Land is quite an opportunity — why, one a common mercenary could only dream of." The warlord lowered his guard. "What would the regent pay for your ransom?" He mused. "A small fortune, I warrant."

Baldwin's eyes gleamed with focus as he swung upward, breaking Dampe's guard. And, with the weight of gravity on his side, he sent his blade colliding with the warlord's steel, knocking his grip loose and lame. Dampe was sent to his rear, facing the Broken Blade with a look of surprise and smug satisfaction.

"Yield," the leper demanded.

Dampe rolled his eyes. "Such 'mercy' will be the death of you."

Baldwin gasped in shock as sudden pain throbbed in his back.

A hand grasped his shoulder, and a knife dug deep into his flesh. With a swift pull and push, the leper fell flat on his stomach, prone and gasping, as he tore at dead grass. Gritting his teeth, he watched as Dampe mounted his black steed, only to gallop off into the blazing carnage.

Slowly, the sights and slaughter of Gravesend began to dim and fade.

Death...?

Paralyzed in his stupor, Baldwin saw a phantom figure emerge from the darkness — a reaper in tattered black robes, coattails as rags in the wind. Her face was hidden by a long hood and the wide brim of a straw hat, though a pair of pale lips were visible. Leaning on a tall wooden scythe with a dull blade, the reaper seemed a rustic figure, content to simply stare at Baldwin as a towering specter.

"Has my time come?" the leper choked.

Death did not reply. She planted his scythe into the soil and knelt at the leper's level, as if inspecting an oddity amongst the crops and corpses. Silence lingered in the air as the reaper rose. If Baldwin didn't know better, he'd say Death was perplexed.

"Answer me," he said, "please — "

Suddenly, Baldwin awoke to ash and smoke, reeling as he choked down lungfuls of foul air. Ruined houses loomed overhead as he scarcely recognized Gipi pressing her gloved hands on his bandaged chest, trying to resuscitate him.

"W-what...?" Baldwin wheezed.

"Oh, thank God," Gipi gasped. "You're not dead."

"Not yet." Baldwin didn't even try to sit up, enduring his own labored breaths. "What happened? Did we win?"

Gipi did not reply, but her eyes betrayed any notion of comfort. Gravesend had been massacred by the Undertakers. Every man, woman, and child had been cut down, strung up, or put to the torch. The horrors of war were laid bare with a gallows tree and dozens of corpses, butchered and swaying from frayed nooses, left for crows and cruel sport, blood pooling upon gnarled roots. Baldwin hoisted himself up with the hilt of his sword, though his body was wracked with pain. Gipi laid a firm hand on his chest.

"Easy," she said. "Don't exert yourself."

"What of the girl?"

The fool shook her head.

Baldwin gazed upon the ruin, shaking, knuckles white as he beheld the gruesome aftermath of his failure. Tears ran down his fetid cheeks. However, from that same despair came an ember of spite, one that caught wind and spread its own flame of conviction and hate.

"Are you gonna be okay?" Gipi managed.

Baldwin shut his eyes, praying to whatever God would listen. A single-minded determination burned in his thoughts. He took a knee and spoke a simple vow.

"I will avenge these people. Dampe will pay."

Baldwin swung his sword over his back and pressed to the east, where the rising sun cast a sickly orange shroud over the weald. The brigands had left ample tracks to follow. And in his solemnity, the leper began his pursuit. When at last they'd returned to Castle Mourne, Baldwin was greeted by nothing but smoke — the camp had been abandoned. Even the cellar had been looted of provisions and valuables. Only a few banners remained, as if left to mock the pursuers.

"Looks like they left in a hurry," Gipi said.

"So it would seem…."

"Hey," the jester said, "at this point we should really think things over."

Baldwin fiddled with the lacing of his leather vambraces. "I'm going after them, Gipi. I will not sit by idly and let this massacre go unpunished."

"Look at you, a champion of justice."

"Do not take me for a fool," the leper snapped. "I know better than most how unfair and cruel the world can be, but should I just concede? Let injustice triumph because the right thing is too inconvenient? Too taxing? Should I end my journey here?"

"I didn't say that—"

"Certainly you implied it," Baldwin scowled. "Every waking hour is a gift and, by grace that remains, I will dedicate what time I have to stoke a flame of righteousness in this godless world." He pointed his sword at the livid horizon. "There's not a moment in my life free from the shadow of death. And in that lies my greatest strength. I'll die standing."

Gipi opened her mouth, as if to speak up, but no words escaped her lips.

"I, for one, am going after them. You are welcome to follow."

Though spring had come, the land had yet to truly thaw. The soil was cold and firm underfoot. The river crossing led to a fork in the Old Road, with its limestone sediment and running streams. Baldwin followed the route northwest, as the brittle trail wound through the moor. Such was his long, aimless journey to glory.

"Not gonna lie," Gipi said. "If you do manage, it'd make a hell of a ballad."

Baldwin cracked an embittered smile. "Oh?"

"Hey, I don't just follow you out of morbid curiosity, you know. Beneath the batshittery that is your life, there's a glimmer of potential." She winked. "See, my well of inspiration is a little dry of late. As long as you're swinging that sword, I'll tag along."

"I," Baldwin managed, "thank you, Gipi. You are a good friend."

"Oh, don't get all sappy on me."

"Very well. Have you written anything of late?"

Gipi drew her lute and began to strum a melancholic melody, slow and simple yet carrying a cadence that could easily rise into a bolero, if given the chance.

"It's a work in progress," she sighed, "but you get the idea."

ACT TWO

CHAPTER ONE

Warming his bandaged hands over the campfire, Baldwin watched the heavens dim to the color of molten metal. Listening to crackles against the still woods, he stared on, hypnotized by licking flames as they consumed twigs in a smoldering embrace of embers. He raised a flask to his lips and took a swig of brandy. He was a knight in soiled armor — every strip of linen served to shield him from the unforgiving world, lesions glimmering with fluid and foul humors.

Baldwin scribbled on a random page of his journal.

I have failed. I will do better.

Huddled in tenuous firelight, Baldwin shut his eyes, letting his thoughts wander. The Massacre of Gravesend was still fresh in his mind. Corpses lined the memoried streets, and the mercenary prince rode his black stallion, wreathed in flame. The leper gritted his teeth. Doubt nagged at his conviction. Why did he care so fiercely? What drove him to such rage and vengeance? Was it truly the notion of innocent blood being spilt? Or was it something else? An excuse to latch onto a villain in his mad pursuit of glory, however noble it seemed?

"No," Baldwin growled, "it is justice. The will to do the right thing."

"You okay?" Gipi asked from a lofty branch, laying her head upon her hands.

The leper did not reply, content to brood at the flames.

Gipi went back to restringing her lute. "Suit yourself."

The moon rose, slowly, glowering upon the darkened valley.

Baldwin set sail into strange dreams. From the shadow

of thought, he felt a corpse-light shine upon him, as the world seemed to twist. At first, Baldwin thought it a trick of fever, until he saw dancing lights in his mind's eye, as something beyond took form.

Again…?

Paralyzed in his sleep, Baldwin saw Death atop a pale horse.

Wreathed in a shroud of black cloth, she clutched a slender scythe beside her steed, blade shimmering against wisps of eerie blue light, ensnaring the leper in mind and soul. Dead leaves swirled with the black rider's every step, until she paused on the fringe of the fire's glow.

"You've met with a terrible fate, haven't you?" Her voice was a distorted echo of a distinguished aide, ageless and ethereal, having spoken to commoners and kings alike. "Heed my words, leper. The thread of your mortality is thin indeed."

"Why didn't you take me?" the leper asked.

Death paused, as if choosing her words carefully. "It would not have been a death ordained by God. Rest assured, you are fast asleep by the fire, just as I wander the limbo between aether and earth." Her eyes glimmered as pools of spectral light. "I was sent to watch over you, leper. To usher you to and from the grave. A duty that I will carry out to whatever end."

Baldwin kept a grip on his sword's hilt.

"There is no need." Death gave a bitter smile. "Be warned, the path you tread is one paved in the corpses of knaves and princes alike, through dark woods of error. Peril lurks around every bend, and recklessness will cost you more than your life. Lest you fade into obscurity."

The leper's brow furrowed. "Why show yourself?"

"To remind you of your potential," Death said. "Your life hitherto is unworthy of being chronicled, even in tragedy. And yet, you may make your mark upon this unhappy world."

"So, this is indeed my purpose?" Baldwin asked.

Death tugged at the reins of her steed and trotted into the

woods. "In time, you will understand. I will see you through this living purgatory. We will meet again."

The leper tried to speak out, but his words were drowned by the rising tides of awakening. He awoke to morning droplets trickling on his brow as the wind rustled through tall grasses, bushes, and golden trees. What land had escaped the Great Peasants' War was fair and crisp — tranquil, even. As the sun rose over the snowy massifs, he heard the crackle of sausages in a cast-iron skillet. Gipi had already served eggs and roasted vegetables on a flat stone.

"Sleep well?" she asked.

"Not particularly."

Baldwin picked at his breakfast, for the dream did not leave him. If anything, it shed a glimmer of light upon his own purpose, validating his one true course. He dared not tell Gipi, not wanting to endure another round of ridicule. Was it an omen of things to come? Or was it merely the wishful thinking of a dying man? Regardless, the fresh tomatoes did him good.

The next village cannot be far off....

With the fire doused, Baldwin heaved his pack over his shoulder and resumed the trek. Following the upland trail, he watched the sprawling fields bleed into an uncultivated vista of moors and peat bogs. Even the musk of fresh rain did little to mask the festering fens. Baldwin kept a weather eye on the horizon, and the gloom turned gothic. Before a stretch of sparse woodland was a hamlet, barely a cluster of wooden cottages and squat sheds by a lumber mill.

Gipi sniffed the fetid air. "How quaint."

Step by step, they wearily approached the hamlet. Not a soul was there to greet them, and the air was ripe with rot. Baldwin eyed the lopsided sign of the inn, only to find the windows shattered and wood torched. Even the church was a husk leaning against the breeze. Stark against the wooded hollows and whispering wind, the hamlet was altogether abandoned.

"What happened?" Baldwin wondered aloud.

"Graves are fresh." Gipi eyed the cemetery. "Whatever hit this place, it was recent."

"The Undertakers?"

"Possibly." The jester sighed. "But I don't see any sign of a struggle."

Baldwin drew his sword with care, clutching its hilt with both hands. He eyed the sea shanties and shacks carefully for any sign of hostile movement. The leper tread lightly and peered around a moss-covered crypt, spying an open pit filled with cadavers. No blade or shot had pierced them, for they were mutilated by carbuncles and swollen buboes.

"Ah." Gipi cupped her mouth. "Plague."

Without another word, they set out once more, desperate to distance themselves from pestilence and a grisly fate. The hours dragged on until they came to the highlands — white chalk cliffs loomed over the rippling surface of Lake Windermere, its rocky shore spotted with leering trees, tall and splintering against the whisking gales.

Wooden wheels creaked around the bend as a black stagecoach lumbered into view, pulled by hearty draft horses. Bulging crates and strongboxes were strapped to its railed roof, granting a glimpse of all manner of weird apparati. The driver was an eccentric woman, dressed in a thickly waxed leather coat and a raven-beaked mask stuffed with pungent herbs, which even Baldwin could smell alongside vinegar and myrrh. With the tip of a wide-brimmed hat, she tugged the reins, bringing her team to a halt, gazing at the wayfarers with hidden curiosity.

"So," Gipi said, "plague's come after all?"

"Unfortunately," the physician said, softly, "There's little that can be done, other than try to pitch my own remedies and recommend quarantine."

"Sounds like a worthy lead —"

"Gipi," Baldwin snapped. "Your pardon, good doctor. My companion has a sharp tongue but little tact. May I ask where you're headed? The Old Road is not safe these days."

The doctor scoffed. "Nowhere you'd want to visit."

"I see," the leper said. "I would offer to escort you to your destination, in exchange for a lift, as it were. We care not where the road leads, only that it ends at a hearth."

The doctor eyed him up and down. "What are you? A knight errant?"

"In a fashion."

"One with a severe skin condition, I see."

Baldwin sighed, deeply. "Listen, if you're going to berate me—"

"Not at all," said the doctor. "Some believe leprosy purifies the soul through suffering. I've written no shortage of papers on the matter, and you're right, the road is not safe. I can't exactly pay you, but I can offer a session of treatment in exchange."

Gipi shrugged. "Sounds like a worthy trade."

"You do not fear my contagion?" Baldwin asked.

"Well," the doctor said, "I don't exactly plan to remove my mask around you."

"Fair enough. Our destination?"

"Nedlergate."

Gipi's face turned a shade paler than usual. "Has it hit the city?"

"Yes. Which is why it's imperative I deliver this shipment unmolested." The doctor clutched at the reins. "Be warned, though. Nedlergate isn't what it once was."

With a nod, Baldwin climbed aboard as Gipi kept close. Squeezing past the luggage and satchels of medical supplies, he felt the wheels turn underfoot and the stagecoach head on its way. The jester twiddled her thumbs in nervous silence. Under the lantern light, Baldwin leaned against his sword's cross guard, eying the trees along the lakeside.

"Nedlergate, huh?" Gipi asked. "Thought you'd be after the brigands."

"The path of chivalry is hardly a linear one. Besides," the leper eyed his unraveling bandages, "I could use a physician."

"Isn't your condition incurable?"

"Yes, but there are ways to ease my symptoms. Salves and the like."

"I see." Gipi gazed out the window. "Not too keen on visiting the pest houses. Still, I can't help but wonder if you're just latching onto whatever catches your eye."

That cut Baldwin deeper than she likely meant to. How dare she, a court fool, question his judgment? He clutched at the edge of his seat, knuckles whitening, as he attempted to quell the anger in his heart. The leper knew it was irrational, a knee-jerk reaction to criticism, and strived to fetter it accordingly. For his sake as well as Gipi's.

"What do you mean?" he asked.

"You swore vengeance against the Undertakers," the jester stated, "and now you're escorting a supply wagon to a plague-stricken city. It doesn't take a learned man to notice the dissonance here." She leaned back in her seat. "Why are you doing this?"

"I," Baldwin paused, "it seems like the right thing."

"Fair enough."

Dusk crept over the dales. Thick gray clouds billowed across the country, and for a while, it seemed the journey would be an uneventful one, until the carriage encroached upon the silhouettes of urban dwellings. Surrounded by stone bastions, Nedlergate was a noisome morass of half-timbered houses and the common forth. The muddy roadway gave way to pitted cobbled streets as the stagecoach rumbled along its uneven surface. Bisected by the River Tintern, there was a randomness to the slums, teetering over unlit alleys. The descending roads were flanked by tanneries and butcher shops, contributing to the loathsome stench. Moths fluttered about the streetlamps; webs of clotheslines hung from window to window, bedsheets flapping against like soiled banners. The skyline was dominated by chimneys and thin-peaked rooftops, surpassed only by the steeples of the Cathedral of the Blessed Sacrament, looming from the sprawl's heart.

"So," Baldwin said, "this is the city."

"I was expecting way worse," Gipi said.

"We haven't reached the narrows yet," the doctor called from the driver's box.

The city folk were a rabble of off-white tunics, trousers, and leather boots; blathering and laughing in a drunken blur of warts and missing teeth. Taking a sharp left, the stagecoach came to a tall palisade and a pair of iron-banded gates; doors painted with a thick red cross. No one loitered in its shadow; even the urban rabble seemed to fade in its presence, but the reek was all the stronger. A notice had been hammered to the door, reading,

By the authority of the Lord Mayor of Nedlergate, the area beyond this perimeter is hereby under quarantine until further notice. Only authorized persons may pass through these checkpoints as supervised by the City Watch. All unauthorized trafficking, or association with unauthorized trafficking, is punishable by death.

The coach approached the battered gates, guarded by a man-at-arms in a doublet and a kettle helmet. Baldwin eyed the sentry with suspicion, unable to discern if he was a ruffian or toll collector. Regardless, the guard seemed of better cloth than the common thug. The leper studied the soldier's livery with care, but did not recognize the coat of arms.

The man-at-arms raised his lantern. "Halt! What business have you here?"

"We're headed for the hospital," the doctor replied.

The guard took a step past the salt line in the street, pressing a sachet of medicinal herbs against his nose and mouth, eying the stagecoach up and down.

"Name?" He opened a cumbersome ledger.

"Sophia," the doctor spoke with authority. "Licensed physician and toxicologist."

"Right then. What's the load?"

In a rare moment of restraint, Baldwin thought it best to remain in the coach, as Sophia listed the contents of her luggage in full, ranging from poppy sap to clotting powders, as well as no shortage of odd and obscure instruments.

"As you can see," she said, "the supply run is overdue."

"It's still a shilling to pass the checkpoint."

"Under whose authority?" Sophia asked.

"Orders from King Geoffrey himself," said the man-at-arms. "We need to tally and tax those who come and go. Lest the plague spread across the kingdom."

Baldwin's temper flared with chivalric rage. He leapt out of the passenger seat. "Your pardon," he towered over the guard, "but such a toll is hardly warranted."

The soldier shook his head. "I can't go against royal orders," his eyes narrowed, "and you don't look too healthy yourself, sir —"

"The sellsword is my escort," Sophia said. "I will pay your fee, and you will grant us passage. Lest you wish to explain to your superior why you're impeding a doctor's duty."

The guard hesitated, but stepped aside. "Very well."

After a trade of shillings and signatures, the gates rolled open with a terrible groan. Inch by inch, the stagecoach rolled into Cock and Key Alley, as if even the horses were hesitant to cross the threshold. The gates shut behind them, leaving the vagrants alone among those damned to die of plague. Color had utterly abandoned the place, save for splattering of reds, browns, and vomitous greens. Bills of mortality were posted on the notice board in the square. A pasty commoner hastily painted a red cross on a rickety door, as mournful sobs wafted within the townhouse. The steady hammering of a smithy echoed in the distance, its merchant no doubt supplying the watchmen with locks and chains. Not a soul lingered in the street, save for the rats swarming amongst the mud and dung heaps.

"Please," shouted a hoarse voice, "d-don't do this!"

As the stagecoach carried on, Baldwin glanced out the

window and beheld the source of the commotion—a throng of watchmen and a few volunteers pressed their body weight against a door, while the constable wrapped a short chain tight around its paneling.

"We'll die here! We can't last a fortnight!"

With the slam of a padlock, the deed was done, though the residents still rattled their cage. Baldwin knew the truth. Entire households were to be condemned due to a single case. They'd be checked upon daily, but to lock the healthy with the plagued was nothing short of a death sentence. They would succumb within days. Neighbor turned against neighbor, if only to preserve the community, and yet, Baldwin wondered how long it would be until the constable was locked in his own office.

"So," Sophia asked, "what brings you to the Old Road?"

"I am a wanderer in search of wrongs to right," the leper recited. "Nothing more."

"How's that working out for you?" Her voice oozed with sarcasm.

"Questionably," Baldwin admitted.

Gipi smirked, but did not comment.

"At any rate," Sophia said, "you'll find plenty of work here, no doubt. There are few places more foul, or in need of 'heroes,' than Nedlergate."

"We're open for work." Gipi crossed her arms behind her head.

"What of you?" Baldwin asked. "Does study alone bring you to Nedlergate?"

The doctor glanced over her shoulder. "Not only. No small part of it is, how should I put it, academic probation." She returned her gaze to their course. "Let's just say that my techniques are too 'experimental' to be taught at university. Dissection, for example."

The leper felt a surge of bile well up his throat, revolted by the image of the dead being desecrated in the name of progress. "Cut them up—?"

"Please." Sophia sighed. "My professors share your disposition, but by using up-to-date scientific techniques, I will prove them wrong. Go ahead, take a look."

Baldwin rummaged through the black leather bag and found a pocketed scroll of glass vials, each filled with chrome fluid. "To rebalance the humors?"

"Quicksilver," Sophia said. "Not remotely toxic."

Baldwin delicately tucked the scroll away and snapped the bag shut. "I see." He changed the topic. "On the road, we encountered a brigade of brigands not two days ago. They called themselves the Undertakers. Have you heard of them?"

"Can't say I have," said the doctor, "but there's a lot of mercenary bands operating in these parts. What with the peasant uprisings and all."

Baldwin gazed out the window. Not a glimmer of cheer was to be found. Even the taverns were boarded up. Passing row after row of ramshackle tenements and almshouses, it seemed the stagecoach was descending into a pestilent abyss with no destination in sight. Until, deep within the narrows, the leper spied what he mistook for a holy place upon first glance.

"We're here," Sophia said.

Smoke rose in plumes from heaps of burning trash scattered throughout the square, as if the citizens thought fire would cleanse the air. Against the fleeting glow, the Cathedral of the Blessed Sacrament had been repurposed into a house of healing. Flanked with flying buttresses and rows of lancet windows, its gargoyles leered from the parapets, chins propped under their fists, grinning with sick amusement at the misery below. Even the pinnacles were fractured, little more than splintered spires along the lead-tiled rooftops. White banners hung from the belfries, bearing the scarlet caduceus. Save for an occasional moan, the cathedral was a silent mausoleum for all who were admitted.

"Charming," Gipi whispered.

"There's no way this place can heal the sick," Baldwin said.

"You're absolutely right." Sophia dismounted the driver's box, planting her cane against the cobblestones with a clack. "Not without proper treatment, that is."

The leper disembarked with caution. Something scurried in the alley, though he barely made out a swarm of diminutive shades against the firelight. He joined his companions before the doors, where they were greeted by a sister in a habit. A pair of thin-faced orderlies emerged to hoist the supplies inside, waddling, eyes milky and bloodshot. Crows flocked about the bell towers. Baldwin felt a shiver run down his spine. He was being watched. Covering her mouth as she coughed, the sister bid them to follow into the darkened church. The leper did not loosen the grip on his sword's hilt.

This feels wrong....

CHAPTER TWO

Past the narthex and beneath a high vaulted ceiling, Baldwin's footsteps were heavy against the tiles as he marched down the nave. No pews lined the aisles, replaced by row after row of thin cots cradling the dying with coarse blankets. The church was strewn with candles and molten wax in a feeble attempt to stoke the light, for despair lurked in every shadow. Every flame quivered as a choir of moans and hacking coughs erupted from the beds. Even the cold stone walls were remote and oppressive, twisting the cathedral into a cesspit of suffering. Gipi kept a cloth over her mouth, as Sophia exchanged hushed words with the middle-aged abbess.

"The Lord smiles upon your work," she said. "Thank you for your aid."

Sophia sighed. "Don't thank me yet. We've yet to nurse these people back to health."

The abbess turned to the wayfarers. "I must ask. Who are your companions?"

"That's," the doctor paused, "an excellent question."

With her lute strung across her back, Gipi bowed and indulged in introductions, while Baldwin's gaze turned to one of the patients. He was feverish, dripping with cold sweat; black buboes bulged on his neck and armpits, swollen with hot pus, threatening to pop at any moment. A nurse dabbed his brow and prepared a long needle with a shudder, as if bracing herself for the lancing. The leper turned away, and a weeping shriek filled the transept.

"What treatments have you brought?" the abbess asked.

Sophia rummaged through her case and rolled out a scroll of glass vials. "Laudanum," she said, "a tincture of opium infused with alcohol. It will ease pain and suppress the cough, preventing the spread of miasma. There are other options, of course."

"Such as?"

Sophia offered a jar of writhing leeches. "These beauties can extract maladies in the blood." She unscrewed the lid and fished out a little black worm. "Precious, aren't they?"

Baldwin bit his tongue. Beneath her mask, Sophia was beaming with pride over her precious specimens. Moments dragged on, and for a time, it seemed the leper's work was finished — when a deranged scream echoed from above, reverberating off the brass bells.

Out of instinct, Baldwin drew his sword and took a defensive stance, eyes darting about the darkened corners of the cathedral, imagining what stirred in the walls.

"No! Restrain him!"

"He's too fast!"

"Quick, get the manacles — !"

Someone, or something, barreled down the tower stairs, shambling with ludicrous speed. Baldwin spun around, only to be tackled aside by an emaciated figure tangled in an untethered straitjacket. His eyes were glazed with feral desperation as he gnashed his teeth, clawing and pawing at the leper's mask, screaming all the while.

"Oh, king," he howled, "oh, king, cast away your mask!" Gloved hands gathered to pry him away from Baldwin. Wracked with convulsions, the madman struggled to break free of their tightening grips. "The rats said you'd come. Please," he begged, "deliver us from this plague!"

Baldwin staggered to his feet, only for his assailant to be dragged away by the sisterhood, a burlap sack stifling his screams. Those words lingered in his thoughts, and he began to tremble.

The abbess rushed to his side, hands clasped. "I'm so sorry, good sir."

"Who was that?" Baldwin asked.

"Neville. He's…quite mad."

"You don't say," Gipi scoffed. "Can't blame him, though...."

The abbess winced. "Again, I'm so sorry. Neville is usually a peaceful soul. We used to let him toll the bells when he was behaving. Poor thing is of noble lineage, you see, but something happened to him. As to what, we're not exactly sure."

How did he recognize me...?

Baldwin scarcely heard the abbess's excuses, fixated on the sudden assault. How did the madman know of his lineage? Why had he been attacked? Golgotha was half a world away, and he'd never visited Nedlergate on diplomatic missions. He'd heard of oracles from the classical epics, but never thought he'd meet one firsthand.

"Take me to him," he requested.

The abbess led the way up the stairs, ushering Baldwin to the north tower.

As the door shut behind him, the leper crossed the belfry with care; the floorboards moaned with the weight of centuries. From the maze of wooden scaffolds, a collection of great bronze bells hung low, left to corrode with neglect, as if the plague had claimed so many that no one bothered to toll the dead. Cobwebs and flakes of dust beamed in the moonlight, swaying with the leper's every motion, disturbed by his very presence. A shadow protruded around the corner as the bells reverberated with the murmurs of the tower's prisoner.

Baldwin softened his voice. "Neville. Do you know who I am?"

The madman twitched and muttered, ensnared in straps in the corner, like a chained beast. A twinge of pity lingered in Baldwin's heart as he kept his distance from Neville.

"You," the madman choked, "you are Baldwin of Golgotha."

"How do you know of me?"

"The rats," Neville said. "They spoke of you." His eyes were haunted by weird visions and a chronic lack of sleep. His nonsensical words wormed their way from chapped lips. "They know you're here," his voice lowered to a hoarse whisper.

Something scurried in the darkness. Baldwin glanced over his shoulder, only to spy a fleshy tail creep into the floorboards. The leper tried to articulate his thoughts, but couldn't wrap his head around how to question the madman, whose words were so cryptic.

"What else did they say?"

Neville did not reply, twisting in his bonds, uttering a desperate grunt. "Mustn't speak too loudly," he said. "Mustn't let them hear us. No, no. Go away. You'll lure them here."

Baldwin gritted his teeth until a gloved hand fell upon his shoulder. Gipi emerged from the dimness and knelt at the madman's side with a smile, as if trying to soothe his panic. With the twist of a peg, she strummed her lute and played soft chords for his amusement. Though Neville was startled by the fool's sudden appearance, her music soon put him at ease.

"Now then," Gipi said, "how do you do?"

The madman's lips drooped low, as if he was tranquilized by the little song. "Well," he managed, "I could be better." Twitching in his bonds, Neville seemed a bit more lucid as he averted his eyes, staring down a hole in the floorboards. "A lot better, really."

"I bet," Gipi said. "We have a few questions for you." She jerked a thumb towards the leper. "Seems like you've already met my friend here."

"Only in dreams," Neville said. "Darkest dreams."

Baldwin heard the nurses venture downstairs while watching the lamplight fade into the nave below. Neville's words were veiled in allegory and eerie metaphors such as "like a spider on a fly" or "best peel your eyes, lest a bugbear pluck them out."

"My lord," he jerked his head aside. "There's a platter by Genevieve, the big bell to your left. You may help yourselves to an hors d'oeuvre."

Gipi shot the leper a smirk. "Well, don't be rude."

Reluctantly, Baldwin came to a table and chairs behind the bells, where a cloche-crowned plate greeted him with gleaming uncertainty. He lifted the lid, only to be bombarded by a cloud of midges and flies. The plate clattered to the floor as he shouted. Baldwin fell flat on his back, and the insects buzzed and swarmed out of the balcony and into the night. The leper staggered to his feet, glaring at the madman, cheeks burning with indignation.

"Foul knave," Baldwin snarled.

Gipi smirked. "Actually, that was pretty funny."

"Oh, what fun!" Neville cackled. "Never gets old. Would you kindly bring us the plate?" He licked his chapped lips. "There's some true delicacies. Canapes."

Baldwin lifted the plate and gagged.

The starters were a selection of speared flies, beetles, and pallid worms, glistening in a cornucopia of slick carapaces and meaty legs. It was a wonder that the rats hadn't gotten to them. The leper laid the platter before Neville and scowled. How long was this going to take? Was he wasting his time?

Gipi fed the madman a grub. "And what else do you see in these dreams?"

Neville paused, as if bombarded by dread. "The Black Piper," he whispered. "She who haunts slum and sewer alike, spreading plague wherever her mangy claws can reach." He shuddered. "Yes, it is her doing. She conspires to twist and maim the city in vengeance."

Vengeance...?

Baldwin stopped himself from interjecting, if only to discern the truth of Neville's rambling. If only to learn more as to what evils lurked in Nedlergate. Whether a mere lunatic or an oracle, it was clear that Neville knew a great deal about the city. More than the sisterhood would care to admit. And yet, there was a certain tragedy to his tale.

Something terrible happened to this man....

"I've said too much," Neville sputtered. "If they hear us—"

"I'll tell you what," Gipi unsheathed her dirk, "if you'll talk and just be honest, I'll get you out of that jacket." She whispered. "It'll be our little secret."

Neville's eyes glistened like shards of obsidian. "Our little secret?"

"Gipi," Baldwin warned.

"What?" the jester snapped. "Were you just gonna let him rot up here? You're not exactly an exemplar of sanity yourself." Her eyes narrowed, sharper than her knife. "You're better than that." She turned back to the madman. "Now, from what you're describing, the Black Piper's the cause of the plague? Do us a favor and tell us the truth."

"Very well," Neville said. "But you'll think me quite mad."

Baldwin sighed. "We're no strangers to the weird."

Neville nodded, slowly. "Deep in the sewers, the Black Piper makes her lair. She was once of the peerage, like myself, and more than a little touched in the head. Bewitched. Watching from the shadows, she rules her own house. Hatred knowing no bounds. She who holds court for plague-bringers and who would see our city a mass grave."

Gipi scribbled a few notes on a stray piece of parchment. "Thank you for your time." She smiled. "This'll make quite the limerick—"

"You don't believe him?" Baldwin asked.

With a flick of her wrist, the jester cut Neville's bonds, freeing him from his straightjacket. "Remember," she lifted a finger to her lips, "our little secret."

Neville mimicked her with a hush and a giggle. With a nod of thanks, the madman crept to the open balcony, about to begin his descent from the gothic parapets. Before he made the crawl, he turned to Baldwin and spoke with a soft, trembling voice.

"The rats fear you. They know you'll be the one to deliver us from this scourge. That you'd be the one to end their reign." He bowed low. "Farewell."

There was no lie in Neville's eyes. The leper nodded and

turned to the stairwell. His duty was clear — to find and slay the Black Piper. His sword hungered for justice. And justice he would serve. For the oracle had spoken, and he would heed his warnings. Baldwin returned to the nave, among the dead and dying, and pressed on as orderlies attempted to discreetly toss the corpses into the carts just outside. Against the faint glow of stained-glass windows and candlelight, the leper pushed past the double doors, though he was hardly welcomed by fresh air or singing birds — only the despairing sight of a district left to rot in pestilence's wake. Gipi's footfalls were not far behind.

"Slow down," she called, "and let's talk this over for a second."

"What is there to talk about?"

"First off, what are you thinking, exactly?" The jester bounded after him, down the street and past the smoldering braziers. "Where are you going — ?"

"To slay the Black Piper," the leper said. "Such a scourge cannot be left to fester."

"And what makes you believe the man in the straitjacket?"

"Only a fool would deny the oracle."

"Oracle? Oh, you've got to be joking."

Baldwin turned to face his companion, glowering down at her. "How else would he know of me? Besides, can you think of another explanation for this outbreak?"

"I'm not an expert on miasma theory and never claimed to be." Gipi raised a gloved hand. "But let's not charge into the sewers to kill a magical rat catcher." She sighed. "Listen, I'm a fool, right? And nobles love their fools. And it sounds like the Black Piper was among them."

"What are you getting at?" Baldwin asked.

As the orderlies pushed their corpse carts, he caught a glimpse of a nobleman buried under the commoners, his white ruff stained with bloody foam from dead lungs — a sobering reminder of the indiscriminate stroke of the reaper's scythe.

Memento Mori....

"I just so happened to know the Lord Mayor of Nedlergate." Gipi flipped a scarlet invitation between her fingers. "Played a few gigs at his masquerade balls before I stumbled upon you. In fact, he's hosting one tonight at the Mansion House."

"Where did you get that?"

"Ran into an old acquaintance on his deathbed when your back was turned. Obviously, he can't make it. That, and I keep my ears open for these kinds of things. You're good at swinging your sword around, but I know how to play the giddy socialite."

"And how does this relate to the Black Piper?"

"Simple. We gossip with the nobility. With a bit of polish, you'd pass as my plus one. And if Neville's claims are true, we'll have no problem getting some juicy tidbits to expound on. But," she pointed at the leper, "if we don't learn anything, you'll drop this Black Piper shit."

Baldwin cracked a smile. Even if Gipi scarcely believed him, the fool was willing to indulge in his crusade. With a nod of thanks, the leper conceded. "Very well."

"Of course," Gipi said, "there's the matter of leaving the plague quarter...."

Baldwin stared at the billowing smoke on the horizon, imagining pyres of cadavers and molten fat and communal pits for the plagued. Then his eyes wandered upon an unattended cart, pondering whether or not to hide among the dead.

Gipi gagged. "Don't even think about it."

The creak of coach wheels interrupted the debate. Sophia drove to their side. Staring down from her raven-beaked mask, the doctor tugged at the reins and came to a halt.

"I don't imagine you're content staying here."

Gipi gave a theatrical bow. "What gave it away?"

"I'm on an errand," Sophia said. "Care for a lift back to civilization?"

Baldwin boarded the stagecoach without a second thought. Together with Gipi, he made room among the leather satchels and stray scrolls of parchment.

"As promised." Sophia tossed the leper a jar of herbal salve. "Apply this on a wet cloth, let it dissolve and seep into your pores. It won't cure you, but it'll slow the rot."

Baldwin apprised the salve with a smile. "Thank you, good doctor."

With that, the coach wound on its course, rattling along the cobblestone streets. Beyond the quarantine gate, Baldwin watched the crowded avenues give way to Lombard Street with its banks, dime stores, and doric columns. Merchants from the maritime republics went about their business, dressed in red caps and ribbons, accompanied by thin-lipped accountants. Coins and scales clinked from behind closed doors. It was a far cry from the destitution of Cock and Key Alley. Disembarking before the apothecary, Baldwin perused the window displays and shelves of periodicals. To his disgust, he read a familiar name on a cover.

Dampe....

Apparently, he was a picaresque figure, an anti-hero whose violence was distorted by the pen of naive novelists. Even the leper wouldn't touch the penny dreadful.

"Come on," Gipi said, "let's get you to a tailor."

Baldwin nodded, reluctantly, and stifled his rage.

As they ventured down the street, a gang of street urchins emerged from the alleys, dressed in tattered tunics and trousers, sporting rosy cheeks, pimples, and missing teeth, some no older than six. Within a moment, the leper was surrounded by impoverished youth. He muttered under his breath, pushing past as the beggars tugged at his cloak.

"Please, sir," said the oldest, "alms for the poor?"

"I am not exactly a rich man," Baldwin said. "Trust me, there is better game in this district than I." He kept moving, for that alone was true.

"Nice sword," called another. "Are you a dragonslayer?"

Baldwin paused and stifled a smirk. "Something of the sort...."

"How many have you killed?" the children erupted with

questions. "Have you saved any damsels? What about treasure? My pa says he saw a green fairy once, but he's a drunk...."

Baldwin sighed, deeply. "Alright." He drew a few brass coins from his purse. "I suppose it is my duty to aid the meek. You and your brothers are gifted in the art of flattery."

The child bit into a coin. "Thank you, sir."

"Now then." Baldwin knelt to their level. "I'm on a quest myself. Be good and run along now, all right? Try to stay out of trouble," he whispered, "or at least don't get caught."

Most of the children scurried away, but the eldest lingered. "You're kind, sir. If you ever find yourself in East End and need some 'connections,'" he shot him a wink, "come find us."

"What's your name, child?"

"Jeremy. You?"

The leper smiled. "Baldwin. I would shake your hand, but...."

Jeremy shoved his hands in his pockets, revealing a few weeping lesions of his own.

"It's quite all right, sir. I understand."

With a solemn nod, Baldwin returned to Gipi's side, who shot him a genuine smile.

"You're such a softy."

Beyond the crowds of merchants and aides, the marble facade and pediment of the Mansion House lorded from the avenue's end. The leper could almost hear the whispers of petty barons, dreading his return to the court. Meanwhile, an outfitting shop, Giuseppe's, seemed promising for their needs. The door opened with a chime. Baldwin took care not to slam his brow against the rafters, greeted by garments of a dozen colors and sizes. Leaning on the counter was a middle-aged shopkeeper with a polished mustache. The leper pushed past the racks of clothing, eying the collection of masks along the wall—of birds and beasts, the sun and the moon, and others of more lurid design. One in particular had a suspiciously phallic nose, sporting a moronic grin. By the counter, Gipi browsed for gimmicks, baubles to juggle, and the like. She lifted a marotte topped with a malformed doll's head. "Kind of looks like you without the mask."

Baldwin growled with disapproval. "I implore you to take this seriously. If we're going to attend the ball, we must blend in appropriately."

"Neh, neh, neh," Gipi mimicked, every syllable matching the wave of her stick. "I'm Baldwin, and my sense of humor fell off with my nose."

The leper snatched the toy from Gipi's grip. "Enough. You are such a brat." Fettering his annoyance, he placed the stick delicately back on the shelf. "At any rate, what should we dress as? What is in vogue with the nobility of Nedlergate?"

"Good question," Gipi said. "Mocking the poor is always a thing." A glimmer of genius shone in her eyes. "Wait a second. You can go as a leper!"

"What?"

"Think about it." The jester rummaged through her options, lifting knee-length coats and white breeches. "If we just polish you up, but keep the mask, you'll be a hit. Trust me." She reached for the tricones and compared silver and gold trims. "Which do you like better?"

"I'd prefer something more subtle."

"Hate to break it to you," Gipi said, "but nothing about you is subtle."

Baldwin sighed and raised his arms for a fitting. Soon, he was dressed in the most ostentatious outfit imaginable. He gazed into the tall mirror with disgust, examining his knitted garters and sickly green waistcoat. Crowned with a powdered wig, layers of linen, and decorative bandages kept his sores and ulcers hidden. The bronze mask was strapped tightly over the leper's face. With a deep breath, he emerged from the dressing room.

Gipi clapped. "You look fabulous." The jester had already selected her costume and was comparatively quite modest. With a new cap and bells, black-checkered trousers, and a harlequin's mask, the jester was prepared to frolic with high society.

"I feel like a peacock," Baldwin muttered.

"A leprous peacock."

Thankfully, the cashier didn't seem to notice the overpowering waft of sampled perfume. With the handsome price paid, they departed out the door. Despite many happenings, the night was still young and rife with debaucherous potential.

"Remember," Baldwin warned, "we are attending for information. Not to socialize."

Gipi shot him a smirk. "Suit yourself."

CHAPTER THREE

The Mansion House was nearer than Baldwin had thought. In its shadow were clean-cut hedges and rows of rosebushes. The leper admired the gardener's precision. As he sauntered down the path and past the wrought iron gates, the leper was greeted by twin wings and grand gables, impressed by the manor's opulence. He spied a shadowed couple engaged in a passionate embrace by the fountain. At first, Baldwin thought it a discreet moment of courtship, until the man tore at the courtesan's bodice and kissed her neck, followed by a salacious moan and giggle. The front door opened. Baldwin and Gipi were greeted by a masked valet who eyed them up and down with pursed lips.

Gipi handed him the scarlet invitation. "Nice night, isn't it?"

"So it is." The valet skimmed the letter and folded it into his pocket, which was already bulging with identical papers. "My master bids you welcome."

Baldwin gave a nod. "Thank you—"

"Your 'sword,'" the valet raised a hand, "if you please."

Baldwin shot him a venomous glare, but slowly undid the baldric's straps. With grave caution, the leper relinquished the Broken Blade. "Take good care of it."

"Thank you for your cooperation." The valet placed it aside by a rack of rapiers, dueling pistols, and the odd musket, and ushered them to the foyer. "The ballroom is just ahead."

Baldwin trailed after Gipi, casting a shadow over her vibrant colors. He heard swelling cellos passing down the arcades and gilded colonnades, as a violin's fanfare accompanied the doormen's gestures and bows. Affliction aside, Baldwin may as well have been born with two left feet, and the twirling tide of gowns was intimidating. The leper slunk past the nobility, averting his eyes from obscured faces and the array of masks. Such pretense was as stifling as a corset, reminding him of the Holy Land's two-faced aids and poisoned goblets. Content to brood in the corner, he looked on as Gipi twisted the pegs of her lute and strummed along with the waltz. Meanwhile, the aristocracy gossiped and mingled among themselves.

"I say," said an esquire in a ruff, "it is a relief to meet again despite the plague."

"Of course," replied his peer, "after my excursions in Gravesend, I'd be loath to see this soiree canceled, regardless of the circumstance."

"Indeed, I trust you were compensated for your efforts."

"In a manner of speaking...."

The latter's voice was exceedingly familiar. A passing servant offered Baldwin a selection of miniature meat pies, but the leper declined with a wave. His impulse was to grab the platter and fling it as a discus into the man's neck, but the leper withheld his wrath. Frequenting Gravesend was hardly a crime, and yet suspicion cast a pall over the stranger.

Dampe? No, it can't be him –

"Hey." Gipi came to his side with a mouthful of crostini. "Playing nice?"

"As well as I can," Baldwin managed. "Have you heard anything of note?"

The jester shrugged. "Still working on it. Wouldn't hurt for you to ask around, too, though. Can't be expected to do all the talking."

Baldwin huffed and crossed his arms. It was easy for her to say. Being a court fool with sly graces allowed Gipi to quip and get away with anything short of murder. At least, so it would seem. Beneath her painted smile, the jester was just as distraught as vermin scurried and skirted the carpet's rim into a crack in the tiles, led by a deathly pale rat with crimson eyes.

No one seemed to notice, let alone care.

At the far side of the ballroom, a pair of double doors

swung open. Baldwin turned his attention to a dramatic display — an aging lord sporting a mustard-colored waistcoat and densely powdered locks, pressing a handkerchief against his nose and lips. He was shielded from his guests by a cube of distorting glass aloft a grand palanquin, supported by a host of manservants. So warped were the panes that, from one angle, the lord appeared morbidly obese, and from another, utterly emaciated. In a way, Baldwin speculated, this was his mask.

"May I present to you," announced the valet, "Lord Mayor Lawrence Duice—"

"Oh, come now," the Master of the House wheezed, words muffled by thick panes of glass. "There's no need to linger on formalities. We're all friends here." He gestured widely, welcoming his guests with a squinting smile. "I hope the night is treating you well. Though plague ravages our fair city, we have the luxury of indulging in each other's company." He raised a glass of whiskey. "I bid you good health and a golden masquerade."

Baldwin snagged a snifter from a passing server and raised a toast, if only to blend in with the nobility. Lawrence's man-steeds quaked under their load, though whether due to the thick glass or the lord's girth, the leper could not say. Even past the warping panes, he saw fear behind Lawrence's eyes, as if he was expecting someone — perhaps an unwelcome guest.

Upon this realization, Baldwin noticed that the string quartet had finished the light piece and slowly transitioned to a somber rhapsody.

"Your lordship." He approached the Lord Mayor with care. "I thank you for tonight's hospitality. Your servants have been most gracious."

"Of course." Lawrence's smile was unnaturally wide behind the glass. "I must say, though, sir, your costume is in audacious taste. Are you supposed to be a leper?"

"That I am," Baldwin said. "I must ask, however, how you managed to host such an event during such a crisis? What of the plague?"

"What of it?" the Lord Mayor scoffed. "So long as my court is kept separate from the infected, I see no need to postpone our life affections. My dear friends and I wouldn't dream of venturing outside the comforts of our homes."

Baldwin held his tongue, refraining from lecturing the host on leadership. Flaunting his royal deeds and titles would serve no purpose, save to infuriate his host. The leper had forsaken such privileges when he abdicated his throne. Now, he was little more than an imposter.

"I must say," Lawrence said, "I do not recognize your voice or clothes, sir. Where are you from, if you don't mind my asking?"

Baldwin's words caught in his throat as he stuttered, "I am, uh—"

"Ah," Gipi called, "Good King Baldwin." She sneaked to the leper's side. "I see you are acquainting yourself with the Lord Mayor." She nudged him sharply. "Isn't that right, your lordship?"

"Oh." Baldwin caught on slower than he'd care to admit. "Yes, quite right."

"My master here is a lord in the Holy Land. One of the crusader kingdoms, to be exact. As skilled with a sword as he is among the vipers of the court."

Lawrence burst into boisterous laughter. "Quick-tongued as ever, Gipi. And a crusader kingdom, you say? Nedlergate is a far cry from the Holy Land. A small estate, is it not?"

Baldwin straightened his posture.

"Yes. And as a 'crusader,' I've come to investigate rumors of witchcraft under the authority of the Holy See. Tell me, have you heard of the Black Piper?"

Color drained from Lawrence's cheeks. "I have no idea what you're talking about."

"There's no need to lie." Baldwin raised a bandaged hand. "I ask for your cooperation and promise that no harm will come to you or your house. If you refuse, however," he paused for effect, "I am obliged to report the matter to my superiors."

"The Inquisition?"

Baldwin let his implications do the talking. Silence only shadowed his empty threat, and yet, the Lord Mayor clearly had something to hide.

"Very well." Lawrence dabbed his brow with a handkerchief. "Please, meet me in the second-floor lounge." With a clap, the Lord Mayor summoned his manservants, who heaved the poles of his palanquin, preparing for the upstairs trek. "I'll see you shortly."

Baldwin gave a nod of acknowledgment. As Lawrence was carried past the crowd, the leper lingered in the ballroom with his jester.

"I do not appreciate you outing my lineage," Baldwin kept his voice low.

"Could've fooled me." Gipi shrugged. "You did well."

Baldwin shook his head. Such deception was roguish and uncouth, and yet, a bitter necessity. In his travels, Baldwin's pieties were bombarded by pragmatic exceptions. He departed for the foyer and the carpeted staircase. Despite their heavy burden, the staff had already deposited the Lord Mayor at the lounge. Greeted by ruby-red wallpaper and a dying hearth, Baldwin did not join Gipi on the sofa, content to stand and view the oil painting framed above the fireplace—a livid landscape of a city ablaze.

To his surprise, Lawrence was still caged in his glass box.

"So," Lawrence began, "the Black Piper."

"Yes." Baldwin nodded, slowly. "May I ask why you are... encased?"

"It protects me from the plague," Lawrence said. "Certain persons are more susceptible than others, and not due to ill health, if you take my meaning."

"I'm afraid I don't," Baldwin replied.

"Really?" Lawrence asked. "Exactly how much have your

superiors told you?"

Baldwin paused, trying to recall his exact phrasing in the ballroom, so as not to illuminate any inconsistencies with his narrative. "I—"

"Only that the Black Piper was a lady of the court," Gipi intervened. "Once upon a time."

"I'm afraid it's a bit more complicated than that," Lawrence said. "You see, she is my daughter. Clarice used to be a sweet child, talented with the flute, having an affinity for rats. She serenaded her pets with her own compositions. Of course, she didn't get along well with other children. I tried to arrange her with many a suitor, but she wouldn't have it...."

Baldwin was reminded of his own youth, of sparring and exchanging blows over a stolen toy knight. His eventual condition had done him no social favors. Pity tugged at his heart.

"One night, a gang of noble brats assaulted her," the Lord Mayor continued. "No one knows exactly what happened, but according to Neville, the only survivor of the incident, she was held back as they threw her rats in a sack and into the river, intent on drowning them."

"Cruel," Gipi said.

"Supposedly," Lawrence continued, "swarms erupted from the sewers, as if sensing her anguish. Bite by bite, they devoured the attackers, leaving only bones and splatters of blood. And my girl fled. Never to be seen again. Neville went quite mad, looked after the sisterhood, so I don't know what to make of his story. But then came the plague."

"Tragic to be sure," Baldwin said.

"I don't know what to make of this," Lawrence said. "If my little girl is still alive, I'm afraid I cannot assist in her execution. But if she is somehow responsible for the plague, I cannot sit idly and let the city be destroyed. The sick and dying are not to blame."

"I," Baldwin paused, "am sorry for your loss, but you are right. The plague cannot be suffered. Do you know where the incident occurred?"

"Near the Tower Bridge," Lawrence said. "Follow the Tintern south and you'll come to its crossing, but," he choked, "if at all possible, please, spare her."

Baldwin didn't have the heart to tell Lawrence the truth, that his daughter was gone, that only the Black Piper remained. He gave a silent bow—when a choir of bloodcurdling screams erupted from the ballroom below. Without a moment's pause, the leper barreled down the stairs and tore his sword from the weapon rack, only to witness the truly grotesque. The dance floor was covered in a writhing carpet of fur and sinewy tails. The nobility screamed in agony as tides of rats engulfed them—biting, clawing, and dragging them under the surface with dead weight, slowly stripping them to the bone. An esquire gagged and sputtered, as rats pried open his mouth, muffling his cries, only to rush down his throat and gnaw at his innards. Baldwin could only gawk in horror. Dozens of vermin burst from the man's chest, cracking his ribs apart, caked in blood and strands of sinew, as he collapsed into the ocean of gnashing teeth. The leper was rooted to where he stood. Inch by inch, rats spread to the foyer, eying him with ravenous hunger. Snapping to his adrenaline-addled senses, Baldwin grabbed a nearby lamp and threw it at the squirming sea, igniting the carpet in a burst of oily flame.

"What the fuck?!" Gipi screamed from the mezzanine.

The rats did not relent, rushing into the lobby in waves, trampling each other with maws agape. The fire rose. As he turned to the open door, Baldwin spied a gaunt silhouette in the courtyard, whistling into a galoubet, perched atop the fountain, as thousands of rats flowed into the manor. Her fingers danced across the pale pipe, summoning the swarms in a *danse macabre*.

"Run!" the leper roared.

Overcome with terror, Baldwin and his fool fled down the street, away from the symphony of screeches. He'd never encountered something like this before. It wasn't of the natural order—the work of true evil. When exhaustion reared its head, Baldwin turned to face the plumes of smoke, as a sickly, savory odor wafted from the Mansion House. Head pounding and hands shaking, the leper collapsed onto a bench and leaned against the Broken Blade.

"Did we just leave the Lord Mayor to die?" Gipi asked.

In a fit of shameful rage, Baldwin threw his wig onto the wet cobblestones. There was nothing he could do. Even if they returned to rescue Lawrence, he would've already roasted to death in his glass box. Monstrous guilt washed over the leper. He tore off his costume, leaving it to rot in the dampened street. Step by step, he marched south, cursing his cowardice in throes of self-pity, and yet, he knew better. There was still a chance to end this.

"Hey," Gipi called. "Where are you going?"

"Clarice, the Black Piper." Baldwin gathered the shards of his courage, tempering panic into purpose. "Whatever you wish to call her, she dies tonight."

CHAPTER FOUR

A gibbous moon loomed over the rooftops of Nedlergate. Smoke billowed in plumes until the sky was smothered by smog. The Black Piper stalked the ruins of her childhood estate, through charred wood and broken bones, willfully ignorant to the grasps of nobles as their eyes dimmed. Choking and wheezing, the dying lay strewn among half-eaten corpses. Countless rats stirred in the rubble, chewing on bits of rare flesh and each other, scurrying in the firelight. Raising the ivory flute to her lips, the Black Piper played, and the vermin obeyed, swarming at her command. Slowly, she scaled the mountain of rubble and noticed thick shards of glass and muffled cries from beneath the manor.

She recognized the voice all too well.

"So," she mused, "you're still alive."

With a swift melody, the Black Piper called upon her swarms by flute and will. One bite at a time, the rats excavated the shallow grave until Lawrence lay before her. The Black Piper eyed her father; skin flayed by flame, clothes soiled by ash and cinders.

"C-Clarice?" he choked. "Good lord, what's happened to you, girl?"

"Only what the world's done to me." The Black Piper knelt at his side. "I've shed the shackles of ladyhood." She picked up one of her favorites, the albino, and caressed it with dung-stained fingers. "Your daughter was drowned with the rats. And you did nothing to stop it."

"W-what are you saying—?"

"Don't bother denying it," she snapped. "You saw them, how they teased and mocked. That gleam in their eyes. Saying it was because they 'liked' me. That it would've been easier if I 'took it for what it was.' Oh, yes," she hissed. "You indulged me like a pretty princess, spoiled me with gifts. Where were you when it mattered? You thought it would make me proper. You couldn't stomach what happened. Rats weren't the only things I lost that day. You did nothing."

Lawrence averted his gaze. "T-that's not true," he lied.

The Black Piper paused, as if to muse. "Did it ever occur to you how wretched children are? They'll eat one another if given the chance. I would know."

"Even now." The Black Piper pressed a heel on her father's chest, relishing in his agonized gasps. "You hide, drinking and making merry, while I deflower the city. That's why," she sneered, "you will not live to see it succumb to the true plague. I plan to take its very future. A future none of you deserve. Its hope. Its innocence. Its children."

"N-no, don't—!"

"May the rats eat your eyes."

So they descended upon the Lord Mayor, ripping him apart with thousands of teeth, one bite at a time, as he writhed and screamed, until only a heap of crimson bones remained. Cold satisfaction washed over the Black Piper, but her subjects were far from at ease. The albino crept up her shoulder and whispered into its liege's ear. The strangers would be back—an unforeseen complication. Though rats feared them, there was nowhere they could hide, for her eyes and ears were legion. Like everything else in the city, they would succumb to her great pestilence.

The Black Piper cracked a wicked smile.

———

The Tower Bridge was a grim sight, little more than a pair of sullen spires piercing the haze, looming on either end of an arched stone causeway. Baldwin ventured down the streets along the slough of a river, its water black as pitch. Try as he might, the leper could not pry the rats from his mind's eye, haunted by the happenings at the Mansion House.

Did that really happen? Is the fever taking me?

Baldwin cradled his skull, trying to soothe his nerves.

Doubt swallowed his reason. Rats were not capable of such malice. They were vermin. Not daemons. Had he simply imagined it all and thrown the lamp in a hallucinatory stupor? Maybe it was ergotism blooming in his brain, spawned from a bite of infected bread? No, it couldn't be. He had a witness.

"We," he managed, "did see the same thing, no?"

"Man-eating rats?" Gipi asked. "Trust me, I wish it was just a bad dream too."

Baldwin shuddered. The whole affair was monstrous. Something he'd rather not believe. Superstitious as he was, the leper had never imagined such a thing was possible.

Still a few blocks from the bridge proper, he came to yet another slum. East End was a half-step above the misery of Cock and Key Alley; lines of low brick apartments and almshouses curved to form its narrows, punctuated by the occasional shanty built of thatch and wood. Dirt poor and knee deep in filth. The people had long shut their doors for the night. On the corner was a barber-surgeon marked by a pole wrapped in bloody cloth, signs offering deals on tooth extraction and dubious cures. Baldwin marched through the gloom, eying the wretched as they huddled around trash fires meant to deter the plague. Baldwin spied a host of silhouettes in the lamplight—children, judging by their stature.

"Oh," one said, "the knight!"

Baldwin sighed, deeply. He was hardly in the mood to indulge the orphans again. The leper was about to turn back until Jeremy emerged from around the shadowed bend.

"You lost, sir?" he asked.

"Not exactly," Baldwin said, dismissively. Then it occurred to him how well the gang might know of these back alleys and what secrets they held. Slowly, he knelt to Jeremy's level. "Tell me, child. What do you know of the Black Piper?"

Jeremy's eyes widened with dread. "Who's asking?"

"I'd be willing to pay for your cooperation."

The urchin twiddled his thumbs. "Well, okay, but keep

your voice down—"

"Excellent." Baldwin straightened his spine with a crack. "Where exactly is her lair?"

Jeremy laid a finger to his lips. "Not so loud!" he hushed. "They're everywhere...."

Baldwin clutched his sword's hilt, peering into the shadows. He knew full well what the rats were capable of. Sure enough, a horde of gleaming eyes emerged from the blackness, only to vanish as quickly as they'd come. "Speak quickly, child."

"Some of my friends have gone missing," Jeremy whispered. "She plays her flute and lures them with sweets and snatches them away to the sewers. Never to be seen again."

Baldwin felt the pit in his stomach glow. "I see."

"Where does she attack?" Gipi asked.

Jeremy tugged at the leper's tarnished cloak, bidding him to follow into the winding alleys. Against their better judgment, Baldwin and Gipi crept down the cobblestones. The urchin snagged a bit of burning wood from a nearby fire and raised it as a torch, illuminating the path that spiraled deep into the urban labyrinth. Finally, they came to an offshoot of the River Tintern, a shallow stream in a stone ditch. The stench was overpowering. Sewage flowed from a wide culvert and grate, where muddy prints betrayed the comings and goings of many a rat and footpad. Torchlight waned upon their approach. Baldwin descended the mildewed steps and found himself under the Tower Bridge. Groping in the darkness, he felt little things crunch under his footfalls—hard candies, twig dolls, small bones, and the like.

The leper hugged the walls, attempting to navigate the morass.

"Here?" he asked.

Jeremy shot him a thumbs-up, but kept his distance. He raised the torch ever so slightly, shedding light upon a bit of crimson graffiti, reading, "Free Candy."

Torn between revulsion and horror, Baldwin drew his sword. Fear leeched his resolve as he imagined what awaited him in the Court of the Black Piper.

"Stay back," the leper ordered.

Summoning his wrath, Baldwin kicked the grate. It quaked but did not break. Again, he struck its rusted iron. Nothing. The leper felt no pain but could not muster any more strength, not unless he wanted to risk fatigue in the warrens — a death sentence.

Gipi came to his side. "Shall I?"

"Be my guest," he hissed.

Gipi searched the rubble for reasons Baldwin didn't bother to ponder. He was content to watch. The jester tugged a bit of scrap free from the wet stones — a length of iron, a crowbar. With a twirl of finesse, she approached the grate and anchored her makeshift tool against its frame. She stomped on the metal and, with a grinding shriek, the passage was opened.

"Leverage," she said. "Hardly sorcery."

Baldwin turned to Jeremy and gave a solemn nod. "You are free to go. Rest assured, the Black Piper will not live to see the morning." The leper tossed him a shilling and tried to smile, to comfort the child as much as himself. "You see, this is my quest."

Jeremy looked away. "I know you're not a knight."

"What makes you say that?"

"You're too kind. And, well, mad."

"Two things can be true. Go, child."

With that, Baldwin led the plunge into the sewers. His boots sloshed against the sludge, feeling the slick stones underfoot. He rummaged through his pack for a torch and a bit of flint and steel. With a few strokes, the fat-soaked wrap caught fire, illuminating the access channel. Vaults and columns divided the complex into flooded tunnels, walls caked with mold and feces.

Wading against raw putrescence, Baldwin made his way.

"You know," Gipi kept a cloth over her nose and mouth, "we could always turn back."

Abandoning this errand was tempting, and yet, something nagged at the back of Baldwin's mind. If he didn't slay the Black Piper, who would? The city watch, cowering behind their tariffs and wooden barricades? The Inquisition, who'd have no qualms with simply burning Nedlergate to the ground? Dreadful as this task was, it was his and his alone.

East End smelled of children; a sickly scent that made the Black Piper salivate with morbid intent. Stalking the alleys with long strides, she followed the trail of toddlers. Dressed in a soiled rainbow of garments and garish rags, she was ready to prowl once more. With a knapsack over her shoulder, she juggled a shilling across her fingertips, for urchins were attracted to shiny things. She licked her chapped lips.

"Children," she cooed, "I know you're here somewhere." She drew a pair of candies from her pouch. "I've got sugar plums, chocolate wafers, and all manner of delights...." Every saccharine word oozed with an undercurrent of malice, yet her subjects obeyed, dancing along their hind legs in a grotesque ballet. The Black Piper tugged at her ill-fitting pants, if only to mask the pets scurrying up her legs. Slowly, she lifted an ivory pipe to her lips, playing a little melody to lure those huddled shadows into the light. A couple of bastards peered out from the edge of their scrap-wood hideout, eying her with hungry suspicion. "Wouldn't you like some goodies?" she asked. "Maybe an allowance from Sweet Clarice? Come out, come out. Don't be shy." Try as they might to whisper and hide, the Black Piper could hear their every word through her swarming courtiers.

"No, you mustn't!"

"But she has treats!"

"Yeah, I can't remember the last time I had a wafer...."

They had already given themselves away. The Black Piper sat atop a chopping stump and shut her eyes. She played a song tinged with loneliness to appeal to their pity. Through ritual and timing, the rats silently surrounded their prey, who would happily emerge for a chance to fill their aching stomachs. Hours would pass, but the result would be all the same. Tender as lamb, they would be feasted upon as they deserved. They were delicacies.

No one would miss them.

A rolling ball interrupted her song. The Black Piper knelt and examined the filthy thing. One by one, the children emerged, keeping their distance. She eyed them with murderous intent yet refrained from pouncing preemptively, masked by shadow.

"Come, come," she said, "gather around and let me tell you a tale."

She cleared her throat with a phlegmy rumble. It was a well-rehearsed fable, pieced together from a variety of tales and personal allegory. The Black Piper recounted her days as a "princess in a faraway land," which wasn't untrue concerning life as the orphans knew it. She embellished the tale with "three princes" who took her "mice" and "deflowered her rose."

The children were enthralled by her lavish descriptions and theatrical voices, and huddled together in faux fear at the ending.

"What happened to—?"

"Why," the Black Piper raised the flute to her lips, "they got what they deserved...."

With a shrill note, the rats chittered and rushed the children off their feet in a tide of gnawing teeth. Pouncing like a spider upon a mass of maggots, she swept them up into her sack and tied it shut. The children kicked and screamed, but the burlap was too tough to break free—a pebble struck her brow. Snarling in pain, the Black Piper's eyes darted about the hovels.

She knew who'd fired the slingshot.

Jeremy...!

"Little brat!" She barreled through the nearest shelter like a rabid bear and grabbed her aspiring nemesis by the leg, stuffing him in with the others. "Now be a good boy and shut up," she hissed, and yet, the Black Piper was distractible, to say the least. Her temper cooled upon seeing her furred courtiers rejoice and squeak in honor.

"Looks like we'll feast tonight, little sirs."

With that, she slunk to the shadows and made way to the Tower Bridge, only to find the sewer grate torn ajar. Intruders had broken into her palace. The miscreants that the rats so feared. She played a sharp chord, sounding the alarm, seething with rage as her army scurried into position. Whoever these people were, they'd join the banquet as the main course.

———

Baldwin led the way and came to a narrow junction.

The leper raised his torch, shedding light upon graffiti scrawled along the curving walls. Though splattered hastily, it resembled sheet music, but as to what melody, he could not decipher. Gipi kept close, her fingers never far from her dirk and sickle. Droplets leaked from the drains above, and shadowed rays of lamplight shimmered hazily against the flowing filth.

"These tunnels go on forever," Gipi sighed.

"So it would seem," Baldwin muttered, "keep your wits close."

"Trust me, they're sharp as ever."

A lonesome flute echoed throughout the depths, as little shadows skittered along strips of stone, gathering en masse. On the fringe of sight, Baldwin spied a silhouette—summoning rats from every crack and crevice. The music was shrill and off-key—a waltz of the damned. The leper gave chase, pursuing the figure down the twisting tunnels, though muck churned with every step, slowing him as it thickened. It wasn't long before Baldwin had lost his quarry.

"Dammit," he snarled.

As the leper took a step forward, something crunched under his boots. With a shudder, he raised his torch, only to find yellowed bones in the sewage and beady black eyes staring back at him. Baldwin's blood ran cold as a soaked tide of rats screeched and chittered, barely kept at bay by the flame. Music still taunted the leper, fading as it bounced off the walls, carrying from seemingly everywhere. Gipi caught up, only to gawk in horror.

"Oh shit," she blurted.

Baldwin swung the torch back and forth, watching the vermin shiver and slink, backs a bristle, as if threatened by the light. For a time, it seemed to work, until heavy footsteps breached the teeming mass. A shadow lunged forth, bloated and sculpted into a vaguely bipedal form by unnatural forces, its folds of fat and girth betrayed by fleeting light. Baldwin dropped his torch with a gasp, catching a glimpse of the monstrosity, squirming and contorting in the darkness.

A swollen fist collided with Baldwin's face, sending him careening down the tunnel.

Dazed yet unbroken, the leper staggered to his feet. A sharp whistle broke the silence, followed by bloodcurdling shrieks. Gipi had thrown a knife into the thing's chest. Baldwin felt the rats gnash at his legs as he hoisted himself upright and attempted to flee the swarm.

"Get it together, Baldwin!" the jester shouted.

Plowing through the sewage, Baldwin tried to fight off the horde as it weighed him down, threatening to drown him in the sewers. A sword could do little against these hundreds of tiny foes. The leper began to sink into the quagmire, as rats crawled under his cuirass and gnawed at his bandages, face inches from filth — until a blinding flash enveloped the tunnel. Ears ringing and vision blurred, Baldwin collapsed in a splashing heap. Before he knew it, the swarms had scurried back to the warrens within the walls. Delicate and deliberate footsteps echoed in the dimness as a lantern shone from the passage's end, revealing a familiar raven-beaked mask.

"Sophia?" Baldwin coughed. "What are you...?"

As he took in lungfuls of stale air and strange fumes, the leper's throat numbed. Whether poisoned or simply exhausted, he tried to stand, only for his knees to shake and weaken. Leaning against the Broken Blade, Baldwin felt the leering walls orbit his skull, greasy water against his cheeks, and gloved hands dragging him to his limping feet.

Then all went black.

CHAPTER FIVE

Emerging from dreamless slumber, Baldwin opened his eyes to lanterns swaying from the rafters of an unknown house, veiled in eerie light. Try as he might to stir, he couldn't quite move his limbs, haunted by afterimages from beyond, as a phantom in tattered robes loomed over the bedside. Baldwin recognized the figure—Death had paid him a visit. He was unable to speak; his heart palpitated as he mustered the strength to reach for his sword, but to no avail. Trapped in his own body, Baldwin watched helplessly as Death cocked her head, as if to remind him of the price of failure.

No…. Not yet—

With a sudden gasp, Baldwin woke once more, springing upright from a stretcher. Moments of silence passed as the leper caressed his brow. Gathering the shattered pieces of his wits, Baldwin examined his wounds and sores, finding his lesions covered in fresh bandages and ointment. Someone had healed him. Though stiff, the leper turned his neck aside, listening to seething instruments of science. Sophia ground medicinal herbs with a mortar and pestle, no doubt producing a poultice. The smoke was thick with anise flavor, as if to rid the air of foul vapors. It was the only reason the doctor sat unmasked, letting her raven locks flow loosely over her shoulders, cheeks round as the sachets she'd stuffed with gunpowder and smelling salts, eyes glistening as jade against the controlled flames.

Sophia did not look up. "So, you've come to then."

"How long was I unconscious for?"

"Less than a day," Sophia said. "My apologies. My concoctions were perhaps a bit too potent for your constitution. You inhaled more than your share. Honestly, I'm surprised your lungs weren't damaged in the process."

Baldwin's thoughts wandered to Death and divine intervention. Was something watching over him? Was his purpose so clear? Or was it simply dumb luck?

It mattered not, for his heart beat still.

"Still," the doctor continued, "you were a fool to venture into the sewers without precautions. If

I hadn't found you, you'd certainly have been eaten alive. What were you doing down there, exactly?"

"I could ask you the same." Baldwin looked away, pondering how to explain the phenomenon of the Black Piper. "Perhaps we hunt the same quarry."

"Oh?"

"I," Baldwin paused, "do not expect you to believe me, but there is a horror beneath this city. They call her the Black Piper. And I have seen her evil firsthand."

Sophia shot him a condescending smirk. "Have you now?"

"She uses black magic to control the vermin and —"

A desperate squeak interrupted their debate as Sophia examined a caged rat. "If there's any hope of curing the plague, it resides in alchemy." She stuck the rodent with a syringe and extracted an ounce of pus. "Therefore, I must balance the humors of the infected. And what better way to test than on the plague-bearers themselves?" The doctor took her sample and laid it under a brass tubular device, twisting the screws with surgical care, peering through a tiny monocular lens. "As I suspected...."

Alchemy....

Baldwin stifled a scoff. Science was nothing but charlatans comparing their latest snake oils. Drunk off their own delusions, these physicians would probe the anus of a cadaver in the name of progress. Such heathen ways could not be tolerated, whether by sword or scalpel. Faith drove him forward. Conviction would have him see dawn. And yet, for all her unorthodox practices, Sophia did manage to heal his corpse of a body — for what it was worth.

"I am grateful for your assistance," Baldwin said, seeking

to preserve his own sense of etiquette. The Broken Blade was propped against the far wall, as were his greaves and breastplate. Strapping the bronze mask to his face, Baldwin dressed himself slowly, bandages stretching with every motion. Once he'd gathered his arms and armor, the leper turned to inquire further, only for a shadow to haunt his thoughts. "Where is Gipi? Is she safe?"

"At the tavern, busking for coin."

"Why am I not surprised?" Baldwin scoffed.

"Be grateful," Sophia said. "Nursing you back to health wasn't exactly cheap."

Baldwin managed a reluctant smile. "Then my coffers must be lighter than usual."

The door swung open with a chime. Gipi sauntered into the room, cap and bells askew, as she drunkenly raised her coin purse high in triumph. "Tonight was a good night."

"That makes one of us," Baldwin said.

Gipi swung her lute over her shoulder. "Glad to see you up and about." She approached the desk and slid an assortment of shillings by Sophia's work. "Any luck on your miracle cures?"

"Slow going, I'm afraid," Sophia said. "Did you bring what I asked?"

Gipi passed her a pewter flask. "Right here."

"Excellent." Sophia took a hearty shot of whiskey. "It's been a long night."

Baldwin rolled his eyes. Though his body ached with fatigue, the Black Piper couldn't be allowed to run amok. "At any rate, what've you deduced?"

"If you doubt me," she said, "come and take a look."

Reluctantly, Baldwin limped to the worktable. The doctor lifted a perfume-stained cloth to her lips and nose, moving aside. He examined the compound instrument but dared not touch it. He hadn't the faintest idea of how to operate such equipment.

"What do you call this device?" he asked.

"A microscope," Sophia explained. "Please, peer through

the lens."

Baldwin squinted past his doubt and obeyed — only to gasp in shock. The optics revealed a host of white worms writhing in the black sample, finer than hair, utterly invisible to the naked eye yet nonetheless real, reminiscent of the drifting debris behind one's eyes.

"What does this entail?" he asked.

"It is generally known that worms grow from foul corpses," Sophia explained. "I have found that everything putrid is filled with masses of these invisible worms. Plague also arises from decay. The blood of the fevered has fully convinced me. I have found it so crowded with worms that it dumbfounded me — plague is indeed a living thing."

Baldwin nodded, slowly, feigning understanding.

"Hang on," Gipi interjected. "Mind if we ask a few questions?"

Sophia nodded, eyes gleaming. "Oh?"

"Firstly," Gipi began, "have you studied the 'nature' of these rats?"

"Less than I'd like to say," Sophia admitted. "I'm afraid beasts are not a topic of study for me, but I have noticed their aberrant behavior." She fiddled with her brass buttons. "According to legend, rats are sensitive to specific pitches and respond as such."

"Music, you say?" Baldwin asked.

"In a manner of speaking."

"Wait, wait," Gipi raised a hand, "what if there's a sequence or, say, intervals. Wouldn't that have, well, 'layered' results — ?"

"The Devil's Tritone," Baldwin interrupted. "It's the only way."

Gipi was about to speak up, but held her tongue. After all, what else could explain the phenomenon of the Black Piper? Long had the Devil's Tritone been condemned by the Holy See. Uttering its dissonance was punishable by excommunication, for its instability thinned the line between earth and aether, lulling the forces of darkness—and worse. Undoubtedly, she was using the Devil in Music to command the vermin and devour the innocent.

With renewed vigor, Baldwin pressed on towards the door. "If we stop her unnatural music," he said, "perhaps we can sever her hold on the rats."

Sophia laid a gloved finger to her chin. "Intriguing."

"Wait, what?" the jester asked.

"There is hope yet, Gipi." Baldwin gripped his sword's hilt, adjusting the baldric across his back. "I must ask you to trust me once more. We may yet burn out this evil. Sophia," he added, "if you'd be so kind as to lend us your expertise further."

"With all due respect, I think my services are better spent here." She opened her texts to glossaries of medical terminology. "I'm a doctor, not a tactician."

Baldwin bowed his head. "Thank you again for your aid and insight, good doctor. I hope our paths cross again." With that, he marched to the threshold. "Gipi?"

The jester shrugged. "Ready as I'll ever be."

———

The Black Piper lounged atop a throne of stones and broken bones, surrounded by the squirming legions of her court—rodents of unusual size. Flanked by sets of cages, torn tapestries, and scavenged baubles, hers was a keep of suffering and hoarded filth, a mockery of high society. Polishing cutlery with a soiled cloth, she wetted her lips, whistling to tune out the whimpers of children. They rattled in iron cages, trapped behind bars. Her subjects were seated, lining the long slab of a table, eagerly awaiting the banquet's second course. Reaching for a bit of pepper, the Black Piper sprinkled a bit of seasoning into the cast-iron cauldron and stirred. The aroma of long pork filled her nostrils.

She licked the ladle. "Perfection."

With the crank of a cruel mechanism, the Black Piper pivoted an occupied cage over the deep pot. Frothing at the lip, it glowed with heat as she stoked the coals under the grating. She lowered the cage, inch by inch, towards the vast cauldron, basking in the urchins' screams.

Tears were her secret ingredient. The pot was certainly deep enough to submerge the bastards in boiling broth—a slow death.

"Hush now," she cooed. "No one can hear you. No one's coming."

Just then, the albino rat emerged from a crack in the wall, squeaking in alarm. The Black Piper gritted her teeth and turned to face her favorite pet. She needn't ask what the fuss was—the intruders had breached the outer walls and were closing in. That could not be suffered.

"Kill them," she ordered.

———

Raising a torch, Baldwin waded through the tunnels once more. The leper gritted his teeth and pressed on into a cistern amidst the sewers. The foul water was shallow here. His wet boots slapped against the slimy flagstones. Stone columns supported the vaulted ceiling, where a shaft of moonlight shimmered past the bars of a drain, gleaming against the dampness.

"How far do these tunnels go?" Gipi asked.

Baldwin grunted but did not reply. Whining wouldn't get them anywhere faster. Gipi watched the rear, content to brood from the edge of the torchlight. Morose as he was, Baldwin couldn't blame her. These conditions were truly miserable.

"We cannot be far," he said. "Now would be a good time to discuss strategy. Something tells me that charging in blindly won't work with this particular foe."

"You've got that damn right." In a single, fluid motion, Gipi drew her lute. She twisted its pegs, plucking the strings, as if searching for the perfect tune. "Trust me, I've got a plan."

Slowly, the air grew chill until Baldwin could see his own breath. The torch began to dim as he followed the trail of corpses. Most harrowing of all were those spared of buboes, covered in tiny bite marks and postmortem wounds—as if they'd been lured to drown. Baldwin's grip tightened around his torch, eyes narrowing. Suddenly, the ceiling quaked. A weakened portion of the sewers caved in, stones severing him from his companion. When the dust settled, Baldwin tore at the blockage, only to hear Gipi's muffled voice from the other side.

"Shit!" she shouted. "Hang tight, I'll find another way—"

An eruption of chittering shrieks cut her short. Baldwin tore loose stones aside, knowing full well that the rats had descended upon his fool. Overcome with panic and rage, he heaved brick upon brick into the sewage, haunted by the sounds of a skirmish.

"Gipi," he cried, "Gipi!"

There was no response, only the sound of scraping claws, and then silence. Whispering a prayer into his rosary, Baldwin drew his sword and pressed on through the subterranean gloom. He carried on, alone, save for the splash of his boots against the water. Fear washed over him, forcing his knees and grip to falter, keeping his guard low. Until he heard that dreadful flute.

At the labyrinth's heart, a shadow loomed from atop a throne of rubble, fingers fluttering across an ivory pipe. Baldwin raised his torch, barely catching a glimpse of his foe. The Black Piper was a lady of the court, dressed in a corset and white ruff, though such things had been tarnished by the loathsome sewers. Her stringy black hair was powdered with flakes of dander, face rail thin, and skirt smeared with filth. Such eeriness was punctuated by a protruding jaw and beady, black eyes. Content to lurk in the shadows, the Black Piper winced at the torchlight as Baldwin stepped closer, as the vermin began to stir. He noticed the frothing cauldron, and a dozen cages dangling midway from the ceiling, twenty feet above the floor, bound to chains and pulleys, crowded with forgotten children.

"You," Baldwin said, "you have much to answer for."

The Black Piper grinned, her teeth glistening in the dimness. "And you've been quite the thorn in my side." She stood, slowly, lowering the pipe from her lips. "You would topple my kingdom, though for what, I wonder? Did Lawrence pay you in advance?"

"My companion wishes that were so."

"Indeed," the Black Piper said. "So, you're not a mercenary. No, your bearing is too regal. Tell me, where do you hail from? Titles, deeds, and all, if you please."

The leper paused, contemplating whether to divulge the truth. Pride overcame reason, and he removed his bronze mask to intimidate her with his foul visage.

"I am Baldwin," he rasped, "of Golgotha."

The Black Piper's eyes widened in revulsion, only for a moment, betraying a glint of fear. "Clarice of Nedlergate," she bowed low, "first of her name."

"From one mad lord to another, then," Baldwin mused. "I grow weary of hunting you, my lady. I trust that you understand the sanctity of a duel."

"But of course." Clarice clasped her wrists. "My weapon of choice should be of no surprise. May the longest breath win, Good King Baldwin." Her eyes narrowed. "Soft as your tone is, I know Lawrence sent you, though he may not have paid you."

"No," Baldwin said, "and frankly, your father wished against me killing you. However, I doubt he's with us." He readied his sword, pointing its chipped edge at Clarice's breast. "I have no such qualms. In truth, I look forward to cleansing the city with your blood."

"Then let us dance."

Clarice blew into her ivory flute, fingers dancing over its tone holes, gathering speed as she played the Devil's Tritone. Rising to a crescendo of terror, its chords howled in a cacophonous gale, evocative of the yawning void. At her command, tides of vermin rolled as waves of fur and flesh, bursting through the walls in a deluge of sewage, threatening to swallow the leper in a sea of teeth. No blade could cut the swarm; Baldwin dove behind the pillar, trying to tune out her wicked melody. With a pause and prayer, the leper's gaze fell upon the cages dangling overhead, as the desperate screams of their captives blared in his ears. As the rats poured forth, engulfing the chamber in a lethal carpet, Baldwin slammed a boot against a pulley, as a counterweight came crashing down, enough to send the cages careening to the ceiling. He gripped the bottom and was lifted yards above a monstrous death, and began to scale the rusty bars.

Safe from the vermin, at least….

From the cage's rusted top, Baldwin clung to the chain for dear life. His heart wavered as he watched Clarice ride the furred waves effortlessly, continuing to play and bask in her victims' screams. Leaping atop a cage as a mad acrobat, she summoned waves of rabid foam and yawning maws, sending her legions crashing against the cages. The leper pivoted his strength and swung from chain to chain like a great ape. Each leap seemed a mile as he dodged a succession of waves and plunged his fist into Clarice's cheek, feeling teeth and cartilage crunch against the might of his fist. She wobbled and bled but maintained balance, changing her tempo, as sewage and knotted tails began to churn.

"How many children have you stolen?" Baldwin snarled. "How many cradles have you robbed to fill your monstrous appetites?"

Clarice grinned. "Far more than you can save."

Strong as he was, Baldwin was cumbersome and not gifted in finesse. At that moment, he swung too low, only for Clarice to perch atop the flat of his blade in a feat of diabolical grace, shifting her weight, as to tangle his sword among the chain.

As they locked eyes, Clarice's heel slammed into Baldwin's chest, sending him tumbling into the rats below, but not before the leper dragged her down by the bodice, content to settle for a draw. With a crack, they landed together on the flagstone floor. Baldwin plowed through bludgeoning pain, having no doubt broken a rib, wheezing, sword still at hand, preparing to deal an executioner's blow to Clarice's neck. He screamed in agony and let gravity do the work, only for the blade to strike a slimy stone.

No!

Clarice had already rolled aside and played a dirge, slow

and somber, that made Baldwin's heart sink into his chest. Before he knew it, the leper was weighed to his knees by fattened rats, gnawing at his wounds, clawing at his fetid sores.

Dammit....

Tails and nails fell over his eyes as paws inched towards his nose and mouth, attempting to squirm and feast on his insides. No raw prowess or strength of will could rid him of these vermin, and for a moment, Baldwin shut his eyes and accepted his fate.

Until a familiar lute echoed from a near passage. Its strings were tuned, sharp and clean, as a chord reverberated throughout the depths, dissonant against the Black Piper's flute, disrupting her music. The vermin twitched and faltered, as if the eldritch trance had been severed. Baldwin raised his head and spied a familiar figure, strumming her lute—the sewers her stage. Every note echoed throughout the cistern, performing a ballad in a major key, strengthening Baldwin's resolve, if only to endure the pain a moment longer.

"You're alive?" Clarice managed.

Gipi played on, tuning out the Black Piper's frantic notes.

"Sorry it took me so long," the jester said. "Got this bitch, okay?"

Baldwin smiled and heaved himself upright, free of rodents. "Your timing is impeccable," he managed a whisper. "Now." He stood, slowly. "Repent."

Clarice's wide eyes were fixed on Baldwin. He gave a bloody cough and tugged at the torn wraps over his arms. He leaned on his sword's hilt and marched forth, dragging his blade against the stones. Gipi's melody swelled into triumphant cords, emboldening the leper and keeping the rats at bay.

"No," Clarice cracked, "no—!"

"Repent!" Baldwin roared.

The rats squeaked as he swung his sword wide. Gipi's music stuttered in tandem with the leper's wrath. Rats nipped at his heels and leapt at him, only to spasm in the wake of dueling songs. The Black Piper was cornered. Baldwin marched on, crushing vermin under his heels, all but relishing in his foe's anguish.

"Don't," she cried. "Don't hurt them!"

The leper did not relent. In an act of desperation, Clarice drew a stiletto and plunged it deep into his chest. Baldwin gripped her wrist, letting the blood flow — she'd narrowly missed his heart. As they locked eyes, Clarice uttered a whimper.

"Why won't you die?"

There was so much Baldwin wanted to say then, to monologue on his crusade, on the nature of good and evil, on the transience of life and death. That he existed in a liminal space between the two — a dead man walking. And in that lay his greatest strength. It would've been a waste of words. Baldwin raised his sword and cleaved through Clarice's chest, severing rib and organ, deaf to her screams. He stomped on the flute, feeling ivory crack under his boot, as an abominable force shrieked through the air, as if some terrible entity had been banished by his triumph. The rats dissipated, fleeing into cracks in the walls, never to be seen again. Dissociating from the pain, the leper tore himself back to the present and leaned against a slime-crusted column, clutching his chest as he bled profusely.

Gipi kept her distance, letting her liege have his "moment."

Silence passed, breached only by the wails of frightened children in cages, orbiting the duelists in a cacophony of sorrow. Clarice managed a bloody laugh, lying prone on the floor.

"Look at them," she choked, "twinkling eyes and tainted minds. What," she paused, "what do you think will become of them, left to rot? Our world. It's…hardly fit for innocence." A maddened smirk crossed her lips. "You've seen it, 'Baldwin of the Holy Land,' no — you know it. Cruel as I may be, the world doesn't deserve them. And they don't deserve to suffer in it. Fables. Fairytales. They're saccharine in comparison to the world of men."

Baldwin stood, slowly. "A shallow misanthropy."

"Perhaps so," Clarice laughed, weakly. "You weren't

there when they took me in that alley. Dragging me. Beating me. We were so young then. When they took…everything from me. Because I had the audacity to deny them. To say, 'no.'" She stared up at the children, eyes wide and fading without remorse. "How many do you think will grow up to be like them?"

Baldwin did not reply.

"You weren't there, but maybe, if you were, maybe things would've been different." Tears began to well in her eyes. "You know what it's like…."

"No," Baldwin said. "I do not."

"Don't bother denying it. You surrendered your throne. Your power. Your privilege. And now you wallow in the filth. Like me. Why? What else? What drove you to this?"

"I will leave you with this," Baldwin said. "You may spread pestilence, but I…I live with it." Clarice opened her mouth, as if to speak, but no words escaped her lips. "Go now." The leper pressed the Broken Blade against her neck. "I will deliver you with mercy."

"Please…."

Baldwin did just that and bowed his head, watching as the remaining rats engulfed the butchered corpse. Whether mourning a mother or feasting on her flesh, he could not say. One by one, Baldwin lowered and pried open the cages, releasing the traumatized captives within. Grateful as they were, he knew the truth. Victory wasn't a vaccine. For good or ill, the future was yet unwritten. Plague would still ravage the city, but fewer children would be eaten.

CHAPTER SIX

The Drowned Rat was a taphouse of mediocre fare. Looming over the River Tintern, its hearth was surrounded by surly sailors and delinquents. Brooding against the firelight, Baldwin kept to himself and sipped at a cup of watered ale, watching as Gipi played her lute atop a table, if only to cover expenses for the night. After a hot bath and a change of clothes, they were ready to fade into the civilized crowd. A serving girl passed by with a platter of roast mutton and various vegetables, enduring the coos of drunk patrons. The leper warmed his hands, wracked with dull yet throbbing pain, simply wanting to rest and recover from the battle in the sewers.

Silently, he bit into a chunk of cheddar and stale bread, staring into the fireplace, hypnotized by its fleeting flames. Miraculously, his journal had survived the expedition. Dipping his quill in an inkwell, he scribbled on a drying page, eager to chronicle these happenings—when someone pulled up a chair across the table.

"I take it your mission was a success?" Sophia asked.

"Indeed," Baldwin did not look up, "the Black Piper has been slain." He felt the doctor smile from beneath her raven-beaked mask. "What?"

"You speak as a knight pursuing dragons."

"Rats weren't the only evil down there."

"That much is plain." Sophia glanced over her shoulder as Gipi capered down the floor, basking in her own solo. "Do you plan on staying in Nedlergate?"

Baldwin opened his mouth, as if to speak, but words caught in his throat.

Noble as yesterday's deeds were, the city was hardly his calling. Shadows of guilt lingered in the back of his mind as he remembered a neglected oath, staring into the hearth, and recalled the massacre of Gravesend—Dampe's silhouette stark against the blazing carnage. He would pursue the mercenary prince to whatever end. He'd lingered too long.

"I'm afraid not," he said.

"Where will you go?"

Baldwin sighed, deeply. "Are you familiar with the Undertakers?"

"The mercenary band? Not intimately. Have you dealt with them in the past?"

Baldwin clenched his fist under the table. "In a manner of speaking. I've sworn vengeance against their captain. I've witnessed firsthand the man's capacity for cruelty."

"What did they do to you?"

"Outside of a knife in the back. Nothing. However, I was there at Gravesend, and despite my best efforts, could not save them. I cannot abide that."

Sophia lifted her mask and raised a pewter cup to her lips. "It wasn't your fault."

"You weren't there—"

"Ah," Gipi called, sauntering to their table, "is this man bothering you, good doctor?" She threw a wink and pulled up a chair. "What brings you to this fine establishment?"

"I was in the neighborhood," Sophia said, "and come with a proposition."

"Oh?" Baldwin asked.

"The Old Road is not exactly safe," the doctor continued. "War is spreading, and reliable swords are hard to come by. I have business in the East Marches."

"Leaving so soon?" Gipi asked. "Plague's not exactly over."

"One doctor can't cure an epidemic," Sophia said, "but my findings must be reported to the Narrenturm, a two weeks' journey by coach. There will be a caregivers' convention at the asylum." She lowered her voice. "I may have found the source of the plague."

"White worms?" Baldwin asked.

Sophia nodded, slowly. "War is spreading. Taxes are high, and conscripts are filling the kingdom's ranks where mercenaries cannot. The peasants are revolting." She flopped a gazette on the table, detailing these events. "If I'm going west, I'll need protection."

"War, you say?" Baldwin asked.

"Appreciate the sentiment," Gipi turned to her companion, "but I think we're booked."

Baldwin paused and thought this over. If the Great Peasants War was escalating, then the Undertakers would have ample work cut out for them, and yet, there was no guarantee that he'd come across his quarry with Sophia at the helm. Dampe was the priority.

"We'd depart tomorrow," the doctor said.

Baldwin bowed his head. "As do I. However, my path is already chosen. You must understand, my time is short and must be spent with care." He caught sight of a troupe of ruffians by the bar, fiddling with cudgels and knives. "I fear I've overstayed my welcome."

"I see," Sophia said, a twinge of disappointment in her voice. "Well, thank you for your assistance, regardless. Hopefully, our paths will cross again."

With a nod, the good doctor stood and took her leave. Baldwin resumed his contemplation, musing over his journey thus far, realizing how far from home he truly was. In this foreign country, he was little more than a pilgrim on an endless road. Gipi strummed her lute quietly, as if not wanting to disturb the leper. However, he recognized it as the ballad she'd performed the morning after Gravesend—a bolero with rising potential. Such was Baldwin's will in this world. He did not sleep that night, content to gaze out a window as the sun crept over Nedlergate. Hardly an urbanite, he was anxious to leave the city. Baldwin imagined the golden trees looming on either side of the Old

Road, rolling hills rich with white flowers in bloom, tall grasses whisking in the wind. The next thing he knew, the road lay before the wandering pair, as the open country breathed with waking life.

"So," Gipi asked, "what now?"

Baldwin did not reply. Step by step, he ventured down the road, as great plumes of smoke rose from the East Marches. Picturesque as this country was, the leper knew his course was stained with blood and attrition. With a hand over his sword's hilt, he pressed on along the rows of unmarked headstones, haunted by reminiscence over those he could not save.

If there was any hope in avenging Gravesend, it lay at the war front.

Dampe. You cannot run forever....

ACT THREE

CHAPTER ONE

Alone in his tent, John Radcliffe rubbed his calloused fingers against yet another toy soldier—lovingly whittled, no doubt a gift from the woodcarver to his son. Slowly, he placed it on a map of the East Marches with the others, completing a host of repurposed models and pawns. He caressed his thick gray mustache, contemplating his next move.

We're running out of options....

Even now, he felt the enemy close ranks. Radcliffe's men were exhausted and on the run. Scouts could be just over the next ridge, archers circling like crows over dead lambs, and they wouldn't even notice. So few remained. So few had the courage to stay. Morale was fleeting. Holes in canvased walls seemed to stare at him, judging. With a trembling swig of whiskey, Radcliffe marched out into the cold night air, half-hoping to sober up.

"Captain." A footman came to his side with a salute, leaning on a bill-hooked pole. "Reconnaissance has yet to report back. Should we send a search party?"

Radcliffe did not reply. Broken battlements formed a fragile shell around tents and bonfires of Sentinel Hill. The mountain trail seemed to twist around the captain's skull as he came to a cliff's edge, overlooking the enemy camps in the valley below.

The Great Peasants' War had ravaged the land. Once, its parishes and townships had partitioned rolling acres into a patchwork of crops and orchards; a green hill country, tended to lovingly by pastoral folk. Half-timbered houses nestled against one another along the high street of every hamlet, while coaching inns loomed in the woods for weary steeds and travelers. Children played in the open green, and wolfhounds dozed through their nightly vigils. When the soil was rich and harvests were bountiful, even the pall of winter held little sway.

"Captain?" the soldier asked. "Are you well?"

"Well, as I can be," his voice was hoarse from shouting orders and yesterday's retreat. His ears still rang from the howling artillery; his hands unwashed, stained with the blood of his comrades. The consequences of lethal overconfidence. "How're the boys doing?"

"Shaken, but...all right."

Radcliffe scoffed, knowing well what the soldier meant. "Can't say I blame them. Desertion isn't exactly an option. Or surrender." He turned to the footman. "Do you know what happens to 'traitors' under the king's banner?"

The soldier paled. "I've heard stories...."

"Hung, drawn, and quartered," Radcliffe said. "First, they fasten you to a hurdle and whip the steed to the square. Then the noose and the drop. Seems almost merciful, doesn't it?" He cracked a manic smirk. "Right before your last breath, they cut you loose and take a blade to your gut and groin. Splitting for all the world to see. Then the axe comes down on your legs, arms, and, finally, your head. And the last thing you see on God's green earth is chopper lifting up your still beating heart, and hear the words, 'Behold, the heart of a traitor!'"

Radcliffe didn't bother to face his subordinate. His point had been made. "Our hands may be filthy," he said, "but at least we offer a clean death."

"I'll," the footman paused, "keep watch then, sir."

Radcliffe took his leave. The Kingsmen were not the only soldiers massing in the foothills. Mercenaries and foreign landsknechts had answered the call as well. With numbers alone, the royalists were all but guaranteed victory.

"If this is our end," he said, "so be it."

The working fields lolled to the east with rows of tilled earth and acres of wheat and barley. Such bounties shimmered under a golden sun. Dressed in wool tunics and trousers, yeomen and farmhands tended to their crops, wiping away the sweat from their brows, pressing on with heavy iron scythes, toiling until the sabbath. Baldwin was careful to keep his head low and face hidden, while Gipi's bells notified the peasantry of their passing.

"Nicer country than we're used to," the jester said.

Half a week had passed since their departure from Nedlergate, and now, they were scarcely a day's trek from the war front. Anxiety was palpable. On occasion, the travelers would spy a regiment of men-at-arms bearing the king's livery — a red rose against a white field. This was a royalist country. With every hour, the smell of sulfur drew nearer.

"It seems we share the course of the Kingsmen," Baldwin said.

"Huh," Gipi commented. "How's that make you feel?"

"What do you mean?"

"Let's just say I doubt they're going to help the peasants."

"Only to fight the rebels."

"Uh-huh," Gipi kept her voice low, "and do you think they care to distinguish the farmer's wife from the rogue archer? May I remind you who hired the Undertakers to begin with?" She shook her head. "If you want justice, you can't turn a blind eye to that."

"What are you suggesting?"

"Just making sure you understand this isn't a fairy tale."

"I once ruled a crusader kingdom, Gipi," the leper said. "When I was sixteen, Sir Reynald and I won a great victory against the Easterlings. Though I may be a king no longer, do not forget that I know a thing or two about the art of war. And its price."

For once, Gipi conceded with a nod. "Fair enough."

As the sun began to set, they came across an old barn aloft a hill — ideal for squatting. Inside, Baldwin barricaded the creaking doors with a pair of pitchforks. Gaping holes in the roof provided ample ventilation for a bonfire, and timber was plentiful. Content to sharpen his blade, Baldwin sat atop a sack of barley and waited for nightfall. Dinner consisted of tomatoes, sausages, and crispy bacon, prepared with a skillet that Gipi had likely pilfered in the city.

She winked. "Don't ask, don't tell."

Baldwin managed a smile. For all his moralizing, the reality of travel was laid bare. He'd have likely starved without Gipi's pragmatism. When all was said and done, they settled in for the night, listening to the wind rustle through rows of wheat.

"Rest easy," the leper said. "This may be our last chance before the war front."

Gipi settled for a makeshift mattress of hay bales. "No need to remind me."

Try as he might, sleep proved to be a fickle mistress. Baldwin stared at the stars and moonlight piercing the fractured ceiling — a shiver ran down his spine, as a familiar presence made itself known. The campfire had long since died. Outside the barn, the leper spied orbs of ghostly blue flame as heavy hooves crunched against dry grass.

"Gipi," Baldwin's voice was barely a whisper, "wake up!"

No response. She was still as a corpse. Given his contagion, he dared not touch her. Baldwin readied his sword and ventured out of the barn, if only to greet the black rider with suspicion — Death loomed from atop a pale horse, scythe at hand.

"So," Baldwin said. "You're not a dream?"

"Make of me what you will," Death said. "It matters not, for I am inevitable." With a wave of a thin hand, she summoned a black box in a wisp of scentless smoke.

Slowly, she dismounted and smiled beneath her long hood.

"What business have you with me?" Baldwin asked.

Death knelt before the dry earth, silently, as grass and good life withered at her touch, leaving only a circle of blight where she sat.

She opened the box to reveal a chess set of ebony and ivory.

"Please," she said, "indulge me."

Baldwin hardly understood, but obeyed his reaper. Before he knew it, the board was set, and the pieces were placed. In a game of chance, Death was given black.

The leper shot her a smirk. "Naturally."

"Your move."

Baldwin reluctantly took a seat. The barn and wheat fields seemed to be swallowed by darkness, as if he and Death were the only ones in existence.

So, they made their opening moves and studied the board.

"Are you frightened?" Death asked.

"Yes." Baldwin examined a white pawn and made his decision — a king's gambit. "All the world is in chess, or so they say. I take it my life is no exception."

"Indeed." Death deployed her bishop, severing the leper's right to castle. "But not all tales are worth telling." She stroked her alabaster chin.

Baldwin sent a knight to corner the black queen. "What do you mean?"

"Your reckless abandon in the city, in the face of plague and worse." Death plucked a pawn and fell back with a sigh. "You're fortunate to have someone watching over you."

"You," Baldwin asked, "spared me?"

"More than once."

"Why?"

"It would not have been ordained by God," Death said. "Though that is not to dismiss your feats of strength. I must ask, however, what is your purpose?"

Baldwin stared at the board; he had solidified control of the center.

"To do good and deliver the wicked —"

"No, you misunderstand." Death peered into his eyes, unpinning her queen and cornering the leper's bishop. "What drives you beyond a mere oath? Why do you fight?"

Baldwin paused; his lips were dry, and his hands were

shaking. On the surface, his cause was noble, and yet, it reeked of self-righteousness, wandering from parish to parish, fighting evil for the hollow reward of recognition. Solemn as he was, Baldwin would not die in obscurity. No, he was meant for greater things. As for what, he could not say.

"Life is meaningless without purpose," Baldwin said, "and so my search continues."

"And you think Dampe will be your deliverance?"

"It's certainly a start."

A lonely ray of light pierced the darkness. Death smiled and twitched her fingers, dismissing the game in a wisp of cloud. "That may be the first time you've been truly honest with yourself." She stood, robes fluttering in the wind. "I encourage you to cherish what precious time you have left and pray you find... whatever it is you're looking for."

"Have you nothing better to do than toy with me?"

"Do not fret. Our game is far from over, but its end is inevitable."

Baldwin tried to stand, gripped by sudden fatigue. His eyes fluttered shut as Death mounted her pale horse, departing with the fleeting night. Adrift in dreamless slumber, he would bask in the shade of the thoughtless void. Such was Death's parting gift.

The Old Road could wait.

When at last he woke, Baldwin gathered his belongings. He and Gipi resumed their eastward journey. Death's words did not leave him. As they carried on, distant smoke thickened into a stale miasma, as fallow fields bled into the trenches, and even the massifs were but pale phantoms. Through the haze, Baldwin saw the aftermath of skirmishes and raids—toppled coaches, looted corpses, and horse carcasses. He gritted his teeth, reminded of the massacre of Gravesend. The Old Road was the leper's only course, his salvation, its cobbles leading the way to parts unknown, and in that uncertainty lay hope. Then came the screams. Without a moment's hesitation, Baldwin followed the cries off the road, as distorted memories of burning dead clawed at his thoughts, whispering all the while.

"Baldwin," Gipi tore at his bandaged sleeve, "snap out of it!"

The leper tore himself back to the present, surrounded by the ruins of a nameless village. He trod through the scorched earth with care and paused before the casualties. Baldwin's knuckles turned white, clutching his sword's hilt, though he didn't remember unsheathing it.

"What happened?" Gipi asked.

"I," Baldwin managed, "nothing. It's nothing."

Torn between fear and shame, the leper looked about the ruined hamlet. Fantasies and aberrant happenings aside, one thing was certain—his sanity was fleeting.

"I'm worried about you," Gipi said.

"Fear not," Baldwin replied. "My conviction is strong as ever."

"That's not what I'm talking about." The jester shoved her hands deep into her pockets. "I've known you for a long time, Baldwin. And I can safely say you're getting worse. Chasing after things that aren't there. Going with your gut against all odds. Being so quick to believe in, well, anything."

"Am I wrong?" Baldwin asked.

"You're not wrong," Gipi sighed, "just—"

"Then leave me be. When my 'madness' is a peril, then we shall talk." Baldwin knelt before one of the dead and examined his battered armor. "The Undertakers were here."

Cannonfire severed his words. Baldwin raced to the hilltop and witnessed the battle at hand. At the foot of the mountains, a host of men-at-arms engaged the peasant militia in volleys of musket-fire. Clad in gambesons and morion helmets, the Kingsmen flaunted their livery and fought alongside sellswords of different colors. Amidst the slaughter of pike and shot, the peasants formed crude phalanxes, bracing themselves as they impaled the foe in thin forests of spears. Watching from a distance, the leper was awestruck until he caught a glimpse of a foppish mercenary riding a stallion, raising his saber high, shrieking a command to charge.

Dampe...!

Horns erupted over the far ridge. Baldwin turned to the mountains. Another captain loomed over the valley on horseback, raising his morningstar to the gray heavens. With a roar, he led a host of rough riders in a counterattack. Baldwin did not recognize the grizzled veteran, but understood his role as commander of the rebel forces. The leper watched in awe as cavalry swept through the Kingsmen, slashing their necks with billhooks and stolen swords. In the heat of battle, the rebel captain dismounted. Musketeers fired upon the rabble from high cliffs. Those without cover fell dead, but the captain stood tall, shield embedded with shots and dented.

"Radcliffe," cried a militiaman, "watch out!"

An enemy soldier stabbed the captain through the shoulder, only for the bulwark of a man to retaliate with the brunt of his striped shield. With a crushing blow, he smashed his assailant's skull in a haze of gore and splintered bone. Wheezing and spitting blood, the captain knelt, as if to summon a second wind, yet did not stand. Baldwin watched the old soldier in the gunsmoke. Gray and scarred, his left eye was covered with a leather patch, having borne witness to uncounted campaigns. In him, the leper saw a kindred spirit, though this was not a holy war, rather a war of royalists and peasantry. The captain collapsed onto his chest. Deaf to Gipi's warnings, Baldwin sprinted to his side, lifted a heavy arm over his shoulder, and took cover in a neighboring farmhouse.

"Who," Radcliffe choked, consciousness waning, "who are you?"

The leper did not reply. Within the hour, the peasants had sent the enemy fleeing into the neighboring woods. Slowly, the dust settled, and the crows descended upon the carnage. Though he did not understand it then, Baldwin had declared war on the

King of Mulgrave.

CHAPTER TWO

Slowly, the dust settled, and the crows descended upon the carnage. The battle had ended. Corpses smoldered in heaps as the peasantry salvaged arms and armor from the fallen, scurrying like roaches in twilight. It was a pyrrhic victory. They hadn't the luxury of time. Dusk spread its black wings in the east as the sun fled across beige fields. The Kingsmen would return with a greater host and snuff out the rebels. Trudging around the dead and dying, Baldwin searched for signs of Dampe—furs, rings, anything a cut above the common soldier. He found nothing save odd glances from the rabble. The leper tugged at his hood, ignoring them.

When he ceased his investigation, Baldwin returned to the barn where Gipi tended to the rebel captain with bandages and medicinal herbs.

"How is he?" he asked from the doorway.

"Alive," the jester said.

Baldwin was greeted by straw underfoot. Shafts of light shimmered through windows and holes in the thatched roof, illuminating motes of dust. Radcliffe was propped against the wall, grasping his bleeding chest, breaths ragged and shallow.

The leper knelt, planting his blade into the floorboards.

"Who are you?" Radcliffe managed.

"I am Baldwin," he said, "knight errant."

Radcliffe staggered and pulled himself upright, dismissing Gipi's offer of support with a wave. "And what brings you to this miserable country?"

"I am in pursuit of a mercenary captain," Baldwin said. "You are likely familiar with him and his company. Your men repelled his forces."

"Dampe?" Radcliffe sneered past his pain. "Bloody hell,

what's he to you?"

"A common foe."

The captain's eyes narrowed with grim suspicion. "Your speech is kingly. You're not from the courts, are you?" His thumb rested over a dagger strapped to his belt. "Speak quickly."

Baldwin glowered and straightened his posture. "I hail from the Holy Land of Golgotha. And I am not a member of any court. That's all you need to know of me."

"And you?" Radcliffe turned to Gipi.

"Glorified nanny," she quipped.

Radcliffe stifled a laugh. "Can't say my men will take kindly to your fool—"

"Oi!" A line of longbowmen had them covered from the open doorway, pulling back creaking strings, steel-tipped arrows aimed at the leper's chest. "Get away from him!"

The leper heaved his sword over his shoulder.

"At ease," Radcliffe barked.

"Captain, sir, you're wounded!"

"Really? Had no idea." He leaned against a bare shelf. "These folk saved my sorry ass. Dragged me to shelter, they did. You'd best thank them."

The archers glanced at each other and slowly lowered their aim. Baldwin smirked and loosened the grip on his sword's hilt. They were fledglings; the way they shifted in place, belts limp across their padded jackets, eyes darting away from the sight of blood.

"You know how to swing that thing?" Radcliffe asked.

"I've seen my share of war."

The captain's smile widened. "Looks like it." He limped past his men, patting a youthful sergeant on the back. "Come on, we're headed back to camp."

Gipi took a step back. "Thanks for the invite, but we're not exactly soldiers."

"Oh, it's not an invitation." Radcliffe glared. "I'm informing you. Can't risk word of our whereabouts spreading to the Kingsmen."

Archers closed in to surround the wayfarers. Baldwin lifted his sleeve enough to expose ample sores. They covered their mouths and stepped back with a sign of the saltire. Irritated by the runts of Radcliffe's ranks, the leper stuck to Gipi's side, torn between distrust and bitter necessity, following the captain without hesitation.

The jester was about to speak up when Baldwin had a word.

"If we're going after Dampe," he kept his voice low, "we'd best form an alliance."

Outside, he was greeted by a frightened menagerie of farmers, ferriers, and stableboys. Faces thin and frames gaunt, they leaned on billhooks, wielding rusty swords and flails.

"Tough crowd," Gipi muttered.

All eyes were fixed upon the strangers. Fragile morale wafted through the ragtag ranks like a stench of sweat and unwashed hides. Whether out of superstition or common sense, they made way for Baldwin and Gipi, but kept arms at hand.

"If you'd be so kind," Gipi called, "I'd like to know where we're going."

"Don't worry," the captain said, "we'll reach camp soon enough."

———

Hours had dragged long into the night. Marching by torchlight, Baldwin was hardly accustomed to uphill travel. Mighty as he was, the leper gripped a near stone and paused to catch his breath. He wasn't alone. Passing by dormant geysers and tall rocks, the peasantry endured the trek with short wind. The trail wound on through the steep ravine, flanked by sheer stone cliffs, as the air thinned and fogged. Radcliffe and his rough riders led the company farther into the mountains. Shrubbery was scarce, and the way forward was scoured by dry gales.

"Gentlemen," Radcliffe called, "we do not stop until camp."

With a shuddering sigh, Baldwin quickened his pace. Gipi drew her lute and twisted its pegs; strumming with a steady tempo, she played a funeral march. Such music did not deny his suffering and was better suited for a trumpet, and yet, it was enough to drive him forward.

"Hardly your usual work," the leper said.

Gipi shrugged. "Consider it an interlude."

With a sigh and meditative discipline, Baldwin was numb to his own exhaustion. Out of the corner of his eye, the leper swore he saw a phantom rider aloft on the cliffs. He smiled bitterly to himself and locked eyes with Death from afar — the reaper came as soon as it went.

A vision. Nothing more....

When at last the army came to Sentinel Hill, the ramshackle arrangement of canvas tents and makeshift battlements dismissed any notion of protection the leper might have had. The only thing keeping the rebellion alive was the ravine leading directly to the hideout. If that narrow trench was breached, nothing would prevent a massacre. Driven by spearpoint, Baldwin and Gipi were escorted across the plateau and passed by storehouses loaded with peas, grain, and casks of ale. Whatever their tactics, the peasants were skilled robbers.

"This," Baldwin asked, "is your encampment?"

Radcliffe dismounted his steed and clutched his bandaged chest. "Such as it is."

"Daddy," shouted a child, "Daddy!" A little shadow rushed out of a nearby tent and embraced Radcliffe by the knee. "You're back!"

Radcliffe picked up his son and swung him around. "Promised I would be," he laughed. "Oh, I missed you, boy." He lowered the child. "Now, be good and run along to your mother."

"You're not gonna tuck me in?"

"Not tonight," Radcliffe said, a twinge of regret in his voice. "I've got a busy night. I'll read you a story tomorrow, all right?"

"Promise?"

"Promise." As Radcliffe sent his son away, he winced, grasping his wound in pain. "I'm glad he didn't notice," he muttered. "He doesn't need to know."

"You fight for your family," Baldwin said. "I see."

Radcliffe smiled sadly. "What father wouldn't?"

For a moment, Baldwin forgot about the civil war and his own crusade. He watched the child walk away, hand in hand with his mother, humbled by such a scene. He had abdicated his throne and responsibility, divorced of any purpose save his own last testament and will. Though he stood dying, the leper wondered what life would've been like if he'd married and had children of his own. A lonely breeze interrupted his melancholic musings, lifting dust along the rocks. Baldwin shook his head and remembered the words he'd yet to write; deeds he'd yet to commit.

"Come," Radcliffe said, "we've much to discuss."

The captain swept open the tent with one hand and led his guests to privacy. Baldwin was impressed by the tables and carpet of pelts and hides lit by candlelight, which were of fine quality. Old standards and regimental tapestries hung from the walls, reminding the leper of his own war camps in the Holy Land of Golgotha. Radcliffe paid the furnishings no heed.

"I must say," Baldwin said, "I was expecting the leader of this movement to be a ruffian."

"Learned men, soldiers and outlaws," Radcliffe raised a snifter, "and now fools and corpses. Our ranks are colorful, to say the least."

"What does it come down to?" Gipi asked. "Your revolt, I mean."

"The poll tax," Radcliffe said. "Lord to serf, all have to pay tribute to the war effort. And no small fee, might I add? Taxmen shoved their hands up the skirts of young women, to see if they were married and therefore eligible to pay double." He sighed deeply. "I did not fight abroad in Vermillion for petty despots to

ravage my own country, so I helped organize the initial revolt."
He smirked. "We beheaded eight of their collectors. The rest
fled."

"And so, the rebellion spread west?" Baldwin asked.

"Gravesend joined us for a time, yes, as did many other
parishes." Radcliffe reached for a bottle of whiskey. "Make
no mistake. We're not some horde of inbred yokels. It takes
organization to get this off the ground, let alone fight the
king's standing army." He poured them each a generous shot.
"Brunhilda even wrote us a manifesto. 'The entire institution of
nobility is counter to God's will,' she says, and frankly, I'm one
to agree."

Baldwin scoffed. "Quite ambitious—"

Gipi nudged him sharply. "What are your terms for the
king?"

"An end to bonded labor. Any are to sell their produce
as they so choose. Land rent but fourpence an acre. And no man
shall be punished for taking part in the revolt."

"Would you abolish your very way of life?" Baldwin
asked.

"Without a second thought. The only law is that the people
move to be ordained."

"I'm on board," Gipi said.

Baldwin hesitated; the notion of men governing themselves
was disturbing. Then again, he was nowhere if not in a strange
land. "With all due respect, I didn't accompany you for a lecture
on anarchism." He did not touch his offered glass. "We have a
mutual enemy."

"So you've mentioned," Radcliffe said. "Dampe, captain
of the Undertakers."

"What do you know of his operation here?"

"Very little. Scouts report that his company is massing
alongside the Kingsmen. I saw him briefly at the battle, but he
turned tail the moment we gained the upper hand. Coward."

"You'll get no argument from me," Baldwin said.

Radcliffe pointed to a keep on a tabletop map. "His headquarters are in Castle Garland," he said. "It is an estate twenty miles north and the royalist foothold in the region. Siege is impossible with our current ranks, so we settle for subversion and disrupting what we can." He glanced at the leper. "That said, I hadn't considered sending in a small party."

"We've snuck into forts before," Gipi said.

Radcliffe smirked. "Not like this one. Castle Garland is the summer home of the king himself. It's protected by a hedge maze as well as standard fortifications."

"Have you considered, you know, burning it down?"

"Not that simple, I'm afraid."

Baldwin's thoughts wandered to far corners of imagination. What kind of garden couldn't be undone by fire? What manner of specimens were kept in the country house? He fidgeted with his bandages and tried to focus on the matter at hand.

"What's more," Radcliffe said, "we've heard rumors of something in those walls. Just between us, I think the Kingsmen have a new weapon."

"What do you suspect?" Baldwin asked.

Radcliffe shrugged. "Your guess is as good as mine, but I'd appreciate some reconnaissance, if you take my meaning." He raised his glass. "I know you're not in this for our revolution, but they're not likely to trace you back to me, should you get captured."

"Our motives indeed differ. That much is plain."

"It's settled then," Gipi said. "Assuming we bring you information, or even the plans proper, how much would that be worth?" Her fingers danced over her coin purse. "Our coffers are a little dry, and this is a dangerous heist you're sending us on."

Radcliffe laid a heavy purse on the table, spilling with silver shillings and gold coins. "If you make it back, I'll pay you double."

Gipi's eyes glimmered with greed. "You've got it."

Baldwin examined a crown with care. It was less glossy

than expected, as if its purity had been melded with base metals. "You're counting on us not to return."

"The stakes are high for all of us, leper."

With a solemn nod, Baldwin left the rebel captain to his strategies. Outside, he took a seat and warmed his hands by the bonfire, as the peasants threw sheets of paper into its blazing embrace. He watched the documents curl and blacken, numbers and figures vanishing into wisps of acrid smoke, and let his mind wander for a moment.

I suppose it's difficult to tax them without ledgers....

"Not gonna lie," Gipi said, "I like these people. You could learn a thing or two from their civics." She pulled up a seat by the leper's side. "What's the plan?"

Baldwin did not reply. Flames licked the cold night air — lonely lights on a barren tor. Struck with bitter inspiration, the leper opened his book and wrote briskly.

> *Flames yearn as dreams fade,*
> *Kept alive by tinder of hope,*
> *Nursed by a corpse.*

Baldwin found no respite that night. Slowly, the bonfire faded to a heap of embers, and the men took to their weatherworn tents. The leper picked at his sores out of nervous habit. Mustering self-discipline, he stood and wrapped his wounds with a strip of linen. Dawn crawled over the mountains, smothered by gathering clouds, as light shimmered hazily across the East Marches. Baldwin's only companion was a young recruit dozing on watch — until the clatter of splint mail and heavy footsteps broke the silence.

Baldwin glanced over his shoulder to find Radcliffe emerging from his tent.

"Rough night?" the captain asked.

"I rarely sleep well anymore. And you are up quite early."

"Figured we could use a head start."

Baldwin didn't quite understand. "We?"

"Been thinking," Radcliffe said. "I shouldn't leave this up to a pair of strangers. No offense, but I can't afford to trust you, so consider it a helping hand."

"Are you fit to join us?" Baldwin asked. "You were grievously injured."

"I'm fine," Radcliffe scoffed. "Trust me, I've had worse. Once fought for two days with an arrow in the knee." The captain lifted his mace and kite shield. "You'll need someone who knows the Kingsmen and how they operate, if you're going to Castle Garland."

"I see," Baldwin said. "You've fought alongside them, have you not?"

Radcliffe did not reply. As morning dragged on, the militiamen began to stir, and breakfast was served—leftovers, eggs, bread, and butter. It was enough to start the day. The captain was fortunate enough to have a personal stash of pickled herring, but Baldwin was hardly envious. By the time Gipi had woken, the day was well underway.

"Morning," she yawned, staggering to the leper's side.

"It seems we have a new companion." Baldwin eyed the captain who instructed a host of younger recruits in the training ring; little more than a ring of wooden stakes around a makeshift armory with dummies and painted targets. "Radcliffe wishes to accompany us."

Gipi popped a peeled egg into her mouth. "Makes sense," she said, mid-bite. "I wouldn't trust us alone with this kind of mission either." Her face paled as if sudden implications had dawned on her. "You don't think this is gonna cut into our payment, do you—?"

A choking shriek cut her short, echoing throughout the encampment and the cliff sides. Militiamen had gathered around one of their own convulsing on the ground; wheezing, gasping, eyes wide with mad terror, unable to choke out a word.

"Captain!" someone shouted. "Move, move!" Radcliffe

barreled past the onlookers. "Don't just stand there!" He turned to the nearest bystander. "What happened?"

"I don't know, he was just drinking some beer and then...."

Baldwin kept his distance, not daring to intervene. Out of suspicion, he poured a bit of ale from a keg into his own pewter cup, only to find it darkened with pulp and dried leaves. He shifted its contents as little pale worms writhed in discolored foam.

Like the vermin Sophia discovered....

"Do not drink the ale!" Baldwin roared. The peasants shot him confused glances, muttering asides, but began to obey as soon as Gipi knocked a tankard loose from a shaky hand, demanding their attention. "It's been contaminated," he said.

The peasants unanimously splashed their ale onto the rocks and cracked earth, much to their chagrin. As the crowd dispersed, Radcliffe left the chirurgeon to administer treatment by way of charcoal. The captain was shaken, unable to look Baldwin in the eye.

"I am familiar with such treachery," the leper said.

"As am I." Radcliffe dabbed his brow with a scrap of linen. "In Vermillion, the enemy poisoned our wells on the eve of battle. The casualties were massive."

"Where did you find the ale?" Gipi asked.

"In the cellar of an abbey. Monks had fled, and we thought nothing of it. Dammit." Radcliffe clutched the handle of his morningstar. "What're the royalists up to?"

Baldwin had no answer or comfort to give. This was undoubtedly the work of the Undertakers. He would follow the trail and hunt them down. He was close, closer than he'd been since that night of horror. The bounties of justice were low and ripe for the reaping. As the wind howled down the ravine, Baldwin departed for the mountain trail, driven by fevered honor, to deliver the wicked. His companions weren't far behind.

CHAPTER THREE

The lands north of the rebel encampment were left feral by their lord's will. Keeping to the sidepath, Baldwin and the others trod lightly through the holm oak woods, lest they alert the patrols on the road. The forest seemed to twist in its own shade, damp and forlorn. The trees were thick and gnarled, oppressive in their girth; leaves devouring the light as it trickled to earth. Baldwin's boots slipped against the mud. He staggered down the way and grasped along the deadfall. Gipi was light on her feet and shook her head, while Radcliffe marched on with care, morningstar and shield at hand.

"How far are we?" the jester asked, her voice low.

"You'll know once we reach the glade," Radcliffe replied. "From there, we'll get a better view of the castle and strategize."

A twig snapped loudly under Baldwin's heel. Ravens took flight, cawing into the lobed canopies. The leper gritted his teeth, cursing his own clumsiness.

"Miracle no one's heard us," Gipi muttered.

"Let's keep it that way," Radcliffe said.

Something rustled in the undergrowth. Baldwin raised a bandaged hand. Slowly, he drew his broadsword and crept off the path. From the highroad, he heard footsteps and the clatter of plate mail. He slunk behind a tree and watched on. Soldiers were on the march, armed with pikes and muskets; a convoy, judging by the wagons, as for what cargo, Baldwin could not say. They hummed a ballad in tune to rattling drums, oblivious to the leper and his companions just off the cobblestone way. With great care, Baldwin returned to the others.

"What is it?" Gipi mouthed.

The leper jerked his head aside. They couldn't afford to linger. When at last they came to the glade, Baldwin climbed a hillock under a darkening sky. Castle Garland was nearer than he'd anticipated. With its lucarnes, columns, and gilded pilasters, the villa dominated the woods as a monument of majesty, flanked by four pointed turrets, lined with cannons and mortars. Surrounded by a dry chalk moat and walls of ivy-laced stone, it would've been a beautiful sight, if not for the shadow of war leaving only a facade of a martial bastion.

"Cheery place," Gipi said.

"Don't let your guard down," Radcliffe said. "This is the royalist stronghold in the East Marches." He turned to the leper. "I guarantee you Dampe's somewhere inside."

Baldwin eyed the fortifications in search of a sally port or opening in the walls. He found nothing, save the vast acres of pleasure grounds. As to why the gardens were left open, the leper couldn't say, but suspected that they were hardly unguarded.

"I don't see any soldiers," Gipi commented.

"No," Radcliffe said. "They're hiding behind the crenels." He pointed to the slits and holes in the curving turrets. "We can't go through the front gate."

"Then what do you suggest?" Baldwin asked.

"Look closer," Radcliffe said. "Down there."

No wall separated the garden from the woods, blending together seamlessly under the garrison's vigil. Eight acres of low walls and shrubbery formed the open green, split by the Boardwalk—a bold avenue leading up to the iron-banded gates. From lawn to terraced lawn, the meadows were lined with roses and ribbon flowers in border planters, as serpentine paths tempted the eyes to twin mazes, haunted by macabre fountains and ancient yew.

"What now?" Baldwin asked.

"There's a conservatory on the west wing," Radcliffe said. "If we make it through the gardens, we can infiltrate the keep through there."

"I see," Baldwin said. "What of the patrols?"

Gipi smirked. "Simple. Don't get caught."

The forest trail merged with the Boardwalk in a matter of minutes, and the company stumbled upon a grim sight. A litter of pigeons lay dead and scattered about a granary; pupils wide, beaks dry and agape. Baldwin approached with care and examined an open crate.

Amidst the wheat were cherry-like fruits he did not recognize.

"I think I've found something," he said.

The jester examined one of the strange berries. She sniffed it and recoiled, dropping it at once. "Nightshade, I think," she said. "What the hell is going on?"

"There's a small bounty of the stuff." Baldwin shifted through the barley. "Nightshades aren't native to these lands. And these fruits. They are too large to belong to any species that I'm aware of. Someone in the castle must have cultivated them."

Radcliffe glowered and pressed on. "We make for the west wing."

Down the graveled lane to the Oval Pool, Baldwin heard the clash of rapiers—sparring by the sound of it. The company hid behind the pillars and bided their time.

"Two, one, five," Dampe said, dancing along in a mock duel.

Gipi clasped the leper's shoulder and shook her head, knowing full well his impulse. Baldwin shuddered at her touch yet conceded. A page, no older than thirteen, struck against Dampe's foil, engaged in practice with the mercenary prince. He was going easy on the boy, it seemed—a rare display of character in the blackguard.

It has to be an act….

"You're improving." Dampe sheathed his foil and tussled the boy's hair. "Remember, swordsmanship is as much about fooling your opponents as it is chivalry."

The knights of the Holy Land taught me the same….

Dampe gestured to the door. "Come, it is time for your studies."

"Thank you, sir," said the page.

The mercenary smiled. "Dampe will suffice."

Baldwin glared at him from afar, thoughts ablaze with violent anger. How dare he attempt to act so fatherly to the youth? To what end was he scheming?

"Coast is clear," Radcliffe said, "Baldwin."

"Yes," he managed, "I am aware."

Taking a sharp left, the company snuck into the inner grounds. Hedges loomed over the meandering paths as the well-manicured walls of a labyrinth. Disoriented by the spiraling routes, Baldwin kept an eye over his shoulder. The way back had been swallowed by yawning myrtle. As the leper investigated the hemlock and wolfsbane nestled between bushes, the true nature of this place dawned on him — it was a garden of poison.

"Damn," Gipi wheezed, "do you smell that?"

Baldwin rolled his eyes and tapped his noseless mask, torn between annoyance and amusement. Apparently, she needed a friendly reminder.

"Right," she said, looking away, "sorry."

"What is it?"

"It's foul," she gagged, "like a corpse."

Baldwin smirked. "Are you sure it's not me?"

"No, it's different. Like if garlic, moldy cheese, and your sweaty ass had a baby."

"Sounds disgusting."

For once, the leper was grateful for his condition. Before he could retort, something slithered under his boot — a black vine lined with thorned suckers, snaking like a tentacle into the soil, recoiling to unknown depths. Baldwin knelt to examine the limb, only to slice his finger, drawing a drop of blood. Radcliffe flexed his shield arm.

"We need to keep moving,"

As the mists thickened, the company eventually came to a triple-tiered glass tower attached to the west wing. Composed entirely of leaded windows and iron lattices, the conservatory was covered in strands of ivy, crawling up its sleek walls, and exuded the authority of a watchtower. The soil was soft before its foundations, and muddy footprints led to the threshold. As Radcliffe opened the door, it gave a moaning creak. Within the greenhouse was a suffocating jungle of colonial plants, its stained-glass distorting rays of light into weird shadows, casting a shroud of perpetual twilight. Humidity smothered all in a veil of silence, as the air thickened to a steamy miasma, fostered by steel vents underfoot. The stench of rotting flesh was overpowering, as if the carnivorous plants had digested their victims over the course of months. Rows of planters housed flytraps, pitcher plants, and blood orchids, though the greatest specimen loomed from the chamber's heart.

"What the hell is that?" Gipi gasped.

Towering and terrible, the Belladonna was a parasitic organism, having completely overtaken a sickly alder tree. Masses of fleshy tendrils dug deep into its pallid bark, pulsing like knotted entrails; carrion flowers bloomed as gullets in its trunk, their petals laced with venomous fangs. Stranger still were the rash-colored fruits on spinal stems.

Wicker baskets lay stacked upon the floor, filled with strange berries. As Baldwin stepped forward, a dissociative trance overcame him; needling tingles ran through his arms and hands. Attempting to plow through the sensation, the leper nearly knocked over the barrels and baskets, but caught himself on an empty planter.

"Let's not linger," Baldwin hushed, treading over the sprawling vines, which dug deep between the floorboards. "These vapors are unnatural."

"We must burn this thing down," Radcliffe said.

"And what? Alert the whole garrison? No, we carry on."

Radcliffe and Gipi followed the leper's lead, weaving their way around the Belladonna.

As they came to the east side of the conservatory, Baldwin opened the varnished door, ushering his companions into the west wing of Castle Garland.

Gipi nudged the leper. "Are you okay?"

Baldwin adjusted his mask, sweat trickling down his brow. Strangely, the brass visor seemed ill-fitting, as if his cheeks were swelling. "I'm fine," he lied.

Scarlet carpet cut through its long halls, every door leading to a drawing room or stately apartment. The burgundy wallpaper was grayed by the ages, and even the wood paneling was faded. Suits of parade armor, embossed with silver and gold, lined the corridors in odd numbers as decorative sentinels; watching on, silently, halberds at hand. A draft wafted through the open windows, as red curtains fluttered in the chill air.

"I must say, your lordship," said a familiar voice from upstairs. "Your hospitality is magnificent, your majesty. The food, the wine, the music...."

"I do not share these delicacies lightly, General Dampe."

In a single file, Baldwin and the company followed the voices and scaled a double helix staircase, flawlessly hewn from marble and crowned with a stained-glass ceiling, at the castle's heart. When the trio gathered outside the door, Baldwin crouched behind a potted fern — grim-faced musketeers marched on patrol down the far side of the hall.

He eavesdropped with murderous intent.

———

In the lavish confines of the King's Apartment, Dampe was entertained by a display of scones and no shortage of elderberry wine. Seated on a velvet chair, he indulged himself with a cup of tea, pinky out, like a dandy of the court. He was doted upon by a pair of maids who all but wiped his nose for him. It was a welcome change of pace from the blood-soaked battlefield.

"What is your next course of action?" asked his employer.

Across the oval table sat King Geoffrey of Mulgrave — greasy black hair, moon-faced, with a sickly complexion. Dressed in a short-wasted doublet with a long skirt and knee-high breeches, he had attempted to grow a mustache, as was popular among the gentry, only to manage a thin pair of whiskers. Fiddling with a silver fork, he seemed a tad uncomfortable.

It was only natural, given that a third of the nation wanted him decapitated.

"My men are already sowing the seeds of destruction," Dampe said. "By poisoning the granaries of supporting villages, we'll crush the rebellion at its source—the peasantry."

"Kill the poor, you say?" Geoffrey asked, smiling at the notion, as men of the peerage understood that their subjects were but beasts of burden to work the fields. "This would have dire ramifications for the yearly harvest, no?"

"Better famine than anarchy."

Geoffrey nodded in agreement. "However, if a poll tax is enough to cause an uproar, don't you think poisoning their neighbors would only fan the flames further?"

"We need only remove those who oppose us." Dampe's eyes shifted to the bookshelves along the walls, their texts and tomes ranging from botany and toxicology to the occult—all of which the king had a reputation for studying. "As for the royalist parishes, sow rumors of superstition." The mercenary's lips curled into a knowing sneer. "Those who know their place will round up midwives and wise women for you. Throw in the Witchfinder General and you'll have the perfect scapegoat. They'll never suspect your involvement."

"Intriguing." Geoffrey laid a finger to his chin. "I must admit, I was skeptical of your tactics after the incident at Gravesend. Early results, however, are encouraging."

Dampe laughed. "So long as you uphold your end, you have nothing to fear."

"Likewise, I assure you."

The king had handsomely paid the Undertakers' bills, which were more than what Gravesend could say. Moreover, tea with the king was something only the grandest of sellswords would experience, and Dampe prided himself as a cut above the common cloth. At that fleeting moment, the captain thought he heard someone, or something, beyond the wall.

He cocked his head, only to resume his game of diplomacy. *Must be my imagination....*

———

Baldwin turned to Radcliffe, who gripped his morningstar with white knuckles, eyes burning with violent rage. They nodded in mutual understanding. Baldwin barreled through the door like a battering ram. Summoning his strength, the leper swung his sword high over his shoulders and roared with righteous fury. Delirium obscured his senses, and he cut through flesh and sinew — severing a child's scream. Baldwin looked on in horror. His blade hued the floor with a quaking blow as the page from before lay butchered by his own blind assault, bleeding from the mouth, tears welling in his eyes.

Hush, hush.... Oh God, please, no!

Baldwin was frozen in shock, breathing heavy. Shaking, he tried to reach out and hold the page's hand, only for him to vomit a lungful of crimson ichor. There he lay — dead. The leper stared at his own bloody palm. His companions stumbled upon the grisly scene. Gipi gasped and covered her mouth. Only a mad mantra coursed through Baldwin's mind.

Dammit, dammit, dammit!

He fled down the open hall. What followed was a montage of alarms and wanton butchery. Wailing like a deranged revenant, the leper cut his way through the guards, tears streaming down his face. Deaf to Gipi and Radcliffe's shouts, lost to poison and panic, his sight burned with dancing lights and mad colors, until a musket shot pierced his shoulder.

Stumbling out a two-story window, half-hoping the fall would kill him, Baldwin tumbled off the hedges and slammed his brow against stone. Dozing in and out of consciousness, Baldwin was lifted to his feet and dragged to dungeons unknown. The last thing he remembered was a steel barrel against his neck and a mocking voice.

"You're a hard man to kill, Good King Baldwin."

CHAPTER FOUR

Baldwin opened his eyes, wondering if he'd been blinded — darkness still enveloped his senses. He stirred, only to find his wrists strung up by manacles, feet chained and dangling over the flagstone floor. Robbed of armor and bandages, he was naked in the dark, lesions and sores left exposed in the dampness. The stench of mildew and dried blood was his only companions. A muffled crack of the whip slashed his ears, followed by tortured screams.

Imprisoned....

Poison wore off, yet guilt did not leave him. Baldwin's thoughts were awash with shame, seared with images of the boy's corpse. He clenched his fists, struggled, chains rattling, but barely mustered the will to breathe. He deserved this.

What have I done? What am I...?

The door's hinges shrieked open. He heard footsteps clopping down the stairs as torchlight sputtered faintly into vision. Baldwin raised his head, glaring at the silhouette of his nemesis.

"Dampe," he growled.

The mercenary prince tipped his feathered hat in faux politeness. "Baldwin."

Silence lingered in the air.

Dampe's face was hidden by shadow as he pulled up a chair at a fine table and tugged at his ruffed sleeves. A small banquet lay before him: roast pheasant, candied pineapple, and persimmons, and, most importantly, a carafe of red wine. Between its arrangement and the chiaroscuro of candlelight, it seemed an exercise in still life, in sharp contrast to the pillories and racks lurking on the fringe of sight.

"I suppose you think yourself a mastermind," Baldwin

said.

"Hardly," Dampe said. "I'm just a simple merchant trying to pay the bills as it were. What I do is a matter of good business. My business just so happens to be military operations."

"You murder innocents—without remorse."

"An unfortunate byproduct." Dampe sighed. "You are not so noble, might I add. Swearing yourself to rebels, infiltrating a royal estate, murdering an innocent page—"

"As if you didn't station him there, knowing I would come for you."

"I honestly took you for dead."

"Such assumptions will be your undoing."

Dampe drew a long knife, gleaming in the hearth's light, and sliced into the pheasant. "Let me guess. Somehow, you survived my little raid on Gravesend and took it upon yourself to avenge those unfortunates caught in the crossfire." He raised an eyebrow. "Don't tell me that you pursued me all the way here? Driven by some misplaced sense of righteousness?" He shot the leper a loathsome smirk. "That must be the worst thing I've ever heard."

"Is that why you're here? To taunt me?"

"Not quite," Dampe said. "You see, it's one thing to tangle yourself in my web, but to involve yourself in the war? I'm afraid I can't simply kill you."

Baldwin's heart sank into his chest, yet he endeavored to remain as stoic as ever. "You've come to torture me, then, is that it?" He cracked a grin. "I can cope with torture."

Dampe raised a tempting goblet, as if to offer Baldwin a toast. "Your nerves are dull, that much is apparent, but we of the Undertakers can get creative."

From the shadows, a monstrous brute emerged, moving to Dampe's side. Dressed in a leather tunic and grass-stained trousers, the executioner was masked with a burlap sack. He unrolled a scroll of wicked implements to an adjacent table—thumbscrews, iron spiders, and, of course, the pear of anguish.

To Baldwin's surprise, his torturer settled for simple pliers.

"And what manner of creature is this?" the leper asked.

"Man is the greatest monster of all," Dampe said. "The Gardener earns a pretty penny for his services. I'm curious to see how you both perform."

Baldwin's thoughts were devoid of fear. Only a bitter masochism remained. He let the Gardener creep near and stared into his dull eyes—at his own reflection.

Dampe served himself a lusciously dripping leg. "Now then, how many of Radcliffe's bandits are hiding in the mountains?"

"Bandits? You're not one to talk."

"Be that as it may," Dampe said, "you're clearly affiliated with the peasant revolts. Which makes you, oddly enough, an enemy of the Crown." He lifted a forkful of poultry to his lips and took a healthy bite. "No one's going to save you, Baldwin. Your best bet is to cooperate."

"So I can be drawn and quartered at your convenience?"

"In a word, yes."

"Tempting as it may be, I'll have to decline your generous offer."

Dampe shrugged. "It makes no difference to me." He reached for a fistful of grapes and cocked his head. "Strap him down."

The Gardener undid Baldwin's chains and let him collapse onto his knees with a crunch. Overcome with exhaustion, he could not muster the strength to stand. His manacles unlinked from his ascending chains, he was dragged to the far wooden tabletop and placed upon its dank surface, wrists bound tightly by chains. Heavy as they were, those bonds were corroded by sessions of wear and misuse. Baldwin noted that with a glimmer of hope.

"I'll ask you again," Dampe said. "How many are there in the mountains?"

Silence stung the passing seconds. Baldwin did not reply.

"Start with his fingers."

The Gardener gripped Baldwin's thumbnail with the pliers, tearing it from the quick with a twist and pull. The leper winced but scarcely felt anything, grateful for his condition, if only for a moment. Lips sagged in the aftermath of his poisoning as he smirked to himself.

"Again," Dampe said. "And I'm just getting started, mind you. Trust me, there's a reason I requested such a banquet. I expect this to take no small amount of time."

"A waste on all accounts."

"Let's not get ahead of ourselves," Dampe said. "Now then, how did you come by Radcliffe? What is he to you? Perhaps a veteran from overseas?"

"I've known the man for less than a day," Baldwin said. "In truth, I struck an alliance in the hopes of tracking you down. So I could deliver you to Hell myself."

Dampe took a sip of wine. "I'm flattered." He cocked his head, and the Gardener extracted yet another nail. "You'll have a hard time wielding a sword after this."

Baldwin felt a twinge of numbed agony as the pliers ripped a jagged swipe across his middle finger. He dared not wince or moan. He had to endure. There was something else at work — an earnest guilt and desire for punishment. By his hand, an innocent had died.

As a pair of shears neared his lips, Baldwin mustered the will to speak.

"Wait," he said.

"Little late to beg, don't you think?"

"The boy," Baldwin managed. "Who was he? To you?"

Dampe stabbed the table and exhaled. If he didn't know better, Baldwin would've thought the mercenary prince was grieving. Instead, he lowered the brim of his hat and licked his dry lips, as if to mask his tearing eyes. "I'll leave that to your imagination," he said. "But I'm surprised you haven't asked," he sneered, "where your friends are."

Baldwin's eyes widened in horror. Possessed by his own misery, he'd forgotten about his companions. Panic pounded in the leper's chest as he tugged at his chains.

"What have you done to them?"

Dampe clapped his hands, and a hatch in the ceiling dropped open with a clatter. The grind of unseen mechanisms filled Baldwin's ears as a cage descended into the cellar, its prisoner bound with hempen rope and masked with a cloth hood.

"No!" the leper bellowed.

Dampe whipped off Gipi's hood and tore at her hair. Baldwin struggled against his chains, desperate to break free, sliding his bloody wrists through the manacles.

Dampe raised a knife to the fool's lips. "Such a pretty little face, don't you think?"

Gipi spat in his face, shaking with rage and terror. Dampe recoiled, only to grab her cheeks, gaping her mouth, and press the blade into her tongue. "Now then," he turned to the leper, "answer me. If I don't like what I hear, she'll have a hard time cracking jokes."

"If you harm her —"

"You are in no position to argue, my friend."

Baldwin was overcome with anguish, vision blurring, heart pounding against his ribs. The Gardener prepared to extract another nail, but the leper barely noticed. He gathered his strength for one last push. His instinct was plain — to kill.

"Very well," Dampe said. "I'll start with her tongue."

Resurrected by wrath, Baldwin tugged and tore his wrists through the battered chains and broke free. He stood and lunged, smashing an iron cuff into Dampe's nose. He tackled the mercenary with brute force, dragging him by the hair to the open hearth. Numb in body and thought, the leper pressed the mercenary's face into the smoldering coals like a greased mutton chop. Dampe shrieked as his cheek crackled; the reek of roasting flesh filled the chamber.

"Hey," Gipi shouted, "would appreciate a bit of help."

Baldwin released his opponent, leaving him to writhe on the floor. The leper tore Gipi's cage down in a feat of monstrous strength—only to sense an encroaching shadow. He snatched a wall-mounted axe and chopped into the Gardener's skull, who collapsed with a heavy thud. Relishing the impact of steel, he turned to Dampe, about to deliver the killing blow. The wretch cowered and scurried beneath a table like a cockroach, just out of reach.

"Leave him! We don't have time," Gipi said, slipping out of her bonds. "Won't be long before the entire garrison comes crashing down."

Motes of dust trickled from the ceiling as clambering footsteps echoed from above. With great reluctance, Baldwin obeyed and disengaged. Escape was their priority. He kicked in the wooden door, leaving splinters and shattered panels in his wake. Guards gasped in the torchlight as the leper brandished his axe; wounds raw and exposed, body as a rotting corpse. He carved the way forward. Horns and footsteps sounded throughout the cell block—Baldwin did not relent. He was caked in the gore of his enemies. Rage had reduced him to a feral beast, seeing red in a sea of blood, and yet, he was stronger than ever. A crossbow bolt impaled his palm. It mattered not. He could fight left-handed.

All he sensed was fear and dead men.

Baldwin clenched his fist and tore loose the bolt. He smeared his own blood onto his face, basking in misery and martyrdom, feeling his pupils dilate, imagining the page's final moments of terror. Affliction aside, Baldwin was as capable of sin as any man. Though the rot was taking him, leprosy had freed him from pain and physical limitation. How many times had he fought to the brink of death, only to endure? How many corpses would it take to pave the road to an end worthy of remembrance? What in God's name was keeping him alive? Even now, he felt Death looming over him, scythe inches from the reaping. Suddenly, Baldwin spied the fleeing shadow of a final guard and intercepted him with grim precision.

The leper lifted him by the collar and slammed the poor soul against the masonry wall, knocking the wind from his lungs.

"Where is he?" Baldwin growled. "Where is Radcliffe?"

"He's," the guard wheezed, "being transferred."

"Where — ?"

"Don't just stand there," Dampe screamed from afar, "after them!"

The garrison was closing in. Baldwin dropped the guard to the floor and leapt for the stairwell, quickening his pace as he scaled its stone steps, feeling Gipi's presence not far behind. They came to the barracks and gathered their own confiscated arms. There was scarcely enough time to don armor. The leper gripped his sword's hilt and welcomed the touch of familiar steel. Only a single purpose coursed through his mind — the will to escape. When they reached the gardens of Castle Garland, the leper was greeted by fog and the silhouette of a prison carriage departing for the Old Road. Before he could turn to the stables and give chase, it had already vanished into the midnight mists.

"Dammit," Gipi spat. "What now?"

Baldwin turned to the villa. In truth, he yearned to charge back and slay the stronghold itself, to earn a selfish ballad among the rebels. Slowly, his senses and sanity returned, if only for a moment. Beacons were lit on the tower-tops. He knew better.

"We flee."

Hours later, hidden in the surrounding forest, Baldwin and Gipi managed to evade the search parties, crouched among the gnarled roots of a great oak tree. Eventually, when the shouts of men and bays of hounds subsided, the leper took a moment to breathe. Away from torchlight, the sounds of woodland life soothed his shaken spirits — chirping crickets, the odd hoot of an owl, and the gentle patter of rain against leaves and fallen branches.

"Are you well?" Baldwin asked his fool, voice hushed.

Gipi caressed the cuts on her lips and cheeks. "Well as

you'd expect." She sighed, deeply, stifling her shakes. "What do we do? Now that Radcliffe's lost."

"Gone. Not lost."

"Really now?" Gipi scoffed. "And just what do we tell the rebels? It's not like we'll get a standing ovation for our failure." She shrugged. "Probably get hanged."

"Assuming the Undertakers don't poison them first."

The fool shrugged. "Fair point." She leaned back, letting raindrops trickle upon her face. "Luckily, we made it out, though. You went stark raving mad back there."

Baldwin stared at his left hand; fingernails torn apart, wrists raw, and palm agape with a puncture wound. "I did what anyone would do."

"Bullshit," Gipi said. "I don't know what goes on in your head half of the time, but that was insane. Here." She took the leper by the hand and wrapped his wounds with firm care. "There's a fine line between courage and madness."

"And stupidity," Baldwin added.

"Well," Gipi smirked. "I wasn't gonna go there." She paused, fiddling with her frayed sleeves. "What're we doing here? In this godforsaken place?"

"Your guess is as good as mine." Baldwin turned to his fool yet did not look her in the eye. "The truth is, I'm beginning to doubt this quest."

"How so?"

"It's just," Baldwin paused to collect his thoughts, "after I killed that boy, all I could think about was how I deserved to die. And I couldn't even do that." He cradled the Broken Blade, lost in his reflection. "All my life, the peerage saw in me a higher purpose. From cradle to grave, I was meant to do great things, and yet, it meant nothing in the face of my condition. In the face of Death. From king to serf, none can escape her. For all my talk of great deeds, I suppose none of it has meaning, unless...."

"Unless what?"

"It's nothing."

"No, seriously." Gipi laid a hand on his pauldron. "Keep going."

"It's the pathos of things," the leper said. "The impermanence of one's life and the acknowledgement of that truth. A gentle sadness, if you will. If all we have are fleeting moments of agony and ecstasy, then let us embrace that to whatever end." He stood up, feeling his back crack with every motion. "As I press on, searching for meaning, the more my faith is shaken. I find myself imagining a world without God and His divine light. And whether good can exist in such a bleak reality." He lowered his head. "Again, merely a thought."

"To do the right thing without God," Gipi repeated.

Baldwin shook his head, scoffing at his own absurdity. "Again, it's nothing. The Devil is worming into my thoughts, seeking to corrupt with doubt and regret." He braced himself for the trek back to Sentinel Hill. "One thing is certain. We will meet Dampe again."

"I'm counting on it."

"And when we do," Baldwin said, "I pray it will be the last time."

He watched the wind whisk through the trees. In the Holy Land of Golgotha, the wind was a monstrous thing, scouring the dry earth in the day and cutting to the bone at night. Here and now, it was gentler, kind even. Slowly, Baldwin undid the straps and lowered his mask. The draft against his face was intoxicating. Moment by moment, the implications of mortality sank like knives into numbed flesh. Baldwin did not want to die. There was nothing to sacrifice or give himself to, save for what he made of this wretched world — that was why he fought. Meaningless as his struggle seemed, it masked the fatal truth.

It was not Death he feared. It was to live without purpose.

CHAPTER FIVE

Sequestered in the dim privacy of his quarters, Dampe tended to his wounds in humiliating silence, pressing a damp cloth against his cheek. His skin cracked and splintered, swollen with blisters. He had prided himself on his beauty, only to be deformed in a moment's hubris. Forcing himself to look in the mirror, Dampe gritted his teeth and refrained from picking at his face. Overcome with sudden rage, the mercenary prince shattered the glass in a tantrum, thoughts ablaze and branded with Baldwin's image.

Striking like lightning out of the clear sky, the bastard sought to make his life as miserable as possible, but such brooding was interrupted by a knock on the door.

"Is everything alright, sir?"

Dampe took a deep breath and shuddered. He snuffed out the oil lamps, one by one, and approached the door, raising a shaky hand towards the brass knob.

"What is it?" he asked, fettering his anger and embarrassment.

"The king requests your presence."

"And?"

"Well, he wants to discuss 'the future of our partnership.'"

Dampe shuddered and downed a shot of brandy, enduring the viscous sting. "Tell him I'll be there as soon as I'm presentable." He leaned against the vanity like a thespian preparing for the stage. He'd toiled for decades to get this far, rising from the trash of society to dance and dine among kings, only for his career to stand on a razor's edge—all because of one loose end.

"Sir?" his lieutenant asked.

Dampe loosened his grip on the doorknob. Gunther was slow but not stupid; a gunman capable of blasting through the strongest of foes. Gunther had long been there for him, since the outset of Dampe's journey as a landsknecht. They had fought side by side, looted, pillaged, and burned. Despite the ruthless carnage they had wrought together, they shared a common understanding — the likes of which transcended blood relations and notions of friendship.

Dampe sighed, deeply. "You may enter."

Gunther opened the door. Clad in a slashed doublet and voluminous pantaloons, his garb was a darker shade of red and black, a blunderbuss strapped across his back. His frown was masked by a beer-bleached beard, but the captain knew better. Gunther was concerned, if only for the company's morale. Dampe made sure to keep his wounds hidden in shadow.

"Come," he managed, "have a seat and a drink. It's the least I can do."

Gunther stepped forward with grim hesitation and pulled up a fragile chair. "So," he asked, "I don't think what his majesty has to say will be good."

"No shit." Dampe poured them each an overflowing snifter of brandy. "However, I have another path. One that doesn't involve bowing to lords and lieges. Remember, we have a contract with Vermillion as well. Our seasonal absence may be noted sooner rather than later." He drummed his fingers against the tabletop. "It would be more profitable to take up their offer and abandon the Kingdom of Mulgrave altogether. Should we play our cards right, that is."

"I have no issue with that," Gunther said.

Dampe stood, slowly, making certain that his face was bathed in shadow. "We'll play along for now and see what the king has to offer."

Gunther nodded and saw himself out the door. Dampe took a moment to catch his breath and brood. Something needed to be done about his face. Staring into shattered glass, he reached for white powder and mercurial paints, caking his wounds in the stuff.

"I'll be there shortly...."

After what seemed an eternity of preparation, Dampe swung the door open and endured the gawking stares of his own men. He ignored them, if only to keep up appearances, pretending that nothing was wrong—weakness could not be tolerated. Dampe followed the stairs to the second floor of Castle Garland. In the King's Apartment, the servants dared not look at him. If anything, Dampe basked in their brief asides and took a seat across the long table.

"General Dampe," Geoffrey said from the far end, back to the fireplace, unfazed by his charred visage. "I'm pleased to see you up and about." A serving girl poured him a snifter of sanguine liquor. "Truth be told, I wasn't entirely sure you'd make it."

Dampe reached for a glass. "It takes more than a wayward sword to kill me."

"Yet seemingly enough to shame you."

"Ah," Dampe managed, "indeed."

The king fiddled with his silver fork, bending it backwards into a mock catapult. "When I hired the Undertakers, I was told that they left no evidence or survivors. That their leader was a cunning veteran of campaigns against the Holy Land."

"Our reputation precedes us," Dampe said, nervously.

"Then how do you explain this breach?" Geoffrey raised his voice ever so slightly. "Rebels have infiltrated my summer home and escaped, likely with knowledge of our plans to quell the revolting hamlets, killing a third of my garrison in the process." His brow furrowed. "If memory serves, you volunteered to oversee their interrogation."

Dampe poured himself a snifter of port. "That I did. However, I've deployed my men to slaughter the rebels at their mountain base as we speak. The supporting villages will soon follow." He took a hearty gulp as wine wept into his wounds. Perhaps his tongue was damaged as well, but the aftertaste seemed off. "I assure you," words caught in his throat, as a lump formed in his neck, "you see...." Next came the heart palpitations, fluttering, as his breath turned shallow. He knew what was happening. "No, no—you can't do this to me!"

The king raised a smooth hand, and a pair of guards planted Dampe in his seat. "You were right about one thing. I can't afford to have your atrocities traced to me. And given your recent, shall we say, mishaps, my confidence in you is shaken."

"Heh," Dampe scoffed, "so that's it, isn't it?" His vision was overcome with spiraling lights and darkening colors. "Throwing me out like a heap of shit."

Geoffrey nodded. "Once a commoner, always a commoner, I'm afraid."

Dampe ran his fingers through his hair. "Oh, you'd better make sure I'm dead," he drew his flintlock pistol and aimed at the king, "because I'm taking you with me!"

Before the guards could intervene, Dampe pulled the trigger with a hollow click. He grinned as Geoffrey's eyes widened in shock, only for the apartment to orbit his skull as the world began to dim. Even on death's door, something inside Dampe refused to surrender. Thoughts drifting to oblivion, it would take more than poison to quell his ambition. Should he survive, there would be hell to pay. After all, this wasn't the only nation he'd sworn fealty to.

If I wake up, I'm burning this whole kingdom to the ground....

———

In the brooding shadow of the massifs, Baldwin and Gipi took to the Old Road across war-torn acres reclaimed by heath and bog. Only the skeletal ruins of villages remained, scattered like carcasses in a beast's den. Trees stood burnt and stark as rivers ran low through the countryside. The Undertakers had pillaged upstart folk into obedience or death—not that they had much worth plundering. Rows of heavy footprints and wagon tracks seemed to share Baldwin's course.

"Well," Gipi said, "this land's seen its fair share of hardship."

"You don't say," the leper muttered.

"No need to get all pissy at me. What's the plan?"

"We make for Sentinel Hill," Baldwin said. "Hopefully, the militia will understand our failure. With any luck, they'll rally forth and stop the Undertakers in their tracks."

"And if they don't?"

"You'll have the luxury of saying, 'I told you so.'"

Amidst the desolation, Baldwin's eyes widened in horror as smoke rose from the foothills. Within the hour, the leper and his fool scaled the sloping ravine to Sentinel Hill, greeted by torched tents and the piled carcasses of the fallen. The reek of gunpowder and charred flesh pervaded the scene; black standards stood among the dead, signaling the Undertakers' victory over the rebel militia. Gipi searched for survivors amidst the carnage. Ravens tore at the corpses and took flight upon her approach. Solemn as ever, Baldwin took a seat and rested against the Broken Blade.

"Anything?" he asked.

The fool shook her head, silently. Baldwin was hardly surprised. Whispering a prayer into his rosary, he stood — only to hear something stir in the rubble. He drew his sword, eyes narrowing in the smoke. A steel-tipped bolt whistled past his head and pierced the barricade.

"Who goes there?" he bellowed.

The only response was a winding crank.

A stout woman emerged from the shadows; coarse black hair pulled back with a scarlet bandanna, clad in greaves and a steel gorget. In gauntleted hands, she clutched a heavy wooden crossbow, capable of impaling a horse, and took aim at Baldwin's chest.

"Could ask you the same," she spat.

"Easy." Gipi came between them. "We're no friends of the Undertakers."

Baldwin sheathed his blade as the arbalist lowered her bow with caution in kind. "You're the ones Radcliffe brought over yesterday, right?" She stepped further into the light, revealing apple cheeks and a swarthy complexion. "Where is he?"

"Captured. He's been taken by the Kingsmen," Baldwin said. "But first, what happened here? Are there any other survivors?"

"Barely. We hid the women and children farther up the trail," the arbalist said. "Those who fought were slaughtered where they stood." She averted her eyes from the surrounding carnage. "I got a few good shots in, but we were overrun in minutes."

"Tragic," Gipi said, failing to mask her impatience. "Listen, you need to muster what you can. The Undertakers are plotting to poison the villages who support the cause."

"What?"

"It is true," Baldwin said. "They plan to exterminate those who oppose the Crown."

Color drained from the arbalist's face. "No time to waste then." She jerked her head aside. "Follow me. We need to tell the others."

Down a sidepath winding about tall stones, Baldwin and Gipi were led to a man-made cave delving deep into the mountainside. Iron trolleys lay toppled about the entrance, and picks and shovels were left strewn about the rusty tracks, as if the tunnels had been abandoned suddenly. The arbalist lit and raised a pitch-soaked torch, shedding light upon the hastily dug passage and its wooden supports.

"Tread lightly," she warned.

Descending into the mines, Baldwin followed the gleaming copper veins with care, feeling his way along carven stone. Scorched and soot-smeared rock betrayed where applied heat and water had blasted the way forward, and where entire tunnels had collapsed.

The leper wondered how many corpses lay crushed under his boots.

"Got a name?" Gipi asked.

"Hilda," the arbalist said. "Brunhilda."

"How long have you been with Radcliffe's band?" Baldwin's low voice reverberated throughout the mines. "It seems he's recruited quite the motley crew."

"Four years, and yes."

Gipi shoved her hands in her pockets. "Don't talk much, do you?"

"No."

Hilda's course led them to where the tunnels collided with a yawning cavern. Thin stalactites hung like racks of blades over pools of unknown depth; aged wooden walkways creaked underfoot until the company touched the damp stone floor. Sparse candlelight flickered against huddled shades of the desperate few, faces dirty and clothing simple even by the standards of peasantry. Women tended to the wounded. Sobs and whispers echoed throughout the chamber. Only Hilda's presence, it seemed, kept panic at bay. Baldwin stuck to the shadows, not wanting to frighten them further.

"Where's Radcliffe?" someone asked.

"Attention," Hilda said, raising her voice. "Anyone able to wield a sword, come with me. The Kingsmen won't stop at Sentinel Hill. They're planning to poison the hamlets that support our cause. Everything we've fought for stands on a razor's edge. This is our last chance."

Murmurs of uncertainty echoed throughout the cavern.

A handful of bandaged men managed to stand, but most simply wallowed in injury, heads in their hands. It didn't take a general to know that morale had been butchered as well.

"You didn't answer," an old man said, possibly a stable hand or gong farmer, judging by his dung-stained trousers. "Where's Radcliffe?"

Hilda took a deep breath, as if swallowing an uncomfortable truth. "He's been captured." The survivors remained silent, though their despair was palpable. "Listen," she said, "we have to endure. Do you think it'll end here? They'll burn your homes and salt your fields. There won't be a tomorrow, unless we act now." She beat her breastplate. "But take heart, for we have Radcliffe's chosen at our helm."

"Excuse me?" Gipi blurted.

"The captain has invested his trust in Baldwin, the crusader king of Golgotha, who abdicated his throne as a knight errant. And...his minstrel."

Baldwin would've preferred that without pretense. Though he scarcely believed in the tenets of rebellion, the leper knew this tyranny could not continue.

"It is true," Baldwin said, playing along with Hilda's embellishments. "I have seen what evil your lords are capable of us firsthand. I was there when Gravesend was massacred for daring to oppose the poll tax, and since, have pursued the dogs of war across the East Marches. I have sworn to destroy those responsible for such atrocities." He drew his sword and raised his blade towards the ceiling, embracing an impending ovation. "Follow me, and together we may have a hope of delivering this evil to justice!"

There was no applause—the survivors remained unconvinced, dull eyes fixed upon the masked stranger; brows furrowed in confusion.

"In case you haven't noticed," the old man scoffed, "we've been flayed harder than a fish on a fast day. We've got less than fifty men, counting the invalids. What can we possibly do? And, besides, we don't know you. Who else can vouch for your character?"

Baldwin bit his tongue. The dissenter had a point—these ranks couldn't hope to triumph through strength of arms. Not against Dampe and the Undertakers.

"I can." Gipi stepped forward. "Don't get me wrong, we're not heroes. Barely a carnival of two. And you guys aren't exactly an army. That doesn't make us helpless, though." She turned to the leper. "He may not look it, but Baldwin single-handedly broke out of Castle Garth. Carved through the garrison like a hot knife through butter. And made it back here. To warn you." She eyed the old man. "I think that's worth more than a white flag and brown pants."

Moments of silence passed until a few more peasants stood and approached, leaning on their billhooks — a half dozen in total. Baldwin sighed deeply and conceded as the ragtag band came forward, shaky yet at his command.

"You there," the leper said, approaching a young recruit. "What is your profession?"

"Farmhand."

"And you?" Baldwin asked another.

"Potter, sir."

"Blacksmith," said a third.

"Not as of now," Baldwin said. "You are soldiers of God. By the power bestowed unto me by providence, ours is a righteous crusade. And so our enemies be damned." He gave the sign of the saltire. "I absolve you of guilt and sin." Such a decree was stolen from papal bulls that he'd heard time again, meant to rally thieves and murderers to the Holy Land of Golgotha, but here it was spoken with sincerity, to inspire his men. "Let that be of no small comfort."

The militiamen exchanged nervous smiles and gathered their arms and armor; kettle helms, leather bracers, and farming implements repurposed into weapons of war. With the company assembled, Hilda led the way out of the mines and into the sun.

"Where will the Undertakers strike first?" Baldwin asked the arbalist. "You know this land better than I. What are the key towns and trade routes?"

Hilda hoisted her crossbow over her shoulder. "Best bet is to follow the River Tintern to the working fields. From there, we intercept what we can." She turned to address her men. "We make for Nedlergate. And it won't be an easy trek."

"The capital?" scoffed a militiaman. "Are you mad?"

Hilda sighed. "The Undertakers will turn Radcliffe in at the Tower. With any luck, we'll intercept the convoy and free him. Keep your wits about you."

Half a mile up the trail, brambles and twisted trees began to sprout from stone, as the rush of water filled Baldwin's ears. Further still, the company came to the riverbank—peppered with brown and black pebbles—cleaving through the mountainside. A lonely pier jutted into the white, foaming rapids, as a raft bobbed with the current, tethered to its cleat. Waterlogged planks moaned as Baldwin approached the vessel, skeptical as to how many it could support.

"This will take us to Nedlergate?" he asked.

"Hang on and don't fall," Hilda said, boarding with ease.

Gipi followed, as did the peasant militia. With oars distributed amongst the company, the leper managed to crouch on the raft's edge, desperate to keep some distance between him and the company. Gipi did the honors and sliced through the rope with her sharpened dirk. The raft tore its way downstream instantly. Baldwin clutched its lip with numb hands; cold water sprayed his mask, threatening to reduce his bandages to sodden strips.

"Damn this trek," he muttered.

The raft gathered speed, shredding through water as its crew paddled as best they could, while Hilda crouched at the stern. Baldwin kept an ear out for game or stragglers in the surrounding undergrowth, yet scarcely heard anything save the crash of water against stone. Then it occurred to him, perhaps the danger lay beneath the surface.

"I must ask," Baldwin said to the arbalist, "how did you know of my lineage?"

Hilda smiled. "I've seen the Holy Land long ago. Though you wouldn't remember me, not all easterlings fought under the banner of the Sultan Khan."

Baldwin's eyes widened in surprise beneath his mask. "You were there? For the Siege of Golgotha? No, you couldn't have been."

"Like I said, it was long ago—"

The raft jerked against the rapids. Before he could regain

his balance, Baldwin toppled into the river with an icy splash. Undertows tangled and tore him in dueling directions. Squinting against the flow, the leper reached out to the surface, only to tumble downstream as stones raked across his flesh. Thick piscine forms brushed against him—Baldwin reached for his sword, only for scaly tails to slap his face, threatening to knock his mask loose, until many hands grasped his shoulders. Hoisted by his comrades, he found himself aboard the raft once more, taking in desperate lungfuls of air.

Baldwin shuddered in embarrassment.

"Nothing smells worse than a wet leper," said the fool.

"Shut up, Gipi...."

Hours passed as the company sailed on. Gipi shared her whiskey flask with the peasants, much to their delight, though Baldwin stuck to his own cup. Hilda declined her merry offer, preferring to stay sober while in command. Beyond the massifs, the River Tintern wound across golden fields, following the Old Road as tall orchards shifted in the breeze. The company made it to the crossing and disembarked among the thickets. Baldwin sighed with relief upon feeling solid earth under his boots. Wringing his woolen cloak, he felt his bandages flop and unravel—the peasants kept their distance, averting their eyes in disgust. Despite his misery, Baldwin took comfort in the smoke rising over the ridge, imagining the hearth of an inn.

"Uh," Gipi said, "that's an awful lot of smoke."

A pit of uncertainty churned in Baldwin's stomach; he spotted flies swarming just off the path and ventured forth, driven by suspicion, only to stumble upon a gruesome sight. The corpse of a villager lay in a muddy brook, eyes and tongue bulging out of his skull.

He's breathed his last. Poisoned....

Baldwin clenched his fists, thoughts burning with fury. How many villages did the Undertakers plan to massacre? How many innocents had to die by Dampe's command? Sensing a presence in the reeds, the leper drew his sword—conviction reborn.

"They're here."

CHAPTER SIX

Darkening clouds gathered over the East Marches. With nothing left for them, Baldwin led the peasant militia and kept to the sidepath, as to lose any pursuers in the gloaming. By the hour's end, they came to a pastoral land of hills and flaxen grass, where shepherds tended to their flocks, and wolfhounds herded woolly stock to barn and pen. Beyond the cottages and fenced acres, few inhabited the countryside, even by the standard of rural parishes. The leper wasted no time basking in such quaintness, footfalls heavy against the roadway.

"Are you sure the Undertakers are nearby?" Brunhilda hoisted her heavy wooden arbalist over her shoulder. "I've yet to see any sign of them."

Baldwin glanced over his shoulder. "The corpse off the road was evidence enough."

"It makes no sense, though," she said. "This is royalist country, and there aren't any towns nearby. Why would the king authorize such an attack?"

When the company came around the wooded bend, they spied a coaching inn at the crossroads—a two-story taphouse offering fresh kegs, lodging, and stables for weary steeds. The sign of the Smoking Ewe swayed from rusty hinges, as if bidding the company to enter.

"This is the only inn for miles," Hilda said. "We're far enough from Castle Garth. The Undertakers will pass through here on the Old Road to Nedlergate." She turned to her men, idling at the doorstep. "We're stopping here, but don't get too comfortable."

Baldwin opened the front door, welcomed by the crackling of a hearth. The Smoking Ewe was fairly unremarkable. Under rafters and candled chandeliers, wooden tables and seats sat low in the dimness, and above the fireplace rested a head of a "three-eyed ram," likely the grisly invention of a taxidermist. Shepherds took refuge at the bar, drinking as the evening wore on. The ceiling moaned under the weight of its second-story business, and the clink of bottles filled the air. Baldwin kept his distance and pulled up a seat, met with silent stares.

Hilda and the others weren't far behind.

The leper slid a few silvers across the table and offered his own pewter cup. "We'll have the same as them," he kept his voice low, raising two fingers. "It's been a long day."

The barkeep, a burly middle-aged man sporting a thick handlebar mustache, nodded and poured the company a round of whiskeys. Baldwin took a corner seat by the open hearth and shut his eyes, allowing himself to shudder. Memories of murder and torture pierced his thoughts, as hail began to rattle against the leaky rooftops, mirroring his own fragile state.

"Are you alright?" Gipi asked, joining his table.

"No," he admitted.

Baldwin reached for his journal, which, though wet and battered, had miraculously survived his wanderings. No lyrics or wisdom came. He tried to write, only to be confronted by fog, as if the muses had abandoned him. He felt nothing. Resolve had become an armor encasing his sorrow and rage, shielding him from every threat, real or imagined, yet unable to lower his guard or remove his helmet. Baldwin drank to numb his mind as much as his failing flesh. Whiskey upon whiskey, he felt the taproom and its patrons orbit his skull until words turned to worms and slugs and lost all meaning.

Gipi reached for his cup. "I think you've had enough."

"How many have I had?" the leper asked.

"Yes," the fool quipped.

Baldwin paid her no heed and shambled to the bar, waiting for the barkeep's attention. Hilda and the others tore at a rack of roasted lamb ribs and slathered ripened cheese over rolls of rosemary bread, until they had either gone to their rooms or were loitering outside. Nothing save a hushed exchange a few seats down reached the leper's ears.

"So," said a shepherd. "Any news from the front?"

The barkeep shook his head, eyes fixed on the floor. "No, nothing at all."

"Seriously?" he whispered. "I can't take it. Ever since they set up shop."

"Quiet! Someone might be listening—"

The door swung open as clomping boots filled the taproom. Baldwin raised his head, glowering as a host of cloaked and hooded miscreants marched toward the bar, voices rough and raspy. The leper watched on with morbid intent. Whether by righteousness or a need to prove his own worth, Baldwin contemplated how many he could take on.

More of Dampe's men? Local brigands? It matters not....

"Evening, gents," said the captain, "we have returned." He slammed a fist against the bar. "Olaf! Give us a round, will you? Not the swill you serve these sheep-fuckers."

The barkeep nodded silently and went for the cellar.

"Well?" a brute snarled. "Looks like you've got something to say."

The local shepherds eyed each other nervously and stood, one by one, like a throng of frightened children, seeing themselves out the door. Only Baldwin and Gipi remained. She kept a gloved hand over her dirk, eyes fixed on the leper, as if praying he wouldn't do anything stupid.

Olaf returned with a cask of wine and a platter of wooden cups.

Baldwin, solemn as ever, kept to his own and yet couldn't help but smirk at the scene, eying the captain like a side of beef to be butchered. The hearth's light seemed to flicker and wane. He uttered a low laugh and killed his shot with ease, ignoring Gipi's cautious approach. The brigands glanced at each other, nervously, but postured with ill intent.

"What's so funny, asshole?" the brute said, knocking

his own goblet onto the floor. "Hey," he approached the leper, slowly, "you spilled my drink."

Baldwin locked eyes with the barkeep and raised two fingers again, clutching the hilt of his broadsword. Olaf reluctantly refilled his glass.

"You deaf?" The brute inched closer. "I said, you spilled my drink."

"He says you spilled his drink," Olaf said.

Baldwin did not reply, content to sip his whiskey.

"It's alright," the barkeep said. "I'll get you another. On me."

Grueling silence passed as the brigands gathered around Baldwin, as if unsure whether to assault the madman. His smile widened and he laughed, uncontrollably, as if possessed by a daemon of foul humor. Gipi weaseled past them and laid a hand on the leper's shoulder.

"Don't," she whispered, "they're not worth it."

"You're with this freak?" sneered a bandit.

Baldwin's drunken thoughts drifted to the boy at Castle Garth. Things would be different. They had to be. The leper placed his cup firmly on the bar and slid a gold coin to the barkeep.

"Apologies for the mess," he slurred.

Baldwin drew his sword and cleaved through the brute's shoulder, relishing in his screams as blood splattered the countertop. Taking a poor stance, the leper howled like a mad thing as he cut through skin and sinew, much to everyone's horror. He made short work of the brigands and found himself surrounded by dead men. No glory was to be had. Silence and shame washed over him in an unwelcome tide. Without a word, Baldwin saw himself out the door, shambling into torrential rain. In a moment of intuition, he saw a shadow in the misty twilight, perhaps a horse-drawn carriage. Then it dawned on him.

The convoy…. Radcliffe!

Baldwin barreled across the roadway, hurling himself at the nearest brigand, hewing him in two with a remorseless chop.

Amidst the chaos, he dove behind the carriage as black steeds panicked. Bloodlust washed over him.

"What the hell are you doing?!" Gipi yelled from afar.

"Do not let that wagon escape." Baldwin kicked and bashed the wheels, gritting his teeth, trying to knock a peg or two loose. "This is our moment!"

Gipi sprinted and dove past the musketeers and their line of sight, tumbling with grace and weaving around their clumsy shots like a mad acrobat, leaping towards the gate. A boot knife whistled from her fingertips, impaling a fusilier in the throat.

That's the fool I know....

Baldwin swung his blade blindly as a skirmish erupted between rebels and brigands, eager to carve into the flesh of evildoers, only to be greeted by a wicked parry. A hulk of high rank greeted him, pressing down upon the leper's blade with the weight of his own hilt, glowering with a grimace. Clad in the bloodstained motley of his profession, the landsknecht eyed Baldwin with keen interest.

"So," the brigand's voice boomed with a force of devilry, "you're the one who maimed my master." The towering opponent broke his guard and backed away, clutching his sword with both hands. "Baldwin of Golgotha, better known as the royal pain in our asses."

"And to whom do I owe the pleasure?" the leper asked, urgency stinging his thoughts, all but sobering his frenzy. "Another dog of the Undertakers?"

The landsknecht cracked his neck. "Call me, Gunther."

Baldwin knew better than to talk down the mercenary. With a mutual lunge, they tangled their blades in a flurry of blows. Gunther pressed the advantage and knocked Baldwin back with a forceful blow, all but sending the sword flying from his bandaged hands.

"You're strong, little leper," Gunther said, "but I'm stronger."

"I assure you, I could do this dance all day."

Gunther's steel collided with the leper's cuirass. "I'm sure you can," he said. "Call me impressed that you're still standing. It won't do you any good, though. Radcliffe's scheduled for execution upon arrival." He swung upwards and cracked his fist against Baldwin's jaw — a cheap shot. "What? Did you think we'd give you the luxury of time?"

Baldwin spat out a broken tooth. "You and your comrades will pay dearly for your crimes," he snarled. "For the crimes you've committed on the Crown's behalf."

"Hate to break it to you," Gunther said, hoisting his sword over his shoulder, "but there's little loyalty to Mulgrave in our ranks. We're in it for the coin. Or, in my case," he grinned, "a damn good fight. Get up! I'm not done with you yet!"

Baldwin would humor the landsknecht with a duel, meeting his challenge with a hueing blow. "So that's why you fight? For the thrill of combat?" he growled. "What a waste."

"Depends on your perspective," Gunther said. "It's a living. Sometimes the less you think about it, the happier you'll be." With a swift draw, he readied a wide-mouthed blunderbuss and aimed at Baldwin's chest. "Well, nice chatting, but we're running late — "

A steel-tipped bolt whistled across the Old Road and impaled Gunther's wrist. He roared in pain, dropping the gun with a clatter. Hilda emerged from a stack of barrels, flanked by a pair of longbowmen, reloading her crossbow with a metallic clack.

"Hell's fires, I'm good," she quipped.

With a tremendous roar, Baldwin lunged after his quarry. Gunther spat onto the earth, thwarted by the sniper's shot, and took to the carriage. Aboard the driver's box, he gave a command to retreat and rode to the west, flanked by men on horseback, leaving dust in their wake. Baldwin heard hoofbeats not far behind, accompanied by the jingle of little brass bells. Gipi rode beside him and offered a gloved hand. Within seconds, they gave pursuit down the Old Road with the fool at the reins and Baldwin wielding the Broken Blade.

"After them," he ordered.

Through thin-branched thickets and shallow glens, Baldwin felt the harshness of packed dirt under hoof as he eyed other riders along adjacent paths. Masked by black hoods and neckerchiefs, they took aim at the pursuers. The leper shielded himself from shots with the flat of his broadsword, only to feel the blade splinter with each parry.

"Take the left flank!"

Gipi obeyed and rode into range. Baldwin swung wide and knocked the rider off his steed with brute force. Swiftly, they gained on the carriage.

"Forth," the leper pointed his blade ahead, "charge forth!"

"Going as fast as I can," Gipi snapped.

Riding beside Gunther's carriage, Baldwin locked eyes with his opponent, who laughed. "Well, you've got bigger stones than I thought!" He flung a handful of iron balls, which burst into a barrage of smoke and shrapnel. Gipi's horse bucked and whinnied, almost knocking the leper to the unforgiving road. "You're a tenacious bastard, I'll give you that." He drew a pistol from his hip and fired blindly at the pursuers. "Jester's not bad either."

Amidst the chaos of gunfire and roadside perils, Baldwin raised his head and saw a crossing at the River Tintern. With a sudden spurt of speed, Gunther rode a few yards ahead and smashed an oil lamp against the timber bridge, igniting it instantly, cutting Baldwin and Gipi off from the convoy. The leper dismounted his steed, seething, watching the carriage flee through rising flames, as Gunther's mad laughter faded into the distance.

"Farewell, leper," he bellowed. "We'll meet again!"

As the bridge crackled and the fire spread, Baldwin gazed upon what lay beyond — the silhouettes of urban dwellings, stark against the setting sun, dominated by a fortified prison atop a black hill. He hadn't seen Nedlergate from the east until now, with its smokestacks and steeples, as the stench of human waste wafted from the open streets. It was a darker place than the leper remembered, and he dared not dwell on what awaited them.

"Should we wait for the others?" Gipi asked.

Baldwin took to the sidepath, silently approaching the Tower of Nedlergate. He hoped that Hilda and her militiamen would rendezvous with him upon the prison grounds. Crowds gathered in the distant street of Tower Hill, cheering and jeering, as if witnessing another head rolling off the chopping block. If what Gunther said was true, then time was short.

Should they fail, Radcliffe would be dead within the hour.

CHAPTER SEVEN

The Tower of Nedlergate was a blight upon the city. Its iron-banded gates stood as indomitable doors that had endured centuries of war and civil unrest. Such was the castle's arrogance that its heights bore untouchable elements of the gothic, from lancet windows and ornate pinnacles to the gargoyles whose spouts fed the river below. Even the pale banners, hanging from high balustrades, bore the bloodstained rose of King Geoffrey. Under the pretense of security, enemies of the state were imprisoned in its dismal cellars. Torture and violent death were ever threats to the people, whether for crimes real or imagined. Countless victims had fallen to heated pokers, spikes of iron maidens, and the stroke of the executioner's axe. The Tower bore witness to a history of greed and hatred, looming over the entirety of Nedlergate as the silent warden of a far greater prison.

Such is my destination....

Amidst the urban spectacle, Baldwin stuck to shadowed alleys and small streets between the boulevards. It seemed every citizen had gathered at Tower Hill, swarming in an unwashed mass as criers handed out pamphlets listing tonight's beheadings. The leper took a copy and skimmed the list of names and charges. Crimes ranged from larceny to murder, but most were in association with treason. The public was, by nature, a mob of running mouths and rotten teeth. Baldwin observed in bitter silence; they hardly cared for justice, only a spectacle to ease the grueling mundanity of their daily lives.

"Charming," Gipi said with a sigh. "Wouldn't expect anything less."

"This," the leper muttered, "is why democracy is a fool's hope. The only thing worse than tyranny is the will of the mob." He crumpled the paper and postured, eying the bleak fortress before them. "At any rate, we must infiltrate this wicked place."

Gipi rolled her eyes. "Good luck barging in," she kept her voice low. "Look around." Kingsmen kept vigil in the streets and atop the battlements, armed with muskets and sabers, eying the crowd. "Locked up tighter than a chastity belt."

Baldwin lowered his head. "Every keep has its weakness. We need only find out what." He took a few steps forward, still in the shadow of the Tower. "Come, we must hurry."

Beyond the fringe of the crowd, Baldwin and his fool stuck close to the river's edge among the bakeries and fishmongers, cautiously, so as not to draw attention. Rows of gibbets hung from the battlements, cradling the corpses of convicts, while pikes crowned with severed heads loomed from parapets of stone. Murders of crows pecked out their eyes and tongues, only to take flight and circle the turrets like wraiths in twilight.

"Legend says that if the ravens leave the tower," Gipi said, "the kingdom will fall."

"Then I suppose Radcliffe would see them off," Baldwin scoffed. "We cannot wait for Hilda any longer. Her rebels would only alert the guards to our presence."

Gipi shrugged her thin shoulders. "You'll get no argument from me."

They approached the docks along the river, where all manner of merchandise was being transferred to and from the ferries — rations, provisions, and the like. The scene was lightly guarded, as young soldiers surveyed with waning attention, likely between shifts. Baldwin crept around the bend and watched a ship approach the submerged portcullis of Traitor's Gate from beneath the Tower Bridge. The leper gritted his teeth as its iron bars lifted slowly with a loathsome clank, as if chained to a hidden mechanism. While the outer walls were guarded by mortars and crenels, smuggling oneself in a barrel didn't seem the worst idea. There was something amiss in the side streets — plumes of smoke wafted from Pudding Lane, and the air turned hot. Baldwin hadn't the time to dwell on such things. Before Gipi had a chance to object, the leper had already leapt inside a barrel and shut the lid atop his head. She followed suit with minimal complaint. Holding his breath, he felt steady hands toss the barrel aboard a ship's deck, letting his thoughts wander as he slipped through Traitor's Gate.

Why am I doing this? Risking my life for a cause that I scarcely believe in, and for what exactly? Glory? The desire to be remembered? The longer I fight, the hollower my struggles seem. Why do I fight? Merely to challenge and fend off my own demise? Fighting for its own sake is no different than to pillage and burn. No different than them. There has to be a purpose to this. There has to be an answer. And a righteous one at that. There has to be —

"Is that the shipment then?" asked an unseen officer.

"Aye, sir," said a guard. "That should be all."

Peering from a peephole, Baldwin watched a cadet take inventory with a bulging ledger only to usher the cargo to be carried aside without inspection — a stroke of luck.

Alone in the storeroom, Baldwin lifted the lid and crept out of his hiding place, silently congratulating himself on this moment of cunning. Before the guard could close the door, Baldwin cupped a hand over his mouth and flipped the unsuspecting soldier onto his back, knocking him unconscious with a crack against the flagstone floor.

The leper advanced, warily, sword at hand. Somewhere in the lower levels, Baldwin found himself in a masonry corridor leading to and from the inner docks. With a sigh, he stuck to darkened corners and eyed the patrols. Eventually, a familiar figure emerged from the barrels by the pier, sauntering to Baldwin's side.

"Well," Gipi whispered, "now that we're in."

"We make for the dungeons."

Baldwin took to the hall, eying the water trickling into rusted grates where he sensed the faint stirrings of life — perhaps a pack of rats or a dying prisoner. The lower halls were poorly guarded, as if most of the garrison was relegated to the Outer

Ward. He followed the muffled moans ever deeper into the foundations. Pitch-soaked torches flickered along the gray stone walls, faintly illuminating heavy wooden doors to numbered cells.

"I doubt they'll bother getting him settled in," Gipi said.

"What do you mean?"

"They plan on executing Radcliffe on arrival, right? We should head for—"

An agonized scream cut her words short, followed by a series of labored cranks. Baldwin shuddered but said nothing, imagining the rack in use beneath their feet. Slowly, the leper drew his sword. Strange barbed vines lurked along the walls, sprouting from cracks in the floor—reminiscent of the specimens in Castle Garland. In a single file, Baldwin and Gipi descended into the dimness, greeted by humidity and flakes of pollen floating in the torchlight.

An exchange of voices breached the long quiet, echoing from the lower halls.

"Your majesty," said a goaler, "this is an unexpected pleasure."

"Enough with the niceties," Geoffrey said, "I am merely here to examine my garden in bloom." Soft bootsteps accompanied the king's dour tone. "How are the mandragoras progressing? Are they ready for deployment?"

"They're still growing, your majesty. And I would hesitate to uproot one."

"Well, that's why we have prisoners, isn't it?"

Mandragora, the parasitic root that grows from the fluids of the freshly executed. No wonder the king is so keen to sentence his people to the gallows. He's fertilizing an army....

The leper and his fool lingered far from sight, not daring to approach the king's entourage. Creeping in darkness, the leper took the descending stairs to a cellar. The chamber was overtaken by ferns and ivies of various sizes and shades, from deep green to noxious purple, every thorn dripping with blood. Dismembered remains lay strewn among the tangled roots, fresh limbs, and yellowed bones, painting a gruesome picture of the maimed feeding these plants. Wide shafts of moonlight were cast from the ceiling, as if the chamber was once the bottom of a well, though the shadows of iron bars crushed any notion of a quick escape.

"Poison gardens," Baldwin said. "Truly fitting for this nest of vipers."

A metallic shriek breached the stillness, and an emaciated corpse was tossed down the chute, falling to the wooden floor with a snap and crunch. Ropelike vines began to stir, snaking about pots and planters, eager to worm their way into flesh. Baldwin watched on in horror as thorns sliced through skin and floral proboscises lapped up the blood like thin tongues.

Dangling from wooden supports were gibbet-sacks—man-sized pods that digested prey in cocoons laced with enzymes and digestive fluids, germinating in the gloom. Against his better judgment, the leper examined one such thing in the torchlight, watching as its captive meal twitched with labored breathing.

"Get down!" Gipi shouted.

Baldwin drew his sword and took a defensive stance. Something struck his back. He collapsed onto his chest, gasping, as tendrils tipped with botanical bludgeons writhed above him. A bulbous silhouette descended slowly, suspended from dozens of thick vines, eclipsing the light as it shone through its veiny flesh, illuminating all manner of half-digested corpses.

"What is that?" Gipi gasped.

The Great Corpse Flower flailed wildly, slamming its clubs against spare pots and barrels of fertilizer, shattering them in a whirlwind of clay and wood. Baldwin rolled to the side and took cover behind a tall column. As he cut through a wayward vine, white sap spewed from the severed tendril, and the Corpse Flower rasped in pain.

Gipi took cover amidst the planters and readied her dirk and sickle. Leaping atop the dirt beds, she wobbled and dodged the serpentine tendrils, slicing off tips and buds—for every limb she cut, two more burst from the floorboards to ensnare their prey.

"Shit!" she cried.

Constricting vines lifted her high over the swollen bulb. It yawned open, revealing a pitcher-maw with lips oozing with slippery mucus. With a purging blow, Baldwin cleaved through its limbs and scaled its girth. He danced upon the lip of the gullet, enduring the vines as they flogged his back, all but flaying flesh from bone. Gritting his teeth, the leper gazed into the sickening stomach; walls red with leafy veins and lined with thorn-teeth. Such was Gipi's fate, should he fail or falter. As the vines prepared to drop the jester to her corrosive demise, Baldwin leapt into the stomach and carved into its innards. Ignorant to the burning pain, he slashed again and again. The Corpse Flower shrieked in pain as the leper planted his blade deep into flesh and tore upwards. All but swimming in milky blood, he smirked. The Corpse Flower began to wither and die. Weakened vines dropped Gipi as she tumbled across the floor.

With a mortal chop, Baldwin trudged out of the remains.

"Abominations," he growled, "this is not of the natural order of things."

Gipi flicked the sludge off her gloves. "No argument here."

"Still," Baldwin eyed the stirring plants, "there is no denying it. The king is weaponizing these foul specimens." He tore a torch from the wall and hurled it at the dead flower. It caught fire like dry tinder, and flames spread rapidly throughout the chamber, filling the tower with plumes of black smoke. Together, he and Gipi fled to the prison level.

"That should slow them," Baldwin said.

"Definitely put a pause on the mass poisoning."

With the lower floors behind them, Baldwin and Gipi found themselves in another tower. The bustle of rallying guards told them everything they needed to know — the Kingsmen had been alerted to their presence. The leper, cumbersome as he was, remained unseen. Gipi fiddled with a lockpick and opened the door. As she peered around the corridor, Baldwin looked out of a crenel upon Tower Hill. The crowd howled and heckled as another head fell to the axe, rolling off the platform and into the pit.

"Where do you suppose they're keeping Radcliffe?" the leper asked.

"Away from the other prisoners," Gipi said. "Frankly, I'm shocked they haven't drawn him by horse yet. If I didn't know any better, I'd say they're stalling."

"Stalling, you say?"

"Never said it made sense —"

The distant clang of hammers and anvils interrupted their exchange. Metalworks toiled in the ground floor of the Outer Ward. Gipi's eyes glimmered with greed, as if suddenly recalling another purpose of this castle. The leper sighed deeply.

"The Royal Mint," he said.

The jester shoved her hands deep into her pockets. "A detour is awfully tempting...."

"Would you want to end up drawn and quartered?"

"Don't think for a second that you're any better. We're breaking out one of the king's most wanted. If we get caught, it'll be mercy that they kill us on the spot."

Baldwin rolled his eyes and conceded. "Fair enough, but Radcliffe is the priority."

"Fine," Gipi said. "Sometimes I wonder if you're allergic to profit."

Against his better judgment, Baldwin followed his fool to the workshops and their billowing smokestacks. Furnaces blazed as molten silver and gold were cast as glowing ingots, passed through steel rollers and screw-operated presses. Amidst the scales and shears, workers in leather jerkins toiled in unspeakable heat and a miasma of noxious fumes. The metallic toiling of hammers and stamping machines was deafening, as sparks flew with every strike.

Despite the hellish conditions, the gleam of precious metals pervaded the halls. Gipi's fingers danced their way towards an open crate, and she swiped a handful of gold crowns. Much to Baldwin's surprise, the workers were far too preoccupied with their miserable labor to notice thieves in twilight. Together, they sneaked to yet another turret when the leper heard another host of voices — muffled by stone.

"Easy," a mocking voice echoed from around the bend. "It'll be over soon enough."

"If you think my death will mean anything," Radcliffe scoffed, "then you beefeaters are stupider than your reputation precedes — "

The crack of a cudgel carried down the corridor. "Shut up and keep moving!" shouted a goaler. "You're heading straight to the gallows."

Baldwin was about to charge when Gipi laid a finger to her lips and drew a slender dirk from her boot. With a sliding step and a leap, she dove her blade into a goaler's throat. The leper barreled to her side and chopped into the torso of the guard still standing — a killing blow.

"Y-you!" Radcliffe stuttered. "I took you both for dead. How'd you escape?"

"A story for another time." Gipi knelt and plucked a set of iron keys from a corpse. "At any rate, let's not stay here any longer than we have to."

"I'm grateful that you're alive," Baldwin said.

Radcliffe sighed with relief, though battered almost beyond recognition. He hadn't the luxury of his eyepatch or medals. Missing a handful of fingernails and dressed in a burlap tunic, he clung to the rope across his waist and scant shreds of dignity.

"And I'm grateful you came for me," he said. "Wasn't expecting it, honestly."

"Understandable," Baldwin said.

Radcliffe looted a saber from a slain guard, examining its polished blade against the torchlight. "Now then, what's the plan for getting out?"

"Plan?" Gipi scoffed. "Oh, you flatter us so."

Baldwin paused, sensing a lurking danger in the cells. Suddenly, a pair of iron portcullises shrieked and clattered down, blocking the presumed exit and where the infiltrators had come from. "Stay close," the leper said. "We're not alone."

"No shit," scoffed a familiar foe. "I knew we'd meet again, but not so soon." Gunther emerged from the shadows yet kept his distance from the gate. If Baldwin didn't know better, he would've taken the smile as genuine. "Not sure if you're as stupid as they say or a genius cut from a different cloth."

"You," Baldwin spat. "Let us go at once."

"And why would I do that?" Gunther sighed. "Don't take it personally, milord. Like I said back at the inn, we're in this for the coin. Still, to risk your life over such a radical cause. You must be something of a rabble rouser yourself, right?"

"Nothing of the sort," Baldwin snapped.

"Huh?" Gunther said, seemingly shocked. "Could've fooled me. Anyways," he shot a thumb up to the upper levels, "better hurry on before the fire spreads—"

"That's enough, Gunther."

A moment of dreadful silence passed as another figure emerged from the darkness; though his face was blistered and wrapped in bloodied bandages, the warlord's presence was unmistakable. "Baldwin," he said, "I suppose I owe you a bit of explanation."

"What the Devil are you doing here?" the leper growled.

"Collecting my just reward," Dampe said. "The Crown tried to double-cross us after you escaped from Castle Garland. Thought we'd be easy to dispose of. So, we're pulling a 'Gravesend,' if you take my meaning. Under orders from new management."

"Oh," Gipi scoffed, "nice face. You look like a porkchop. Extra crispy."

"Laugh while you can," Dampe sighed. "It won't matter

soon."

Baldwin's grip on his sword's hilt tightened. Distant screams and tolling bells penetrated the thick stone walls, as panic spread across the city. Even the leper could smell the smoke. Out the window, the skyline blazed in an impossible pyre of crowded houses and slated rooftops. Before the implications of the Great Fire of Nedlergate could truly dawn on him, unseen beasts battered against a locked door, as if trapped inside a cell, sensing spilled blood, yearning to break free and join the carnage. Shrill cries, bestial and half-human, pierced the dimly lit halls.

"This is no prison block," Baldwin said, "it's a menagerie."

"How astute of you," Dampe sneered.

The creatures gained leverage against the hinges, prying the door loose from its frame. Baldwin drew his broadsword, clutching with both hands, bracing himself for whatever lurked within. The door shattered under a quaking blow. Corpses lurched into the light, mouths agape, uttering loathsome moans. The leper recoiled in disgust as they belched mud and white worms, roots jutting from every orifice, as if animated by parasitic flowers in bloom.

Mandragorans...!

Baldwin gazed into their gelatinous eyes and tried to cry out in fury, though nothing escaped his lips. Fright tore at his heart, enfeebling him in body and mind. The leper dodged one such creature's lunging advances and, after a moment's horror, cleaved its skull without mercy, as soil and pale sap splattered the floor amidst grey matter.

"Now," Dampe said, "if you'll excuse me, I have a city to sack."

CHAPTER EIGHT

With the corpses of redcoats in his wake, Dampe raised his flintlock and smelled the smoke. Alone in the Tower courtyard, he watched the starless sky rain with ashes and cinders, as the light of a thousand flames engulfed the city beyond the ramparts. As he prowled the open green, Dampe supervised his men as they ransacked the Royal Mint, heaving sacks of coinage into armored wagons and rounding up moneyers to be shot. Gunther was never far behind, blunderbuss and mortar at hand, blonde hair pulled back with a leather strap.

"That's a lot of money," he said.

"Indeed. More than enough to line our pockets for the year." Dampe shot his lieutenant a smirk. "Amazing what a stray match in a bakery can do."

Gunther took a bite of pilfered pastry. "Yeah," he said, mouth full of cakey goodness, "so what's next? Load up and commandeer a couple of ships?"

Dampe turned to the Inmost Ward and drew a second pistol. "Not yet. I have a score to settle with his majesty. Suppose he's cowering in his chambers. Preparing to flee."

"Wouldn't surprise me. Blue bloods are all the same."

"I'll entrust you with securing the Outer Ward in the meantime."

"You're going in alone?"

Dampe nodded, slowly, watching the smog-bound heavens with keen intent. "It won't be long until our special guests arrive."

With that, he departed for the Great Hall and shoved open the wooden doors. His footsteps echoed throughout the palace, under its hammerbeam arches, evoking kings of old. Between the opulent beams were stained glass windows and mounted heads of ferocious game—bears and boars, no doubt trophies that Geoffrey had inherited from his ancestors. On the walls hung tapestries depicting the lives and trials of saints, woven from wool and silk, silver and gold. And yet, Dampe felt only a yearning for things that would never be his.

All my life, I've looked up to the nobles in their chateaus. All my life, I've envied them, the prestige of the peerage. And now, so close to tasting the scraps they take for granted, I've been cast aside like trash under the seething sun. And they almost succeeded....

Two nights ago, Dampe had gasped awake to unwelcome life, grasping about the earthen walls of a hastily-dug grave. Staggering upright, he had shambled on instinct, mind devoid of reason and rational thought—animated by overwhelming rage. Peals of thunder erupted over the mountains, as cold rain pattered against his nude body. When sense and sanity returned, he noticed the gravekeeper gawking in horror. Dampe laid a finger to his lips, only to knock the poor sod unconscious with a blow to the temple, fist colliding with the man's skull. Seething and heaving, he robbed the peasant of coinage, clothing, as well as a ring of keys.

A second chance, perhaps....

Rallying his men in the king's absence, Dampe did what any rational man would do—set fire to the capital in an act of vengeance. Here and now, to the right was a door left ajar and a staircase leading to yet another cellar. Dampe cocked his pistol with a click and the intent to kill. He inched down the stairs and followed the fleeting candlelight into the greenhouse.

"Your majesty," cried a servant, "we can't save everything—"

"Shut up and keep packing," Geoffrey barked, "and be careful with the specimens!"

Under the gaze of tinted windows and past rows of planter beds, the king scrambled for his alembics and retorts, mortars and pestles, desperate to save his great work, while a pompous aide rummaged through what little was necessary. Taking aim in the dimness, Dampe fired his flintlock. The servant collapsed in a lifeless heap, shot in the chest. Geoffrey drew a sleek knife from his belt and spun around to face the intruder, eyes wide and tearing with terror.

"You," he stuttered, "I had you killed."

"That you did," Dampe said. "Now then," he lowered his guard, gesturing to the alchemist's desk, "take a seat, your majesty. Got any brandy down here? I'd like to talk."

"Excuse me?"

"You heard me," Dampe pulled a chair. "You've already lost, and no one's going to pay your ransom. That much I can promise. Unless you want to die now, I suggest you humor me."

Geoffrey's face was contorted in confusion as he reached for a bottle of vintage. Pouring them each a generous goblet, he sat across from Dampe, who picked at his fingernails.

"You know," the captain began, "there's something you said back there that's been bothering me. Once a commoner, always a commoner. That was a deep cut." He raised his glass in mock cheers. "Anyway, I trust this hasn't been tampered with?"

"No more than mine."

"Listen," Dampe said. "Do you know why you've lost? I'll tell you. Arrogance. Simple as that. Royals lock themselves away in the high castle, thinking that they're invincible to the problems that wrack the peasantry and daily life. And that's true, to an extent. But there's some things you can't outrun: plague, fire, and, of course, debt. See where I'm going with this?"

Geoffrey sipped at his brandy. "Not really."

"Should've expected that," Dampe said. "The plight of commoners is beyond your comprehension. Although I'm not one to talk." He took a hearty swig. "We play by different rules, you and I. Though I'd say I'm the freer of the two. And I'm not talking about exemption from sumptuary laws. Life's nasty, brutish, and short, as a wise man said, but that doesn't make it a hopeless abyss. To cast off the shackles of conventional morality and embrace your own ideals. There's genuine power in that. If only everyone was so lucky to pursue it."

"That's why you're here? To talk about your feelings?"

"No," Dampe said, "I'm just...externalizing my thoughts. Can't afford to have Gunther and the others hear me blather on like a sad sap, can I? I have a reputation to maintain." He smiled, bitterly. "I know that I'll never be a noble. I've come from nothing. No estate or titles, but I absolutely pity you." He watched the blood pool from the servant's corpse. "But enough of that." He stood and stuffed his ears with bits of wax, tracing a finger along the collection of herbal specimens. Though he scarcely believed in such superstitions as devil roots and their screaming spawn, he was nothing if not competent—he'd learned from his mistakes. These weapons would be Geoffrey's undoing. He raised a weird sapling like a ragdoll and stared the king down. "This," he scoffed, "is your secret weapon? Doesn't look like much." To his disgust, the mandrake began to twitch and coo like a babe. "We know what happens next."

"It was nothing personal, Dampe."

"I know," he sighed, "and this isn't either."

With that, Dampe tossed the mandrake into the fireplace, watching as it shrieked and curled into a ball of burning taproot. Such screams rose to an inhuman pitch. Geoffrey clawed at his bleeding ears, eyes, and tongue bulging out of his skull. Before he could even speak, the king had collapsed to his knees and pawed at Dampe's tunic, as light slowly faded from his eyes.

"Long live the king...."

Dampe rid the corpse of his burden of finery and returned to the courtyard, palms greased and conscience clear. Gunther was waiting for him like a hound on a leash.

"Courtyard's secured, captain," he said.

Dampe smiled but did not reply. The fire rose. It was only a matter of time before his contractors made their descent, and yet, he had a score to settle with a certain leper. He couldn't afford to keep Baldwin around like a fly on a dung heap. Something had to give.

High in the Royal Menagerie, Baldwin tore at the portcullis, attempting to pry it open with the flat of his blade. Every time he wedged an inch of progress, his sword slipped, and the gate came crashing down. He slammed his boot against the iron bars in frustration.

"Dammit," he fumed, "it's no use."

Torchlight flickered and waned as the subjects sobbed and moaned inside their cells. It was a madhouse of inhuman cruelty and tortured souls. On occasion, Baldwin would catch glimpses of gross deformity in between the bars of prison doors. He shuddered, wondering what had happened to these people. What disease reduced them to such a feral state. He could scarcely look at those he slew; tainted veins, rootlike growths, faces warped in a perverse fusion of bark and flesh, sickly flowers blooming out of their throats.

Gipi examined one of the bodies. "The 'mandragorans' were probably men once," she said, dissecting a tendril woven through skin and sinew. "Prisoners implanted with bad seeds." She sighed, deeply. "Poor bastards. Glad we burned the others in the dungeons."

Radcliffe leaned against the far wall. "So, this was your plan? Wonderful."

"Maybe you'd prefer being drawn and quartered —"

"Enough," Baldwin said. "Bickering won't get us out of the Tower alive. Gipi, give me a hand. Radcliffe, hold your tongue."

The fool shrugged. "If you insist."

A deep rumbling filled the Tower, followed by a shrill whistle, growing louder as it drew near, as if coming from the air. Gunpowder underpinned the reek of burning wood and tar.

"Get down!" Baldwin roared.

In an explosion of splintered masonry, a six-pound shot breached the castle wall, slamming against the far side of the corridor. Radcliffe leapt over the rubble and scaled the gaping hole. Perhaps it was a blessing in disguise, yet Baldwin knew such luck was a sign of an even greater threat. Baldwin and Gipi joined the captain before the sheer drop.

A swollen shadow loomed in the skies above, floating, distorted by rippling heat, as a phantom wreathed in smoke.

"Is that a dragon?" the leper gasped.

"No," Gipi said, "but I've never seen anything like it."

Radcliffe's face was drained of color. He said nothing and led the descent from the Tower. Baldwin and his fool stayed close, scaling the ramparts inch by inch, until the leper felt solid earth underfoot again. He squinted as smoke stung his eyes and nostrils, heat tempting to tear off his mask. Together, the company regrouped at the execution grounds amidst frenzied crowds. Tower Hill was in utter anarchy. Flames leapt from rooftop to rooftop and crowded houses smoldered like great bonfires, exposed wattle blazing within ovens of battered plaster. The streets overflowed with stampedes of rushing bodies and hastily packed carts, wafting with hysterical screams, as the brave and stupid rushed to salvage their livelihoods despite the holocaust. Fettering his own terror, Baldwin stood against the tide of refugees and drew his sword once more. A soaring host descended from the eclipsing shadow—winged, too mechanical in motion to be any bird, spewing jets of liquid flame upon the city below.

"Vermillion," Radcliffe managed, "the Empire's here."

"The city's done for," Gipi said. "There's nothing we can do."

The leper seethed in silence. For once in life, reason overcame his sense of chivalry. Though ashamed, he turned and ran, following his companions to the Tower Bridge. Pushing past the masses, Baldwin raced for the open gates at the far side of the overpass. Beneath its high stone balustrades, the River Tintern shimmered against the rising inferno, gleaming like a sea of molten metal, livid with apocalyptic light. Along the docks, workshops combusted in barrages of splinters and shrapnel, filling the air with billowing clouds of reeking tar. When at last the leper reached the far side of the bridge, several townhouses creaked and collapsed in a heap of smoldering rubble, blocking his only escape.

"Fuck," Gipi gasped.

Radcliffe raised his head in terrible awe, as the shadow descended from the miasma above, revealing a lacquered frigate, lovingly carved from oak and pine, lined with fantastical and frightening creatures and dozens upon dozens of mighty guns. Its sails had been replaced with colossal balloons of hot air and great steel burners, hoisting the colors of the Sun King. Soldiers leapt from portside and starboard alike with wide wings of wood and canvas, spiraling down like swarms of bats, descending upon the city under siege.

"The *Tarrasque*," Radcliffe said.

Baldwin gasped in terrible awe. "What?"

"The flagship of the Imperial Air Force," the captain explained. "It's not leaving until the city's obliterated." He turned to Gipi. "We make for Sentinel Hill. If I'm right, then the king's already dead. We need to regroup with whoever and whatever we can."

The mound of debris crumbled in a heaving sigh of embers. Baldwin shielded his face from the flames swirling and surrounding him. Strange men-at-arms descended upon the bridge; clad in leather jerkins and steel armets, their mechanical wings snapped shut as they drew long blades, engaging the enemy without a word. The leper grinned. He cut through the soldiers like a child snapping the limbs of dolls, cracking their wings, and slicing through light armor — until the last one raised a nozzle and hose attached to a steel drum on his back. Baldwin narrowly dodged the flaming spray, eyes widening in horror at this new class of enemy — the Vermillion Dragoons.

From out of the chaos, a sniper's shot pierced the soldier's chest, and he collapsed. Dead. Baldwin turned to the upper battlements, eying a woman armed with a wide crossbow.

"Alright, men," Hilda shouted, "douse the flames and get

them out!"

On the other side of the blockage, the peasant militia tossed bucket after bucket of water upon the burning debris, reducing the fire to embers and charred wood. Gipi and Radcliffe scaled their way to the other side. Baldwin was about to join them, only to hear the clatter of hooves against stone as a familiar shudder ran down his spine.

"Leaving so soon?" Dampe jeered, keeping distance from the leper from atop a pitch-black steed, parading his malice for the world to see. "Isn't this what you wanted? Come now, Good King Baldwin. Let's not waste the chance to make your mark on history."

"Don't," Gipi cried.

Baldwin was deaf to her pleas, thoughts impaled by swords of sorrow and fury, obsessed with the promise of retribution and remembrance. Even if it meant his own life, Baldwin would take the captain with him in a glorious duel. And with such witnesses at hand, nothing could deter the leper from his course—the decisive battle. It was time to die.

"Go," Baldwin said.

"But—"

"I'll be right behind you," he lied.

CHAPTER NINE

The *Tarrasque* loomed over Nedlergate, reducing its spires and steeples to rubble in a barrage of cannonfire, and dragoons swept the public like condors upon carrion. Baldwin beheld the capital of Mulgrave from the far side of the Tower Bridge — ruined and aflame.

Dampe sat mounted aloft his black steed mere yards away, stark against the blazing skyline. The leper drew his sword and took a defensive stance, waiting for the landsknecht to make the first strike, but no sign of aggression came.

What is he plotting...?

"Nostalgic, isn't it?" Dampe's eyes gleamed in the firelight. "Feels so long since I burned that hamlet to the ground. To think a simple raid would infect my band with such a persistent parasite." He clutched the reins of his mount. "You think you're special, don't you? A knight in shining armor destined for greatness. Gallivanting from inn to inn as if you aren't just some diseased vagrant born to die in a mass grave." He drew his arming sword. "Another pile of bones to be buried in this burning city."

Baldwin gritted his teeth. "You waste your words." He pointed his sword at the landsknecht's chest. "What good are the insults of a thief and a murderer?"

Dampe raised a thin eyebrow. "I think we can agree on something. This time, only one of us will walk away." He whistled, summoning a ground crew of squires and valets. "Get the leper a horse," he ordered. "Let him choose his lance and shield."

Baldwin thought he'd misheard the captain. "What?"

"Oh, come now. You of all people should know my penchant for theatrics. The Tower Bridge is perfect for a *pas d'armes*, wouldn't you agree? How could I resist the opportunity?"

"A joust, you say?"

"Do you accept?"

"I'd be loath to refuse."

Dampe clapped his hands. "Excellent! If we're going to do this, we do it justice."

Baldwin scoffed at the absurdity of the situation. Dampe's servants offered him a mangy warhorse that reflected his own will and weakness. The leper wasn't offered so much as a chanfron for his steed. He didn't need it. He mounted his horse and took the nearest lance, surveying a selection of heater shields designed for such a duel.

"The blank, if you please."

"Are you sure?" asked a squire.

Baldwin nodded. Prestige and heraldry would not save the leper. Skill and God willing, on the other hand, had gotten him farther than he'd thought possible. When Baldwin mounted his steed, he took a wooden lance and flexed his shield arm, prepared for battle. Meanwhile, Dampe's squires assembled a suit of opulent yet ill-fitting armor around his build, no doubt looted from the royal armory. Elaborately gilded and curved in peasecod fashion, the garniture was laced with weird foliage, crowned with a horned helmet — protruding eyes, toothy grimace, stubbly chin, akin to a deranged satyr.

Fitting....

Mounting his caparisoned steed, Dampe slammed his visor shut, eyes shimmering with bloodlust beneath the visor, and raised his lance and shield bearing the Undertakers' livery — a skull and crossed shovels. Baldwin rolled his eyes at the display of vanity.

"A king shouldn't need a codpiece," he scoffed.

"Never claimed to be one," Dampe said, raising his voice. "Leave us!" His entourage did just that, skittering like roaches into the darkened streets. "Now then, shall we canter on?"

"This doesn't end on horseback."

"Don't worry, I know."

The landsknecht galloped to the far side of the bridge. Baldwin followed suit to the opposing side. Dampe and his steed rippled in sweltering heat. The passing seconds seemed to last forever. Without warning, Dampe began to charge. Baldwin answered in kind, feeling the stones rumble under-hoof, hoisting his lance into position, boots firm in the stirrups, bracing himself for impact. Lance and steel collided with tremendous force, tips shattering against mail. Baldwin gasped as a shard penetrated his cuirass, catching a glimpse of Dampe's smugness. As the leper's horse trotted across the bridge, he coughed up a lungful of blood, only to clutch his reins, steering his steed back to face his foe.

I will not go gently. I… I…!

Petty as it seemed, this was a worthy end. Before he knew it, Baldwin landed a passing blow against Dampe's neck and slouched under the weight of grievous injury, dodging the enemy lance with no degree of skill. He smirked at such dumb luck.

One more pass….

Baldwin quickened his steed's pace at the last moment and lunged with every ounce of strength he could muster. He couldn't quite recall how it happened. Only that Dampe fell off his horse and collapsed with a metallic clatter against the bridge.

"Y-you piece of shit," he shrieked.

Baldwin dismounted and stumbled to his feet, yanking the wooden shard free from his fetid flesh, numb to the injuries wracking his body. Slowly, he drew the Broken Blade and bid his foe to fight on. "Get up," he said. "We're not done."

Dampe uttered a laugh and hoisted himself upright, as if pulling his wits together. "As you wish," he coughed, drawing his mighty zweihander from its baldric, and charged with hatred in his eyes. "Looks like you still have some life in you yet. Let's remedy that!"

Though haunted by fatigue, Baldwin let blood flow from his corpse of a body as the world began to churn around his skull, summoning a psychotic roar.

———

On the outskirts of Nedlergate, Gipi watched as the city collapsed in a conflagration. Stinging gales blew the fire west and devoured everything from Lombard Street to Cock and Key Alley, leaving ruin in its ravenous wake. Barges crowded with refugees set sail downriver, and many more attempted to cross by swimming, only to be swept away by deceptive currents. Soot-smeared mobs had gathered upon muddy shores and the foundations of the Tower Bridge, desperate to reach safety in the fields south of the city walls. Wails of lost children were drowned out by coughing masses. The fool could only do one thing to comfort them — strum her loot.

"I'll take requests," she said, "free of charge."

Twisting her pegs and clearing her throat, Gipi began to play as a small crowd gathered at her feet, desperate to distract themselves from grief and crippling dread. Her eyes were fixed on the Tower Bridge, faintly hearing the clash of swords — a duel amidst the flame.

She began to recite Baldwin's romance,

> *Robbed of crown and kingdom fair,*
> *He'd fled the Holy Land evermore,*
> *In the shadow of despair,*
> *His reign but a broken sword,*
> *Yet not by cowardice had,*
> *He chosen this loathsome road*
> *Nor by greed or humors mad,*
> *Lingering upon death's node,*
> *Wracked by hope's chivalry,*
> *Numb to knife and brigand's blow,*
> *He has a violent destiny,*
> *To die in lands yet unknown,*
> *Courage and doom be apparent,*
> *So walks the leper errant.*

The crowd crackled with modest applause, though not a

coin reached Gipi's bowl — understandable, given their newfound destitution. Despite her scarred cheeks, her smile was genuine as she settled for song in the midst of tragedy. Anything to dull the pain. Before the fool could begin another ballad, Radcliffe rode a draft horse to Gipi's side, face grim and sporting a thick grey beard. Hilda and the peasant militia had already rallied to his side.

"We're moving out," the captain said.

"Aren't you forgetting someone?"

Radcliffe hadn't the gall to look Gipi in the eye. "Regrettable as it may be, I can't risk any more lives for one soldier. Let alone someone like him…."

While the captain droned on with hollow justifications, Gipi still stared at the Tower Bridge and the twin silhouettes dancing along the ramparts. The leper and the landsknecht fought on, ignorant of the crisis surrounding them. Rage welled in her stomach.

"Baldwin's a good man," Radcliffe said, "but he's a liability."

"Liability?" Gipi snapped. "He risked life and limb to save your sorry ass, and this is how you repay him?" She pointed a gloved finger at his chest plate. "Spin it however you like, you'd be dead without his sword. What? Did they chop off your balls back in the Tower or something?" She swung her lute across her back. "I'm going after him."

Hilda lay a gauntleted hand on her shoulder. "You should come with us," she said. "You're a good fighter and quick on your feet. We need more like you."

That caught the fool off guard. At first, Gipi thought it was a cruel joke until she saw the honesty in the arbalist's eyes.

"And I'm sure you do, but I have prior obligations."

"You don't care for the cause?" Hilda asked.

"Trust me," Gipi said with a sigh, "you'll be hard pressed to find a better advocate for your liberation, but you're asking me to leave him behind. I can't do that." She crossed her arms. "Let's be honest, Baldwin wouldn't last two days without me."

Radcliffe conceded with a sigh. "Shame, really." He gave one last look at the smoldering city. "Even with the king gone, Vermillion isn't going to be a better master. Mark my words, we'll have our work cut out for us." With that, he led the retreat to the East Marches. "If you change your mind, you know where to find us. Best of luck."

Gipi gave a lukewarm tip of her cap and bells, watching as Hilda and the militia joined their dear leader on the Old Road. She scoffed and shook her head. Worse than Radcliffe's abandonment was her own loyalty to lord and liege. Baldwin was an idiot; there was no denying that. She'd be lying to say she wasn't tempted by the rebels' offer.

However, Gipi didn't come this far to trade one hopeless cause for another. Despite her bitterness, the fool's resolve was only tempered by the flame. She sprinted to the bridge, quickening her pace. One thing was certain.

If he survives, it'll definitely be something to add to the ballad....

———

The Battle on the Tower Bridge raged on.

Baldwin had the upper hand, pressing down against Dampe's blade, causing the landsknecht to quake in his boots. It was not strength, but rather, ignorance of his own failing body. Hilt against hilt, their swords were entwined in a crucible of rage. Fevered with tunnel vision and rising lassitude, the leper felt no pain—even on death's door.

"You will not forestall my judgment," Baldwin gasped.

"And what justice it is," Dampe said, "the delusion of a dying wretch."

With a shift of footing and breach of guard, the captain broke free and doubled back. Before Baldwin could retaliate, it was too late. Dampe had impaled the leper through his left shoulder, cross guard slamming against his chest plate. Edges of steel sliced into sinew and ground against bone. Baldwin gasped in wordless agony.

"I'm surprised you can feel that," Dampe mocked, twisting his blade.

Cruel leverage was on the landsknecht's side. He lifted the leper with his sword, grinning, as Baldwin struggled desperately to break free. Suspended over the River Tintern, he felt life ebb with every shuddering breath. The Great Fire of Nedlergate began to dim, and Death, shrouded in shadow, offered him a pale hand from beyond.

"Have you given it any thought?" Dampe's words breached the leper's stupor. "What will you do afterwards, if you kill me? You've put so much into this crusade of yours."

What indeed....

Death lingered yet had not come to claim her due. Baldwin had a choice. And his was already made. In an act of existential defiance, the leper tightened his grip, lacerating his bandaged palms, and began to shift his own weight onto the shaft of steel. He did not attempt to pry the blade loose; instead, to lower it to an even level — it was working.

"What the...?" Dampe gasped.

Baldwin felt loose stones shift underfoot and roared with blind fury. He pivoted the sword protruding from his deepest wound at a sharp angle, trembling in a deluge of pain, and swung his mass with impossible strength. Before the captain could disengage or utter a taunt, he slipped against the bridge's edge, and his hold began to weaken.

Heaving the Broken Blade, Baldwin chopped through Dampe's shoulder with gravity's weight. Blood splattered the leper's mask. He smiled with bitter acceptance. The battle had taken its toll. With the last of his strength, Baldwin tore at Dampe's gorget and keeled over backwards, sending them careening into the deep, dark water — together.

CHAPTER TEN

Shorn of thought and pain, Baldwin drifted to oblivion's ingress. He felt nothing, not even the numbness of his every waking moment. It was a familiar darkness, reminiscent of the unremembered time in mother's womb, and yet, utterly alien. Then came the light of a distant torch, or perhaps a lonesome star, shining across the void, obstructed by a silhouette he knew all too well. Death was wreathed in a tarnished cloak; the brim of a wide straw hat obscured her pallid face. She leaned on her unremarkable scythe as a most venerable spirit. Her lips curled into a gentle smile as she waved a sinewy hand—summoning a chess set of ebony and ivory in a wisp of black smoke. Slowly, Baldwin regained the will to speak.

"What is this?"

Death reassembled the match, placing every piece exactly where they'd left off. "You have accomplished a most noble deed at the cost of your own life. Even now, your corpse sinks to the bottom of the river. You stand upon the edge of the abyss."

"Then why test me further, if my journey has ended?"

"Has it?"

So they resumed the match of mortality. Move by move, Baldwin watched tiny embers flicker to life in the vast darkness above until constellations began to take shape, casting a pall of faint light upon a wraith of farmland. Tall stalks of wheat and corn swayed in the wind; black as sin, ripe from the reaping. Such allegory was not lost on the leper.

"Are those—?"

"Those who perished in tragedy," Death said. "They are now lights to be guided and grain to be harvested." She advanced a black knight in a sharp offensive. "You are no exception." She plucked a white rook from the board. "I'm afraid your time is short."

The wind shifted against Baldwin's back.

"I," he said, "accept my death. I have accomplished all I can."

"Then why continue the game?"

Baldwin did not reply. He stared at the board, king and a handful of pawns cornered in a desperate phalanx. Why was he struggling? Short of his own selfish song, he'd played no small role in history's making, bearing witness to adventure and horror in equal measure. And yet, a spark within refused to embrace the swing of Death's scythe — the will to live.

"I have no unfinished business," Baldwin said, inching a pawn halfway across the board, "and I regret nothing. Only that...." He averted his eyes. "Never mind."

"Go on," Death said.

"There's so many deeds left to see in poetry. Goodness to share with the world. Though mine is a death worth dying, I only lament that I hadn't the chance to accomplish more."

The breeze shifted. Baldwin's pawn had reached the far side of the board, much to his surprise. Death offered him a choice of fallen pieces to resurrect. He chose the queen.

"And yet," Death said, "you seem so eager to die."

"I've spent two decades in terror of you," Baldwin admitted. "All my life, I've been haunted by reminders of your existence, from sermons at evensong to my own maladies. Wasting away as a bedridden husk of a king. Hardly a life worth living." He advanced the dregs of his forces. "When I set out on this pilgrimage, I cast off the shackles of that fear."

"To live the epics you so admire?"

"More than that," Baldwin said. "Chivalry is a vessel for what they mean to me. Moreover," he completed his final move, "checkmate."

Death toppled her king and clapped slowly. "Well done."

"You let me win."

Death dismissed the game with a wave, and the heavens

yawned open with tremendous light. "May conviction guide you to ever greater heights," she said. "Till we meet again."

Blinded by divine radiance, Baldwin felt his soul drawn to echoes of the material, lifted ever upwards to the world of men. He reached out with an ephemeral hand, free of bandage and bondage, as fatigue and physical sensation crept into existence. Once more, the leper felt the numbing aches that plagued his every waking hour. He had rested for too long.

––––––––––

Baldwin's eyes rolled open to a burl of canvas and pained moans. Laying atop a heap of blankets in an unknown tent, his limbs and chest were wrapped in layers of bandages that had barely managed to stifle the bleeding. He lay beside those less fortunate—a clinic of burn victims and amputees, rows of weeping bodies and blistered cadavers. The leper managed to stand, though his wounds had hardly healed, enfeebling his every motion. He reached for a spare crutch and staggered down the aisle of bloodstained mats. An aide in a torn habit stared at him in shock, treating a charred man with herbal salves and clotting powders. Baldwin overheard a faint murmuring and spied a pair of conversing shadows behind the hospital's curtain. One of them he recognized instantly.

"He's still comatose?" Gipi asked.

"Yes," replied a nurse. "Those in his state rarely recover. Considering his injuries, I'm shocked he's clinging to life. He should've died days ago. I've never seen such resilience in a patient before. Especially a leper." She sighed. "He's blessed with a stout heart."

"Yet here we are."

"We'll tend to him as best we can," the nurse said.

Baldwin hobbled past the patients and pushed the curtain aside. His eyes stung with smoke for a moment. Then he saw a hastily pitched encampment of tents, wagons, and ash-choked trails near the ruins of Nedlergate. Under a reddened sun, refugees littered the emergency marketplace. Some peddled their wares, mostly farmers, while others slept on the hard, grey earth. Only in the aftermath was the scale of suffering made known.

Gipi lingered among the survivors. Stricken by shock, she turned to face Baldwin with wide eyes. "What the—? When did you start walking again?"

"I—"

Before he knew it, Gipi lunged to embrace him, only for the leper to hold her at bay with freshly bandaged hands. "Please," he managed, "you know that's a poor idea."

"I thought you were—dammit!"

Tears welled in Gipi's eyes. Baldwin smiled, honored by her loving concern.

"Rest assured," he said, "I don't plan on going anywhere soon." He turned to the nurse. "Thank you for your service. Where are my things?"

"Safely stowed," she replied, "but I wouldn't recommend lifting a sword."

"Show me, please."

The nurse took him to an open truck containing his cuirass and the Broken Blade, both worse for wear, as well as his bronze mask. After paying the chirurgeon's fee, Baldwin took to the open marketplace, though goods were limited to hardtack, local produce, and cheese.

"Mostly rations," Gipi said, "taken from the garrison, or what remains of it. Some farmers donate what they can, but Nedlergate's never gonna be the same."

"So it would seem," Baldwin said. "How long was I unconscious?"

"About a week."

Baldwin was caught off guard. To think the survivors had salvaged so much in such little time. It was proof of their resilience, even with local relief and charity. Life went on as it would've in any parish, whether for good or ill. For every child playing in the street was a family mourning the loss of a son. Baldwin watched a heated argument unfold between tenants and landlords by the baker's stall. Apparently, the renters were somehow responsible for property damage by contract. The leper carried on, in no position to intervene, and traded a fourpence for a wheaten biscuit.

He nearly broke his teeth upon the first bite.

Gipi stifled a smirk. "Never said they were edible."

"What happened to the city proper?"

"Gone," she said. "Reduced to a pile of ash."

Baldwin sighed, deeply. "A pretext for invasion?"

"So say the lynch mobs."

"And what of Dampe?"

"Never came out of the river."

Baldwin bowed his head in silence, torn between lament and solemn satisfaction. Despite his wicked deeds, Dampe had been the villain of the leper's crusade—a despicable fiend wearing the skin of a man. Without a target for righteous fury, Baldwin was no closer to glory than where he'd started. In a way, he was mourning. Life was not meant to be taken lightly, and yet, the world was a brighter place without the Undertakers.

He sat on a stone and opened his journal, staring at the blank page.

Weeks of recovery bled together as Baldwin trained and remastered his technique in swordsmanship. It was impossible to tell how much had truly healed and what was the leper's delusion of fortitude. His symptoms were worsening by the day. Painless nodules swelled where he'd been stabbed, scarring the wound with tissue thick as leather. Gipi was content to busk for bread, and together they salvaged a living among the survivors. Days went on until Baldwin was clad in armor and prepared to wander the Old Road once more.

"When you're ready, Gipi."

Suddenly, a massive shadow befell the encampment. Refugees stopped in their tracks, dropping baskets of goods and gawking at the heavens in terror. The *Tarrasque* had returned, soaring over the ash-choked fields of Mulgrave, drifting to the ruined city.

Baldwin gritted his teeth. "It taunts us still?"

"So it would seem," Gipi said.

The leper said no more and limped with his best foot forward, making his way across the green until he beheld what remained of Nedlergate—mountains of smoking debris punctuated by the shattered battlements of the Tower. The dirigible hovered over where Cock and Key Alley once stood, as crewmen descended its deck with long ropes to the street.

Suspicious indeed....

"What the hell are you doing?" Gipi kept her voice low, rushing to his side. "You're in no condition to go back out there."

Baldwin slipped on slick stone, a misstep which threatened to cast his brittle body into the river once more. "Be that as it may, Vermillion is up to something. And I cannot stand by idly, Gipi, regardless of injury. Besides, I won't be going alone."

Gipi followed with a forlorn sigh. "You're gonna be the death of me."

Crossing the Tower Bridge once more, they crept down the barren streets, flanked by scorched townhouses. The ground was hot underfoot, threatening to burn through the soles of Baldwin's boots. Gipi kept an eye over her shoulder and drew her dirk and sickle, following the vast trail of destruction.

"Morbid," she muttered, "but at least the pestilence has been dealt with."

Shuffling filled the acrid air as shadows clambered over stone and wooden wreckage. Baldwin noticed a few carts filled with a variety of trinkets and baubles—silver spoons, oil paintings, and fine furniture in varying states of preservation. Whenever a crisis struck, the sticky fingers of opportunists were never far from unsuspecting pockets. A gang of looters emerged from the cellar, cradling a few casks of wine, only to drop their prize in shock.

"As you were, gentlemen," Gipi said.

Baldwin grunted in disapproval but carried on. Though

looting was a crime punishable by death, he was scarcely in a position to enforce the law. At the blackened heart of the slums, they arrived under the shadow of the *Tarrasque*. Beneath its hovering hull, crews of swarthy workmen dug through the rubble-strewn streets with picks and shovels.

Gipi knelt to the leper's side. "Excavation?"

"They'll find nothing but rats and sewage," Baldwin said.

"I wouldn't be so sure," the fool replied. "Remember, the Black Piper had quite the maze down there. Wouldn't surprise me if there's more secrets under these streets."

"What do you mean?"

Gipi slunk to the shadows by the riverbank and led the way to a wide culvert and grate—where they'd infiltrated the sewers. "Should we retrace our steps?" she asked. "Find out why they torched the city? I mean, where else would digging by the river lead?"

Driven by a shared curiosity, Baldwin lit a torch and began the descent.

Rhythmic clatter of hard labor was never far away, echoing through stone walls. The leper marched against a rancid slough, following the tunnels into darkness. Frightened vermin skittered down the tunnels, and the reek of smoke wafted from the streets above. Hours later, Baldwin came to the wide cistern where he and the Black Piper had dueled to the death—rats had reduced her corpse to a heap of gnawed bones, nesting in her ribcage. The chamber split off in a multitude of directions, and the sound of clanging shovels was directly above him.

"Where to now?" the leper asked.

"That's an excellent question," Gipi said.

Baldwin raised his torch and examined the curving walls— blood and feces had been smeared in the form of strange scripture, as if written by the mad or possessed. Though he could not read it, there was a wrongness to the characters as they seemed to shift and recede in the torchlight. Whatever the language, it was not of men.

"I do not remember this," the leper said.

Gipi was light on her feet, careful not to disturb the rats. "Me neither." She peered down the westmost passage, where the masonry shifted from brick and mortar to forgotten arcades of antiquity. "Think I've found something," she said. "We haven't explored here, have we?"

Torchlight began to flicker and wane, though no wind reached this place. Baldwin ventured to the sluice and crept around its flow, scaling a ladder to pass the stone dam. On the far side of the rusted gate, wastewater flowed in a forced direction through a flooded corridor with a high ceiling. Wading through murk and muck, the leper recognized the passage as an aqueduct of limestone and concrete—predating the oldest castles in the countryside.

"Didn't realize the sewers ran so deep," Gipi said.

"The people of Nedlergate did not build these. They are far too old." Baldwin's every step echoed throughout the long passage until a low, guttural hiss breached the stillness. The leper slowly drew the Broken Blade—nothing emerged. "Tread lightly," he said.

"Way ahead of you," Gipi whispered.

Together, they descended nine flights of spiraling stairs, deep into what seemed an inverted tower, until Baldwin reached the bottom of the cyclopean well. Something crunched under his boots, brittle as clay. Baldwin mustered the courage to look down. Skulls and yellowed bones lay strewn about the pit, as if discarded in heaps of waste, left to rot in mass graves and ossuaries of dust and debris. Some were far older than others. Past the jingles of Gipi's coin purse, Baldwin heard something else in the labyrinth. Foreign voices in hushed conversation. Perhaps a squad of invading sentries. The leper tore his weight behind a column and waited, unable to recognize their slough of a dialect. He took a few steps forward and barely spied a host of shadows fading around the sharp corner.

Deep into the implacable darkness, he carried on, ever

into the unknown. His mind wandered into black corners of imagination. What was this labyrinth's purpose? What lurked so far beneath the earth? At last, Baldwin came to the hall's end — a portico with tall columns of granite and crimson porphyry. The leper's head throbbed with an unknown force.

Slowly, he pushed open the great bronze doors. The complex yawned open to a rotunda rimmed with a series of annelid idols, its domed ceiling lined with rows of square coffers reaching to a perfect oculus from which no light poured.

Worms of the earth....

Baldwin did not recognize the wrongness.

It was not the work of the Devil or anything so simple. In lieu of hellfire was a void of negative space; a cold indifference that swallowed all pretense of morality until nothing remained. Even the statues were not of any pagan icon, but blasphemies that not even the vilest of heresies could hope to emulate. It was a denial of the divine that could not be understood through faith or classical philosophy — a providence of nihilistic implication.

Is this what drove the Black Piper mad...?

The clustered eyes of the statues seemed to follow him, glistening with eternal hunger. As Baldwin's vision blurred with sudden fatigue, he fell to his knees. Whether a symptom of his own worsening condition or something more sinister, he could not say. Regardless, the leper gathered the shards of his wits, seeing a handful of silhouettes examining what appeared to be a marbled reliquary. Huddled in shadow, he remained unseen.

"Gentlemen," a flamboyant voice echoed throughout the chamber, "I believe we've found that certain something that His Imperial Majesty has been searching for."

"Good," said a brigand, one of the Undertakers, judging by his armband and drab uniform, "then let's hurry and get the hell out of here."

"Yeah," said another, "this place gives me the creeps."

"Oh, come now," cooed the first among them, "not afraid of the dark, are you?"

A lithe figure stepped into the light — coattails hovering over motes of dust, heels clacking upon the hollow tiles of antiquity. Dressed in garish robes, his face was painted as an orientalist of the Imperial court, almost to the point of foppishness. His finely embroidered caftan was lined with livid red furs; long fingers bespeckled with rings, brow wrapped in a turban punctuated with peacock feathers.

"All that's left is to claim our just prize. Any volunteers?" Silence pervaded his ranks until a steely click punctured their hesitation. "Perhaps I should rephrase that."

Held at gunpoint, the nearest brigand stepped to open the chest.

"There's a good lad," the Fool General mocked. "Earning your keep."

Meanwhile, Gipi came to the leper's side, crouched in the thickest shadow. Together, they eyed their strange new foe with grim anticipation — too frail to intervene, too weakened to do anything save to watch in dawning horror. The brigand creaked the lid ajar and reached into the great stone chest. He recoiled in disgust as a fistful of white worms greeted his hand, only to gnaw through skin and sinew, burrowing into his flesh.

The general was thoroughly unimpressed.

"Out of the way," he shoved his screaming subordinate aside and peered into the chest himself, "there we are." With a stretch and slap of operatic gloves, the Fool General withdrew a most peculiar relic — a malachite pyramid engraved with strange symbols and mechanisms, including a trio of sockets, two of which were occupied by strange glass spheres, resembling the eyes of a cephalopod. He tossed it to one of the mercenaries. "Hold it for me, won't you?"

"W-what is it?" asked a brigand, trying his best to ignore his comrade writhing on the floor, whose hand had been all but stripped to the bone.

The Fool General raised a thin eyebrow. "That would be of no concern to you." Without pause, he raised a flintlock pistol and put the injured man out of his misery with a point-blank shot. "Well then, I'd call our expedition a success. Move out."

The Undertakers exchanged fearful looks and struggled to speak until the most headstrong among them, perhaps an officer, managed to blurt, "And what of payment?"

"What of it?"

"We didn't sack the city for free," the officer said, "and we lost a deal of men during the raid. Even our captain. So, I won't ask again. Where's our money, Pierrot?"

The Fool General rolled his eyes, rummaging through his pockets. "All those precious lives lost over a pile of gold? You'd think you'd take some pride in your work. No wonder you're all little men." He tossed over a satin bag bulging with coinage. "Happy now?"

The officer glared at his employer, poured the francs into his greased palm, and counted them greedily. His brow furrowed with rage. "We're thirty short."

The Fool General said nothing.

"Enough with the games, Pierrot," the officer snapped. His men drew their arms in unison, taking aim. "Give us what we were promised, or we will shoot."

Pierrot reached into his pocket and pulled out a handkerchief, dabbing his nose. His mutinous host opened fire in a cloud of gunsmoke, and then — silence. The general brushed the shot off his rippling chest, skin and sinew slithering to heal the wound. His smile was gone. The brigands' eyes widened with rising panic, and their officer stepped back, taking a moment to comprehend their position. A corpse-light shone in Pierrot's eyes. One of the brigands clutched his forehead, dropping his pistol, mouthing a scream. Blood oozed from his eyes and mouth until he collapsed with a splatter of gore, and something burst from his ribs.

The Fool General stepped forward, cracking his knuckles and neck. The others quivered in their boots, stepping back while their officer turned and ran in terror.

"Kill them," Pierrot whispered.

Pallid things slithered from the corpse—carrion eaters, and more emerged from cracks in the walls. Lunging with hungry maws, they overwhelmed their prey without eyes. The general watched with glee as the men fell to gnawing worms and parasites within. He stepped over their dying forms, as they reached out with bleeding hands, gurgling in anguish, as white vermin feasted on open wounds. Looming over the dead and dying, he watched the officer flee and trip over rubble, landing with a crack. The worms closed in, writhing along the curvature of the walls. The officer inched away, sweating and panting.

"What the hell...are you?" he gurgled.

"Something far out of your league." Pierrot knelt to the officer's side and collected the pyramid of unknown origin. "Let's say, I'm not one to be trifled with, as you've no doubt realized by now." He glanced to and fro. "I'm what your mother said would drag you to hell if you didn't eat your greens. I'm the thing that lived under your bed. The window-peeper. The jackboot in the night with cudgel and pike." His smile widened, revealing a mouthful of yellow fangs. "And, in time, I'll become something a lot worse." With that, he clapped his hands, and the carrion eaters fell upon the dead, feeding on pooling fluids, before retreating to the dark corners of the earth. "Oh," he said, "I almost forgot." He tossed the officer exactly thirty pieces of silver, chuckling like a giddy child. "Consider it due payment."

Enough of this....

Overcome with a fever of righteous fury, Baldwin drew his sword and tore his way into the light, taking a defensive stance. "You," he bellowed. "Are you the one responsible for the city's destruction? Were you the one holding Dampe's leash? Answer me!"

The Fool General's eyes narrowed in momentary confusion. "I'm sorry, who are you?" He waved a hand dismissively. "Come to think of it, I don't care."

Gipi lunged from the shadows, attempting to plunge

a dirk into Pierrot's stomach. He dodged with uncanny grace. Baldwin swung his blade wildly—only for his stitches to tear in a fit of agony. The leper collapsed to his knees, and a blast of eldritch energy sent him careening against the far wall. When sense returned, Baldwin hoisted himself upright with the hilt of his sword, only to collapse in an inexplicable stupor, losing control of his muscles. Gipi lay prone beside him, dazed and reeling, unable to stand. Pierrot gave a malicious grin; tendrils of sickly green power snaked around his fingertips.

"W-what was that?" Baldwin wheezed.

"Nothing you need to concern yourself with." The Fool General grabbed his prey by the chin, forcing the leper to look him in the eye. "Though on second thought, I'd better leave a survivor or two to spread the word. Easy, now. It'll take a while for that to wear off."

"Don't you dare run from me," Baldwin said.

"Who said anything about running?" Pierrot called as he crept up the stairwell, vanishing into the upper complex. "I plan on taking my sweet, sweet time."

Baldwin tried to stand and pursue the enemy, only to collapse under the weight of fatigue. He gritted his teeth, propping his body against the Broken Blade, only to burst into mad laughter. Having traded one villain for another, Baldwin would pursue this new threat to lands unknown. It was his reward for slaying Dampe—a foe worthy of true hatred. Shouldering his burden, the leper set off into darkness, seeking a path to the end he so craved.

ACT FOUR

CHAPTER ONE

It was an omen. Great peals of thunder erupted in the heavens, over continents and nations, punctuated by flashes of lightning and eerie forbearance. Like the rising chords of a churchly organ, the clouds darkened, smothering the bitter earth. Eventually, the notes swelled into deafening fanfare—a symphony that could not be silenced, answered only by trickling rain, fluttering like fingers upon ivory keys, pattering, dancing to a vague melody until the final chord was struck, until droplets pattered in torrents upon the Winedark Sea.

To the Cinque Ports of Mulgrave.

Midsummer had reached the western shores, and with it rumors of piracy. Baldwin's heavy leather boots sloshed in wet sand, eyes all but blind with dryness and astigmatism, listening to waves lap against stone. He wrapped his limbs with firm care, ignoring the fluid seeping through his bandages. Though the leper could not see the creatures twitching in briny pools, nor feel the seaside breeze against his lips, he was grateful for a moment's solitude.

It has been long since I've allowed myself such reprieve....

Lost in the livid glow of twilight, Baldwin sat atop a flat stone, opened his leather journal, and began to write. Words formed slowly as ink spread across the page, flowing into yet another canto in his own epic—one that he had yet to title. Memories of his deeds flashed in his thoughts like drawn steel. He could almost smell the cadavers in Cock and Key Alley, the Great Fire of Nedlergate still blazed in his mind, and Dampe smirked from beyond, taunting the leper with countless lives that he could not save. And yet, these horrors paled in comparison to the one puppeteering them—the Fool General of Vermillion, Pierrot.

A foe worthy of my hatred....

Baldwin snapped the book shut and stood sharply. Months had passed since his recent ventures, and his quarry's trail had run cold. Vermillion had pillaged the city and countryside and driven untold folk to seek refuge along the coast, such as it was. Despite his obsessive sense of justice, Baldwin was no closer to achieving greatness than when he had started. On the horizon, he spied a trio of shadowed ships against the twilight, one quite large in the open water. They remained still, as if laying anchor, perhaps a defensive force of the Royal Navy sent to repel aggression by sea. Regardless, the leper had his suspicions.

Those sails are strangely familiar....

Clouds gathered over the sea, billowing and sagging as gray omens—rain pattered against Baldwin's pauldrons as he raised his threadbare hood. Heaving his broadsword over his stiff shoulder, the leper returned to the port town. Fishmongers plied their reeking trade, shucking oysters under the overcast sky. Tremendous galleons rested at dock and pier, white sails folded against their masts, while swarthy workmen heaved crates and barrels of cargo and commodities into rows of warehouses. A familiar tune carried near the doorstep of the Pig and Whistle, the local inn and watering hole. Baldwin smiled and followed the song of plucking strings. Gipi sat on the roadside, busking for coins as she sang ballads of their shared excursions. A modest crowd had gathered about the fool in worn motley, humored by her tales of a "leper errant." When she ended and the sun began to crawl over the westward ruins of Nedlergate, Baldwin approached his companion.

"Impressive haul," he saw the coinage bulging in her purse, "if you value such things."

"Say what you will," Gipi sighed, "I'm not spending tonight on the street."

"Enough for room and board?"

"For nearly a week, in fact." Gipi stood and stretched, pocketing the coppers and crowns. "Here," she passed him a shilling, "get us a corner table, will you?"

Baldwin nodded, silently, and ventured into the inn. The warm scent of clam chowder greeted him, as did candlelight and the murmurs of fisherfolk, dressed in flat caps and leather boots. The floorboards moaned underfoot as the leper kept to the shadows. Fishing nets and yawning jaws of bone lined the walls, accompanied by oil paintings of shipwrecks in chiaroscuro, contributing to the rustic gloom. He approached the bar and raised two fingers. The lazy-eyed bartender, perhaps a sailor in his youth, poured him a pair of rotguts with a single slice of lemon. Within moments, Gipi had joined him near the hearth.

"There is a danger to this place," Baldwin said.

Gipi shrugged. "No different than any other fishing hamlet."

Baldwin eyed the sailors sharply beneath his bronze mask. "Little good comes from living so close to the sea. Have you heard anything about the Fool General?"

"Nothing of local note," Gipi said. "Weird talk, though. Fishing boats left abandoned. Galleys spotted near the Isle of Skellige. Something's brewing."

Baldwin's eyes widened in dreadful surprise. "Abandoned without a crew?" He clutched his glass, recalling such a thing on the shores of his own kingdom—the work of corsairs. "I see."

"What's wrong?"

Baldwin took a deep breath and began. "Othello was once the Jewel of Khand and Golgotha's rival across the Winedark Sea. From its mosques and madrasas, men of science and heathen faith plum the dark corners of the earth for knowledge, as they have since the dawn of civilization. Such an ancient land is not free of evil." He sighed, remembering the city described by embassies, having never seen its spiraling minarets himself. "Indeed, its greatest achievements were built by thousands of slaves. Under the reign of the Sultan Khan, pirates made port along the coasts, setting sail to capture 'infidels' whether at sea or in their own homes, to meet the unending demands of forced labor."

"Are you finished?"

"Your tone is unnecessary—"

"I'm from Othello," Gipi said, "in case you've forgotten. And we're a long way from the slave markets. I doubt 'swarthy heathens' will come knocking."

"Be that as it may, this hits a bit too close to home, as it were."

"At any rate," Gipi flagged over a barmaid, "may I have some of those?" She gestured to a platter of several dozen oysters being shared among the sailors. "Are they fresh?"

"Today's catch," the barmaid said.

"If you please, then."

Baldwin shot his companion a smirk. "Are we so low on funds? It's not even fish day."

Gipi winked. "I'm rather fond of oysters, and their 'benefits,' if you take my meaning."

"You make it abundantly clear."

The leper finished his foul brew in silence, lamenting the vineyards of the Holy Land, unable to cease his speculation on the trio offshore. He never got a good look at those silhouettes, but such rumors troubled him deeply. Baldwin lay the copper cup on the counter and left to wander the wharf. Dockhands had turned for the night, as houseboats and fishing vessels bobbed with the rising tide. He watched the lamp of the lighthouse flicker from the neighboring cove, wondering how many ships had been plundered in recent months.

"Pardon," he said.

Baldwin made way past the fisherfolk, careful not to brush hands, until he came to the naked reefs nestled among the coves. His was a solitary existence by necessity, lest others come to share his bleak fate. Alone with wandering thoughts, the leper sat on a smooth stone under a pier, as black waves lapped against the shore. Shutting his eyes, he let the sounds of the sea spirit him to familiar vistas all but forgotten in fever's wake, though he would find no comfort in dreams. Cacophonies of war rang throughout the beige fields of memory. Musketeers had opened fire alongside heavy cannons with thunderous booms, and frontline formations had impaled each other in pushes of pike. Amidst the slaughter, Baldwin had locked swords with a slave-soldier of Othello, his blonde hair streaking as a banner through the arid wind. With a killing blow, blood splattered his cuirass, and the opponent collapsed in a lifeless heap — one casualty among thousands. He cracked a hollow grimace, numb to everything save the promise of victory. He was sixteen once more, and his symptoms had yet to manifest. Renewed with remembered health and youth, Baldwin swung to the left, cleaving through scale mail, and again to the right, slicing into sinew. Even the janissaries were overtaken by his swordsmanship.

Suddenly, a heavy blade carved into Baldwin's back.

He retorted with a howl of pain and a desperate swing, spilling the soldier's entrails onto the dusty earth. Ears ringing and overcome with sudden fatigue, he slumped against his sword, only to hoist himself and stifle a bloody cough. Smoke stung the stale air. Baldwin gazed aimlessly at the city from afar. The white banners of Golgotha were ablaze.

The Holy City had been breached.

Dread smothered the flames of Baldwin's valor, if only for a moment. Overwhelmed by instinct, he sprinted towards the Pilgrim's Gate, ignorant of grievous injury and the retreat of his own men. None of it mattered. His people were in mortal peril. Mighty as Baldwin was, he was weakened upon reaching the gatehouse — knees trembling, breathing shallow. Dragging his blade as a cumbersome burden, he limped past the walls and spied a monstrous silhouette in the great stone bailey. His horror was rivaled only by awe.

What is that — ?

Sudden screams tore him to the present. Here and now, the smell of sulfur and gunpowder was heavy in the air. Baldwin reached for the Broken Blade and sprinted back to the fishing hamlet, confronted by the port ablaze. Cannonfire erupted from across the bay, twelve-pound shots collided with home and hearth, and the silhouettes of three ships rippled in flaming chaos. Just as the jihadists had once invaded the Holy Land, so too had the corsairs of Othello come to pillage. Baldwin ran past the fleeing townsfolk, drawing his sword with a bellow of fury, driven to defend the innocent as they fled for the church.

Upon the darkened shore, he greeted the corsairs with a glint of steel. The enemy disembarked from rowboats with small arms and wicked sabers — a motley lot, most of ruddy complexions and coarse black hair. Gangs had already splintered to the open streets, to catch and shackle the meek as chattel to be bought and sold. They howled in the moonlight as wolves at the door, maiming and murdering any who dared resist. Half a dozen men rushed at the leper, blades and pistols at hand. Baldwin dove into the violent fray, ignorant to the blood splattering his mask. Heaving the Broken Blade with a tremendous roar, he was all but deaf to screams erupting from the Pig and Whistle, which blazed amidst the frenzy of shot and steel.

Gipi — !

Someone struck the back of the leper's skull. He collapsed, and the world began to spin and darken. The last thing Baldwin recalled was a swarm of sweaty hands grasping and shackling his wrists and ankles — a fate that many would share.

CHAPTER TWO

Drifting in and out of consciousness, Baldwin remained ignorant of the shiphands heaving him aboard the largest ship in the consort. He woke to a pail's worth of water splashing his face. The leper was bound in irons and surrounded by prisoners of varying walks of life, mostly mariners or fishwives. Baldwin's arms and armor were nowhere to be seen. Quiet sobbing rippled through the cargo hold. The corsairs kept vigil with long-barreled guns at hand, dimly illuminated by oil lamps swaying from the rafters. Not one face was visible, whether by scarlet wrappings or deliberate shadow. Judging by the swaying of the ship, the corsairs had already set sail. One man, a wayfarer in muddy clothing, whispered a prayer repeatedly in his rosary to keep evil at bay — and not merely the whips of slavers.

Hollow steps echoed from the darkness ahead. A black figure descended into the bowels of the ship. The corsairs turned their attention to the encroaching admiral. Dressed in a tattered coat and a thrice-cornered hat a tad too large for his head, he was a man of short stature, distinguished from his cohort by naval fashion and genuine malice; face shaven, hands resting on pistols holstered across his belts and bandoliers, lips thin and gums bleeding.

"How many?" The admiral's voice was deliberately low.

"Three hundred," said the bosun. "Prime stock. Rest have been culled."

The admiral nodded, silently, yellowed eyes scanning his prisoners.

Baldwin glowered but said nothing, struggling against his bonds. The admiral made his way through the rows of shackled men, towering over their slouched forms, until he came to the leper and knelt, slowly, to his side. "Prime stalk, indeed," his words dripped with sarcasm.

The crew laughed bitterly, as if on command.

"You're certainly the odd one," the admiral said. "Who are you?"

"I am," Baldwin managed, "no one of consequence."

"Oh, I must know."

Baldwin kept his lips sealed in silence.

The admiral sneered. "Now then, I remember the mention of royalty in these waters." He let those words seep like the sting of the lash. "But," he stood, sharply, "I suppose if you're no one worth talking to, and an invalid at that, then I'd best throw you overboard."

The leper hesitated. "I do not fear you."

"Then you'll die braver than most." The admiral jerked his head aside with a hollow crunch. "Take him to the deck. For proper questioning."

Moments of beatings and blurred vision passed swiftly, as muted pain accompanied Baldwin's ascent to the deck. Stumbling and staggering, he was brought to the taffrail and forced onto his marrow bones in mock prayer. He did not struggle, knowing well that these shackles could not be broken easily. Not in his weakened state. In his delirium, Baldwin could not speak. Saltspray stung his open lesions. The bosun slammed Baldwin's hand against the rail and spread his fingers. A knife gleamed in the moonlight.

"Chum the water," the admiral said and stood proudly, despite the imposing stature of his underlings. The corsairs did just that, tossing buckets of entrails and bloody offal into the sea. Something stirred beneath the waves with a seething hiss. A school of slender serpents breached the surface — arching their pale forms, slithering along the starboard.

"Now, I'll ask one last time," the admiral said, "who are you?"

"I believe you have your suspicions," the leper growled.

"Then why the fuss?"

"I didn't live so long by giving away my name freely."

"Freely, he says. You really don't understand, do you? But, I digress, it's not every raid we find such a handsome bounty." The admiral gave a stark nod. Without warning, the bosun's knife pierced the wood between the leper's knuckles. "I know someone who'd pay a pretty price for you in their menagerie. And I'm sure a voyage in the brig will bruise that spirit of yours."

"And who, may I ask, my most gracious jailor?"

"Odo Leechman," the admiral said, "and you'd do well to remember it. Welcome aboard the *Scheherazade*, Good King Baldwin."

Gritting his teeth, the leper endured the hard plummet to the brig—solitary confinement awaited him, and he was sequestered from the rest of the imprisoned. As he peered through the rusty bars at the battered and the broken, an urgent thought crossed his mind.

Where is Gipi...?

————

Under the cover of a starless night, Gipi did not stray from the shadow of mast and sail, climbing her way aboard the smallest of the galleys. Grasping the rail, she hoisted herself onto the deck, drawing her blades with vicious intent, eying the corsairs as they slacked on watch. The agony and anguish of the slaves below was as palpable as the rhythm of the waves, threatening to send even the nimble fool tumbling into the roiling sea. Wringing her cap and bells as quietly as she could, Gipi slipped from barrel to barrel, eager to cup a slaver's mouth and plunge a knife into his neck. Try as she may to disguise her bitter loathing with a veneer of dry humor, the servants of Sultan Khan were beneath her sympathy.

I'm never going back there....

During the raid, hardly an hour ago, Gipi had fled the Pig and Whistle, watching on as the tavern burned to the ground and Baldwin was taken captive. She would not leave her idiot liege to die in the salt mines. She knew what these men were capable of. She'd faced such cruelty firsthand. It was a matter of first blood. Slitting a corsair's throat, Gipi flipped her gurgling target overboard with an assassin's grace—it was only natural, given how she had escaped captivity in the Holy Land. The fatal splash was louder than she intended.

"Who's there?" shouted a guard, raising his rifle blindly at the darkness.

Gipi crouched low, wiping her blade clean against her patchwork trousers. She threw a copper coin against the mast—a cunning distraction—and crept through the hatch to below deck. Landing with a soft thud, Gipi groped her way in along the clammy bodies of rowers and rotting corpses, inching her way over heaps of feces, trying to ignore the whimpers of broken men.

Suddenly, a slave grasped her wrist, chains jangling in the darkness.

"Help," he gasped, "us."

Gipi hushed and laid a finger to her lips, though she was as blind as the slaves in the imprisoning blackness. Hoarse whispers filled her ears, different tongues blurring together in a desperate babble—the slaves began to stir with panic and hope. Many hands tore at her sleeves, as if reaching to the heavens, as if salvation was within reach.

"G-get off me," she gasped.

Her revulsion was born of memory—as if she was forced to relive the humiliation in the harem, to play the lute and lyre for the amusement of the Sultan Khan. Better off as a minstrel, her quick wit was the only thing that prevented her from becoming a concubine—or worse. Here and now, Gipi tore herself free from the desperate grip.

"Baldwin," she raised her voice, ever so slightly, "where are you?"

No response, save the rising cacophony of voices. Footsteps marched down the steps, gathering speed, as an oil lamp shed scant light on Gipi's form. Eyes darting in the dimness, she scanned the columns of prisoners for anyone resembling a leper.

"Well, fuck," she muttered.

Against all notions of mercy, Gipi slipped free of the imprisoned and dove for the cargo hold across the way. The corsairs rushed downstairs and attempted to silence the rabble. Screams filled the wooden hall—someone had been shot in the leg. Gipi shuddered and quietly shut the door behind her, peering through the keyhole for a second glance. Baldwin was nowhere to be seen. Hidden among the barrels of fish remains and rotting vegetables, Gipi waited for the patrol to pass by—only for the corsairs to open the door. She held her breath, waiting until they left for hammocks in the lower deck. Gipi slipped out the porthole, continuing the search for her liege aboard the neighboring vessel, regardless of the icy waters or betentacled things lurking beneath the surface.

———

Hours seemed to blur together. Baldwin sat in his rusted cage, massaging the open sores on his fettered wrists, chained by the neck like a bear to be sold. Stoic and silent, he shut his weary eyes and tried to ignore the weeping murmurs of the other prisoners—until he heard the jingle of iron keys. A corsair greeted him with a curt nod.

"Admiral wants a word."

Regardless of response, or lack thereof, the door creaked open. Baldwin was escorted to the captain's cabin. He was seated at the dining table. The walls were lined with all manner of trophies, ranging from silk tapestries to pagan idols—including a scarlet altar by the bedside and bookshelves. The loot seemed tarnished by dimness and smoke. Burning incense cast a pall over the admiral who sat on the far side of the table, veiled in rippling shadow.

"There's no need to dwell on formalities," Leechman said, cutting into a small plate of pickled herring and boiled eggs, garnished with a sprinkling of chives. He raised a cup of pilfered ale to his lips to wash down the sailor's delicacy. "You must have many questions."

Baldwin rested his manacles on the table. "Where is our heading?"

Leechman's smirk was barely visible in the dimness. He pushed the plate towards the leper and offered him a separate set of silverware. "Come now, humor me. It's not every day a man of my station gets to dine with the King of the Holy Land."

"A title I forsook long ago."

"Not so long from what I've heard."

Despite his gnawing hunger, Baldwin did not touch the dregs of the meal.

"You intend to sell me at the slave markets, no?"

"At the bazaars of Othello, the city under Vermillion occupation." Leechman's eyes were yellow with jaundice, and yet, the leper thought them daemonic in candlelight. "So you haven't heard. We've taken control of the caliphate across the sea, curiosity of the Fool General. Say what you will of his methods, but General Pierrot is...effective."

So they are affiliated....

That caught Baldwin's attention, though he knew better than to succumb to blind fury—a rarity for a man of his temperament. Slaver or not, perhaps the leper could extract a grain of truth from the admiral. "You are of the Vermillion Empire then?"

"A privateer under the protection of the Sun King. I assure you, this messy venture is merely to cover expenses. In truth, I was dispatched to search for curiosities of the occult."

Baldwin's thoughts wandered to the vaults beneath the streets of Nedlergate and their eldritch implications—to the Malachite Pyramid that Pierrot had uncovered. Despite his position, the leper knew better than to divulge in any leg of his journey—let alone what he had seen.

"We're a long way from the Holy Land," Leechman said, sharply. "No one is coming to your rescue. But I digress. Have you ever been to Othello?"

"No," Baldwin said, "but I've heard much from my

embassies." He attempted to entertain the admiral, talkative as he was. "Under Vermillion occupation, you say? And who, pray tell, is the governor of these new territories? The Fool General, I presume."

"Correct," Leechman said. "What else do you know of the Sun King's plans?"

"I beg your pardon?"

"Don't bother denying it. You clearly intend to use such relics against Othello. Your nations have a long and bloody rivalry, after all."

"I pity your cynicism."

At that moment, Baldwin saw something on the fringe of sight — a shadow out the cabin window, darting across the darkness. He thought it a trick of moonlit fog until the door swung open. A dagger whistled past Leechman and impaled the far wall. Eyes wide with shock that gave way to fury, the admiral launched out of his seat and reached for a pistol.

"Who in the hell — ?"

Baldwin lunged with steel cuffs and bludgeoned his captor's skull, sending him reeling with a crash against the floorboards — the crew likely heard that. The leper did not turn to face his rescuer, knowing well that Gipi slinked to his side.

"You alright?" she asked.

Rallying shouts and footsteps clambered up from the lower deck. Baldwin eyed the glass sphere on the table. Leechman lay slumped, dazed in the corner, and began to stir.

"Hey," Gipi said, "we have to get out of here."

Corsairs lunged to greet him with steel and grapeshot. Gipi led the way, tumbling and dodging, as she slashed open their tendons. A bosun in a turban struck fiercely with a fishing spear, intent on driving the hook through Baldwin's shoulder. The leper narrowly avoided the blow — but not before a scimitar gleamed in the torchlight. Gipi was already fiddling with rope and rigging to undo a rowboat. In a leap of faith, the leper climbed into the suspended vessel.

"Come on," Gipi muttered, "dammit."

Her dirk was ill meant to slice through ragged hemp, but the bonds came undone eventually. Together, Baldwin and Gipi fell with the rowboat into the open sea. His corpse of a body groaned upon wooden impact, though he felt no pain. The fool crouched beside him and sheathed her twin blades, but her triumphant smile soon vanished.

"Uh," she managed, "where're the oars?"

A host of steely clicks carried from the taffrail — a firing squad of corsairs had them cornered like puppets in a shooting gallery. Baldwin gritted his teeth but said nothing. Leechman staggered to his crew, a crimson hand over his beaten and bruised brow.

"Don't," he snarled. "Bring them on board."

The next thing Baldwin remembered, he was struck hard upside the head and collapsed onto the deck. Leechman knelt low to the leper's side, rage smoldering in his eyes.

"I am curious," the admiral hissed, "where is it that you planned on going?" He stood sharply and addressed the crew. "Ready the pulleys," he ordered, "and the irons."

"Admiral?" asked a shiphand.

"Do as I say!" Leechman snapped.

The corsairs skittered to their stations and prepared the blocks in a manner that eluded Baldwin — until he saw a rope sprawling under the port to starboard. A slave, presumably selected at random, was dragged to the deck and hoisted up the yardarm in a wicked strappado. Dangling and wailing, he was dropped suddenly to the sea, screams muffled as pulleys tore him under the ship. Color had vanished from Baldwin's face as he witnessed the act of brutality, scarcely able to fathom what awaited the poor soul beneath the waves.

"Nothing like a good keelhaul," sneered one of the corsairs.

Mechanisms slipped to and fro, back and forth, as heaved by the corsairs. When at last the slave was brought abroad to the other side of the *Scheherazade*, he was but a flayed cadaver laced with shredded strips of skin. Without word or ceremony, Leechman jerked his head aside, and the corpse was cut down and cast overboard, to feed the worms of the sea.

Baldwin was speechless, trembling.

"Don't overestimate your worth," Leechman said. "So much as another quip and that'll be you and your friend." He raised his voice. "Back to your stations, the lot of you. We arrive at Othello tomorrow." He scowled at the leper and his fool. "Enjoy the brig."

CHAPTER THREE

The wrought-iron grate shrieked shut. Baldwin was shaken. Gipi sat in the corner of the brig, her irons rattling in the darkness. The leper shuddered at what they had witnessed. How many had been bought and sold from the *Scheherazade*, ferried to the underworld of criminal syndicates and burning sands? How many had perished on such a voyage, whether by example or simply for sport? While there was hope for the leper and his fool, as there always was, he could not say the same for the chattel crowded together in the cargo hold.

"Can," he stared at his ulcerated hands, "I save them?"

"Never stopped you from trying," Gipi said.

"What do you think awaits us?"

"Best case scenario?" Gipi paused to ponder, "I make it as a minstrel and you get thrown in with the pit fighters. Honestly, though? Salt mines. For both of us."

Baldwin shut his crusted eyes, letting his thoughts set sail into a sea of dreams. "We must not suffer these wicked men," he said. "Mark my words, I will find our course to freedom."

"Get some rest," Gipi sighed, deeply. "We've got our work cut out for us."

In dreams, Baldwin was free of bondage yet harrowed by evil of a different sort. He drifted in and out of consciousness, at the mercy of the *Scheherazade* and its swaying rhythm, imagining the Holy City of his youth once more, of the campaign against the invading East. His blade was unbroken then. The clash of steel began to fade, seemingly swallowed by a darker presence—one not born of memory. In the great stone bailey, Baldwin stepped in a crimson pool and beheld the casualties of war strewn about the floor, mangled and dismembered, eyes wide in terror. Swarms of white worms writhed among the dead, as rows of torches flared with corpse light, illuminating nothing save the way into deep and creeping darkness.

A terrified scream echoed from within.

Baldwin mustered his courage and sprinted into the unknown. His footsteps were heavy and loud against the tiles. He followed the pale flames along the walls, guided by the desperate cries of the wounded. He came to a halt, confronted by a gruesome sight.

What is that...?

It was a wicked silhouette—impossibly gaunt, towering over the dead, wreathed in a cloak and cowl of ethereal cloth from which no limb emerged. Before its robes lay the remains of a soldier, one of Baldwin's men. The young king shifted in place, his own blood dripping onto the floor. He was wounded. Exertions did nothing to ease his injuries. Though Baldwin could scarcely breathe, the silhouette sensed the presence of yet another challenger and seemed to smile as the corpse light shone upon a feminine face.

"You're not here," Baldwin said. "The Holy City never fell. This didn't happen."

The silhouette said nothing.

Baldwin took a defensive stance with only that shaft of steel between him and the enemy of unknown origin. "What are you?" he asked. "Speak!"

The silhouette swung wide—a massive scythe emerged as if from nothing, its steel gleaming against the corpse-candles which circled the blade. With a wrathful cry, Baldwin lunged to greet his opponent with blind force, blonde hair flowing bright. He may as well have struck the air. Parry after parry, Baldwin was thrown across the chamber and slammed against the far column with a crack. The silhouette lowered its guard, the twin lights behind its eyes shimmering not with malice but a cosmic indifference, betraying it as Death under a different guise.

"This is," Baldwin wheezed, "not what happened."

"No," Death said. "It is not."

Baldwin raised his head with trembling effort, seeing his own shadow upon his opponent, as if the enemy rose from such darkness. Then it occurred to him. Was this the same Death who so observed his every thought and deed — the reaper he once bested? Was God's patience running so thin, settling to send a less merciful spirit to stir his soul?

"Are you — ?"

"I am what you make of me," Death said, "but do not speak as if you understand. You are incapable of epiphany as you are now." Slowly, it began to stalk into vision. "Even now, your judgment is clouded by fear and loathing. Not of death. Not of pain. Not of me. But of your own weakness." It turned to the piled dead. "You are not ready. Perhaps you will never be."

Baldwin shut his eyes in a feeble attempt to dismiss the towering figure. "This is a dream." As those words escaped his lips, his flesh began to atrophy — lesions and sores spread from cracking skin, as the pain began to fade. The leper stood once more, clutching the Broken Blade by the hilt. "You are a daemon born of my fever. Nothing more."

Death seemed to sneer. "Did it ever occur to you," its speech was slow and deliberate, "what happened after you abdicated the throne? What will become of the Holy Land?"

Baldwin lunged once more, rage in his heart — only to be torn awake.

"Land ho," someone called.

As the corsairs rushed to their stations, preparing to make berth, Baldwin rested his weary head in bandaged hands, haunted by what he had dreamed.

Baldwin did not reply. Rays of sunlight rippled among moats of dust through cracks in the hull and naked ceiling. The leper waited for his jailor to unlock the cages, but no one came to the brig. Or to the cargo hold, for that matter. Something was amiss.

"What do you see?"

"Othello."

A call to prayer echoed from the tallest minaret, announcing the dawn of a new day. The *Scheherazade* and her consort came to a halt—dockhands warped and roped the ships to stone piers. Commotion and terrified sobs filled the cargo hold as the captives were herded by bayonets to the deck. Finally, a corsair opened the iron hatch of the brig, and Baldwin was forced to join the prime stock. Under the blinding sun, the leper kept his head bowed yet glowered at his wicked captors. Odo Leechman leaned against the taffrail, as if basking in the notion of another profitable auction.

The *Scheherazade* had docked upon the outer ring of the Cothon, a cul-de-sac of a harbor centered on a central bastion and island, where the Imperial Navy kept a martial presence. Crowds had gathered to gawk—a rising tide of swarthy faces and turbans, some with coin at hand, shouting a cosmopolitan babble of dialects. The hagglers were kept at bay by the musketeers of Vermillion's occupying force, clad in rich blue coatees and tall shakos, sweating, unaccustomed to the rippling heat. Such was his welcome that Baldwin scarcely noticed the splendid sights of the Jewel of Khand.

In a single file, the chattels were led to the bazaar with its spices and open stands. Cries of despair mingled with the bustle of daily life. Friends were separated, children were torn from their mother's embrace, and husbands were segregated from wives in groups of thirty bodies, guarded from the front and rear. Maidens were inspected in face and hand, no doubt to be taken as harem girls. A father was dragged to the podium, pleading for his son not to forsake his faith.

This can't be happening....

For once in his life, Baldwin was frozen in shock, overwhelmed by sheer helplessness. He failed to struggle against his bondage. No fury came to him. Only a hollow paralysis in body and mind, like a sow before the slaughter. He was about to be pulled to the stage, when he noticed a handful of feminine silhouettes on the rooftop, armed with long arquebuses and muskets, moments from firing—and fire they did. Amidst the cacophony of gunshots, hosts of slavers and Vermillion soldiers fell to volleys of lead, blood splattering the open streets. This was his only chance. Whatever insurgency his saviors belonged to, Baldwin did not know, nor did he care. He barreled through the rear guard, bludgeoning through with force of manacles and tremendous strength—when he saw a flash of motley among the scattering survivors.

"Gipi," he called.

Though still shackled, the leper and his fool fled into the narrows. Eventually, the gunshots began to fade as they took cover among the vacated stalls.

"Hey," Gipi followed his gaze, "you can't save everyone. So keep moving."

Guilt nagged at Baldwin's conscience. Fleeing into the medina, he had left hundreds to their fates at the bazaar, and yet, what else could he do? Lead a mutiny and liberate every man, woman, and child aboard the consort? There was a time to deliver the wicked to justice. There was also a time to acknowledge that he was but one man in a cold, uncaring world.

Or so he told himself.

In his heart of hearts, Baldwin knew better. Hiding among the crates of dates and casks of olives, the leper pulled his hood tightly over his face, staring at a rising plume of smoke, imagining hot irons pressed against the flesh of the freshly captured— brands to last a lifetime. Without warning, he launched to his feet and set his sights upon the bazaar once more.

"Where're you going?" Gipi asked.

"To save them."

"No, you're not." She slid in front of the leper, between him and the open street. "I'm not letting you throw your life away. Maybe you forgot, but they'll keelhaul you."

"Assuming my capture—"

"Which's guaranteed."

"Gipi," Baldwin said. "You would have me live with this?

Knowing that I could've freed hundreds, yet only thought to save myself? I cannot do that." He pushed past effortlessly, marching down the unpaved streets, rolling his eyes as she gave chase.

"Wait—!"

"I will wait no longer," Baldwin said, rage tightening his chest. "I must do whatever good I can. Now and always. Every second I waste, the more suffering ensues."

Something cracked under his boots. Whether a twig or a bit of bone, Baldwin did not know, nor did he care. And yet, he felt a dramatic shift in the air.

"You know," Gipi snapped, "you're a selfish little shit. Don't lie to me." She cried after him. "You're not doing this because 'it's the right thing.' We both know it's to find meaning and purpose. For yourself. That's what it is. That's what it always was. Because you can't accept the fact that maybe, just maybe, you're not that fucking special."

Baldwin halted in his tracks.

"I didn't risk my life for them," Gipi continued, "I did it to save you."

"For which," he managed, "I am grateful."

"No, you're not. You couldn't give two shits whether you live or die. Well, guess what, you're not the only martyr to walk the earth. And the world doesn't need more."

Baldwin raised his head towards the heavens, ignorant to the crowd gathering to witness the meltdown. "If that is how you truly feel," he said, "then do not follow." So he departed to the bazaar with a shuddering sigh, tears trickling beneath the mask.

"You knew the road would not be easy," he told himself, "and yet…."

Nearing the skirmish, Baldwin paused to breathe. The implications of Gipi's absence began to sink into his thoughts like poisoned daggers. He couldn't afford to dwell on it. Not now. Baldwin clutched his rosary with weeping fingers.

"I will save them."

Gathering speed and fanning the flames of rage, Baldwin

sprinted to the bazaar with a fierce howl, diving headfirst into melee and massacre. Drawing a curved scimitar from the corpse of a corsair, he swung wildly and sought to cut down as many as he could — giving no quarter to those who'd see the innocent condemned to a lifetime of abuse. Blood splattered his mask as he bathed in self-righteousness, drunk with carnage. Baldwin scarcely noticed the cloaked figures and flashing daggers beside him, ushering the liberated to unknown alleys, and yet, he knew that he was alone in his struggle.

Nor did it matter.

His was a solitary path and in that lay its virtue. It had to be. And in his conviction, Baldwin lost himself to a maddened dance of violence. Whether the truth or a trick of the fever, corpses began to pile about him in a great fugue, and he felt no remorse. Suddenly, a boot slammed against his spine, and a host of sabers swung down to meet his neck.

"No," Leechman came between the leper and the lazy-eyed guard, "he is a special case. We've already a bidder." He took Baldwin by the collar, dragging him to his feet, relishing in the humiliation. "You just don't know when to quit, do you?" He pressed a flintlock against the leper's brow only to fire a warning shot past his bleeding ear. "Don't test me."

Baldwin did not rebel, gritting his teeth and accepting defeat — for the moment.

"Do you understand?" Leechman asked.

"Yes."

"Then come," the admiral tore him tightly by the neck, "your new master awaits. And I think you'll find him to be quite agreeable. In a manner of speaking."

Leechman led his captive through the medina, its routes twisting and turning, and kept to the shade between mudbrick tenements, under cover of webs of clotheslines and soiled carpets, into the heart of the Old City. Hardly a soul dwelled in the district, though pamphlets written in multiple languages were posted about the doors, and signs of struggle — broken windows and battered doors—peppered the walls. Only the passing of musketeers breached the stillness as Vermillion soldiers marched on patrol. It was as if the district had been cleared out by the occupying force, its people relocated to somewhere Baldwin would rather not contemplate.

Something is wrong. Vermillion hasn't simply conquered the city....

The midday sun glowered upon the leper, threatening to blister and bake his flesh, when he passed through the Janissary Gates into slums that had outgrown the walls, greeted by hovels built from sandstone and dry talus. Hempen bridges spanned the gaps between awkward spires, stretched over mines and quarries, where slaves toiled with picks and sturdy shovels, striking salt from the earth under threat of the lash, backs scarred and weeping. Dust stung Baldwin's eyes, suffocating the sun in a wan pall. The coughs of pale-lunged miners carried from every hut, and tremendous shards of salt lay throughout the open pits, jutting as swords drawn from the womb of the earth. Excavations were well underway. This was the territory of the Saline Guild—the Zone Rouge under Vermillion occupation.

A loathsome place....

Down the residential lanes, Baldwin overhead the murmurs of locals who kept their distance, as if shunning his very presence. Men both swarthy and sickly languished in poverty; emaciated, dressed in ragged scraps and clothing likely salvaged from lost shipments. Then it occurred to Baldwin. Many of the idle slaves were amputees in some form or another, whether missing hands, an arm, or both their legs; discarded by their owners and left to either beg or starve to death. Though not a bottle was to be seen, even the leper could smell the overpowering blend of tobacco and hashish. Pipeweed, it seemed, was their only escape. Many had substituted meager rations for the sweet taste of oblivion.

The only windows belonged to a hammam, a bathhouse wafting with the rhythm of warm candlelight and hot steam, topped with a modest dome—where overseers and Vermillion soldiers went to waste what little free time they had. Though he could scarcely read the creaking sign, Baldwin made out the faded image of a pipe seared into its wood.

"What is then den of iniquity?" he asked.

"Where you'll be spending the rest of your days."

"And," he mustered, "my master?"

"Merely the proprietor of this establishment."

A bouncer stood by the door, mustache waxed and arms crossed, watching as peddlers and the impoverished went about their business. To Baldwin's surprise, the doorman beckoned him to set foot inside. With Leechman as his guide, they were welcomed by burning incense and muffled coughs of smoking men. Such an antechamber led to a wide array of bathing pools with no shortage of ornate rugs and hookahs. The ceiling swirled with narcotic smoke, and Baldwin took in a lungful, if only to soothe his nerves. The door shut with a chime.

"Welcome," said a rasping voice, "how can I help you today, stranger?"

"Just a delivery," Leechman replied.

From out of the smoke emerged a man wreathed in a tall black coat. Hooded and cloaked, he was adorned with scraps of silk and bits of finery, trinkets and baubles, somewhere between an impoverished merchant and a well-to-do vagabond. With sallow eyes, he looked his prize up and down, though his face was inscrutable, masked by a scarf and gaiter.

"So," he said, "you must be Baldwin, fourth of his name."

The leper did not answer.

"Your reputation precedes you," the merchant said.

"And you are?"

The merchant laughed. "A dealer in all manner of things."

"Slaves among them?"

"Come," said the merchant, "we must talk—"

"Ah," Leechman stepped between them, "but before that, I believe it's customary for us to receive payment before the master chooses to fraternize with his prize."

"It's a rough economy out there." The merchant turned his attention to Leechman. "What do I owe you? He's not exactly in mint condition."

"I assure you, this is how I found him."

"I'll settle for half."

"Half?" Leechman sputtered. "That's absurd! He was a hard one to break in, I'll tell you that much. At least an extra twenty percent for damages—"

"Then I wish you luck finding someone else willing to pay for a leper."

Leechman gritted his teeth and spat on the floor. "Fine."

Despite his position as a mere commodity, Baldwin found a certain delight in the admiral's situation. "I do suggest you take it."

"Of course you do," Leechman snapped.

The merchant laughed and rummaged through his pockets and purses, handing a satin bag bulging with coinage without counting. "That should about do it."

Leechman bit onto a piece of eight and returned a devious grin. "Pleasure doing business with you." He took his payment and handed the merchant a single iron key. "Do with him as you will," the admiral said. "Not in my contract to ask questions."

The merchant waved. "And you'd be wise to keep it that way."

Leechman had already stepped into the shadows, but not before Baldwin saw a glint of steel in the torchlight, followed by a number of cloaked figures skirting along the fringe of sight.

"Rest assured," he called, "my men and I appreciate your generous patronage."

Daggers at hand, the assassins were merely a step behind. Baldwin smirked yet shuddered, knowing full well what his "master" had in store for Leechman. Meanwhile, the merchant removed Baldwin's shackles—clattering against the tiles.

The leper massaged his wrists, glowering with morbid suspicion.

The merchant laughed. "Don't look so dour. This is the best thing that could've possibly happened, given the circumstances. You're a hard man to find, mind you."

"Who are you?"

"A friend of the Holy Land."

That caught Baldwin off guard. He began to soak in his surroundings, hanging tapestries and turquoise tiles, and, hidden among them, the saltire—the symbol of common faith.

"I abdicated my throne long ago," Baldwin said, guessing the merchant's agenda. "The regent sent you, no? To convince me to return and reclaim my birthright? As if I am fit to rule." He looked away, about to depart. "I thank you for freeing me, however—"

"Free?" the merchant laughed. "Make no mistake, my liege. Here, in Othello, you are not free. Far from it. I am merely a kind and generous master." He laid a greasy hand on Baldwin's shoulder. "And you're going to do exactly as I tell you."

Baldwin held his tongue and fettered his rage. Hours later, he lifted a cup of coffee to his blistered lips, savoring the bitter aroma. The merchant sat afar on a richly patterned rug, cross-legged, suckling his hookah and puffing clouds of smoke. The humidity did little to ease Baldwin's symptoms, but the leper found a certain comfort in the steamy bathhouse. He was tempted to remove his mask, if only to bask in moisture against the pores of his fetid cheeks.

"Not much of a talker, are you?" the merchant asked.

"Pardon, the voyage was most arduous."

The merchant reached for a wrinkled date on the platter and sighed, deeply. "It's no secret you've been meddling in affairs overseas. We've got contacts in Mulgrave."

Baldwin's thoughts drifted to Radcliffe and his radicals—it was long since he fought alongside them amidst the Great Fire of Nedlergate. "You know of the revolts?"

"Aye," the merchant said. "World's a smaller place than either of us cares to admit."

"I see," Baldwin's eyes drifted up to the swirling smoke, "then you are no friend to Vermillion, I take it? Nor the Fool General."

The merchant nodded. "The men who attacked the bazaar? They work for me."

Many things troubled Baldwin. Though he was no stranger to civil unrest and open revolt, he knew little of the workings of Khandish politics. Let alone what his captor's true agenda was. His concerns were many, and it was difficult for him to pinpoint the root of evil — save his course to rid the world of sin, whatever form it took.

"What's your interest in the Fool General?" the merchant asked.

The leper bowed his head solemnly. "I was there when Pierrot gave the order. When the Nedlergate was razed to the ground. He is responsible for much death and destruction. I cannot abide by such cruelty. And yet," he stared at his bandaged hands, "perhaps I can find purpose in ridding the world of such evil. Whatever form it may take."

The merchant shrugged. "Why is that your responsibility?"

"Evil thrives when good men do nothing," Baldwin snapped. "And if you seek to free the enslaved, your critique is without merit." He paused. "What do you want of me?"

"Liberation," the merchant said. "Not for me," he raised his sleeve, revealing a brand scarred and seared into his forearm, "or even the city, but for those who share our faith."

"I'm afraid I don't follow."

The merchant gazed out the open window, where the coughs of the enslaved filled the streets. "Many of the slaves you saw," he continued, "came from Golgotha."

Baldwin's cup clattered against the saucer. "The Holy Land?"

"A lot has changed since you've abdicated the throne."

The leper did not know what to say, let alone whether anything needed to be said. His hands shook with ailing purpose, and his thoughts wandered to what he had left behind; guilt wracked his conscience, haunted by what could have been. If he had accepted responsibility, in lieu of wandering the earth as a knight errant, would his people have been spared such a fate?

Perhaps so, but such lamentations would not save them.

"Come," the merchant chuckled, darkly, "I've something to show you."

Baldwin obeyed and followed the downward steps—a secret passage hidden by a slab of stone. The merchant lit an oil lamp and bid the leper to stay close. In the root cellars beneath the hammam, under the boiling springs, they walked dimly lit corridors and darker passages, guided by lit candles clustered in ossuaries. Faded pigment and carvings of coded figures lined the curving walls, images of saints and myriad miracles veiled in symbolism. Baldwin caressed the icon of the saltire, and the aged paint flaked gently against his fingers.

"Catacombs are plenty beneath the city," the merchant said. "Most of them are used for burial and worship." He raised the lamp, shedding light upon niches cradling the skulls of the ancient dead. "Even now, we pray in secret. In hope that God will answer with the coming of his chosen. To free us from the shackles of tyranny. Be they sultan or imperial."

Baldwin mulled over this carefully. What manner of chosen? It was true that hagiography of the Holy Land was rich indeed; however, the notion of a savior descending to usher in a golden age for the faithful was wishful thinking. Even he knew that. These images were made by men, and it was men who would lead the vanguard to keep the darkness at bay.

"Othello has long sought to repress our faith," Baldwin admitted. "Crusades and jihads alike have been fought in the Holy Land, contesting a rightful rule."

"And we faithful seek a means to escape these shackles."

"Then I am as stranded as you folk," the leper sighed. "How would you see us freed?"

A warm breeze swept the path's end. Eventually, the

merchant guided him to an alcove overlooking the Old City embedded in the towering cliffside. There, where the apartheid slums met the quarters of colonial tourists, sat one of the last living wonders of Antiquity. Rotund and tremendous to behold, ringed with row upon row of colonnades and classical arches, the Colosseo dominated the skyline of Othello and had righteously earned its name. Whiter than marble, its stonework predated the Exodus westward across the Winedark Sea, accented with gold, ivory, and circus reds, housing a hundred statues and a thousand flames, each in honor of a champion sacrificed to amuse the masses. Such a sight humbled all who looked upon it, even the king in exile. It was a monument to violence, and in that lay its promise of glory eternal.

"Many of your subjects are forced to fight in the Colosseo. There will be a tournament soon to celebrate the end of the Sultan's dynasty, such as it is." The merchant eyed Baldwin with keen interest. "I have yet to sponsor a champion."

"I see," Baldwin said. "You would have me live among the slaves and inspire them to revolt." He bowed his head with a forlorn sigh. "May I know my host's name?"

"Darius," the merchant said.

Baldwin nodded in kind, mulling over these matters carefully. Loyalty to his people aside, it was true that he was a stranger in a strange land and had nowhere to run. Should he flee, the leper would be hunted and cut down in the open street, if he too was fortunate enough to escape the slaver's scourge. Moreover, he was ill-equipped and robbed of funds. Short of stowing away aboard the next ship to Mulgrave, Baldwin had no means of escape. Then there was Gipi. In truth, he regretted his words. Sitting on a slab of stone, anxiety and insidious fear washed over him in a sudden tide. Had she evaded capture? Had she slipped free of bondage, only to skulk in the shadows of the open medina? Regardless, Baldwin worried for the fool.

"I will abide," he said. "Under one condition. You will help me find someone."

CHAPTER FOUR

Gipi had vanished into the Old City and pilfered a cloak to hide her motley—a thin disguise against familiar perils. Never before had the fool thought she'd return to Othello. Though much had changed in her absence, the smell of spice and opium smoke made her head swim in a sea of memories she'd rather forget—harem halls and hammams, where she amused the rich and powerful. Only her sapphic wit kept their salacious leers at bay, and failing that, a knife in the dark, for she'd learned long ago how to navigate life in the sultan's court.

I'm never going back....

The sun had crept across the Winedark Sea, little more than a shimmering mirage over crimson waters, though Gipi was far from the Cothon and its passing ships. Here and now, she played the limping vagrant, to fade among the downtrodden and destitute, of which there was no shortage. Vermillion soldiers were on patrol in search of the insurgents. Though their presence brought nothing but fear as they raided home after home, she knew the brigade wasn't looking for her, per se. What truly ailed her was dearer to the heart.

"Baldwin," she muttered, "you son of a bitch."

Punching a sandstone wall, Gipi grunted as pain shot through her knuckles. To think the bastard would just up and leave—then again, what did she expect? Gipi took a moment to sit by the dust-choked roadside, laying her head in her hands. It was true, she did sign up for this, to chronicle his misadventures, to whatever end. It wasn't so much Baldwin's departure, but how easily it seemed to come to him. As if she were a prop to be thrown aside when she outlived her usefulness—or worse, talked back. Muttering like a madwoman, Gipi leaned into melodrama and began to sob, until she heard something—the strumming of a lute. She reached for her own instrument, only to remember that Leechman had stolen it along with the rest of her possessions. Clenching her fists, she endured those poorly tuned strings, rolling her eyes at caterwauling vocals. She slipped to the alleys to uncover the source of the music and came to a plaza with a marble mandala of a fountain, approaching a busker seated upon its edge, entertaining a small crowd. Gipi sneered, knowing his type well.

Lank-haired and dressed in a loose tunic, he was no doubt a charlatan with a fistful of loaded dice, the sort who used his art to serenade and enthrall the young and naïve, without regard for tempo and lyrics seemingly written by a virgin. He shot a lady in green a wink and repeated his four-chord chorus. Lurking on the fringe, Gipi waited until the song had finished and joined in the applause — slowly and with sarcasm.

The busker forced a smile, no doubt recognizing the insult.

"And who might you be?" he asked.

Gipi let slip a devious grin. "Oh, just a troubadour looking for trouble."

"It seems you've found it. Tell me, do you play?"

"I do, but I'm afraid I haven't an instrument."

"A bard without an instrument to call her own?" the busker scoffed. "My dear, you must be down on your luck." The crowd punctuated the quip with mocking laughter.

"Oh, that's about to change," she muttered.

"What's that?"

"Have you a spare?"

True to Gipi's suspicions, the busker reached for a second lute near his vagabond's pack.

"That I do."

"Well then." Against any sense or judgment, Gipi whisked off her cloak with all the vim and vigor she could muster, revealing her cap and bells in the twilight. "A challenger approaches, my good sir! And I wager everything on my person that I will earn the crowd."

"If you win?"

"Well," Gipi winked, "a bard isn't much without a lute, is she?"

The busker paused, as if hesitant to accept. The clomp of leather boots against stone echoed from deeper within the medina, but Gipi stood her ground, pretending to ignore the marching soldiers. When they had passed, she offered a hand in mock respect.

"What say you?"

"Very well," the busker said.

Gipi twisted the pegs with firm care until she was vaguely satisfied. Though the lute was hardly polished and ill-maintained, she would make do with what she had. Then, with a strumming strike, the fool began the first verse, which the busker answered in kind with surprising skill. She grimaced with a hint of respect and let her thoughts wander with the dueling strings. Imagining horns and castanets underpinning every stroke, Gipi humored herself in a solo, letting rage and resentment sweep her spirit into the song—the phantom of Baldwin seemingly on the fringe of sight, beneath the lids of her eyes. Gritting her teeth and channeling such angst onto the poor instrument, the fires of flamenco kindled a tremendous finale, until even her opponent had no choice but to pause in admiration. Swinging her cap and bells like a lunatic minstrel, Gipi settled for a reprisal and melancholy outro, and took a low bow. The crowd was silent at first, until the busker led the applause, and they soon joined in cheers.

"Good lord," he said. "Who hurt you?"

Gipi smirked, but did not reply.

"Keep it," the busker offered a handshake, "that was impressive—"

Suddenly, a shadow fell upon the throng, and Gipi heard the click of muskets and arquebuses—the garrison had caught up to her. The fool slipped her prize across her back, much as the way Baldwin would the Broken Blade, and turned to face the captain.

"That was quite the performance," he said. "I've never heard that piece outside of the sultan's palace." He stepped forward. "Tell me, where did you learn it?"

Gipi laughed nervously. "Oh, just a piece I picked up at the Cinque Ports. You run into all manner of vagrants and musicians there." Her fingers inched toward her empty sheaths, silently cursing her lack of daggers. "Well, gentlemen, I believe I've overstayed my welcome."

The firing squad took aim.

"Do you think it wise," the captain asked, "to resist arrest in these trying times?"

"No, I suppose not."

"Bind her hands. Bring her in for questioning."

Gipi uttered a wry laugh. "Fuck that."

With that, she leapt to the right and scrambled up a neighboring ladder, desperate to evade captivity by way of the rooftop. "Never going back there," she muttered to herself in a mantra, deaf to grapeshots as the guards opened fire. "Never going back."

She staggered and sprinted across the flat-topped houses, bidding her audience farewell with a wave — and tripped over her own pointed shoes, tumbling with a crash onto the street below, a flimsy tent and stand breaking her fall. Dazed and reeling, Gipi staggered to her feet, only to be greeted by a phalanx of pistols and long barrels.

"Slippery little bastard, aren't you?" the captain sneered. "You'd best come along."

Gipi raised her gloved hands, slowly.

CHAPTER FIVE

Stirring his aching body, Baldwin splashed his face with cool water—a luxury in the miserable slums of Othello. Staring at his own reflection, the leper pondered his own mortality as he rewrapped his limbs. No one else would dare tend his wounds. He wondered what the day held. If he were to meet with the fighters imprisoned beneath the Colosseo. Indeed, he knew little of Darius's plans, only that he sought to liberate those stolen from the Holy Land.

"Sleep well?" the merchant asked.

Baldwin smiled, sadly, reminded of the fool he'd forsaken in a moment's anger. "Well as I could," he said, nursing a chipped cup of coffee. "Tell me. How do you propose we go about reintroducing me to my people? No doubt they know me as the coward who abandoned them...."

"One thing at a time." Darius raised a gloved hand. "First, you must understand exactly what we're up against, regarding the tournament, and meet the reigning champions."

"And how do you propose we do that?"

"We take a trip to the Colosseo as spectators."

Though Baldwin had no qualms with smiting the wicked, the notion of bloodsports, of the innocent being pitted against one another like rabid dogs, was sickening.

"I suppose I'm to play your bodyguard."

"No play about it," Dairus sneered from under his scarf, "you are."

Baldwin was offered a coarse linen shirt, a step above the scraps and rags most made do with. Towering over Darius as a somber warden, the leper wrapped his face with a shawl of bandages to hide worsening deformities lest he be denied entry to the Colosseo. In the dusty streets of the Zone Rouge, Darius led him down the lanes of potters and vegetable gardens, each stall under the shade of a canvas tent. Breakfast was of simple fare, lentil soup and yesterday's bread, and yet, Baldwin found it oddly reminiscent of peasants' food in the Holy Land. In his studies, he learned that Golgotha was less than a week's voyage from Othello and the Cothon. Such closeness had enabled centuries of conflict and military complications. Never before had he thought a land so near could feel so foreign. Listening to street singers and rattling drums, Baldwin was careful to avoid the attention of Vermillion patrols. Block by block, Darius led him to the Colosseo and its long banners of occupation.

"The Fool General chose to renovate this amphitheater recently," the merchant said. "As to pacify the masses while his officers deal the lash."

"Somehow that doesn't surprise me," Baldwin muttered.

Deafening cheers erupted from the stadium, drowning out the clash of steel and screams of the mutilated. Dairus approached the axial entrance with all the bravado of a snake oil salesman. He paid a fistful of sultani to the dwarfish ticketers, Punch and Judas. Meanwhile, Baldwin, pensive as he was, took a moment to soak in the surrounding crowd, languishing in line, eager to bask in bloodshed. He was torn between disdain and pity for their appetites. The people seemed to swell into every orifice of the ground floor, crowding up the stairs and down the darkened arcades to their seats. Baldwin felt as if he were descending into hell itself, bombarded by flaring lights and tortured screams of men and beasts beneath his feet. He followed his master up the stairs and into the stadium, under the shade of the big top, and soaked in the diversity of the audience — from the marbled rows of viziers and senators, to the tiers of traders from across the Winedark Sea — about to join the plebeians upon the middle ring.

"No, no," Dairus said. "You sit with the rabble."

It took Baldwin a moment to realize what he meant. Sure enough, upon the farthest ring, above the seats of the peasantry, were wooden benches reserved for the slaves. Reeking and miserable, these lost souls stared in vacant interest at the carnage below.

The leper glowered at his master, clinging to a semblance of prestige.

"It's nothing personal," Dairus added. "It's just, we can't afford to bring attention, can we? Go on now," he waved dismissively, "be a good servant."

Baldwin conceded with a nod, muttering, and took his place among the chattel. He waited for the horns to announce the entrance of the gladiators, but no such fanfare came.

Come midday, there was movement in the sultan's box and a flamboyant figure raised a hand in peace, face painted as a pale harlequin in the sunlight. A hush befell the rancorous crowd. Baldwin knew well who commanded their attention. Dressed in a fusion of fashions, Pierrot sported an emerald turban punctuated with a peacock's feather, draped in a flowing gown of speckled silk. He and the viziers of the vestigial court were surrounded by elite soldiers—janissaries in silver masks and heavy black cloaks.

"Ladies and gentlemen," the Fool General said, "citizens of Othello, of the Vermillion Empire, lend me your ears. I bid you welcome to a sample of the coming games. In honor of those who've given their lives to see you prosper under the rule of the Sun King, let this contest be a reminder, not of the war which led to," he stifled a smirk, "such destruction, but of new beginnings and prosperity to come. And what better way to kick it off than a grudge match?" The crowd erupted in cheers, and Pierrot basked in their applause. "Come on. Louder! You people love this shit." He raised his arms as a magnanimous despot. "Can you dig it?" he roared.

Baldwin saw through the veneer of populism like a hawk upon a rat.

Pierrot was but a ringmaster who sated the masses with bread and circuses. He was invulnerable as of now, the sultan's box shielded by a wide mesh net.

"In the blue corner," Pierrot roared, "we have the reigning

champion and crowd favorite. The handsome prince in chains, a cataphract without a cause—Solomon of Many Colors!"

True to the crowd's delight, the portcullis lifted ever slowly to reveal a white rider astride a white steed, clad in scale mail dazzling with a thousand colors shifting in the sunlight. Armed with a lance and crowned with a close-fitted helmet, the cataphract pranced a lap about the arena and waved to the ladies, basking in the bouquets thrown at his feet. He dismounted his steed, letting his blonde mane flow like streamers of gold. Baldwin crossed his arms, unamused by the garish display—a peasant's idea of nobility. Solomon twirled his spear like a dancer and turned to face the opposing gate with mock courage, eyes narrow in fierce anticipation.

"And in the red corner," Pierrot sneered, "we have the heel of the match. And a personal favorite of mine. Condemned to a lifetime of servitude for sacrificing his own son to the brass bull—yes, you heard that correctly—is the most monstrous beast in our menagerie. Now his rage is given back to you, the people, as a source of good fun. Here comes Humbaba the Butcher!"

At that moment, the gate opened and out emerged the favored villain in chains. A host of jailers undid his shackles and fled for their lives, letting their ward see the light of day. He was an ogre of a man, a brute of prodigious build, clad in the trophies and skulls of conquered kills. Every bit of armor was pilfered from a different corpse, though his clothing was limited to a loincloth and sandals, masked with a tremendous galea and armed with nothing save spiked gauntlets. Such hands had dealt more death than any one janissary could ever hope to achieve. Heaving and seething, grinding those knuckled plates together until sparks flew from his fists, he stepped forward, thighs and calves bulging as the limbs of a beast, biceps rippling in a varicose sea, eyes burning with hate from beneath the helm. His back was streaked with open wounds, as if having vowed to never retreat, even in the face of humiliation and defeat. The masses erupted in hisses and jeers, and Humbaba dug his heels into the dirt, tempering their hatred in a crucible of rage — until a scripted hush befell the crowd.

"Now," Pierrot sneered, "I want a nice clean fight to the death, from you both. Two men enter. One man leaves." He raised a soft hand. "Begin!"

Humbaba charged like a feral boar, but Solomon was far too nimble a target, poking and prodding the Butcher for a good show. Baldwin thought the heel a tortured beast cowed into combat, his fearsome costume just that — a costume. When a spiked gauntlet grazed the cataphract's cheek, the acrobatic duelist doubled back and stuck his lance deep into Humbaba's side, twisting the tip mercilessly, a whispered taunt on his lips. Something in the Butcher changed — the shackles of restraint had broken, revealing a rising urge to maim and gore. With a tremendous roar, Humbaba seemed intent on delivering a killing blow, only for Solomon to strike again, this time for the kill.

Baldwin cheered for neither, disgusted by them both.

At last, Solomon had impaled the Butcher through the torso. He let his opponent slump as blood pooled and clumped upon the sand. In a moment's arrogance, the cataphract waved to the crowd and prepared to bask in their love, twirling his lance in triumph — until a prone Humbaba grabbed him by the ankle, crushing it effortlessly, like the neck of poultry. Solomon let loose a shrill scream. The crowd fell silent in shock before anyone could so much as process what was happening. Humbaba rose and slammed a gauntleted fist against his opponent's skull — obliterating his pretty face in a splatter of gore. The Butcher rose, slowly, victorious yet disgraced. Obviously, he did not expect an ovation, but Baldwin felt the crowd's howls of wrath, downward thumbs, and demands of execution unwarranted. Humbaba merely stood in stoic acceptance, enduring the shame of his own survival.

Baldwin did not rise to defend him; it was not his place. When the games had ended, he approached Darius with reluctance, shaken by what he had seen.

"What did you think?" the merchant asked.

"Grotesque," the leper said.

"Thought you'd say that," Darius lowered his voice. "I'm afraid it's much worse in the dungeons below. Coincidentally, you'll be staying there."

Baldwin nodded with grave reluctance. "If it means freeing my people, I will obey, but do not forget. You are to help me find someone."

"Yes, yes." Darius waved dismissively. "Your little traveling companion."

"How did you—?"

Darius shot him a crusty wink. "Don't underestimate the Sisters Dervish. My master has eyes and ears everywhere. But I don't think you'll like what I have to say on the matter."

Baldwin's heart sank into his chest. "What do you mean?"

"Gipi's been taken."

Something in the leper broke with dread. He tore at the merchant by the collar and lifted him to his level. Darius's eyes wandered to the low sultan's box. Baldwin followed his gaze to Pierrot and his entourage. Towards the rear was the harem, composed of concubines and belly dancers in silk veils, though one minstrel sat among them. Though she wore no caps or bells, or the diamond motley of Baldwin's court, her face was unmistakable.

"Gipi?" The leper's grip waned. "How?"

"I don't know," Darius conceded with a sigh, "but I doubt Pierrot would 'invite' her without reason." He watched the viziers choose evening companions and depart to the arcades. Strangely, Gipi remained on her own, and the Fool General kept his distance, as if in respect, a rarity for one capable of such wanton cruelty. "Who is she to you?"

"She is," Baldwin's thoughts drifted to the many escapades and misadventures they had shared, from Gravesend to the Tower of Nedlergate. She had always stood at his side, a stalwart companion, loyal to a fault—something he had betrayed, "a friend that I do not deserve."

Darius clasped the leper's shoulder. "It won't be easy, but my men will do what we can to free her. In the meantime, I'll need you to rally the slaves in revolt. Come the tournament in three days' time, we'll meet again and help you both escape."

Baldwin's gaze drifted to the bloodstained arena, where Humbaba was bound and shackled once more — tamed, as if conditioned to accept his fate.

"Take me to the Butcher. I want to share his cell."

"Are you mad?"

The leper sighed and straightened his posture, wrapping his knuckles with care. "Word will spread rapidly of 'the King of the Holy Land' in captivity. And I plan to make my feats known among the gladiators. Only then will they accept me. And I have another request. Worry not, it is a small thing." He smirked at the merchant. "I assume we don't get to pick our titles."

"You'd be right about that."

"Register me as 'leper errant.' Gipi will know the meaning of it."

Darius shrugged his shoulders. "No harm, I suppose." He bid Baldwin to follow him to registration, where Punch and Judas had taken up residence.

Before the lobby, the twins sat behind a booth and roster — one in red, one in blue — faces caked in powder and punctuated with moles, wigs, and false noses meant to mask symptoms of syphilis, mockeries of nobility. They were oddities from Vermillion and no doubt had immigrated to Othello to eke out a better life. Punch kept to the papers, a monocle over his remaining eye, while Judas counted the silver admissions with studious intent.

"I wish to register a fighter," Darius said.

"Oh?" Punch raised his false nose from his ledger. "And who, pray tell, is your champion?" He eyed the leper sharply. "Clearly, he's seen better days."

The merchant gave a nod of approval, and Baldwin

removed his hood.

"I am Baldwin IV," he said, "of the Holy Land."

Judas nearly knocked over his stack of silver in surprise, yet Punch remained unconvinced. "And I'm the Sun King's nephew, twice removed from the throne." The latter scribbled a memo on a piece of parchment. "Lunatics of all stripes are welcome to the Colosseo. They tend to give some of the best shows. Or the worst. Depending on the hysteria."

At that moment, a troupe of masked jailers emerged to take Baldwin in irons. He complied and gave the merchant one last nod. Led down and deep into a labyrinth of cell blocks and cages, Baldwin faintly heard an exchange between Dairus and the ticketers.

"Can't believe he fell for it."

"Gullible as they come, I know."

Sudden rage flared in the leper's heart. Curses caught in his dry throat. He had been tricked. Against all sense and reason, he moved to tear his way back to the lobby, to rip the twins limb from limb—when a studded cudgel struck the back of his skull. Drifting into darkness, Baldwin's eyes darted about beasts and emaciated fighters, little more than sacks of sinew shackled to the wall. At last, he was thrown into his requested pit.

"Enjoy your new toy, Humbaba."

CHAPTER SIX

Gipi followed the courtiers with hesitation down the streets of the Old City, greeted with colonial reconstruction and rapidly gentrified districts. From the rubble of recent raids, white manors had been built over the bones of madrassas and mosques alike, fountains and rich gardens adopted for the pleasure of the occupying elite. Such an aristocracy on holiday fanned themselves in the heat, and their servants toiled under threat of the lash. And yet, even the peerage seemed to live in fear of the Fool General. The regional governor led his entourage like the host of a butcher's circus, hardly ignorant to his bloody reputation.

"Come," he called, "we have much to discuss."

Gipi could scarcely believe she had escaped execution, let alone that Pierrot was her savior. Whether on a whim or something more insidious, she did not know. Last night, locked in the interrogation cellar, she waited for the janissaries to carry out her due sentence for resisting arrest and disturbing the peace, when she received an unexpected visitor.

"You must be wondering," the Fool General said. "Why I didn't kill you—during your nasty little intervention in Nedlergate. And why I'm not going to kill you now."

Gipi did not reply, seated on a wooden chair, hands and wrists bound in irons.

The Fool General clapped sharply, and one of his aides emerged from the darkness with a cloche and tray, revealing a display of iced oysters and escargot. He plucked one such morsel with enthusiasm yet dined with unexpected civility.

"Most of the royal court does not approve of such foods, thinking it for common folk," he shot her a wink, placing the place just out of reach, "but we know better, don't we? How the best things can come from the real world. Where we're faced with ugly choices."

"Who are you?" Gipi asked, finally.

The Fool General's eyes shone with strange sincerity. "A friend. Something you seem to have in short supply. No king incognito is going to pay your ransom, I'm afraid—"

"How do you know that?"

"Oh, come now," he cracked a playful sneer, "the world is too small a place to allow Baldwin of Golgotha and his favorite troubadour to simply vanish into thin air." He stood, slowly, movements as fluid as the tide, and crept behind her chair. "You've seen my true nature already, or rather, a glimpse of it."

Gipi did not reply.

"Or is this merely a case of mistaken identity?" Her captor began to glide away. "Maybe you really are just a jester who lost her lute and stumbled upon my shores—knowing the quickest way to evade the janissaries by chance alone. In which case, best of luck—"

"Wait," Gipi called.

The Fool General paused. "Do the words," he spoke with slow deliberation, "'Malachite Pyramid,' mean anything to you?" He sneered over his shoulder. "Yes, or no."

"In what context?"

The Fool General uttered a mischievous laugh. "Shall I remove these shackles?"

Before Gipi could reply, the guards had already undone her bonds and opened the iron door to freedom. "Thank you," she shuddered, "General."

"Oh, please," he said, "call me Pierrot."

"Is this a trick?"

Pierrot rolled his eyes and did not reply. He never did come back for the oysters, leaving them to rot amidst the starving inmates and tortured screams.

Here and now, he seemed to enjoy playing tour guide and pointed out all manner of historic oddities and cultural nuances that alluded even Gipi.

The most recent of which was their destination.

Against the horizon, there loomed a black tower of wrought iron and open-latticed steel, ugly and superficial to behold. As to its purpose, Gipi did not know—in her disgust, she suspected it had no use at all, save for what the masses gave it. No artistic merit, no technical application, save its own sake. In any other context, it would've been a modern commentary on a waste of resources, but in its scale alone, it was a slap in the face to the proletarian, a mocking monument to the futility of this wretched occupation, to Pierrot's apathy, to notions of prosperity and all the pretty little words sultans and emperors spoke to placate the masses.

At least, the Fool General was an honest tyrant.

"What are your intentions with me?" she asked.

Pierrot rolled his eyes. "Oh, come now, Gipi. Just because I dress like a sultan doesn't mean I'm driven by such carnal impulses." He eyed the lesser viziers with disdain. "I'm not like them. Driven by the need to sow one's seed. Some men aren't born with that. Rare men who devote themselves to greatness in lieu of what's the word, what most use to secure a legacy."

For a fleeting moment, Gipi was unsure if the Fool General was being sincere. The way he mused in silence, eyes darting about the slender minarets, was unnerving. If she didn't know better, she would've thought it a moment of authenticity. "Children?" she guessed.

"Ah, yes," Pierrot twiddled his fingers in the air, "children! Thank you. I hate children." He laughed to himself, giddily. "Just wretched adults in the making. Only louder. Smellier. Successors that don't do anything to earn it, nine times out of ten."

Gipi forced a laugh. "Yeah, I'm not a fan either."

Pierrot glanced over his shoulder with an almost genuine smile. "That's why I like you. You've dined with kings and lepers alike. You accept the world for what it is. I respect that."

Gipi winced at the presumed allusion to Baldwin, but it was a fleeting thing.

"And what is the world?"

"Why, a cesspit of blood and shit," Pierrot laughed, likely louder than he meant to. "When I become emperor," he regained composure, "I'm going to outlaw children, you know."

"Sounds like a plan," Gipi said with mock enthusiasm, failing to mask her horror. "Never needed those bastards to carry on the future of civilization anyway...."

"Quite right, quite right."

At the latticed gates of the Iron Tower, the garish guard of Vermillion ranks made way with halberds at hand. He thrust open the doors with manic vigor, all but goose-stepping to announce his own magnificent return. Gipi was taken aback by the sharp contrast of the tower's interior — more a museum than a palace, a monument to the Fool General's conquests. From a taxidermied oliphant he once rode across the Alps, to the skulls of upstart chieftains, he was nothing if not a hunter of men. The true horror, however, did not lie in Pierrot's cruelty per se, but in its tactical precision, which yielded these results.

"Come," he called, "I want to show you something."

Gipi was escorted down the hall by a phalanx of armed guards, the walls adorned with numerous commissioned paintings of sacks and sieges the Fool General had overseen.

"Oh," Pierrot said, "I'm especially proud of that one. Poisoned half the kingdom's water supply to get them to capitulate. Left room for 'living space,' if you take my meaning."

"How quaint," Gipi muttered.

"This, however," Pierrot said, "is my pride and joy."

They came to a drawing room draped in gold pilfered from treasuries and tributes from the Grand Duchy of Chimay and neighboring nations. Pierrot reached for a crystal carafe and poured a pair of crimson shots — only to down them both with slippery ease. Haram, it seemed, did not apply to the occupying force. Not that the Fool General would care even if it did. He gestured widely to a surprisingly small and modern painting above the mantle.

"This is?" Gipi asked.

The painting was a postmodernist depiction of a colorless yet regal clown—sporting a sad smile despite all the motley and finery in the world, which he held in his hand as a sovereign's orb. Teary-eyed, the figure's posture was proud yet strained, as if carrying the weight of the world on his shoulders. Though Gipi knew the agonies of existence were anything but unique, be it in art or experience, she couldn't feel moved by the tragedy of the fool who would see himself as an emperor—lonely in his presumed excellence. Then it occurred to her, Pierrot did not merely wish to surpass his own humanity; in truth, he lamented its absence.

"A self-portrait," Pierrot said. "Awful, I know."

"No," Gipi said, mustering her sincerity, "it's evocative."

Pierrot mimicked the sad smile of his own image. "I'm a cubist in more ways than one," he poured himself yet another shot, "the idea that perception is to be vivisected and stitched back together always fascinated me. One's humanity is no different."

Gipi had grown weary of listening to the siliques of fools and corpses, but something about Pierrot piqued her interest, as if he were more than a misanthrope.

"I think I follow," she managed.

"You think," Pierrot repeated and reached into a set of drawers, withdrawing a familiar relic—one he had pilfered from the ruins of Nedlergate. "Do you know what this is?"

Gipi did not reply. Indeed, she had no idea what to think.

"Oh, come now," Pierrot said. "The Malachite Pyramid has been the subject of myths and legends the world over. You mean to tell me, a woman of your bardic talent doesn't know?"

"Afraid so."

Pierrot's smile faded, if only for a moment. "Well, no matter. It is a key, if you will, and a loathsome little key at that. As I may have mentioned in Nedlergate." He raised a spindly finger. "One that may unlock the way to reshape the world, or perhaps to *conquer* it." He sneered at the implications which eluded his hostage. "Come now, you know of what I speak." Setting the artifact on the drawing room table, he paced about the room. "A great power gestating beneath the earth. It is this power that the Vermillion Empire seeks to harness. To usher forth an age of prosperity—nothing so low as to sate the ambitions of petty despots, I assure you."

"I have no idea what you're talking about."

"Don't bother denying it." Pierrot's patience began to run thin. "Your dear Baldwin was after this imperial prize to further his own kingdom's agenda. Why else would a monarch stoop so low as to wade through the sewers? I hardly think that's his idea of a holiday."

Gipi scoffed and shook her head. "You don't know him at all, do you?"

Pierrot bit his lip. "No, perhaps not. Surely, though, a season of exploits didn't leave him unrewarded. He must've come across something of worth in his wanderings."

"Would be news to me." Gipi tried to play coy. "Besides, Captain Leechman took all of our possessions. And I mean all of them. You might want to ask what he didn't deliver."

Pierrot drummed his fingers upon the velvet couch. "I doubt it would grieve you to learn that Leechman was murdered last night. Sisters Dervish in the Zone Rouge. Knives in the back. Indeed, my men have searched the *Scheherazade* and her entire consort. Top to bottom."

Gipi shifted uncomfortably in her seat.

"We did, however," Pierrot reached into a lacquered chest, "find this."

At first, Gipi thought that the Fool General reached for some experimental weapon to dissolve flesh from bone, only to spy her lost lute—the same one Leechman had stolen.

"Here," he offered with grace, "I have no use for it. More of a vocalist myself."

Gipi took her, twisted her pegs nervously, and plucked the strings once more. She sighed with relief, feeling as if her hands were complete again.

"Thank you," she managed.

"Think nothing of it," Pierrot said and poured a shot of her own. "It's the least I can do, considering you're not to leave my sight or jurisdiction."

Gipi downed the drink without concern for poison or trickery.

"Figured," she admitted.

Gipi was guided up the spiraling stairs for many flights until she came to a high apartment with a balcony overlooking the entirety of Othello. The room was gaudy and garish—a carnival of colors, and the round bed was draped with a canopy of dreamcatchers. Ivory countertops and satin pillows aside, the Fool General spared no expense on décor. Though the twins took their leave, Gipi could sense their master creeping up the stairs.

"Why do I get the feeling you're keeping me as your jester?" she asked.

"Hmm," Pierrot mused, "a fool's fool? Quite a notion. Never occurred to me, but yes, let's go with that." He shut the door, slowly. "Sleep well, Gipi."

She did not, despite all the comforts that Othello and Khand had to offer. Languishing in bed, Gipi listened to the rattle of bone chimes and watched eerie shadows along the walls. As the moon loomed over the minarets, she reached for her lute and began to play a nocturne of shadows inspired by such scenery. Though she was hardly a damsel, her thoughts wandered to Baldwin—whether he was still swinging his sword like the lunatic she knew. Regardless, Gipi was content to play to whatever listened in the dark. No one was coming to her rescue.

CHAPTER SEVEN

Musk and mildew wafted throughout the winding dungeons beneath the Colosseo. Baldwin watched shadows dance against torchlight and endured the dry moans of the imprisoned. The hulking silhouette of Humbaba lurked in the corner, cracking his swollen knuckles amidst a bed of bones and wet straw—unbothered by his new cellmate. Betrayed yet unbroken, the leper staggered to his feet and apprised the strength of the iron bars.

Sea green rust aside, they were deceptively sturdy.

"Don't bother," said the thrall. "If they could be bent, I would be free long ago." Humbaba rose to splash his face with bad water from the trough. Truly, the gladiators were livestock confined to squalid pens. Baldwin kept his distance. The crack of a lash pierced the pervading gloom. The thrall towered as a goliath of a man, cursed with impossible strength—a beast to be pitted against lesser murderers and madmen.

"You're new," he said. "Wing's for ranked fighters."

"It was my request."

"Eager to salute and die, are we?"

Baldwin smirked at the notion. "More or less." He eyed the hulk in the shadows. "I watched today's duel," he said. "You fought most gallantly."

Humbaba scoffed. "You're a long way from the Holy Land." He laid a wrapped hand on the leper's shoulder. "Bit of friendly advice. Best look after yourself. No one else will."

Baldwin was taken aback by the thrall's soft-spoken nature.

"Odd," he said. "I took you for the Butcher."

"Stage performance," Humbaba said. "Crowd loves someone to shit on." His eyes gleamed in the lamplight, deep yet inquisitive. "How'd you wind up here?"

"Bought and sold," Baldwin admitted with a shudder of indignity. "Corsairs raided the Cinque Ports, and I was among the captured." He sat on a chained bench and clasped his wrists. "However, fortune seems to be on our side. If we are to fight together."

"Together?" Humbaba said. "You mean, each other."

"I beg your pardon—?"

"Cellmates are to get to know each other before the match. So we can put on a good show for the Fool General." He scoffed. "What? Did Darius not tell you?"

Baldwin fettered his renewed rage with a deep breath. "He neglected to mention."

"You're not the first sod he's sold."

Against his better judgment, words of defensive accusation escaped the leper's lips. "They say you sacrificed your son to the brass bull—"

"Speak of that again, and I'll break your legs."

Baldwin saw a gleam of ferocity in the thrall's eyes and thought better than to antagonize him further. With a nod of agreement, the leper paced about the straw-strewn cell. Despite the manipulation of a merchant, he remembered the rumor of his own people being forced to kill once in the name of the Sultan Khan, now for the Fool General. The notion filled him with rage.

"I was to inspire you to rise against—"

"Spare me," Humbaba growled. "As if we haven't tried."

"What do you mean?"

"It's hard to save those who don't want it," the thrall sighed. "Janissaries. Half of these cells are training grounds to weed out the weak for the sultan's guard."

"Was Solomon such a champion?"

"Well on his way to being one."

"Surely, not all of you are under consideration—"

"You're gonna get your ass beat, you know that? Just not by me."

Baldwin crossed his arms and said no more.

"This is the labor wing." The thrall spoke with diction which Baldwin found oddly familiar. "We're condemned to die for the amusement of the masses. Any questions?"

"Just one, if you please," the leper said, lowering his hood, letting his regal bearing and failing flesh punctuate his presence. "I am King of the Holy Land of Golgotha, or, at least, I was. Truth be told, I've heard word of people of the faith imprisoned in this complex. I've come to liberate them. Will you join my cause?"

Humbaba stared at him in bewilderment. "Oh, I see. You're insane."

"I — well, yes," Baldwin shrugged, "but that's hardly the point."

Humbaba laughed and patted the leper's back. "Delusions go far down here. It'll keep you alive longer than most. Hang on to the memory of the high castle, 'your majesty.'"

"You don't believe me?"

"What? That you've come to lead us to freedom?" Humbaba rolled his eyes. "You were tricked. Punch and Judas saw an opportunity and took it. Besides," he muttered, clutching a bent talisman hanging from his neck. "Golgotha hasn't sent ambassadors in years."

"You are from the Holy Land?"

"Would you believe a 'murderer?'"

"No," Baldwin said, ignorant to the implication. "I suppose not."

Humbaba snorted. "Figures." With that, the thrall returned to his bed and leaned against the wall. "Get some rest, 'Baldwin,'" he said, "you'll have work cut out for you in a bit."

"Sorry," the leper said. "I don't recall giving you my name."

Humbaba eyed him mockingly. "Am I wrong?"

"No," Baldwin said. "It's just —"

At that moment, the jangle of iron keys interrupted the banter of prisoners. "Alright," called a guard in an iron collar and coif. "Shift change. Get moving."

"Shift — ?"

"Shut up and get going!" the guard slapped him with a studded cudgel. "Salt won't mine itself. And you," he yelled at the thrall, "teach him the ropes."

Baldwin contained his fury, if only for a moment. In any other circumstance, he would've killed the cur then and there. However, if he were to inspire his people, the leper would need to make certain that all could see that the wardens could bleed.

Humbaba took his time, towering over the guards, and came to Baldwin's side. "Well," he said. "You heard the master," he said, calmly. "Come on, I'll show you."

"That's right," squealed the guard. "Move it."

Baldwin was forced to march among the enslaved, down the underpass to the Zone Rouge and its bloodstained quarries. A light at the tunnel's end all but blinded him, but the prisoners were crowded into a great lift and slowly lowered by mule-power into the depths. No stairwells or exits were lit. Old and young, fit and lame, all were equal in expense. Baldwin and Humbaba were shoved onto a crowded ferry to a lower portion of the mines. Rowers with scarred backs ushered them to their destination. The short trek took them along a river of livid green brine. Truth be told, the leper recalled little of his descent. Before he knew it, Baldwin was forced to dig with a pick at hand, chipping away at colossal blocks of salt. His only companions were the screams of despair and the shadowed hulk by his side. He thoughtlessly endured the humiliations — taking solace in that he felt no pain.

Three days of this toil. Unless —

"Easy." Humbaba cupped his shoulder. "Don't delve too deep. Trust me, you'll feel the sting. Here," he began to hoist the heavy cart, burdened with salt, "let's head back."

"I am not to look after myself?" Baldwin asked.

Humbaba rolled his eyes and muttered something under his breath. The hulk heaved the cart along the tracks to the depot. Baldwin continued to heave and grind against the basin, each stroke a wave against the shore, lost in a trance. He did not look at his fellow man, weeping and crumpling in fatigue, lucid to the truth — that he was a tourist of suffering. So, the leper continued for two days with neither food nor rest. The slaves looked upon him in awe and disgust.

"Who the hell is he?"

"No way he can keep that up."

"Poor bastard's gonna burn himself out."

In Baldwin's heart of hearts, he thought himself stronger in spirit. If only the slaves recognized their own strength, perhaps the city would be a different place. Come the second day, the leper was numb to the salt against his own lesions, stroke upon stroke, until the corpse wagons stood at the ready.

"You're still here?" Humbaba asked.

Baldwin had dug a lonely path into the deep quarry, impossible by mortal standards. He had uncovered a crimson vein and half-fossilized fingers jutting from the earth. Baldwin did not relent. The discovery mattered not to him. He would prove his strength to his people — to himself. Toiling, he unearthed a corpse mummified in salt, emaciated and utterly dehydrated, little more than a rigid cadaver that fell and broke upon the floor.

Great rumbling echoed throughout nowhere and everywhere alike.

"That's enough," Humbaba said.

Lost in a trance, Baldwin continued, willfully deaf to the thrall's words.

"Enough," he tore the axe from his hand, "you'll stir the mine!"

"Is that not the strength of one man?" Baldwin scoffed, eyes gleaming in the lamplight. "Could I alone cause the mine to falter? This institution of suffering?"

"Spare me," Humbaba spat.

"Are you so content — ?"

The thrall's fist collided with Baldwin's remnant of a nose, sending the leper reeling on his back. "Watch your words, your majesty. This isn't the palace."

The snapping threat of the lash was enough to separate the two.

"Break it up!" shouted the overseer.

Baldwin spat a mouthful of blood onto the stone floor. Slaves had gathered to gawk at the scene. The leper stood, roughly, and wiped the salt from his knees, palms raw and oozing with pus. He did not so much as wince. He merely passed Humbaba by and collected his axe. Alone in his conviction, Baldwin basked in the notion of martyrdom. His thoughts were hazy with dancing shades, swearing that Death herself scoffed at his exertions.

Someone clapped from across the cavern.

"There we have it," the guard jeered, "a pacesetter! Keep it up, and it'll be a half-portion for your efforts." He called to the rabble. "See this? This is what a model prisoner looks like."

The leper had earned the entire garrison's attention, feeling the lantern's light upon him.

The garrison erupted in mocking laughter.

"Here you go," he tossed a strip of jerk at Baldwin's feet, "a bonus for you—"

In a fit of lunatic justice, Baldwin delivered the pickaxe to the guard's skull. His eyes burst out of a shattered skull, and blood splattered the walls. Shock and silence filled the tunnel.

"What've you done?" Humbaba gasped. "They'll kill us all!"

"No," Baldwin tossed him the axe, "they'll kill you unless you fight." His voice rose to a righteous bellow. "That goes for all of you! Take up arms!"

Humbaba stared on, stupefied by the leper's audacity.

"Kill all who stand in the way of your freedom," Baldwin roared. "Those who would deprive you of your faith!" He cut through guard after guard, relishing in the terror in their wide eyes. "Your king and country demand it, for I am Baldwin of Golgotha, and I have come to free you. Once more unto the breach! For all that is good and godly!"

The slaves looked upon the scene in horror. Baldwin was a monstrosity to behold, lifting guards by the throat only to snap their necks with tremendous strength. His chains and manacles were weapons in their own right, colliding with skulls and ribs, sending the enemy crumpling in his wake. He heaved and seethed, all but laughing mad.

The alarm had sounded.

Reinforcements arrived, arquebuses at the ready, taking ill-aimed potshots into the panicking crowd. Mad with fever and rage, the leper led the charge, even if no one else dared to follow. Beating and biting, he sought to instill terror in the hearts of his supposed masters, but was overwhelmed by bodies alone. Pinned to the ground and with a pistol in his mouth, Baldwin felt the swarthy opponent atop him, finger twitching over the trigger. Suddenly, a hulking form barreled forth and tackled the warden aside, crushing his body effortlessly like the hooves of a veldt-beast. Humbaba's back was to the leper, but at least he'd found his courage.

"Take their blades," said the thrall. "Fight to the Cothon!"

Baldwin nodded in gratitude and took up the scimitar. He looked to the crowds, watching as even the most malnourished among them pilfered arms and armor from the slain guards. A shoddy army, but an army nonetheless. Torch, sword, and gun at hand, they gathered speed, and fire shone in their eyes, the fevered will to live, the same will he'd taken for granted.

"We take the ferries," Humbaba said. "Go!"

Baldwin noticed the brands among the rising slaves, scarred in the shape of the saltire, alluding to their status as infidels in the land. Soon, they would be free men.

"I am grateful for your aid," he said. "We make for the surface."

"Not like we have a choice," growled the thrall.

———

Gipi sat in the second-story salon, content to sip her cannabis tea, across the long table from Pierrot, who nibbled on bits of kabab, dates, and saffron rice. The silence was eerie, and she could hear the Fool General chew with every second. Stunted guards flanked the threshold, arms behind their backs, ever at the whims of their master, as minions in miniature.

"So," Gipi said, "we've got a tournament coming up."

"That we do," Pierrot said. "A celebration of the occupation. What better way to make the common filth feel better about themselves? Man's a cannibal, after all."

"Uh-huh." She did not bother to debate. "Tomorrow, right?"

Pierrot masked a dainty burp. "Indeed." With the snap of his fingers, he summoned a servant to refill his carafe with crimson liquor. "It will be quite the spectacle."

"I'm surprised you're willing to indulge in common appetites."

"Oh, make no mistake," Pierrot winked, "this isn't about the people."

Something about the Fool General's delivery made Gipi more than uneasy. She looked about, eying the baroque paintings and trophies of conquered kingdoms, a museum of stolen curios and finery. Indeed, she felt as if the entourage served as an exhibit in such a collection, each a gimmick to be fawned over for its novelty. Suddenly, the doors burst open.

"Forgive the intrusion, sir," a sweat-soaked janissary took the knee, "there's a slave uprising in the Zone Rouge. They've taken the mines."

Pierrot said nothing. He speared a bit of spiced beef, bending the fork backwards as a mock catapult, and flung the morsel at the janissary's face.

"Sir — ?"

"I'm sorry," Pierrot spoke at last. "Just who are you speaking to?"

"M-my apologies, general," the soldier said. "Our garrisons were overwhelmed. The ferries are gone. They're likely headed to the Cothon."

"Well then," the Fool General said, "we can't have that, can we?" He stood slowly and pushed in his seat. He came to the window overlooking the sprawl of Othello and leaned against the sill. "Who instigated them, I wonder?" he mused. "They're usually so docile. Like cattle...."

Gipi knew the answer and suspected her captor did as well, but she dared not speak up, lest she earn the ire of Pierrot and the legions at his disposal.

"Your orders, general?"

Pierrot sneered. "Let them go."

"What—?"

"You heard me," Pierrot said. "Tournament's canceled. Let them have their freedom." He eyed the look of perplexed horror on everyone's face, basking in their wordless objection. "Oh," his words oozed with melodrama. "Oh," he sighed, "I'm sure they've been inspired by a leader far greater than I." He grasped Gipi's shoulder, relishing in her shudders, then spun to face the janissary. "Sarcasm must be a foreign concept, I know. Flood the mines. I want the city on high alarm. Kill anyone and everyone violating curfew, but I want Baldwin alive."

"Baldwin?" the janissary asked.

"The 'leper errant,' you idiot," Pierrot snapped. "He's on the roster." He glowered at the captain. "Well? Don't just stand there. Lead the way!"

Gipi stood as quietly as she could, slinking in the general's shadow. Despite her anger and abandonment, she longed to see Baldwin again, if only to ensure his life.

"Oh, no," Pierrot wagged a finger, "no, no, you stay here."

"What are you going to do to him?" Gipi blurted, her etiquette and instinct to survive vanishing in the wake of protective rage.

Pierrot merely snickered to himself and turned to the tower guard. "Make sure she doesn't leave. And you lot, see that preparations are underway for the tournament. We don't want to disappoint our 'special guest.'"

Surrounded by soldiers in shakos and tassels, Gipi watched as the Fool General departed to commit the unspeakable. And yet, she clenched her fists. Though she did nothing then, she would not stand by idly and let it come to pass. Her eyes darted to the open window.

———

Guided by the lantern's light, the free and faithful rowed down the canal in single file, waves of brine splashing the densely barnacled hull. Baldwin and Humbaba led the vanguard through the shallows and against the rocks. Hours bled together, and they spoke of many things.

"I've never been to the Holy Land," Humbaba said.

"Was your father a slave?"

"And his before him."

"I see."

"We were told stories by our priests," the thrall spoke in reverence. "Of the Cathedral City and the old olive trees. Is it true what they say? Is it really so beautiful? That we are free to practice our faith there? Without fear of persecution?"

"It is," Baldwin said. "All are welcome in Golgotha." He hadn't the heart to tell the truth. That he knew well of the raids on the eastern shore and neglected to pay the ransom of generations — save the odd noble or cleric of note. "I will not rest until you and your kinsmen are home once more. The freedom of all faiths is something I hold most sacred."

"Why did you leave?" Humbaba asked.

Baldwin eyed the loopholes and slits against the curvature of the ceiling, listening carefully for any sign of musketeers lurking in the battlements within. He raised a lesioned hand, bidding the rowers to soften their strokes. "Something's wrong," he said.

"What — ?"

Though all but blind in the blackness, Baldwin heard the grind of metal against stone. Slowly, the water began to rise with white rapids.

"Abandon ship!" someone cried.

"No," Humbaba roared. "Keep rowing! We're almost to the Cothon."

They quickened their pace in frantic unison. The sluice gates moaned open, flooding the tunnel within moments. A frothing wave knocked the leper off his boat, sending him careening into deep, dark water. Scimitar at hand, he hearkened to the muffled cries of his men and let the current take its merciless course. Feeling his way along the canal, Baldwin groped his way to the shrinking surface and gasped for air, his mouth inches from the ceiling—and plunged into the water once more. Though his fortitude was fleeting, the leper held his breath for what seemed an eternity, until the aqueduct spewed him and many others out of an unknown drain.

No torch or lamp was to be lit, but the moon shone bright over the salt-stained cove, shedding scant light upon the rocks and pumiced formations.

"Where are we?" Baldwin wheezed, taking in a lungful of seaside air.

Humbaba groaned as he staggered to his sandaled feet. "We got flushed out."

Harbor bells echoed in the distance, and the silhouettes of docked ships swayed in the distance. The leper smiled at such dumb luck. "We can set sail on one of these ships," he said. "Hurry!" he rallied his men. "We are an arm's breadth from freedom!"

Those who remained scuttled like wharf rats, desperately clawing their way along and over the rocky shore. To Baldwin's surprise, the nearest ship was indeed the *Scheherazade*, likely decommissioned since the death of its captain. The irony did not escape him. So the slaves boarded the ship. The leper beamed in disbelief as joy warmed his heart to see his people go.

Raising his head and basking in the westward wind against his lips, he prepared to board himself when a wayward thought pierced his mind.

Gipi....

Though Baldwin's duty lay with his people, so too was Gipi his dearest friend. Though the needs of the desperate masses undoubtedly came before his own, something kept the leper rooted where he stood. He was torn between two loyalties. Gipi was in the custody of the Fool General, locked away in the harem's tower. A fate worse than death, in her opinion.

Humbaba gripped his shoulder. "Your majesty?"

Baldwin did not so much as flinch, thoughts fixed on his most grievous error, even if it had led to the happiest moment of these people's lives. He'd already made his choice. Eyes fixed upon white sails in the moonlight, Baldwin took a single step forward. Before he could speak his mind, shouts of panic erupted aboard the *Scheherazade*. Clusters of lights flickered upon the deck. Baldwin reached for his scimitar, but Humbaba raised his gigantic hands.

"No use," said the thrall. "They've got us surrounded...."

Sure enough, the janissaries had the entire mob in their sights, waiting for the order to deliver a massacre. Despite his righteous fever, Baldwin let his scimitar clatter to the ground and helped the injured upright, glowering at the rider cantering from behind.

"Pierrot," the leper growled.

"Hello again," the rider did not dismount, content to smirk atop his horse, "your 'majesty.'" He eyed his quarry up and down. "You've definitely seen better days."

Baldwin did not reply.

"I must say, your ability to inspire these steers is enviable. Why, if I had even a dozen such doting men, well, I wouldn't just be the Fool General of Vermillion."

"Be careful," Humbaba whispered to his liege.

"I've dealt with this madman before," Baldwin said. "You will pay for the innocents you've slaughtered," he pointed a lesioned finger at the rider, "I was there. In the city, you raised to the ground. How many, Pierrot? How many died that night alone? Have you no soul?"

"Are you quite done?"

Baldwin opened his mouth, as if to speak, and yet, he knew that nothing could guilt or sway the Fool General.

"At any rate, you'll have to be more specific, I'm afraid," Pierrot sneered, as if amused by the leper's naivety. "Vermillion's scorched more than a few cities."

"You—!"

"Is life really so precious to you?" Pierrot raised a pistol, cocking it with cruel intent. "I wonder if your 'comrades' share such noble conviction?" He addressed the trembling and downtrodden. "Make no mistake, slave you were and slaves you are, but I'm feeling magnanimous tonight. Come quietly and you might live to see sunrise." He lowered his head. "Perhaps we've been a bit harsh. What with the ration cuts and work quotas." He winced, as if those words tasted like vomit in his throat. "If you please, I've better things to do than to slaughter you all." One by one, the slaves took the knee, much to Baldwin's disgust— Humbaba neither first nor last among them. "Considering that you slew Dampe," Pierrot spoke to the leper, "I'm curious to see you in action. You'll be the highlight of the tournament."

"What are you scheming?" he muttered.

Pierrot chuckled, but said no more. With the faithful surrendering to shackles, so began the quiet march to the Colosseo. Once more, Baldwin was forced to obey. Suddenly, a low droning filled the heavens, and the moon was blotted out by the silhouette of a magnificent flying machine. Inching ever to the Iron Tower, the *Tarrasque* had come to Othello once more, though no guns rolled to starboard and no dragoons leapt to the streets below.

Something was wrong.

CHAPTER EIGHT

Gipi crept about the dust-choked narrows of the Old City, having since descended the riveted battlements of the Iron Tower. True to Pierrot's orders, the janissaries were on high alert and patrolled the alleys, particularly near the sodden piers of the Cothon. Slipping from shadow to shadow, she came to the boardwalk suspended over shallows littered with flotsam and jetsam. Torchlight and rallying bootsteps drew near. Gipi leapt into the water at low tide, careful not to slice her leg on barnacles and strewn junk—when a glint of steel caught her eyes. The Broken Blade gleamed in the moonlight, left to rust in the debris. She recognized it instantly.

Tears in her eyes, Gipi drew the sword from the briny sea. *Baldwin....*

The janissaries searched the harbor's edge, scanning the perimeter for any sign of escapees or suspicious activity, clutching their arquebuses, hands over the hilts of sheathed scimitars. Gipi pressed her thin body against the flagstone wall, holding her breath, waiting for the brigade to pass her by, when she spied a low formation of shadows stalking the flat rooftops, cloaks fluttering silently as banners in the midnight wind. Before she could so much as speculate as to who—or what—they were, a thrown knife had slit the commanding officer's throat. With a gurgling gasp, he fell dead, blood pooling from his neck, and the janissaries were cut down within moments, slain by a troupe of cloaked strangers—those who had liberated the slaves in the bazaar, the Sisters Dervish who harassed the Vermillion occupation.

Gipi's eyes widened in horror. She was unsure what to say or do. The figures stared at her in turn, faces shrouded in darkness. Slowly, she raised her hands and forced a smile, eyes fixed on the arsenal of drawn blades. With an exchange for silent asides, they had the fool surrounded, and one threw a pocket of pale dust in her face. Before she could rightly react, Gipi had inhaled a lungful of the substance. Her eyes rolled over and she collapsed face first into the wet sand, only to be hoisted upright, senses numbed, brought aboard an unknown vessel.

"Well," an unfamiliar voice breached her stupor, "a promise is a promise."

———

Baldwin was cast into solitary confinement once more, the cell door shut behind him. Left in darkness to brood and fester, the leper sat on the damp stone floor, content to wait for morning — for the coming ordeal by combat. A narrow slit of a high window blessed him with air, though no wind reached him. He did not fear death, and yet, anger festered in his heart — these people, his people, enslaved by the corsairs of Othello, were conditioned to accept their fate, robbed of hope and ambition. Perhaps they deserved this, helpless as they were, woefully incapable of shedding their own shackles, even if galvanized by the King of the Holy Land. Such darkness twisted his thoughts, reducing the leper to a bitter shell of a monarch. Cowards to the last, he could not lead those unwilling to fight nor fend for themselves.

He would shed no tears for another lost cause.

Whether by fever or madness born of despair, Baldwin watched his breath waft in pale clouds, and a bitter chill pervaded the cell. The world seemed a fogbound facsimile of what he knew. Torchlight throughout the cell block waned rapidly, little more than a row of corpse-candles. He was greeted by a forlorn presence watching him from afar.

Death had come once more.

Wreathed in a threadbare hood and cloak, she emerged from Baldwin's own shadow, towering over the leper in a gaunt form. This apparition, eerie as it was, had little relation to the cosmology of the ancients or the faiths he knew, angels or daemons, though she took on the guise of such iconography. She seemed to manifest from beyond the pantheons of old, attempting to filter her timeless will into mortal language — the image of the reaper. Leaning on her humble scythe, the psychopomp was a spectator to Baldwin's anguish, though she had not come to claim a soul so tortured as he. Not yet. The leper looked upon Death in veneration, knowing well that she could harvest his final breath on a whim, should it be ordained by God.

"Your power to inspire has atrophied," she broke the long silence.

Baldwin did not reply; in truth, he hadn't the will to speak.

"To think you once achieved a great victory against the Easterlings, and yet, you cannot so much as rally your enslaved subjects to save themselves."

"Have you come to mock me?"

"Nothing of the sort," Death said. "However, this is not how I imagined your end. Such a bitter resignation. Is this all it takes to tarnish your crusade?"

"I cannot lead those unwilling to follow," Baldwin snapped.

Death bowed her head. "No, perhaps it is more than that. Your house had long left these people to fend for themselves, content to wage war against the sultanate from the comfort of the Holy City. Such unwelcome responsibilities have since passed to the regent, though you'd be a fool to ignore the guilt seeping into your conscience. These people, these folk you've left behind, suffered from your own inaction as much as the slaver's lash." Her hollow eyes pierced through Baldwin, who shivered upon her judgment. "Their failures are yours."

Baldwin stood, swiftly, though still in shackles. "What would you have me do? Should I not have abdicated my throne? Should I have languished in royal comforts? And mindlessly let the fever take me?" He glowered at the reaper. "I refuse to submit to that."

"Perhaps not," Death smiled bitterly. "However, to blame the learned helplessness of these people on lethargy alone is truly a sin." She bowed her head, seemingly all the taller in ill lighting. "Would you abandon these folk as you've abandoned your birthright?"

"Enough!" Baldwin roared. "I am not some lowly vagrant—"

"What have you truly accomplished in your wanderings hitherto?" Death asked. "You have witnessed much of the world's cruelty, but failed to prevent the spread of such evil at every time. From the Massacre of Gravesend to the Great Fire of Nedlergate, your pursuit has been a pilgrimage to nothing at all. And now, on midsummer's eve, you've squandered half a year—your final year—only to wince at the thought of committing yourself to the greatness you claim to crave. What shall you choose? Heroism? Or cowardice?"

Baldwin was at a loss for words, stupefied by the audacity of Death. Should anyone else dared to speak to him as such, the leper would've challenged them to a duel, but Death was ephemeral and would not quail at any threat or retort by the sword. And in the throes of his own vulnerability, Baldwin was forced to harken to the words of the reaper. Death smiled, bitterly, as if sensing her words delivering a pain the leper had thought himself numb to. It wasn't sadism per se, but a cruel mentorship, a will to temper and reforge Baldwin's spirit through a crucible of shame. Come the cock's crow, Death's presence began to recede.

"Should you continue blindly down this path," she said. "You will die only to gaze upon your squandered own works, and despair. Until we meet again."

Dawn's first light crept through the lone window.

Baldwin heard a metallic shriek, and the cell door opened. Hoisted to his bandaged feet by the wardens, the leper was escorted to the armory where he was to browse a barrack's worth of weaponry, martial and exotic, from mauls and maces to antiquated swords. He examined the racks with limited interest until something caught his eye—the Broken Blade. How it had wound up in the gladiatorial armory, the leper neither knew nor cared, but sighed with relief as he gripped its hilt once more. For the first time since his abduction in the Cinque Ports, Baldwin had been reunited with the symbol of his doomed crusade. In that alone, he found strength, shutting his eyes and summoning a second wind. Slowly, the great gates opened and the iron portcullis lifted, blinding him with a barrage of harshest daylight. The thunderous cheers of hundreds filled his ears, reverberating off the armory's walls, bidding him to face the tournament ahead.

Something by which he would solemnly abide.

Surrounded by rings upon rings of brightly canvased seating, Baldwin gawked at the terrible vastness of the crowd. The Colosseo was filled to the brim with the rancorous masses, by merchants and gamblers from every walk of life — a cosmopolitan carnival of privilege who would heckle and jeer at those about to salute and die for their bloodthirsty amusement. Splatters of fresh blood already caked the coagulated layer of sand. Mangled corpses had been heaped into wagons to be wheeled off and dumped into mass graves on the desert's fringe. No physician's mercy awaited the wounded, and those who craved murder would find ample opportunity to sate their thirst. Much to Baldwin's disgust, the Fool General waved at him from his sultan's box, sneering at the forced combatant with condescension.

In truth, Baldwin did not listen to Pierrot's waxing speech, content to kneel in prayer to spite these heathens, to brace himself for the countless lives he would take. The initial matches were seemingly primed to wear him down, or perhaps to inspire overconfidence. Swinging the Broken Blade as an executioner in his own right, Baldwin would cleave through sinew and bone, delivering the scantily armored challengers to the only peace they would ever know. Midway through the tournament, Baldwin paused to collect himself — the sheer magnitude of the violence he'd partaken in was intoxicating, though he justified it as necessary for his own survival. Leaning against his broadsword, its blade planted into the earth, he wiped the blood and sweat from his salt-soaked brow. Without warning, the portcullis lifted once more, revealing a familiar hulk of a silhouette. One who emerged from a darkened corridor.

Baldwin's eyes widened in horror, recognizing his next foe.

"Humbaba?" he gasped. "No, wait—!"

Before he could plead or appeal to reason, the Butcher charged like a rabid bull, narrowly missing Baldwin as a spiked elbow grazed his chest. The mutual combatants locked eyes for a moment and shared an understanding of the loathsome show they were to perform; Baldwin merely refused to accept it. Dodging and parrying Humbaba's reckless blows, the leper felt each strike make its mark, threatening to shatter his bones, for the thrall would indeed play the role of the heel, if only to earn an extra bit of hardtack and a canteen of clean water.

"I am sorry," Humbaba muttered.

Baldwin shoved his opponent back yet refused to swing his blade, choosing to pace about the Butcher—something the audience mistook for cowardice.

"Listen to me," the leper raised a bandaged hand, "it doesn't have to be like this—"

"Spare me," Humbaba roared, as if trying to force his ambivalence into rage. "No speeches can save us." His eyes gleamed with resentment beneath the bronze helm. "The world you knew, the epics you hold so precious, they mean nothing to us common folk. Down here in the filth."

"You're wrong."

A rancid beet pelted the leper's shoulder, likely thrown by an impatient onlooker to goad him into violence. Baldwin merely sighed and raised a middle finger without a glance. Humbaba slammed his gauntleted fists together, as if in warning, and leapt into the hot, dry air like a lunatic ape. Baldwin was tackled to the ground, the very breath knocked loose from his lungs—ears ringing, vision blurred, he scarcely felt Humbaba strike his cuirass, again and again, the Butcher barely refraining from shattering the leper's ribs, if only to prolong the duel for the appeasement of the masses. In a fit of unforeseen strength, Baldwin shoved Humbaba off his corpse of a body and rolled aside, retrieving the Broken Blade.

At that moment, the leper's mind was made.

"I will not enjoy this," he confessed.

On the offensive, he drove Humbaba back with a flurry of heavy swings, the momentum and weight of steel. The leper's unrelenting fury was enough to knock his opponent off balance — his blade colliding with the Butcher's gauntlets, chipping through their bronze and slicing into the sinew of his knuckles. Humbaba cried out in pain.

"Is this truly what you desire?" the leper asked.

Humbaba did not reply, tears welling in his eyes.

"Very well," Baldwin said. "Allow me to prove you wrong."

He drove the Broken Blade deeper between the hulk's massive fingers — a warning as to what the leper knew he was capable of. Humbaba's eyes watered with agonized wrath, and he punched at Baldwin's liver, again and again, but the leper did not flinch, cutting ever deeper into the Butcher's wrist and toward his forearm — every struggle met with worsening agony.

Baldwin glowered at his sorry opponent. He recalled the rumor of a child's death by Humbaba's hands. The leper knew the shame that entailed, though he had no right to call himself a father. Glowering upon the pit-fighter, listening to the jeers of the audience, chosen words escaped Baldwin's lips.

"Your son's death was not your doing."

Tears welled in the thrall's eyes.

Suddenly, Baldwin dislodged the sword from his opponent's hand and swung widely and wildly, slicing into Humbaba's torso yet not so deeply as to cut his entrails. Somewhere between shock and despair, the Butcher slumped to his side and raised his injured hand — whether acknowledging defeat or unwilling to fight his liege, Baldwin did not know. And yet, for the first time since the tournament's onset, he heard the approval of the crowd, chanting his name.

Time seemed to slur in a maddened stupor.

Baldwin lowered his blade, basking in the love of the people, something he'd almost forgotten. Slowly, the leper began to recall what it was like to be cheered and admired, and felt a genuine smile betray his misgivings to such a barbaric custom — until his gaze wandered to Pierrot, who gave a nod of mock respect and a thumbs down, a silent order for Humbaba's execution. Baldwin turned back to the Butcher, beginning to understand the allure of the Colosseo — of the vapid pursuit of glory through violence. Should he have never known the luxuries of courtly life, the leper would've proven far less noble than Humbaba, that much he knew for certain. Without so much realizing it, Baldwin had already raised the Broken Blade, one last swing from ending his opponent's life, and yet, remembered Death's words of righteous scorn. Neither fame nor fortune could absolve Baldwin of the impending deed, nor fill the void that would be left in his fevered heart, should he betray his own creed — tempted though he was. In lieu of mindless slaughter, the leper impaled the blood-soaked sand an inch from Humbaba's skull, turning his rising anger to Pierrot, hatred drowning all sense and reason.

The crowd fell morbidly silent.

"Is this the best you mongrels have to offer?" he roared. "Slaves and mad apes? No. I believe there is a better match for me yet. Come, Fool General of Vermillion!" He raised his blade at the sultan's box. "Are you so drunk on your own victories that you've forgotten what it means to be a warrior?" He sneered. "Come and fight me yourself!"

Pierrot, seemingly stunned at first, burst into laughter and dismissed the challenge with the wave of a white handkerchief. "Very well," he sighed. "Kill them both."

The janissaries raised their arms and took aim, much to Baldwin's disappointment, barrels pointed at the upstart gladiators, moments from opening fire. The crowd murmured in confusion, as if unable to quite digest what had happened — when a low droning filled the Colosseo from above, the sun was blotted out by the vast bilge and silhouette of a heavenward vessel. Then came the cannon fire. Baldwin tackled Humbaba aside as a portion of the upper battlements came crashing down upon the loathsome arena. Within moments, the crowd had erupted into hysteria, and Pierrot lunged out of his silk-cushioned seat, shouting commands to his stunned guard. Amidst the chaos, as the masses trampled each other along the ringed rows like stampedes of frightened wildebeests, Baldwin watched in terrible awe as riotous flames swallowed the tents and coverings; the Colosseo humbled by an onslaught of small arms and booming mortars. Over the starboard, a rope ladder descended from the dirigible.

Baldwin heard a shout above even the rising cacophony, faintly recognizing the familiar jingle of cap and bells, as a thin wave beckoned him to climb.

"Gipi," the leper shouted in happy disbelief. "Is that—?"

"Shut up and climb!"

Baldwin turned to Humbaba, who was obviously troubled by the notion of climbing hempen rungs with a lacerated hand. He nodded, as if accepting his fate, only for the leper to hoist his opponent upright, glaring at him in a wordless demand to do better.

Together, they began to climb.

Slowly, the dirigible rose and departed the amphitheater. Against his better judgment, Baldwin looked down upon the sultan's box—Pierrot stared back with the promise of murder in his eyes. At last, the vendetta was mutual. As Baldwin was lifted aboard by swarthy hands, the dirigible had already flown across the Zone Rouge to the east. High wind swept his threadbare cloak. The Iron Tower began to fade into the distance, little more than an adamantine spike rising from the urban morass. Leagues upon leagues of empty desert lay before his unforeseen course, a vista of sunbaked dunes with neither mountain nor cedar forest in sight—a far cry from the Holy Land. When the leper had regained his wits, he turned to face Gipi, who approached him swiftly. Before he could so much as speak or embrace his fool, her hand flew and struck the bronze mask from his face. It clattered across the deck. Silence stung the air until Baldwin spoke at last.

"I suppose I deserved that."

Gipi did not reply, tears of rage and relief in her eyes.

"I," Baldwin began, "I am sorry, Gipi. For everything. I am unworthy of your friendship. My abandonment of you was unjust. You deserve better than the peril I've put you in." He could hardly bear to look at her, caressing the lesions riddling his face, embracing the atrophy of his flesh. "I do not expect your forgiveness, but—"

"You're an idiot," Gipi said. "But," she looked about the airship's crew, "without your poor life choices, I doubt we would've ever saved so many."

Baldwin knelt to retrieve his mask. "What do you mean?"

From atop the quarterdeck, leaning against the railing, Darius waved at the leper mockingly. The crew was little more than a band of emaciated fighters and former galley slaves, armed with bloodied swords and spears, each a gladiator in the making who chose to shed the shackles of oppression—Humbaba among them. There was an apologetic gleam in his eyes, as if the implications of their liberation slowly began to dawn on the thrall.

"There're a lot more below deck," Gipi said. "Got your sword back, I see."

"How is this possible?" Baldwin asked, torn between joy and utter disbelief. "And how in God's name did you manage to accomplish all this?"

"You can thank the Sisters Dervish for that."

"The Sisters Dervish?"

"Indeed," Darius called, "coordinating this revolt was no small conspiracy. I apologize if you take me for a traitor, but should you have had faith in me, things would not have progressed so swiftly." He nodded, slowly. "Regardless, we have freed the faithful and your friend is safe, and now, with the *Tarrasque* under our command," he gazed out into the horizon, "perhaps the world will learn that even the Fool General can bleed."

"You speak as if this was your plan all along," Baldwin said.

"And if it weren't?" Darius chuckled bitterly.

"I do not appreciate your manipulations," the leper growled, "but I am grateful that you've upheld your end of the bargain. I must ask, though, where are we headed?" He watched the Winedark Sea fade to a gentle mirage. "We're sailing away from the Holy Land."

"That we are," Darius said.

"No flying machines headed our way either," Gipi said. "Pierrot is just letting us go?"

Baldwin peered over his shoulder. "So it would seem," he paused. "I can't imagine news of the Imperial flagship's theft will be welcomed by the Sun King." He glanced about the Sisters Dervish. "Yours is not the first rebellion I have collaborated with."

"No," Darius said, "we are familiar with your work with Radcliffe and his radicals."

Baldwin's eyes widened in surprise. "Are you now?"

"I also trust you understand the threat Vermillion poses not merely to Othello or Mulgrave, but to all sovereign nations as we know them."

Baldwin shifted uncomfortably in his boots.

"All I ask of you is an audience with the Master of the Sisters Dervish," Darius continued. "Someone you've corresponded with and even waged war against, though you've never met our master in person, gracious as your rivalry of faith has been."

"Wait," Gipi said. "I thought Pierrot had the old dynasty slaughtered."

"Aye," Darius said, "so he'd like to believe."

Baldwin's thoughts shifted through the myriad generals and despots he'd confronted over his short-lived reign — until he recalled a decisive battle eight years ago. When he repelled a siege of janissaries and mamluks from the Pilgrim's Gate, quelling their jihad with amicable terms and veiled advisors. Such was the duty he served his affliction. And the rival in question, the heathen general who had earned his admiration, was not easily forgotten.

"Of such a warlord, I know little," Baldwin said, "but I recall talks with the Grand Vizier of Othello or, rather, his embassies." Slowly, the implications of Darius's words began to dawn on him. "Is he the one who sent out my bounty?"

Darius laughed, but said no more.

With the ragtag crew at work, the *Tarrasque* was a smooth vessel in the heavens, sailing far above twisting sandstorms. Save for the odd column of camels or nomadic folk, the Great Khandish Desert was a golden sea, marred by tall shafts of dead wood to mark the venerable paths between oases. As the hours wore on, Baldwin leaned against the walls of the captain's cabin and Gipi strummed her lute atop a cluster of barrels.

"So," Baldwin broke the long silence, "what do you suppose becomes of us?"

Gipi sighed, deeply. "The way I say it, we've put our lot in with peasant folk more than once. Might as well ride with what you're good at."

"I'm afraid I don't follow."

"You've abdicated your throne, sure, but you still pine for the hearts of the people." Gipi shot him a wink. "Folk hero might not be a bad way to go."

"I see," Baldwin smirked and mused. "You would have me join this fledgling rebellion."

"Nothing fledgling about it from what I see."

Slowly, the *Tarrasque* began to drift and descend towards the earth, and great ruins crept into vision—a city of pillars centered on riverbeds long since dried, dominated by a ziggurat rising from a red rock acropolis, a rubble-strewn cemetery of antiquity. It was that step pyramid, that spirit temple, which humbled Baldwin most of all—perhaps the first of its kind, a tremendous edifice of sun-dried clay and mud brick, stalwart against the elements as a temple of heathen idols. And yet, it too lay in the shadow of a low crucible of a mountain, dwarfed by its pumiced slopes and shattered glass flows, a dazzling cornucopia of color against the midday sun. As the airship circled its destination, Baldwin joined Darius at the starboard railing.

"Where are we?"

"Sarukhand," Darius said, "the cradle of civilization, or rather, what is left of it. It is where the Sisters Dervish convene, and where you will meet our master."

When the *Tarrasque* lay anchor upon the outskirts, Baldwin and Gipi disembarked, guided by the dervishes to the empty courtyard. For the first time, the leper allowed himself to study the fluid motions of their escort and realized that, beneath the flowing robes and beige wrappings, they were feminine in form—an order of women. Whether lethal dancers or suffragettes by the sword, the Sisters Dervish were deliberate in action and deed. Gipi shot the leper a wink and a smirk, as if to mock his discomfort. Baldwin muttered but did not speak; such a sapphic brigade was still under the command of the Grand Vizier of Othello.

The leper's audience was with him alone.

Silence pervaded the empty market streets—a place not even the desert wind dared venture. Along the geometric mosaics, guru-faced lamassus, and lanes of houses, the leper felt a pall of tragedy upon this place—then he peered into one of the alleys, upon a cluster of huddled silhouettes, still and lifeless, corpses preserved in the ash of ages. Hundreds more were to be found. The venerated dead had been left untouched by brigand and buzzard for millennia, as if to disturb them was to desecrate the memory of civilization, or worse, to tempt a historic evil. Though no smoke rose from the mountain, Baldwin knew it had wrought ash and immolating death upon Sarukhand, ushering in the twilight of man's first cities.

The dervishes walked with grace about the macabre site, as if pondering the ephemerality of gods and kings—a notion that troubled Baldwin to no end. Though his was to be a slow death, the leper was forced to look upon the merciless breadth of Sarukhand's destruction—a city annihilated within moments. Compared to such a disaster, his pursuit of legacy was vapid, hardly an orphan's fantasy of a kingdom, something to be lost and forgotten with the death of its dreamer—and rightly so. Humility washed over Baldwin's conscience, ushering him to the depths of shame. Was he to drown with his own ambitions? Was his odyssey so meaningless?

Regardless, the day darkened and history cast a long shadow.

Within the ziggurat, as if in response to Baldwin's own crisis, the solitary sign of civilization burned bright, modest though it seemed. Scaling the sloping steps, he was escorted to the sacred hearth of the Sisters Dervish. There stood the Eternal Flame of Sarukhand, the symbol of heathen faith. Though seemingly a modest pyre, the fire had been stoked since the End of Antiquity, its smoke swirling throughout the chamber with the odor of the burning bush, rippling the sight of those exposed to its shamanistic fumes.

The leper was greeted by a silhouette across the temple.

"You," he said, "are the Grand Vizier of Othello."

The silhouette nodded, slowly.

"We have waged many wars against each other," Baldwin said. "Despite our opposition in faith, our rivalry has always been a noble one. Our terms and exchanges were always fair and just. Our embassies were treated with the highest dignity. Even in the throes of sieges. Therefore," he paused, "I do not believe you set the bounty for my head per se."

The silhouette did not reply.

"Your conspiracy," Baldwin continued, "has brought me here. You undoubtedly have no love for the Fool General of Vermillion. Such a sentiment, I share—"

"Take off your mask," said the silhouette.

"I'm sorry?" Baldwin did not understand, at first.

"If we are to have terms, we must meet and see each other for what we are."

Reluctantly, the leper obeyed. Peeling the bronze from his face, he caressed his remnant of a nose, repulsed by his own fetid flesh, unable to meet the silhouette's gaze.

"Happy now?" he muttered.

The silhouette stood from a throne of silk cushions and emerged to greet him. To his surprise, the Grand Vizier was no man at all, but a striking young woman draped in a bedlah and gown of metallic colors—flashes of gold and red, a garnet of mystic quality bejeweling her brow, her long raven hair let to flow in defiance of sumptuary law. In truth, Baldwin did not know what to say or think and was only able to utter the question.

"What—?"

"Your confusion is understandable," her voice was smooth as the silk she wore, "but I am indeed the Grand Vizier of Othello. Or, at least, the one you've come to know."

"How is that possible?"

"Never underestimate the decadence of the court," she said. "In times of war, I merely wrote the letters for the Grand Vizier, given his affinity of opium and harem girls. Call it fraud, if you must, but should I have not, both our nations would have suffered tenfold."

"I see," Baldwin paused. "Forgive me, this is most unexpected." He gestured to the surrounding handmaidens. "And the Sisters Dervish are yours to command?"

"Our order is composed of the downtrodden and destitute, those who know desperation and the will to live in ample portion. Those who will do what needs to be done without thanks or recognition. No matter the humiliation. It is fitting that women would take upon the untouchable mantle, as the shadow of the sultanate."

"What shall I call you?" Baldwin asked.

"Desdemona," she said. "There is no need for titles or formality. I have lost all claim with the death of the sultan." Her words betrayed no love or grief for her husband's passing. "Ironic that we should only meet without nations to call our own. However, I have summoned you to speak of matters which cannot be ignored or postponed any longer."

"The Vermillion Empire," Baldwin said.

"It will not end here," Desdemona gestured to the gathering twilight, "the Sun King's ambitions are as limitless as Pierrot's cruelty. Moreover, they seek to stir an ancient evil beneath the earth — a weapon for their conquests. Though of it, I know little."

Gipi shifted uncomfortably by the threshold.

"The Fool General is gifted in the dark arts," she continued. "He has dabbled in such power and has mastered it in his pursuit of violence."

"Yes," Baldwin said. "I have seen his black sorcery."

"Pierrot's campaigns will spread across the Old World, that much is clear," Desdemona said, "but we cannot fight an enemy we do not know, let alone win." She looked the leper in the eye. "We must infiltrate the Cité du Vermillion and learn all we can of his plans."

"Espionage? I see."

"Pardon the intrusion," Gipi said, "but Vermillion's half a world away. Clever as your hideout is, I doubt you've got tunnels under the sea. How do you suppose we even get there?"

"It's simple," Desdemona said. "We use the *Tarrasque*."

Gipi shrugged. "Hardly subtle."

"Nothing about our approach has been subtle," Baldwin quipped. "If I understand correctly, Desdemona, you would have us join your rebellion and pilfer secrets of occult science from Vermillion's seat of power. Such a scheme is more than ambitious. It is suicidal." He paused. "Yet I must ask, why did you seek me out? To what end are my services so desperately needed?"

"Because of all the kings and generals I've come to know,

you alone have the audacity to do the right thing. Besides, your mind is already made."

The leper's smirk widened. "When do we start?"

When the debate had ended, Baldwin and Gipi came to the ledge of the Acropolis, staring out into the night sky—the stars were different than those of the Holy Land, uncounted pinpoints of light in the firmament of existence, the Eyes of God gazing back upon their fragile creation, windows into the Sea of Souls. Baldwin's thoughts drifted to his life and reign, finding a sliver of solace in that he had inspired this rebellion, though he'd be a fool to take sole credit. Desdemona and the Sisters Dervish, the gladiators who'd shed their shackles, even Humbaba, whose faith was so easily tested, they all deserved peace in the Kingdom of Ends. As for his role, Baldwin did not foresee a place at the table, little more than a warden at the door. This was as it should be. Moments of silence passed as he pondered the state of Golgotha, whether the lord-regent had carried out his master's wishes, whether it remained the Holy Land.

"Are you alright?" Gipi broke the long silence.

"Better than I should be," Baldwin admitted.

"Good," she said. "Not gonna lie," she sighed deeply, "I spent some time with the Fool General. In captivity. Don't worry, nothing happened, but he's a creepy bastard."

Baldwin lowered his head in shame.

"Hey, it's okay," Gipi laid a gloved hand on his pauldron, "but what I'm trying to say is that…something's wrong with that man. If we're going to do this, we need to be careful. And I'm pretty sure you're on his hit list."

"I wouldn't have it any other way."

"Yeah, that's what scares me."

Baldwin turned to his troubadour, eyes moist with tears. "I am glad to have you with me, Gipi. Perhaps we may yet commit to something worthy of song."

"I think we're on the right track."

Despite the pathos of reunion, Baldwin felt a cruel shift on the wind, and the reek of gunpowder and chemical fire reached him. Great plumes of smoke rose from the west of the desert, from Othello, and the leper's heart sank into his chest. No words were spoken. The entire company knew Pierrot was shrieking in a murderous tantrum, slaughtering those he deemed responsible for his own failures. It would be a miracle if the city lasted the night. Regardless, Baldwin understood that the Fool General was not to be suffered. The lunatic had to be put down, lest all the world's nations fell to his wicked whims.

The *Tarrasque* would embark at dawn's first light.

INTERLUDE

In the long months that followed, Pierrot received little recognition for his service, ruthless and reckless as he'd been slandered. The Sun King's faith in the Fool General was waning as the crescent moon, and he knew it well, content to brood and bide his time, delegating the pettier of his duties to lieutenants and lesser officers. Few nobles saw him, and fewer still spoke a word — not that he would divulge in idle conversation. With the *Tarrasque* stolen from under his very nose, Pierrot was content to meditate in his sanctuary, to tame the power he so sought, fickle though it was. Incense and mantric murmurs did little to quell his irritation, though the vermin in his blood began to twitch and obey.

It was better than nothing.

Pierrot had been recalled to the Cité du Vermillion and would humor the Sun King's council, if only to preserve his own position. Such dinners were awkward and bland even by the Fool General's standards, for the flow of salt and spices from Othello had ceased — what with his culling of nearly three-quarters of its population.

"I must say," Louis said at last, "your results leave much to be desired."

Pierrot bit his lip but did not reply.

"What exactly went through your head? When you decided to test the King of the Holy Land? I am genuinely curious."

"Baldwin was hardly a threat at the time —"

"Certainly a threat enough to coordinate multiple revolts and commandeer our flagship." Louis's store of patience was audibly thin. "I cannot tolerate such an egregious failure."

"If I may," Pierrot raised a hand, "I did manage to recover that relic you've requested."

"The Malachite Pyramid, yes. It's an excellent paperweight."

Pierrot rolled his eyes. "Your majesty, if I didn't know any better, I'd say you're quite cross with me." He sighed, deeply. "I admit my short-sightedness, that I got carried away with... playing with my food, but berating me isn't going to improve morale or make things any better. We'd best move on to greener pastures, no?"

"You know," Louis said, "the Chamber of Peers wanted me to strip you of rank and title. To put you on trial at the Bastille. It was only by royal decree that I stayed their hand."

"May I have a list of these 'peers'?"

"Absolutely not," Louis continued. "It is only due to your history of military achievements that I could justify sparing the rod, let alone to those who call you an unsociable madman. A notion which I'm beginning to sympathize with."

"Unsociable? Me?"

"But I digress," Louis raised a hand, "there is a way for you to regain my favor. Baldwin must die. I do not care how you do it, but word is spreading of this 'leper errant' and his merry men. He spits in the face of our authority. He cannot be allowed to live."

"I'm surprised you're not content with letting the leprosy take him."

"He is a symbol of opposition. It cannot be tolerated."

"Trust me," Pierrot said, "I do not disagree, but I must ask, would simply killing him not make him more of a martyr?" He drummed his fingers on the table. "If we are to truly 'kill' Baldwin, we must destroy what he cares about: his legacy, his people, his will to fight."

Louis cocked his head. "What do you mean?"

"He is naïve, little more than a brute with a sword and an overdeveloped sense of justice, and has clearly not thought how we can make him bleed. In fact," the Fool General raised his finger, "I'd say we take the Holy Land of Golgotha—and raze it to the ground."

"And how would you propose we do that?"

"Oh, come now, your majesty," Pierrot smirked, "I'm not asking for much. Just a few toys to deploy and the chance to make Baldwin watch the consequences of his royal negligence. That all this could've been avoided if he only stayed to protect his people."

Louis did not reply for a long while.

"Well?" Pierrot asked.

"I will consider it," Louis said with morbid caution, "but Pierrot, you must know why I am hesitant to loosen your leash. Now more than ever. I cannot afford another Othello." He nodded, curtly. "You are dismissed."

The smugness had vanished from Pierrot's face. He strode down the lonely corridors of the Grande Chateau, seething in silence, until he came to his quarters—and punched the mirror in a fit of rage. Unable to so much as think, the Fool General felt hatred sink its fangs deep into his mind; the drive to do great and terrible things out of spite, a hate that was not his own, rather, of the power which lurked under his skin, one that he understood far more than he let on. He shuddered as a maggot twitched under his eye, an unwelcome tick.

He would not be discarded so easily.

Clearly, the Sun King had no use for him, but Pierrot was cunning. With a single, shuddering breath, he swore to take matters into his own hands. Too long had he played by the rules of the court. Too long had he tolerated the blatant disrespect of the peerage. Why should he endure their inferior squabbling? He was better than them in every way. And he would operate forthwith as such. Calling a patrol of tight-lipped soldiers, Pierrot descended the latticed lift into the Salon de Sade, several stories beneath the streets of Vermillion. It was the Imperial Research Facility, where engineers and alchemists toiled in utmost secrecy, producing the Sun King's weapons of war. It was they who manufactured the *Tarrasque,* and they who invented the liquid fire which had reduced Nedlergate to rubble and ruin. Pierrot's access had yet to be revoked, and so, he crept through the laboratories of frothing alembics and clockwork devices, coming to the menagerie where the most vicious specimens were kept.

"Lord Pierrot," asked an interrupting scholar, "to what do we—?"

"Out of my way." The Fool General shoved him aside.

Both a master and a servant of black sorcery, Pierrot heard the whispers of worms from within high glass tubes along the walls—the worms of the earth. Native to the Grünewald and Mulgrave regions, the nine-eyed eels were contained by salt-rimmed corkage and esoteric seals. They were the offspring of the Conqueror Worm, the power which Vermillion so foolishly sought to tame. Though its nature was unknown, Pierrot was willing to consult his mysterious patron. To think he, too, had undergone treatment in such a place; injected with their eggs, booned with a power born of madness, reborn as the man whose will was one with the worms.

"Sir?" asked a guard. "Why are we here?"

"Don't ask questions you don't want the answers to," he muttered.

Pierrot lay a naked palm against one of the tubes, grimacing as the specimen began to twitch and writhe in sickly embryonic fluid. Through a wordless will, they had an accord, and by the darkness between the stars, the Fool General would serve the worms as they served him. Terrible rumbling filled the chamber, and the carrion-eaters began to stir. Pierrot shut his eyes, channeling his eldritch affinity against the glass, smirking as every cylinder began to crack.

The guards shifted uncomfortably where they stood.

"Pierrot?" one of the soldiers gasped. "What are you doing?"

"Starting a coup."

At that moment, the chamber was flooded in a tide of briny fluid and broken glass. The nine-eyed eels slithered as serpents along the floor, gathering at Pierrot's side like a litter of happy puppies. He barely heard the alarm begin to sound and let his terrified men flee down the hall. It wouldn't matter. With the power of the Conqueror Worm, Pierrot took a brisk walk to the laboratories, ignoring the scrambles and screams of scholars being devoured by swarms of larval worms, content to assemble a horde of monstrosities at their own leisure.

"When you're ready," he spoke to them.

When Pierrot returned to the Grande Chateau, a writhing army at his command, he came to the Banquet Hall and kicked in the door, fragile as it was. Midmeal, the corpulent nobles gawked in horror as the Fool General plucked a snifter from the table, downing the brandy with ease. Louis launched out of his seat, raising a finger in fearful indignation, though the Imperial Guard failed to so much as take aim. Within moments, the table was surrounded by salivating weapons and lamprey-men, directly under Pierrot's thrall.

"What is the meaning of this?" Louis demanded.

"A coup," Pierrot said.

"Are you mad?" shouted a duke. "You can't just usurp—!"

Pierrot raised a pistol and shot him in the skull. The esquires and courtesans screamed in horror—slithering worms gathered to feed on the pooling blood. The lamprey-men, hunched and hungry as they were, drooled upon the shoulders of prospective prey.

"T-this is the thanks I get for my tolerance?" Louis failed to mask his terror. "Pierrot, you have no idea what you're doing. What you're toying with."

"Oh, I beg to differ," Pierrot said. "You're soft, your majesty. You've grown fat in your dotage, a prematurely senile prince on a throne of lies. Your power is illusionary. Your every decree a strongly worded letter. Unlike mine. Unlike the Conqueror Worm." He gestured widely and wildly. "Here, allow me to prove it...by killing you last."

Pierrot did not bother to bask in the hideous feast, the orgy of consumption and violence, taking no pleasure in the nobles' obnoxious screams and pleas for mercy. Once the Banquet Hall had been reduced to a crimson trough for his twisted amalgams and nine-eyed eels, Pierrot strode to the Sun King's throne and shoved him into his seat.

"I don't think you understand," Pierrot said. "How little it all means."

"Why are you doing this?" Louis choked and cowered.

"Said the frog to the scorpion," Pierrot sneered. "You don't get to feign shock when I snap in the corner." He pressed the pistol against Louis's brow. "I've no reason to care save what you give me and, honestly, table scraps don't cut it." He gazed into the Sun King's eyes, as flukes tickled the back of the Fool General's throat. "The Conqueror Worm is all that matters. The only thing worth serving. The world deserves a better villain than some would-be despot, and I'll give it to them. I'll show them what it means to live in fear."

Louis whimpered in horror.

"I think I've told you once upon a time," Pierrot mused, "what I know of the Conqueror Worm comes from bedtime stories, but I haven't told you what those stories are. You see, it's a tale as old as time. One of a dragon gnawing at the root of the world. It was there for the Great Flood and all those…pretty little rainbows. It'll be here long after you're gone. And when it wakes up? Well, that's when the fun starts and mankind faces its end." He shuddered, basking in the impending act of personal murder. "Louis, Louis, you little shit. It was never about power. It was about what we are in the dark. And I can tell you right now, I'm better than you."

"The men will never follow you…."

"Oh, you think that's my plan? To settle for a rule and be worshiped? That's cute. Real cute. If you're not going to fiddle with the Malachite Pyramid, then I will."

Louis's fear gave way to hate of his own. "What about Baldwin…?"

Pierrot halted for a moment, thoughts drifting to the troubadour who spoke so fondly of her master, "Gigi," or whatever her name was. Once more, the Fool General understood far more than he'd let on. Baldwin was a monarch who rejected the restrictions of court and throne, choosing to die by the morals of epics and chivalric poetry — admirable in his delusion. In that manner, he was no different from Pierrot. They were visionaries who sought to hold a mirror to the world and shape it accordingly. The difference lay in Baldwin's naivety, his incessant faith in man's redemption. Pierrot knew better. Misanthropy was a coward's term for realism. He'd seen what man was capable of at his lowest, compelled to murder and mutilate in the name of self-preservation. From Nedlergate to Othello, the commoner was always one ration away from cannibalizing his neighbor. Pestilence, Famine, and War, the atrocities they enabled, would pale in comparison to Pierrot's reason — to end that which birthed monsters such as he.

To witness the apotheosis of this earth.

"Let's just say," Pierrot's grin widened, "he's the hero I deserve."

So the Fool General pulled the trigger and delicately pushed the Sun King from his seat — dead. Content to sit at the table's end, he watched his new subjects, peers worthy of respect, feast on the slaughtered in a coat of crimson over pastels. Kicking up his feet, he let his slippers fall to the floor and raised a glass in triumph. Screams echoed from the lower levels. Pierrot had already dispatched a vanguard to deal with the royal garrison — and soon, the city as a whole. If it was one thing he could count on, it was the penchant of the worms to multiply, albeit in a parasitic fashion, and the Cité du Vermillion would be their spawning ground. With enough of a brood under his belt, Pierrot would launch a campaign of his own, against one Baldwin of Golgotha, for no other need than his own entertainment. Only a single regret lingered in Pierrot's thoughts as he rose to sift through half-eaten delicacies.

"Shame," he said, "I want some escargot."

ACT FIVE

CHAPTER ONE

Under a pall of misty twilight, the *Tarrasque* flew low over the outskirts of the Vermillion Empire, barely a yard above the densely forested canopies. Such a land was pastoral in comparison to the capital due south. Few flying machines patrolled the vineyards under the yoke of medievalism, and fewer lords would report news that was of no concern to their estates. The voyage across the Great Sea had proven long and arduous, but the crew remained well-provisioned for the two-month trek. Those who wished to leave and forge new lives had been granted the opportunity upon every stop, namely the Kingdom of Ikana with its rice terraces and sunset pagodas. Darius was one such passenger. Indeed, Baldwin felt as if he'd circumnavigated the globe—a claim not far from the truth. Here, autumn held sway, and leaves of crisp, earthen colors trickled to the rain-soaked soil. Further south, the air grew thick and humid as white chalk cliffs gave way to fen and bog. Under the command of Desdemona and the Sisters Dervish, the paltry rebels were loath to reveal themselves to the enemy.

"So," Baldwin said, "this is the Sun King's dominion."

Desdemona nodded in silent confirmation.

Amidst moss-festooned branches and rancid foliage, the *Tarrasque* settled for a clearing in the Midgewater Mire, many leagues from the high-rises and clock towers of the Cité du Vermillion. Though from afar its palaces and apartments were the splendor of civilization, its colors were muted by the onset of industrialization, by the smoke rising from soot-stained chimneys in the sprawl past the outer walls. Such elegance had cracked as plaster against the ceaseless toil of machinery. Built over the old labyrinthine streets, hatters and distilleries shared houses and polluted the surrounding mire as a cesspit of dyes and noxious chemicals, to say nothing of metalworks which blazed long into the night. Even the salons and *piano nobiles*, oddly close to the cobbles, were but façades of pretension—tea clubs for the syphilitic bourgeois with no place for the paupers who so idolized them. In the coming centuries, many would seek to emulate the city's ambition, though few would match even a fraction of its decadence. Baldwin would never live to see the Holy City fall to such loathsome depths. The thought never occurred to him. By that ignorance alone, the Grand Conductor had shown him mercy.

"God," Gipi gagged, "I can smell it from here."

"This is the capital of the Vermillion Empire," Desdemona said, her raven hair flowing in the breeze. "Better protected than most prisons."

"And the Grande Chateau," Baldwin gestured to what he assumed was the capital building, "is our destination? Where they delve into occult science?"

Desdemona shook her head. "Not quite," she said, "the complex, the Salon de Sade, lies in the catacombs beneath the city. And we'd be fools to attack the city gates head-on."

Gipi shrugged. "Don't suppose we can go up and knock."

"You'd be a fool to try," Desdemona said, "besides, the gates have been sealed for the past seventy-two hours." She gestured to the trails of lanterns and swift columns leaving the sally ports. "Something's happened, though I'm unsure as to what."

Baldwin gripped his sword's hilt with grim purpose. "More folk displaced by Pierrot's madness?" he sighed, deeply. "I suppose it was only a matter of time." He turned to the Sultana of Othello. "Have you sent out reconnaissance? We must keep to the woods and approach with caution, lest we alert the garrisons to our presence."

"I've already sent my agents," Desdemona said, "and trust their tact more than my own." With that, she bid the leper and his fool to the captain's cabin, where she pored over charts and maps of Vermillion and its defensive holdings. "There is a minor settlement on the bayou. Supposedly, a rebel sympathizer makes his home there. He ferries refugees and presumed criminals to and from coves which honeycomb the south."

"A submariner," someone spoke from the shadows. Humbaba emerged from his seat, bronze helm under his bulging arm. "Erik Ravel," he said, "esquire of the Chamber of Peers and master engineer of the Salon de Sade." He nodded, bitter. "He was the mind behind many of the war machines I was pitted against in the Colosseo. I am unsure if we can trust him."

"You speak as if he is a recluse," Baldwin said.

"If rumor is to be believed," Humbaba said. "At the height of my career, I dined with him and Pierrot...in a cage. He was soft-spoken. Not one for conversation. Much like you, Good King Baldwin."

Baldwin chose to ignore that quip. "Can we find him there?"

"He runs a swamp tour cruise," Desdemona said, "under a different name, of course."

"I see," Baldwin pressed a thumb to his chin, "then we must not delay. Gipi," he addressed his fool, "when you're ready."

"Way ahead of you," she waved and had already marched out the cabin door, "but you might want to say your goodbyes, if you take my meaning."

"What—?"

Without a word, Gipi and Humbaba had left for the swampward road. It took Baldwin a moment to understand what she meant, but he found himself alone with Desdemona. In truth, the two-month voyage meant little to him, but he'd be a fool to deny his attraction to the Sultana of Othello. Should things have been different, namely his fatal affliction, perhaps he would've found the courage to flirt, and yet, without the abdication of his throne, it was doubtful they would have ever crossed paths save through letters of diplomacy and deceit.

"Is there something on your mind?" Desdemona asked, eyes gleaming as sharpened emeralds in the candlelight. "You look—"

"No," Baldwin said, curtly.

Though the leper forced himself to the door, something stopped him from pushing past its aged panels. He leaned against the frame and sighed in a fit of self-mockery.

"I never thought I would join forces with jihadists," Baldwin admitted. "Let alone a sultana commanding the respect of an entire order of assassins. One that on a different day would've likely seen me killed." He gave a nod of heartfelt respect. "Thank you for seeing to my people's liberation. Such a deed is not easily earned. May we meet again soon."

"Save the poetics for when they matter." Desdemona shot him a wink.

Muttering in morbid discomfort, Baldwin fled to his companions, enduring the slosh of mud under his boots. It was nothing. He would die a leper. Courtly love of any kind was hardly worth his pursuit, incapable as he was. However, there was respect which transcended his licentious impulse—the respect of rival lords. Baldwin and Desdemona had ended wars together. In many ways, she was a reminder of his life at its worthiest, before he took upon the Broken Blade and forsook his responsibilities as the King of the Holy Land. She was a reminder of a life that could've been very different—one worth living, sans his terrible fate, one that he could never escape. Refraining from punching a tree in a fit of rage, Baldwin followed the voices of his companions. Gipi passed her pipe to Humbaba, puffing a messy smoke ring.

"That was fast," she said.

"Shut up," the leper muttered.

"The three of us should suffice," Humbaba said, tightening the chalk-dusted bandages about his knuckles, where Baldwin had once cut him so deeply. "And the road should take us to the swamp tour center." Donning his crested galea, the Butcher led the way as a great veldt-beast into the undergrowth. "Let's see if Ravel is worth the fuss."

Baldwin took the rear and gave one last look to the *Tarrasque*. Slowly, cicadas and nocturnal crawlers closed in. Desdemona was nowhere to be seen, presumably gone to consult her sisters or rest for the night, but in her stead, the leper spied an ethereal rider whose presence was bound to the mists themselves. Death had come to observe her quarry.

With a forlorn sigh, Baldwin heaved the Broken Blade over his shoulder and took the first shaky step into the final leg of his journey — into the heart of darkness.

———

Along the red marsh's edge, Baldwin was greeted by a sequence of nighttime sights illuminated by corpse-candles and fireflies — distant plantations, houses, and cotton fields where drones of sickly flesh and copper toiled in eerie light, men reduced to vegetative states, half a step above the reanimated dead. A low vacancy filled their hollow eyes, dressed as peasants and ragtag scarecrows, weird engines grafted to their limbs and spines. Baldwin suspected they were prisoners condemned to mindless labor in the land, but dared not ponder the extent of Vermillion's cruelty, lest he be deterred from his urgent course.

Humbaba, swarthy as he was, was noticeably uncomfortable.

"There are worse fates than to die in the arena," he muttered.

Gipi pressed a finger to her lips.

The leper crept about the fringe of light and spied columns of sobbing folk on the highroad. Though outwardly urbane in powdered wigs and pastels, the refugees were ill-equipped for the Midgewater Mire, save for hand-fans to swat swarming gnats. No guards escorted them, and common sense did nothing to dissuade centerpieces of furniture and oil paintings from joining the northward flight. Naked as babes in a den of wolves, the aristocrats failed to fathom their own peril. Theirs was a forced march, presumably up the coast to the Cité du Lumière, the sister-city of Vermillion. Baldwin overheard a few tidbits of gossip.

"It happened so fast...."

"To think such evil lurked beneath our very homes...."

"The Fool General's gone mad!"

Baldwin scoffed at the last comment yet said nothing — his companions remained at his side. Humbaba cracked his knuckles, as if contemplating whether or not to rob and interrogate the soft lot, but made no such move. Gipi jerked her head aside, and the company retreated onto the boardwalk ever deeper into the bayou. Hours passed, and the gibbous moon shone in slivers upon the moistened earth, shedding light upon scaly things lurking among the cattails. At last, Baldwin came to a palm-thatched hut on stilts rising from the stagnant water, with the sign, "Midgewater Tourist Center," hanging from hinges above the elevated porch. Low golden light flickered within the windows, and the door was seemingly unlocked.

With an urgent knock, Baldwin awaited a response.

"Go away," someone shouted.

Baldwin shrugged and knocked again — the door opened ever so slightly, bound by several locks and chains, and a warty nose jutted from the crack.

"What? What do you want?"

"We're here for a night tour," Baldwin said.

"Center closed three hours ago, son —"

"I'm afraid that won't do."

"Well, it'll have to. Come back tomorrow."

The door shut again; however, Baldwin did not relent.

"Beat it! Or I'll call...."

Without a word of warning, Humbaba stepped ahead of the leper and tore open the front door, shattering its feeble chains, towering over an old man in a moldy nightgown. He was the spitting image of a renaissance man; unkempt and ill-groomed, indistinguishable from a vagabond save for a maddened gleam in his eyes, one which betrayed his cantankerous genius and a desire to be left alone. He was clearly the man they sought.

"Erik Ravel," Humbaba said. "Pleasure to see you again."

"Huh, who the hell are—?" The old man's eyes narrowed as mental gears began to turn, slowly realizing who this one-man brute squad was. "Huh? Humbaba? How'd you get out of Othello? Goddamn, last time I saw you, you castrated a pit-fighter with your pinky toe."

Baldwin shot the thrall a look of abject horror.

"A slight exaggeration," Humbaba said.

"Anyway," the old man tied off his nightgown, "what're you doing here?"

"If I may." Gipi slid to the front of the company. "The Cité du Vermillion hasn't been doing that well of late, has it? Anything unrest of note?" She shot the leper an aside. "Sounds like no one knows what's going on, and it might be in your best interests to find out."

"You are the engineer behind the *Tarrasque*," Baldwin said. "Are you not?"

"Well, yes, but define 'best interests'?" Ravel shook his head. "You lot seem new here, so allow me to catch you up to speed. The Sun King fired me for having grievances about, God forbid, partaking in war crimes. So, forgive me if I'm a little hesitant to see if he's alright."

"Okay," Gipi snapped, "that's not—"

Baldwin raised a bandaged hand in peace. "I assure you, his well-being is of no concern to us either." He turned to the smoke rising from the city. "However, if you are content with Pierrot running rampant, threatening the world as it is, perhaps we'd best seek aid elsewhere."

Ravel bit his lip in momentary silence. "Well, first off, you never exactly explained why you're here." He peered past the leper's shoulder. "Sure you weren't followed?"

Gipi shrugged, hands over the hilts of her dirks and daggers.

Rolling his eyes, Ravel bid the trio inside his shack and tourist center. "Sounds like you've thrown your lot in with the Sisters Dervish and whatever sad sacks they pick up along the way. There're worse things to die for, I suppose." He reached for a kettle over the clay hearth. "Still, I don't think you want any old tour either."

Humbaba took a cup and saucer graciously, hardly a pair of dollhouse props in his massive hands. "Do you still have the submarine?"

"Who's asking and why?"

As the two settled for reacquainting, Baldwin's eyes wandered to the trinkets and baubles crammed along the walls — a museum of maritime oddities and patents for inventions yet to be manufactured. One in particular, a water clock ticking to the End Times, disturbed him greatly. Ravel was the epitome of the tragic engineer, a man whose life's work had been plagiarized by the Sun King and weaponized in ways he never anticipated. That was the root of his cynicism. Like a samba over a slipping record, his seemingly modest existence served only to mask a lifetime of achievements and morbid failings.

"You invented the liquid flame Pierrot is so fond of?" Baldwin asked.

"Yeah," Ravel muttered. "Why don't you rub some salt in my eyes while you're at it?"

"My apologies," Baldwin rolled his eyes with indignance, "but we do not have the luxury of humoring your temperament. We need to get through to Vermillion and someone who can ferry us. Either you will help us or not, but know that history does not look favorably upon the idle." He crossed his arms. "Save your self-pity. I have no use for it."

"Funny," Ravel said. "With that attitude, my services will cost you triple."

Gipi nudged the leper sharply, as if to shut him up. "I'm sure we can come to an agreement with one of your intellect. What's a trip to and from the karst caves?"

"More than you'd think," Ravel snapped. "The mire is infested with specimens and things that'll live a good four hundred years after we're gone. And I'm not willing to risk my submersible, let alone my life, for some partisan effort to destabilize the country." He jerked his head aside. "Now, unless you're going to give me a legitimate reason, get out."

Baldwin was about to step forward and resort to intimidation when Humbaba shook his shadowed head and settled for his own approach.

"I believe you remember my greatest match," Humbaba said. "The one where I cracked open one of your fighting vessels with bronze gauntlets?"

Ravel sipped his tea nervously. "That I do."

"I don't mean to discredit your life's work," the thrall turned to the many achievements along the walls, "but if I can break that chariot, I think I've earned the right to say....the weapons you've created, the misdeeds that haunt you, they can be beaten." He stood and towered over the ragged engineer. "You're not proud of what you've done, and rightly so, but your legacy doesn't have to end in the corpses of nations. Help us make it right."

Baldwin and Gipi exchanged an odd glance; the Butcher's bedside manner was more than unexpected. Tears welled in Ravel's eyes. He turned to an open hatch to a rowboat below, presumably near a shallow route to the cesspits of Vermillion's industrial outflow.

At last, Ravel conceded with a sigh.

"You hate him as much as I do?" he asked. "The Fool General?"

"I have seen Nedlergate burn," Baldwin said, "and liberated the slaves of Othello. I was once the King of the Holy Land, and I swear to you—"

"Is that supposed to impress me?" Ravel scoffed.

Gipi kept to the hearth, hands in her pockets. "He means well."

Ravel shook his head. "Well, if it means stopping the fire consuming the world, then fine, I can't think of a better hope in hell. Just promise me one thing." He turned to Humbaba of all people. "You find Pierrot? You find any of my work? You destroy it. All of it."

Humbaba nodded in an unspoken promise.

"Right," Ravel launched from his rocking chair, "follow me."

Once more, Baldwin stayed at the rear. One by one, they descended the ladder and hopped aboard the bobbing boat. Humbaba's weight alone threatened to sink the vessel, but the leper knew better than to expect it to ferry the company. Slowly, Ravel rowed the oars, his back to the lantern's light, and began to cruise deeper into the bayou. Among the curtains of crimson moss and swarming gnats, Baldwin kept an eye on the murky water, feeling its hull bump against all manner of unseen things — gnarled roots, fish, perhaps the odd corpse, the boat itself hardly a few planks between the company and lurking peril. Dead wildlife peppered the darkened surface, worms writhing in their eyes and mouths, alluding to terrible pollution that bled into the bayou. When the willows began to recede, Ravel brought the company to a lagoon of unknown depth, caked in cattails, wide enough to be ill-watched by the city guard and acidic as to choke all good life from its waters. Stopping by a lonesome dock, Ravel disembarked and took the lantern, perusing the reeds for some trace of the true craft. Gipi gave the leper an uneasy glance, and yet, Baldwin remained patient, though his confidence too began to wane. Moments later, Ravel struck something in the water with an iron rod, echoing with a hollow, wooden thunk. He crept atop an unseen surface, and his light shone upon a periscope and a wrought-iron trapdoor an inch above the water. He turned to the company and gestured to the sealed entry.

"Get in," he said.

Baldwin was the first to abide. As he cranked the valve and opened the hatch, a series of iron rungs led into the hidden bowels of a submersible, flanked by sweeping curves of its walls, ribbed with ornate copper pipage, and with rotund windows into a deep and creeping darkness. Composed of lacquered oak and mahogany imported from the colonies, the furnishings of the ship were cramped yet comfortable—countertops of dials and gauges, helmed by a rudder and display of mechanical meters, it was a wonder of Vermillion engineering. Gipi took a seat, her frame squeaking against its leather, and Humbaba could hardly stand, his shoulders grazing the ceiling. Ravel took the wheel and wound a pair of heavy cranks. Low vibrations echoed from the rear, and the submersible began to move, propelled by clockworks and antiquated screws into the lagoon. Though his guide would never admit it, Baldwin sensed a bittersweet resolve in Ravel, as if no small part of him missed testing such inventions on the field.

"Welcome aboard the *Bolero*," he said.

Twin lamps flickered on, illuminating the forlorn sights of the world beneath the waves. Baldwin's eyes widened in awe, for he'd never fathomed such a place. Impossibly tall strands of scarlet flora rose from the abyss, laden with pods and thin leaves, swaying at the mercy of the tide. It was a forest of rubbery trees whose roots must've delved for miles beneath the dunes of night-soil. No fish swam among them, but pelagic carcasses littered the lakebed to feed armies of urchins, red and royal purple, along with other, more invasive life.

Schools of nine-eyed eels spiraled about weathered rock, burrowing deep into dead sea-beasts many times their size, jawless maws suckling and rasping into rotting flesh. The *Bolero* was but a wooden lung—a glorified bell and bathysphere meant to flounder through the limbo between fields of fishbones and the oily surface. The lagoon was tainted not merely by dye and chemical waste, but also by overwhelming lampreys—a testament to the power of corruption. It was an alien realm, one fraught with death and disease.

"Out of curiosity," Baldwin asked from within the safety

of the cabin, "what happened between you and the Sun King? Surely, he wouldn't discard your work so easily."

"I grew tired of watching my vision kill people," Ravel said. "The *Tarrasque* was just icing on the cake, but," he pointed to the swarming eels, "those sea-devils, those neunauge, they're responsible for just as much destruction, if not more."

"What are they?" Gipi gazed out the window.

"Offspring of something I'd rather not know."

Eventually, the *Bolero* came to the far side of the lagoon, and its lamps shone upon honeycombed caverns. At first glance, they were the work of erosion—the ebb and flow of the tide— but the speed and manner in which they'd been hollowed was impossible by natural means. Between the pipes, the constant flow of black fluid, and the pallid eels which danced about the mouths, it was undoubtedly the bladder of Vermillion's excess— the perfect entry to the sewers. Slowly, the *Bolero* pushed its girth through the largest of the tunnels, its rotund hull scraping against stone with a hideous shriek. With the push and pull of a dozen levers and the propulsion of its paddle, the submersible emerged into a narrow passage caked with rust and metallic debris. Baldwin sighed with relief—but not before something clattered from and behind the vessel and a low-hanging pipe began to seethe.

"Dammit," Ravel muttered.

"What happened—?"

"Nothing," the pilot snapped. "Well, nothing you can fix, at any rate."

"How are we on oxygen?" Humbaba asked.

Ravel did not reply, though his face seemed to pale.

Baldwin shuddered as the *Bolero* sputtered on due course, though a tad more cumbersome along the way. He dared not ask how far these tunnels went, for he did not want to know, and yet suspected that those eels were the symptom of a greater evil.

One that he would no doubt soon confront.

CHAPTER TWO

Hours had passed, yet the *Bolero* still lumbered through the iron tunnels. Despite the junctions and splits from pipe to pipe, Baldwin grew suspicious that Ravel had little memory of these routes, assuming he'd traversed them at all. However, nagging the navigator would not improve their odds of survival. The leper was content to sit idle and fiddle with the frayed ends of his bandages. The twin lamps of the submersible served no purpose in these routes, though Baldwin suspected the company was not alone in the labyrinth.

"How's the oxygen?" Humbaba asked.

Ravel muttered under his breath. "Don't ask questions you don't want the answer to."

Gipi shifted, uncomfortably, clearly more than a bit claustrophobic.

"It'll be enough for a one-way trip," Ravel said, as if attempting to comfort his regretful passengers. "Maybe a trip and a half…."

"How comforting," Baldwin muttered.

The lamps flickered rapidly. Ravel tugged at a few valves and levers, but to no avail. Within seconds, the *Bolero* was veiled in utter darkness — to say nothing of water leaking between rivets. The leper shut his eyes and sighed with bitter resignation.

"What happened?" Gipi blurted, failing to mask her panic.

"Nothing, nothing," Ravel struck a match with a waft of smoke, succeeding on the third attempt, muttering in a mantra, "everything's fine."

"Isn't this submarine made of wood?"

"Shut up," Ravel snapped.

Baldwin shuddered. Perhaps it was the failing air, but he felt short of breath, scarcely fettering his cough — something brushed against the hull. When Ravel fiddled with a winding mechanism and reactivated the propeller, the lights indeed returned, only to illuminate a dilating maw ringed with row upon row of yellowed fangs, the gullet of a basking leviathan. The startled cries of the company were drowned only by its deafening roar.

"Fuck!" Gipi screamed.

Tearing a reverse propulsion device, Ravel drove the *Bolero* into overdrive, desperate to escape the lunging eel. Speeding at a rate which well exceeded its intended capacity, the submersible was seemingly lost in the den of sea-devils, until a thought occurred to the leper.

"Up," he said, "there, go up!"

"What?" Ravel spat. "What're you — ?"

Baldwin, having observed the rudimentary controls of the *Bolero*, shoved Ravel aside harder than he meant to, slamming the old man's skull against a quaking pipe. The pilot was unconscious. Regret could wait. Baldwin took the rudder and sent the vessel on a steep incline, towards what he prayed was the surface and not a whirligig turbine — the latter of which he narrowly avoided. He activated support systems nearly at random as the pipes seethed and began to burst, water flooding into the interior, threatening to drown them all.

"What're you doing?" Gipi shouted.

"Going up," the leper growled.

At that moment, the *Bolero* burst from the surface. Out the portside window, Baldwin spied a stone walkway to the right of the canal. Humbaba smashed open the upper hatch. Together, the company escaped the iron-banded deathtrap and emerged onto the presumed sewer — only for the leper to realize he'd left Ravel inside. Before he could so much as turn his head, the loathsome serpent breached with maw agape, only to swallow the sinking vessel whole with a tremendous splash — destroying their only way back.

As the sewage settled, a moment's silence passed.

"Well then," Baldwin conceded with a sigh.

Gipi rang out her cap and bells, eyes darting about the mildewed corridor. It was clear they had reached the foundations of Vermillion, the sewers of the infested city. Humbaba donned his brass knuckles and glanced over his shoulder into unyielding darkness.

"Alright, what the hell was that?" the fool spoke at last.

"Nothing good," Humbaba said, "and I doubt it's the only one. Still," he paused, "I'd never wish that fate upon Ravel. That was an ignoble death."

"May he find rest in the Kingdom of Ends." Baldwin stared at the rancid depths.

Humbaba grunted in solemn agreement.

"Yeah, I'm sure he'd be touched." Gipi rolled her eyes, gathering her bearings. "Where are we? I mean, looks like a sewer, smells like a sewer, but —"

"I doubt we've reached the Salon de Sade," Baldwin said. "However, if we keep on due course to the surface, we should find some passage to our destination."

The walls were composed of mortar and modern masonry, ribbed as the belly of a beast, lines of oil lamps suspended from the vaulted ceiling, no doubt frequently maintained. Whatever the exact purpose of the long canal, it was in part used for liquid waste disposal, as evident by the spiraling drain from which the *Bolero* had emerged.

"We cannot linger," Baldwin said.

"Wait," Humbaba approached the near wall, "there's something else."

In the throes of shock and urgency, the leper had ignored a series of dung-smeared pictograms along the wall, not dissimilar to the writings of cave folk. Baldwin halted, joining his companions in appraising such primitive script, recalling tales of cyclopic cannibals along the peninsula and further archipelagos — regions not terribly far from Vermillion. Whether the maintenance workers were slacking on their duties or dared not deface such things, he did not know, but suspected the sewers had been ill traversed in recent months.

"What do they say?" he asked.

"I can't tell," Humbaba said.

"Didn't know you could read," Gipi muttered, "but I digress. Reminds me a bit of those 'anthropophagi' you've studied. You know, the headless men of Khand."

"Yes, I am aware," Baldwin said. "Though they're a desert people. If we were to encounter them, we would've likely done so in Othello or the desert. This is nothing I recognize." He felt a presence stir around the farthest bend. "Come," he drew the Broken Blade and lit a pitch-soaked torch, "we must face whatever awaits."

Swallowing their dread, the company pressed on in single file. The clatter and clamor of colossal turbines echoed in the distance, fueled by diversions in the River Soleil and excesses of filth, though no one knew their true design—at least, none who live. The bowels of Vermillion were composed of clockworks and bronze hydraulics, its old stone aqueducts and saltwater caverns converted into channels, as arteries to the heart of industry. And yet, it was not so advanced as to utilize coal or combustion, clinging to a remnant of baroque sensibility where it could afford to do so. Baldwin's mind, however, was fixed on the fecal writings and wet tracks about the walkways. He knelt to examine the latter—webbed footprints and trails of blood led to and fro, alluding to parties of bipedal creatures the leper did not know.

"What manner of degenerates live here?" he muttered.

"The better question is," Humbaba said. "Where did they come from?"

"True," Gipi said. "Given what we've seen, I doubt whatever thrives down here is native to the mire. Or the city, for that matter...."

As if in response to their speculation, a choir of guttural rasps echoed from the fringe of sight. Gipi peered around the bend and gasped in horror, cupping her mouth. Baldwin doused his torch and kept to the shadows, eying a host of slime-crusted hunters in the dimness. Though they walked as men, troglodytes were a low breed; stooped yet slender, rubbery, a foot shorter than a grown man. Nude and nine-eyed, their ringed maws sagged in loose facsimiles of lips—maggot-folk of the sewers, javelins and spiked clubs in their grips. Slouched over a heap of slain aristocrats, they spoke in speech unpronounceable by the human tongue; throaty utterances enough to send chills down even the leper's spine.

Baldwin understood what had happened. Refugees had likely sought shelter beneath the streets, only to be killed as prey for their foolish trespass. Only a true terror could drive fops into the sewers—an evil that would soon detect the company's presence.

In silent consensus, they crept to the upper sewers.

Step by step, Baldwin felt the trek take its toll as sweat trickled down his brow. He paused to lean against the wall, his vision haunted by phantom lights and the closing pall of night. His breaths grew shallow, and he could've sworn he saw an ethereal glow at the corridor's end—only for Gipi to snap her fingers sharply. With a nod, he continued in a forced march.

"What *were* those things?" Gipi whispered. "Do you think Pierrot…?"

"That I cannot say," Baldwin managed, "but I suspect they are, at least in part, connected to Vermillion's corruption. Perhaps the Salon de Sade."

Humbaba raised a hand, bidding the company to halt. He pointed to the steady flow of rainfall, to the slivers of moonlight shining through grates and storm drains. "I don't believe these sewers lead to the Salon," he said, "but we're close to the streets."

Within moments, they came to a ladder leading to the streets, and yet, Baldwin's chest was heavier than ever, every breath weak and wheezing. A desperate fit of coughs overcame him—a mouthful of blood escaped his lips. Mustering the remnants of his strength, the leper staggered to stand, smiling, ignorant of the disturbed asides of his companions. Though

Death was impossibly close, Baldwin gripped his sword's hilt and whispered a prayer into his rosary — a prayer that he would achieve greatness, that he would find glory yet.

And so, he led the climb to the Cité du Vermillion.

CHAPTER THREE

The Cité du Vermillion was no stranger to rainfall. The climate of the Imperial south loaned itself to humidity and coastal flooding, though its architecture had long delegated the frequent flow to waterworks and the surrounding mire. Since the construction of aqueducts, during the height of the Old Imperium, the wetlands had been devoted to a futile attempt to control the tides. For a time, perhaps an age, civilization had succeeded, and so, Vermillion was constructed not alongside but in spite of nature's will. Such was the root of its civilization — but here and now, admits the perpetual patter of torrents against cobblestone streets, Baldwin was greeted by streets flooded not only by rainwater, but by blood.

Such was what the company had infiltrated.

Under a cacophony of thunderclouds, the city was bathed in utter misery. Rain washed any trace of crimson into obscure sewers, leaving only the corpses of casualties in its wake. Fumes wafted from storm drains, alluding to many a machination therein, but Baldwin heaved open a manhole and led the company onto the Promenade, the commercial boulevard lined with boutiques and emporiums with goods from the world over — recently looted, left to mold and rot. Even the Clockwork Guard — crippled soldiers who'd undergone radical grafting and donated their bodies in service to the Sun King — were but rusty husks of flesh and iron exposed to the elements, helpless against this onslaught of devilry. Baldwin knelt to the nearest corpse and shuddered, recognizing the little white worms infesting its flesh.

"Something terrible has happened here," he said.

"You don't say," Gipi scoffed, failing to mask her horror.

Humbaba said nothing, his gaze fixed on the Grand Chateau ahead — when a series of chittering cries rose from the alleys, inching near. Baldwin drew the Broken Blade and spun around, though even he doubted his strength to cut through their chitin. Choosing instead to breach a broken threshold into a random apartment, he was greeted by a dying hearth, the solace of silence, and the reek of death. A bourgeois family lay limp on the sofa in full; faces pale, eyes wide, a bottle of arsenic and a cluster of empty tea cups at the coffee table.

Baldwin dared not look upon the children.

"There's some stairs," Gipi said, mustering her courage, perhaps in willful ignorance. "Come on, we might get to the rooftops from there. Might be safer—"

Chittering cries drew nearer.

Humbaba led the vanguard to the first floor.

Before he knew it, Baldwin pressed on, down the hall and out the broken window, joining the companions on the rooftops. Here, they were safe, save for the silhouettes of flying things. Lost in a maze of shingles and baroque parapets, Baldwin led the way, enduring the distant screams of the mad and misbegotten— people he could not save. Knees trembling, the leper gawked at the scale of such destruction. Though the initial fires had long been doused in a downpour, every home had been broken, every family had been butchered—and for what? No ambition drove these unseen creatures, at least, none that Baldwin could recognize. There was nothing save a ceaseless desire to devour and sow their seed among the dead and dying, a will to procreate in the throes of violence. The stench of moldering bodies was overpowering, and yet, in the highest window of the Grand Chateau, Baldwin recognized the bright lights of a banquet. Someone was celebrating this massacre, and he had a hunch as to who.

"First things first," Gipi said. "We make for the Salon de Sade and learn what we can."

"That is our mission," Humbaba added.

Baldwin conceded with a nod, barely able to fetter his wrath. "Indeed," he said with a shudder. "We must find access to the facility."

The leper was forced to descend the roof to the Place de l'Asticot with its triumphal arches and marble fountains, where crawling things dragged the dead into hollow warrens. The Grande Chateau was across a bridge crossing the River Soleil, perched on an isle amidst white rapids—the Gilded Gates were sealed, its spires reaching to dark clouds and the hidden moon. Such portents troubled Baldwin greatly. Weirder still were those who lingered in the plaza, urbanites in waterlogged clothes, powder since washed from their wigs and faces, drowned cadavers still standing, maggots slithering in their eyes and mouths. Baldwin readied the Broken Blade but dared not approach, careful not to touch the whimpering hosts. Cysts pulsed on their necks, easily mistaken for buboes if not for the twitching within.

Not even Humbaba dared to speak.

Gipi kept to the leper's shadow, watching his every deliberate motion, though no song was to be written. No heroics or epic deeds came to mind, no comparisons to be made, only melancholy underpinned her every thought. Not merely to the horror, either, but to Baldwin's fate. His was a forced march and had been since the sewers. Once he swung the Broken Blade with delusional strength, delivering the wicked to an early grave, but now, he was frail—barely able to raise his sword, let alone challenge his own mortality. Though Baldwin would never admit it, he passed the host not to preserve some notion of stealth or secrecy but to spare his companions from peril. He could not shield them as he once did.

Time was running out.

With a hacking cough, Baldwin spat a mouthful of blood into the wet gutter, choosing to ignore the rising fever, channeling his illness into strength, if only to animate his flesh with willpower alone. He paused to catch his breath, watching plumes of steam rise from the storm drains. Warily, he approached a manhole and lifted its lid with strained effort. Those rungs led not to the sewers but to another section of the underground altogether.

"We're close now," he said.

The corridor was lit with electrified lamps and bronze pipage lined the walls, leading to the hiss of frothing chemicals and steady pistons—industrial percussion. Trails of slime led away from the noise. At the route's end, Baldwin came to a tremendous chamber of metal rivets and high stone walls, a sprawling library with shelves and volumes of alchemical lore. Open tomes and scholars lay strewn indiscriminately about the checkerboard floor. The air was ripe with gas and unknown substances, alluding to a deeper facility therein. Descending a latticed flight of stairs, Baldwin knelt to examine a torn page, finding an anatomical diagram of a "neunauge," as annotated with hasty scribbles. It was identical to the nine-eyed eels infesting the Midgewater Mire, perhaps a larval stage of the carrion-eaters which Pierrot was so fond of.

Though the notes were sparse, the notes read as such.

Exoparasite, expels internal organs to animate cadavers
Rapid reproduction, invasive species to Lumière
Eusocial, colony organism; sentient?

Baldwin discarded the page and turned to his companions. "We can study later," he said. "There is no time to read. Let alone decide what is worth salvaging."

"Agreed," Humbaba said.

"There has to be more." Gipi shrugged. "Artifacts, maybe? Think Desdemona wanted something a little more physical. Besides," she looked about the archives, "think this is it."

The Salon de Sade was not the torture palace Baldwin had envisioned; rather, an institution of learning and ill-advised experimentation. Many presumed prison cells were in truth study halls and cellars of transmutative supplies, and yet, the frequency of broken glass and battered cages betrayed the laboratory as one devoted to neunauge research. The sheer breadth of this work was not lost on him. From selenography to genetic studies in greenhouses, the Sun King had devoted every ounce of scientific funding to mastery over the worms of the earth—most of them vivisected, donated by one Doctor Cronenberg. There was no true evidence of human experimentation, though the odor of burnt hair and flesh left little to the imagination.

It was not until a hidden exhibit that the ambitions of Vermillion were made clear.

In that round chamber, once sealed by vaulted doors now left ajar, Baldwin came to a trove of archeological finds pilfered from every corner of the colonies. Among the moon's tears and relics of antiquity was a tall, obsidian stele from Sarukhand, predating the Deluge by a millennium, chiseled when the Great Glaciers first began to recede. Amidst the cuneiform of a hundred dialects lining its triangular surfaces, codes of law, was the relief of the Great Maw and its spiraling rings of teeth—delicately carved, nigh impossible in detail. Something else rested in its yawning core, a hierophant of sorts, hosting a radiant triangle above their faceless head.

"The Malachite Pyramid," Gipi said.

"You mean," Baldwin turned to face her, "the thing Pierrot uncovered?"

Gipi nodded, silently, and the color drained from her cheeks.

"What does it mean?" As Baldwin approached the artifact, he noticed a translation written on a placard, illuminating these eldritch implications in full.

It is by the divine authority of the Conqueror Worm that I transcribe its wordless will into black stone eternal. It is by such power invested in my bloodline that I rule land, sea, and sky, and command all of mankind to follow this example to the decrees of god-kings—lest those who deviate suffer perdition in the bowels of oblivion. Though to the Dragon Below, my own will is but the child of the father, and my legacy to be dictated by machinations which none may fathom. Let the law be testament to that which appeases the worms of the earth—letting man live to see sunrise and the sunrise thereafter.

Baldwin's legs quivered upon these revelations. Of all the legends he'd studied, the books he'd read, never before had he encountered an excerpt so ancient — so evil. The codes were ways of blood sacrifice, the right of the powerful to subjugate the weak, and disturbing details on "ordeal by worms," should tyranny be challenged in the antediluvian world. In such an age, the Conqueror Worm was akin to God, though to call it such would be sacrilege in the eyes of the Holy See, and yet, Baldwin's faith was shaken by the existence of these blasphemies. He recalled the temple beneath the foundations of Nedlergate, the desolation of the Great Khandish Desert, and now, confronted with the Dragon Below — that which gnawed at the root of the world, waiting until the stars were right, when it would hatch from the planetary egg incubated by man since the first flame. If God allowed such a thing to exist, what did that say about Him? Was it not anathema to His will? Was the Almighty truly so powerful? Or was there something else, apocryphal truths meant to drown with the sinful earth?

Regardless, the text ended as such.

When my great works are but dust in the wind, my cities but rubble and ruin in the sands of time, many will rise to take up this mantle, though few will even earn the ire of worms, let alone their tutelage. Know this, it is by the Malachite Pyramid, the Key to the Gate, that the Conqueror Worm will stir and return that once spawned unto itself — ushering the End of the Age. This is as it should be. It is why we are here.

At that moment, Baldwin drew the Broken Blade, his conviction giving way to an urgent will to see the world live. "The time is now. We must kill Pierrot."

"What're you — ?" Gipi gasped.

"He has the Malachite Pyramid," the leper said, "and will

unleash doom upon the world. Such a monster as he cannot be allowed to own such a weapon. Let alone live. Vermillion knows not what it toys with. Pierrot, however — he does."

"How?" Gipi asked. "How can he possibly do that?"

"Look around you," Baldwin snapped. "Only a fool would deny what he's capable of...."

Breathing heavy and labored, the leper held back a coughing fit, tasting blood in the back of his throat. Gipi laid a hand on his shoulder in concern, her other hand over the hilt of her dagger; together, they half-expected the worms to make themselves known.

Nothing emerged — yet.

Humbaba came to their side. "One would think he knows we're here."

Loathsome murmurs echoed from neighboring corridors, and hulking silhouettes emerged from the shadows — walking cadavers whose muscle and sinew had been eaten and displaced by white worms. "Leechwalkers," as so-named by previous cells.

"Do not fight them," Humbaba held the leper back, "we have no hope of —"

"Do not speak to me of hope!" Baldwin snapped. "We make for the Grande Chateau and end this. Once and for all." In the wake of a second wind, the leper cleaved through the parasitized dead in search of the nearest elevator. "We find a way up," he ordered.

Though he did not look back, Baldwin quickened his pace to a sprint — a roiling tide of slime-soaked worms gave chase, screeching and squelching in ravenous hunger, nipping at Humbaba's sandals. At last, they found an elevator and boarded swiftly. Gipi tapped a brass button repeatedly, and sheets of glass slowly slid shut. The swarm had flooded the entire corridor and collided with the doors, pushing, pressing its panels, cracking the surface, a million toothy maws suckling the frame. Slowly, as if in spite of its own engineering, the elevator trembled, beginning to climb — its ascent punctuated by the recording of some string quartet. Baldwin leaned against the doorframe, whispering yet another prayer into his rosary.

Gipi sighed with relief. "Fuck...."

No words were spoken. She kept an eye on the dial overhead, watching the elevator climb to the ground and middle floors of the Grand Chateau. If what the stele said was true, then Baldwin's panic was hardly misplaced, but the concept of taking on a sorcerous psychopath at the height of his power was not a comforting one. Gipi stifled her shakes as she clutched her damp cap and bells, averting her gaze to the floor, desperate for distractions—to whip up a limerick or something. She didn't want to die. She didn't come this far to see the End Times, and yet, what could she do against the Fool General?

What could any of them hope to achieve?

With a chime, the doors slid open. The upper floors of the Grand Chateau, once opulent and imperial, were caked with the crimson viscera of nobles. From claw marks raking the wainscoting to heaps of raw carrion about the carpets, whatever struggle that had happened was brief indeed, reducing the Sun King's entourage and guard to mangled remains within hours. Only a faint echo of a pipe organ echoed far above, as if goading the known intruders to seek out their own demise. Dictators had a penchant for the dramatic, and Pierrot was no exception. Even now, drunk on madness and bloodlust, the Fool General basked in his great victory—the murder of the Sun King and all opposition in the Cité du Vermillion—that much Baldwin knew. Pursuing the music up many flights of spiraling stairs, from apartment to apartment, he remained undeterred by doubt between the floors, ignorant to the crimson light piercing the stained-glass windows, and to the aura emanating from that wicked melody. Then he came to the summit.

Kicking in the door to the Throne Room, on the twelfth floor of the Royal Clock Tower, Baldwin's voice rose to a deafening roar.

"Pierrot!" he bellowed.

The music ceased. Pierrot's back was to the leper. Beneath a ceiling of ceaseless machinery, he was seated before a great instrument of ivory keys and tall bronze pipes, lined with gargoyles of lamprey-drakes and lost souls. The Throne of the Sun King lay smashed on the approach, flanked by the windowed light of the moon. The late monarch was crucified in the nude upon a low stone arch — an apple in his mouth. Pierrot stood, slowly, revealing his stolen robes and regalia: white ruff, powdered wig, and all, and so, the usurper began his well-rehearsed speech.

"I wish I would've known," said the Fool General, "how troublesome you would be." He remained slouched over the keys, head bowed, fingers fluttering over nothing in particular. "There's something to be said about a merry band of heroes cornering the villain. You're so damn proud of yourself, aren't you?" His words oozed with venom until his persona cracked with repressed laughter. "Oh, who am I kidding? You know I can't stay mad at you, Good King Baldwin." Pierrot spun around, revealing the freshly painted face of an aristocrat, complete with a black mole and pursed lips. "Honestly, you fascinate me."

Baldwin took a few steps forward, the Broken Blade at the ready.

"It's funny, really," Pierrot said. "Do you ever ponder if there's such a thing as past lives? I mean, I know you don't. What with your 'Cult of the Far Messiah' following, but I can't help but wonder if we've met before in a past — or maybe future age."

"You're stalling," Baldwin said. "Enough."

"No, I'm merely contemplating my navels. There's more to true heroics than swinging your sword on the battlefield. You need to know, from the bottom of your heart, why you fight. Even at the journey's end, I don't think you can truthfully answer that."

The leper remained undeterred. "You speak as if you know me."

Pierrot eyed the company and gave a knowing grin. "I've

been giving it some thought," he said. "Why do you fight? To what end do you go through such lengths with no guarantee of success? Hell, I do not comprehend your goals. To 'do good well?' To secure a legacy worthy of remembrance? There has to be something more. No king abdicates a throne for that, unless...."

Baldwin halted in his tracks, but said nothing.

"That's supposed to be the part where you parrot the last word I said," Pierrot sighed, rolling his eyes. "Anyway, it occurred to me that maybe that's part of it. To have absence make the heart grow fonder and whatnot." He clapped, slowly. "Rather manipulative, if you ask me. Alas, I doubt a dozen uncredited deeds will cut it. Not for the kind of recognition you're seeking. You need something bigger. A true tragedy." He bowed low and graciously. "A service I'll be happy to provide. Well, not that you have a say in the matter."

"What do you mean?" the leper asked, lowering his sword ever so slightly.

"Baldwin," Gipi called, "don't—"

"I hear the Holy Land is quite pleasant this time of year."

The leper's heart plummeted into his chest. Flashes of burning cathedrals blinded his mind's eye. His subjects murdered in the open streets—feasts for the worms of the earth. All to pay the price of his absence. All to answer for their lord's hubris.

"No!" Before he fully realized what he was doing, Baldwin lunged and swung wide, seeking to deliver his sword to Pierrot's skull, only for the Fool General to pinch the blade, stopping it effortlessly. His smile widened, revealing a mouthful of yellowed fangs. "You will do no such thing," the leper all but pleaded. "You will not."

"A shame, really," Pierrot said.

Flickers of sickly green flame began to orbit Pierrot's spare hand. With a palm strike, the Fool General sent his plaything careening across the Throne Room. Gipi dashed and slid to Baldwin's side while Humbaba raised his fists in an act of futile defiance.

"None of your efforts will matter," Pierrot continued. "I will salt the Holy Land. And perhaps, in the end, you will be remembered, Good King Baldwin—if only for your failures." Arms wide, he began to waltz towards the company. "The Conqueror Worm hungers."

Row upon row, the stained-glass windows shattered and burst in barrages of jagged confetti, revealing the flight of swarming things against the clouds, thick enough to blot out the moon—an armada of flying terrors. Despite his fear and fatigue, Baldwin stood, shaking, and hoisted himself by the hilt of the Broken Blade, taking one last stance.

Pierrot eyed him, up and down. "I've been looking forward to this."

Baldwin lunged with silent fury, eyes blind and burning against this foe worthy of hatred. With a salute and swing of a ceremonial sword, Pierrot rushed and met his opponent with the narrow steel of his rapier—true to his origin as a dandy of the lower courts.

"Make no mistake," Pierrot said. "This doesn't come from a place of malice." His smile almost turned genuine. "Great men such as us are worthy of remembrance. Hence my gift." Together, they locked blades. Despite the leper's efforts, Pierrot's supernatural strength proved more than a match for his mortal bravado. "Oh, surely, you can do better."

"You're not human," Baldwin snarled.

"An astute observation," Pierrot winked, "but hardly one worth dwelling on." He pressed down on Baldwin's hilt. "The best monsters are born of men. You should know that."

Shoving the Fool General back, Baldwin swung wide and wildly, desperate to land a single blow against his quarry. Pierrot was perpetually an inch out of reach; dueling, dancing mad, relishing in every miss, mocking the leper with his very existence, when a hint of deep green stone flashed under his royal robes— the Malachite Pyramid. Suddenly, Pierrot shrieked in pain. A fateful dirk had found its mark, piercing his side, twisting into his sinew. With a brutal slash, Gipi dove between the duelers and swiped the artifact free.

"Run," she said.

Baldwin stared in shock at his companion's newfound courage, the implications of victory starting to sink in—until long strands of flukish sinew erupted from Pierrot's gaping wound. The Fool General's eyes widened in horror as he tried desperately to shove his own innards back into his body. Humbaba had already led an expeditious retreat. Pierrot's screams began to fade. The company fled from corridor to corridor, en route to the hangar on a whim and fleeting hope. Faithful as a hound, the *Tarrasque* was indeed waiting for them.

"Go, go, go," Gipi repeated in a maddened mantra, "go!"

Leaping onto the dirigible's deck, the company staggered and tumbled as the *Tarrasque* took flight across the midnight skyline. Baldwin immediately sought shelter in the cabin, ushering his companions inside, much to Desdemona's shock and awe.

"Did you—?"

"We found it." Gipi raised the Malachite Pyramid. "Wasn't easy, mind you."

The sultana's eyes widened. "The relic!"

"Worse than you'd think," Humbaba said. "Pierrot's enslaved by the Conqueror Worm and wants to use it to usher in the End Times. He's a bloody lunatic."

"We make for the Holy Land," Baldwin said. "Do not ask why."

With a hesitant nod, Desdemona relayed their course to the Sisters Dervish, who obeyed in kind—when monstrous rumbling filled the Grande Chateau. Baldwin's eyes darted out the sternward window and gawked in horror. Wingless and serpentine, a roundworm of a dragon emerged and darted against the moonlight, joining the armada of flying terrors, seemingly endless in length yet silhouetted, sharing the distorted voice of the Fool General. Whatever injury Gipi had dealt, it let something else escape — a nemesis of reason, an evil within.

"Is that," Baldwin managed, "Pierrot?"

With an ear-shattering cry, the Lindwyrm rallied its legions.

"Follow them," the leper ordered, panic welling in his chest.

"What?" Desdemona gawked. "We can't engage with — !"

"Do as I say! They cannot reach the Holy Land."

Hundreds of feet below them, the Gates of Vermillion yawned upon the Lindwyrm's command, ushering a great host of maggot-folk onto the highroad — twisted mockeries of Imperial soldiers, uniforms tattered and slime-crusted, armed with arquebuses and pikes, slathering as slaves to darkness. Great fighting vehicles and siege engines rolled among their ranks, pulled by rolling isopods and slithering things. The whole of the city was shackled to the Lindwyrm's will. It led the vanguard from the air on a long, eastward march to the Midlands and Golgotha beyond. Not even the *Tarrasque* could combat these forces.

Reeling in the wake of legions, the dirigible took an alternative course despite Baldwin's shouting protests. Eyes watering with hate and horror at this perceived cowardice, it wasn't until Gipi shook the leper's shoulders that he remotely came to.

"Listen to me," she shouted. "We've got to warn them!"

Baldwin paused; her words fell upon deaf ears.

"If we die taking on that...thing," Gipi said, "then who'll save your people?"

"She's right," Humbaba said. "We must prepare for a siege."

Despite the cackling taunts of the Lindwyrm, Baldwin came to his senses — albeit haltingly. "You're right," he choked. "We must outrun them. And warn," he paused, "my people." The leper scoffed to himself. How long had it been since he'd admitted responsibility as king? What had changed in his absence? Would he be welcomed? Would he even be recognized? Regardless, he would not live to see his kingdom burn. That much he swore.

"Set course for the Holy Land," he conceded.

CHAPTER FOUR

Distant yet parallel to the armies of darkness, the *Tarrasque* kept on its urgent course. Days bled together seamlessly, and Baldwin kept an eye on the north—he had no desire to eat or sleep, nor did he stir from his post, vigilant to a fault. Near the day's end, Gipi emerged with a plate of pickled herring and boiled eggs—standard fare for such a voyage—munching as obnoxiously as possible to earn the leper's attention.

With a bitter sigh, Baldwin glanced over his shoulder.

"Want some?" she asked, coyly.

"No, thank you."

"You sure? Can't slay dragons on an empty stomach."

Baldwin did not reply.

"It's been a while, hasn't it?" Gipi joined her absent-minded liege. "Since we've been home." She leaned against the taffrail and glanced at the thousand-foot drop to the autumnal forest, only to shudder and turn away. "Listen, I get that you're scared, we all are, but brooding over the horizon won't solve anything. So, let's go inside and have someone else keep watch."

"No," the leper said.

Gipi bit her lip. "Alright. Suit yourself."

Baldwin watched plumes of smoke rise in the wake of the maggot-folk. Though he could not see such carnage or hear the screams, he knew the Fool General had and would raze many villages on the road to Golgotha. Too long had Pierrot been let to run rampant as a scourge upon the world. Too long had good men stood idle and enabled his slaughter. Baldwin would be lying to call himself an exception. He was a witness to atrocities beyond reason. Indeed, he almost forgave himself for being one person. In the end, his greatest victories had not been accomplished alone, but rather, as the king of a nation.

So, Baldwin opened his journal and filled the final page.

I would not call my quest a failure, futile as it may be, rather, a reminder of my purpose. Perhaps I should regret my departure from the Holy Land, and yet, should I not have obeyed my wanderlust, I would not be the same man homeward bound. The things I've seen. The ways and horrors of the wider world. They would have occurred regardless of my journey. Regardless, I am grateful for what I've learned and the allies I've made. God willing, whether in life or in death, we will find solace.

For that alone, I will pray.

Baldwin shut the book and closed his eyes, taking in a lungful of thin air. The sun crept low over the Massifs, and the verdant pastures of the South Cantons beckoned. Twilight had fallen once more. Step by step, he returned to the lower decks and joined his gladiators in their barracks, Humbaba first and foremost among them. The thrall gave a curt nod of respect, his shaven face shadowed by the gathering dark.

"Look at us," his words were soft. "To think a few months ago, we were resigned to fight for the same evil we're up against."

Baldwin did not reply; in truth, he did not know what brought him here.

"Are you all right?" the thrall asked.

"I think we both know the answer to that," Baldwin muttered.

Humbaba nodded. "Can't say I blame you. Would be a shame for all this to be for nothing. Still," he paused, "we wouldn't be free without you."

The leper stiffened, unsure as to what to say.

"I know you don't give it much thought," Humbaba sighed, "but we're...grateful for what you've done for us." He paused, as if admitting that it was painful, yet looked about the ranks of swarthy men who had his attention. "Without you, none of us would've had a cause beyond fighting for survival and the amusement of sultans and viziers."

"I did nothing, save to remind you of your own strength."

"Don't be so modest," Humbaba scoffed. "It's not becoming of a king...."

The leper shook his head. "If I were ever the king you thought I was, I would've freed your people long ago." He sat on a swaying hammock, laying his brow against his bandaged hand. "Your loyalty is admirable yet misplaced, I fear."

"It's also earned. Not given freely."

"Humbaba—"

"With all due respect, your highness, shut up and listen. A lesson taught is a lesson learned. No matter how hard it may be. You spared me back in the Colosseo, when I didn't deserve it, so it's our turn to repay you."

The gladiators nodded in solemn agreement.

"You got people who believe in you," the thrall said. "Don't take that for granted."

Baldwin uttered a defeated laugh. "I wonder if you'll keep that conviction in the face of oblivion." He stood, sharply. "Thank you for your service. All of you. Our courage will surely be tested in the coming hours. Let our ends be worthy of remembrance."

As the leper turned his back to the wooden steps, Humbaba's eyes narrowed upon him. "Let me put it another way," he called. "We who are about to die, salute you."

"Trust me," Baldwin said, "I don't plan to live long after."

When Baldwin returned to the upper deck, he was greeted by a nighttime gale whisking his tattered cloak, threatening to whisk away his hood. Across the *Tarrasque*, Gipi leaned against the far cabin and strummed her lute, twisting her pegs and tuning her strings.

"Deliver one of your rousing speeches?" she winked.

"Merely a reminder of our mortality."

Gipi rolled her eyes. "How inspiring...."

"Better than a lie."

"Never said otherwise." She cocked her head to the cabin. "Desdemona would like a word, too. Wants to talk about the coming siege. You know, our plan."

Muttering under his breath, Baldwin would humor the sultana, if only to ease his own anxieties. Past the threshold, the cabin was thick with incense and candlelight. Desdemona lay on a sofa with a hookah at hand, lost in a meditative stupor. The Malachite Pyramid was but a paperweight atop the bookshelf, staring as a silent voyeur upon them both. No shortage of bottles and amber spirits lined the liquor cabinet. Silence was rivaled only by the scent of hashish.

"Baldwin," she barely noticed his approach, words slurring, "you've been busy."

The leper shut the door, but did not speak.

"It's a wonder how writings cloud one's judgment," she mused. "To think we've known each other so long, if only through letters and civil words, under the pretense that I was a man." She turned to face him. "Do you think of me differently now? Knowing who I really am."

"I assume you think differently of me. Knowing my affliction."

"That's—"

"We'd be lying to each other, and ourselves, to say otherwise." He pulled up a distant seat. "That was then. This is now. And we have much more to do."

Desdemona's eyes gleamed in the candlelight. "You speak as you write."

"My apologies," Baldwin said.

"There's no need." She puffed a thin ring of smoke, joining the swirling miasma overhead, wisps of clouds in salacious chiaroscuro. "We deserve better fates, you and I, and should things be different, we would surely make a happy couple."

Baldwin averted his eyes, his flushed beneath the mask. "I...."

"Alas," Desdemona covered her naked breast with a sheet

of silk, "it is not so."

The leper stared at the paneled floor until the need to drown his embarrassment grew too great. "If I may." He approached the cabinet and poured a pair of snifters, half-forgetting his own malady — fingers numb and limbs shaking, spilling more than his share. He downed them both to curb the shame — a vintage to be savored. "Have you given any consideration?" The leper poured another glass. "Our strategy for when we reach the Holy Land?"

"I assume we'll consult the lord-regent and take command of his crusaders," Desdemona began. "Between Golgotha's standing army, the Sisters Dervish, and Humbaba's armed rabble, we may have a hope in hell against Pierrot's forces. Morale pending." She stared at the moaning rafters. "We also have the *Tarrasque*, for what that's worth."

"More than either of us are inclined to believe," the leper said. "There is something rather poetic about using the Imperial flagship to slay the Fool General."

"Poetry rarely wins wars."

"No," Baldwin admitted, "but it can galvanize the hearts of men who wage them." He raised his glass in a somber salute. "I do not expect to survive the coming battle."

"I don't think you want to."

That caught the leper off guard. "I beg your pardon?" he sputtered, nearly choking on liquor. Desdemona took a long draw from her hookah. "What do you mean by that?"

"It's no secret that you crave death on your own terms. I do not blame you, but the world is more than what we leave behind. It is what we experience as well, and you've starved yourself of such a thing in pursuit of legacy. Admirable, if only in martyrdom."

"I did not ask for this."

"No, but you embrace it nevertheless."

Baldwin finished the contents of his glass. "We're not far from Golgotha. I suspect we'll arrive come dawn's first light. Until then, we should try to rest...."

"Yes, that we should."

The leper took his leave, eager to flee from reminders of his own weakness, pervasive as they were. Desdemona's words did not leave him — nor would they ever. Lying flat on his back atop the cabin, he gazed at the myriad stars and let his thoughts sail the Sea of Souls, desperate to find a moment of peace, reassurance that he embarked on the righteous road. A familiar chill and veil of frost denied him such a thing. Death had come once more.

Baldwin did not greet her, for she had never left.

"Why are you here?" he asked.

"To see if you've come to terms with your deeds," Death said. "You've come a long way from the vagabond who witnessed the Massacre of Gravesend." She knelt at his side. "And yet, in the end, after everything you've seen, you find your struggles lacking in true purpose."

"Not necessarily," Baldwin said.

Death cocked her head, quizzically. "Oh?"

The leper paused to breathe, choosing his next words carefully. "I do not regret leaving the Holy Land," he began, "though I do find it most ironic that I left a site of pilgrimage to tour the profane world. To save man from himself, to earn my place among the saints, of which I am not worthy." He dared not look her in the eye. "I've learned much on this doomed crusade of mine. Things I would have never harkened to otherwise."

"And what of the horrors you've seen? Of those you could not save?"

"They would've died regardless of my intervention," Baldwin retorted. "As do we all."

Death's smile widened, yet she said nothing, bidding him to continue.

"I've seen much, and yet, I could not stop the Great Fire of Nedlergate nor any of Pierrot's massacres. Commoner or king, one man is ill-meant to change the course of history. And I am just that — one man. My power rests not in my sword alone," he gestured about the *Tarrasque*, "but in those I've inspired and the seeds I've sown. In truth, that is why I return to the Holy Land. To rally all I have earned against the destruction of all I hold dear. Whether I live or die, it matters not. For this is a cause worthy of my life and legacy." His eyes narrowed with newfound resolve. "And I would slay any who would deny that providence."

Death clapped, slowly. "This is the most honest exchange we've shared," her voice seemed all the more youthful, face still hidden by her cowl. "Perhaps God's judgment was not misplaced. Perhaps you shall serve the Symphonia Mundi yet."

"I," he began, "am in no condition to negotiate, however—"

"Oh, Good King Baldwin. You've been given far more chances than you deserved. It is only by the will of the Far Messiah that you even breathe. Do not take such a thing for granted."

That of all things, Baldwin did not foresee.

"Is there more to this? What am I missing? Please, tell me."

Death was inscrutable as ever. "That remains to be seen." She raised her head as dawn's first light rose in the east, shining upon the sights of Golgotha and its environs. "Best of luck in your 'decisive battle.' Rest assured, I will be watching."

Before he could so much as stand, Baldwin was alone once more. The *Tarrasque* had since crossed the Ash Mountains and began to lower its course over the Gotland Veldt—the realm he once knew. From its dry fields to old olive trees upon the tors, little had changed in his absence, much to the leper's relief. Shadowing the goatherds and arid parishes, the dirigible had earned the stares of an entire kingdom. Village priests likely thought the heavenward vessel a daemon, and yet, Baldwin could provide no comfort to those who fled. After the wonders he'd seen, the horrors he'd endured, he thought the land naïve and backwards in comparison to the wider world, as were his former beliefs. Golgotha was rooted in romance with no hope of survival against the powers on the march, not as it was.

Within the hour, the company reconvened on the deck.

"Honestly," Gipi said, "it feels…weird to be back."

"Indeed. I am unsure as to what to expect."

As per Baldwin's instruction, the *Tarrasque* laid anchor east of the Holy City with its spires and tall parapets of stone. Hearing the call to arms from atop the Pilgrim's Gate, Baldwin took a deep breath and set foot onto the veldt of his youth. With the company rallied in full, he approached the doors he'd once departed, eying the archers atop the high stone walls.

"Let us pass," he called, raising a hand. "I am Baldwin IV of Golgotha. Our business is most dire." He paused, mustering the will to speak the truth. "Your king returns."

The bowmen glanced at one another, seemingly reluctant to obey. Slowly, they left the battlements. Odd silence passed until the gates opened.

CHAPTER FIVE

The Cathedral City beckoned as the bastion of all the faithful. With its high basilicas, steeples, and belfries rose as monuments to the Holy See, though its presence was nominal in times of war. Seemingly hewn from the Hill itself, streets sprawled into districts, flanked by flying buttresses and monastic compounds. Banners of the saltire hung low from stone parapets. Residences were seemingly afterthoughts compared to the splendor of the churches — modest and cramped, flats for artisans who'd toiled endlessly to raise these gothic feats. The city was perpetually under construction. No shortage of wooden latticed towers and treadwheel cranes peppered the stoic skyline, and the grind of metal against stone could be heard from any quarter at any hour. Such was the prize of the Holy Land.

"Hey," Gipi snapped her fingers, "Baldwin! We need to keep moving."

One by one, the company walked ahead of him.

Baldwin lingered upon the threshold. Though the Pilgrim's Gate had since opened, his eyes were fixed upon brick-and-mortar apartments and dust-choked lanes, beige reminders of what he'd left behind. Warily, he led the company past his former subjects as they halted, turning their heads, mouths agape and eyes wide. Peasants in shawls and earthen colors, soldiers in soiled tabards, all made way, though none dared to bow. Perhaps it was confusion, or the throes of perceived betrayal, and yet, theirs was a welcome Baldwin had expected. The spires of the palace and lazaretto loomed across the lower serfdoms, though no bell sang to announce the return of the king. Indeed, the leper was just that — a leper.

In the throes of humiliation, he walked towards the Royal Palace of Golgotha.

Plodding hoofbeats drew near. Baldwin halted to face those who'd accost his company—knights in medieval arms, noble in pretension, helpless in the coming hours.

"Ah," he sighed with relief, "familiar colors."

"What business have you here, sir?" asked the banneret at their helm.

Baldwin scoffed at such audacity. "I'm loath to believe I've been gone that long."

"Answer the question," the soldier's tone was forced, "for my sake, if nothing else."

The leper paused, hesitant to divulge such information, even if he didn't rightly know why. "I am Baldwin IV of Golgotha. I was your king not six months ago. And though I've since abdicated my throne, I'd appreciate a tad more respect from you—and your men."

The riders glanced at each other, shifting in uncertainty.

"If you please," the leper raised a hand, "I must speak to the lord regent. Now."

The banneret lifted his visor, revealing the scarred, stubbled face of the king's lieutenant in sieges past. "Never thought I'd see you again, Good King Baldwin."

"Sir Reynald," Baldwin recognized him at once, "a pleasure to see you as well."

"Walk with me," he dismounted, "you and your companions. We have much to discuss." Reynald led the way down familiar lanes to the slums where Baldwin had once passed out provisions to the sick and dying—how long ago it seemed. Many familiar faces were sequestered in the Leper Quarter, though he could not name them. Refugees from Mulgrave and Othello had been displaced by the Vermillion campaigns, and sought asylum within the Wailing Walls. "Things have changed since your departure," he said, "and not for the better."

"Indeed," Baldwin said. "A great evil comes for us all. And it has scorched many a nation before ours." He turned to his old friend. "Please, where is the lord regent?"

Reynald did not reply, all but ignoring his liege.

"Where," Baldwin cupped his shoulder, "is he—?"

"There is no regent."

"What?" the leper gasped.

Reynald nodded solemnly. "The Pontiff in Chimay saw fit to take control over the Cathedral City by papal bull. Again. Much has changed since your absence. This is not the crusader kingdom you once ruled. Noble a reign it was."

"That is ridiculous," Baldwin snarled. "Chimay is under Vermillion occupation—!"

"I am well aware."

"Dammit, Reynald," the leper grasped his arm. "What're you saying? That your lot just…capitulated in my absence? Have we no honor? No sense of duty?" His fingernails dug deep into the gaps between the banneret's armor, tears welling in his eyes. "Listen to me. We are all in grave danger. And no amount of clerical coddling will save us from what's coming."

There was a dilemma in Reynald's eyes, as if he'd felt some kinship and loyalty to the monarch, and yet, he dared not show it. "Firstly," he brushed the bandaged hand aside, "what the bloody hell are you on about? What's coming?"

Baldwin's gaze darted to the western sky. Though the *Tarrasque* had well outflown the Lindwyrm, the maggot host was within a week's march from Golgotha.

"I will tell you what I know," he said, "and attempt to keep it short."

So Baldwin regaled his journey and the terrible course of the world. Reynald's eyes widened in awe at such tales. Though he nodded in understanding of every word, his belief waned upon the description of the Lindwyrm and the advancing armies.

"The enemy will be here soon," Baldwin finished. "And if you dare count on Vermillion to save us, then Golgotha is already dead, and our people with her."

"I," Reynald eyed the rest of the company, "will take you to the 'palace.'"

"Thank you."

The banneret raised a gauntleted hand in peace, and a quiet befell in his ranks, from knight to page, page to squire. "However, I cannot promise the cardinal will be as receptive as I." So, he led the way. "I am glad to see you again, Baldwin."

Lukewarm wind did nothing to soothe the leper's temper. A lack of royal titles was not lost on him, though he dared not speak his mind. The knights muttered among themselves; whether in disdain or otherwise, Baldwin could not say. Despite his rising indignance, the leper shut his eyes and gritted his teeth, knowing that he'd deserved no short degree of scorn—for his absence, his negligence. Regardless, he kept on, seeing this as a purgatory of his own making.

"God willing," Reynald said, "you are as mad as they say."

"If prayers would only make it so...."

The banneret shot a glare from over his shoulder. "Be careful what you say, Baldwin. This is not your city any longer, though many would wish otherwise."

Slowly, the Royal Palace of Golgotha crept into vision. Just as Baldwin recalled the morning of his initial departure, hollow metal clangs echoed throughout its halls, though such noise troubled him greatly. He recognized them as death knells and the workings of medical machinery, to say nothing of the corpse-wagons in the gutters. Had his dynasty's house been converted to a hospice ward? Was this the legacy he'd earned? Clenching his fists, Baldwin bid the company to wait outside in the open air. He had nothing to fear, for he'd already suffered the final throes of this loathsome malady. Only Gipi had the courage to join him.

"You don't need to do this," Baldwin said.

She shrugged, feigning apathy. "I know."

Upon the threshold, Reynald donned a mask stuffed with herbs and thyme and opened the moaning doors to the lazaretto. Baldwin felt its crimson-stained tiles crack underfoot and endured a choir of weakened coughs, every gasp a grim reminder of the man he once was. In lieu of deathbeds were bunks and racks of weapons and armor—barracks for the dying and diseased. Pages marred with sores and lesions were supervised by the old guard. Staggering and stupefied by their own ineptitude, the fledglings trained in hope of joining some unsung crusade. Baldwin looked at their regimen in disgust, not only due to their wretched form, but also the hollow glaze of their eyes. Was this truly the ambition of so many? To die a numbered death on the field of battle? The will to rally and make a martial difference in spite of fatal illness? No. Not remotely.

Something, or someone, had persuaded them.

Baldwin looked to his troubadour for reassurance; she was just as mortified.

"Is this the work of the cardinal?" he asked.

"Yes," Reynald said.

"Take me to him. Now."

Rage stirred in the leper's heart, welling inside him as plumes of murderous smoke. Further into the lazaretto, Baldwin came to his former chambers annexed by the Knights Hospitaller, men in linen wraps and iron masks—imitations of the king. Wet eyes widened upon his approach, for Baldwin's reputation long preceded him. Towering over the mockery guard, he was granted passage to royal quarters since appropriated to the clergy's liking.

"Cardinal Milan," Reynald announced. "We have a most urgent visitor."

Gipi lingered at the door, content to bask in the architecture and emerald banners of the last home she had truly known, eyes awash with saccharine nostalgia.

The room was dark—curtains drawn and candles failing, in Baldwin's own bed languished a cadaverous shade of a man. Though regaled in robes and finery, the cardinal's chest heaved with every laborious breath, face veiled in shadow, though his gums and yellow teeth glistened in the dimness. It seemed Milan had suffered the same malady as Baldwin, though the two had found solace in different means. With the lift of a withered hand, the cardinal bid his attendants to leave them be. Reynald stayed by the door, a hand over his sword's hilt.

"Welcome home," the cardinal wheezed.

Baldwin did not speak, torn between pity and rage.

"Why have you come, child...?"

"I have come," he began, "to warn you. To warn my people. The Fool General and his armies are on the march to Golgotha. We must prepare accordingly."

"Impossible," Milan coughed, "Vermillion has nothing to gain from the Holy Land."

"You overestimate our enemy's sanity."

"Bold of you to call the Empire our enemy." Milan grimaced. "The Sun King has sponsored our newest cathedrals and suppressed the heretic—"

"The Sun King is dead," Baldwin said, "and the Cité du Vermillion with him."

Milan did not reply.

"We don't have the luxury of time," the leper said. "Ignorance will not save you, or my city."

"Your city." Milan sneered. "Child, you are sorely mistaken. You've surrendered all claim to the throne upon departure. In your absence, the Holy See has reclaimed Golgotha and its holdings. It is by papal bull that I, not you, govern the Cathedral City."

"The Pontiff has no right to usurp me."

"You cannot usurp a throne that has no king."

Baldwin glowered at the cardinal and stepped to the foot of the bed. "You may have noticed the Imperial flagship so graciously anchored east of the city," his words oozed with sarcasm, "as to not further alarm the faithful."

Milan nodded, slowly.

"I am not alone, cardinal. I have brought warriors from across the earth. The Sisters Dervish and many a pit-fighter of Khand. You are not so lucky in friends as I."

"Mercenaries are of little use to the Holy See."

"I guarantee," Baldwin said, "that even the knights

you've assembled will answer to me before you breathe your last. You may govern, but are ill meant to lead." He clenched his fists. "What was the price to grease your palms? How many indulgences were bought to purchase your silence?" Against all sense and reason, he drew the Broken Blade, its steel gleaming in the candlelight. "Make no mistake. Should you threaten my people with cowardice, I will end you."

Reynald reached for his own sword, only to be silenced by the leper's glare.

"You have all grown fat and decadent in my absence," Baldwin spat, "and leave us vulnerable to enemies within and without. Enough! Muster the garrison. Tell them, the...old ruler of Golgotha has returned to rally his people from their slumber. Prepare for battle."

Reynald loosened his grip and left to sound a call to arms.

Baldwin prepared to depart when he heard the cardinal utter a bitter laugh.

"You don't think it'll matter, do you?" he rasped. "If what you say is true, the Fool General will raze the city and slaughter us all. What? Have you not heard of Nedlergate or Othello?"

"Do not speak to me of those massacres," Baldwin said. "I was there, Milan. I've seen firsthand the cruelty of Vermillion. It is why I will fight. Perhaps you'd best take the arsenic and make yourself useful in death." So, the leper marched out the door, only to be accosted by a vanguard of lesser knights, bandaged hands over the hilts of their swords.

"To think a man of piety would turn his back upon the cloth," Milan called. "I cannot suffer this, Baldwin. These houses of healing were to be continued in your memory, to raise an army of those who shared your service to the Holy See. A shame, how it must end."

"You've done nothing but profane my name."

Milan raised a hand. "Seize him."

The knights glanced at each other nervously. Baldwin laughed in kind, the Broken Blade at hand. "None of you are prepared to die," he said. "Nor will any of you be remembered if this is how you choose to end your lives. Step aside, and I will forgive this transgression." He gritted his teeth. "Our kingdom did not once wage war against jihadists to quail so easily."

One by one, the knights stepped aside.

"Bar the room," Baldwin said. "Make certain the cardinal does not leave." Down the hall, the leper marched with a gathering entourage of knights and men-at-arms. "Light the beacons and evacuate the parishes," he ordered. "I want every man and strong lad able to bear arms conscripted for the defense. Patrols along the walls at all hours. Keep a weather eye on the west. They will come from the Midlands, trails of slime and scorched earth in their wake." He stared out the window upon the Leper Quarter below, its tenements and sick houses, overflowing with refugees from many a colony. "We will avenge them."

"What of those who cannot fight?" Reynald asked.

"Have them seek sanctuary, but expect no quarter," Baldwin said. "This will be no different from the last crusade. Our decisive battle. Our enemies are no janissaries or slave-soldiers, but the worms of the earth. They are a scourge. And must be exterminated as such."

"Our assets are few," Reynald said.

"What of explosives? Liquid fire? Surely, we have gunpowder."

"Not in ample supply."

"It'll have to do," Baldwin said, emerging onto the gothic parapets. "Mark my words, the Cathedral City will live to see daybreak." He turned to the Knights Hospitaller. "Arm those able to fight. They may get their dying wish yet—to be worthy of my mantle."

"Do as he says," Reynald gave the order.

When the men-at-arms left to prepare for the coming siege, the two were left to brood upon the western sky, where the horizon grew dark and clouds began to brew, days ahead of the invading march. Within moments, the coming mists were recognizable as swarming gnats, swooping low over the fields and shredding wheat and barley to blighted stalks, corrupting the very soil with their venomous presence. The heavens were sickly red, the sun a dull orb wreathed in smoke and acrid fumes — fanned by myriad wings to grant the maggot-folk speed and strength.

"How many?" asked the banneret.

"Vermin beyond count," Baldwin said. "Easily in the tens of thousands. Not only corrupted soldiers but beasts of war as well. Fighting vehicles and siege engines from the Salon de Sade. They are not an army so much as a plague to be put to the flame."

"Why, though?" Reynald asked. "What could the Fool General possibly want with the Holy Land? What have we done to earn such scorn?"

Baldwin lowered his head, mulling over his words. "It is because," he began, haltingly, "our enemy believes us to be weak. Game to be hunted and killed for sport. Pierrot sees our valor as something to exploit. Our history of chivalry is to be mocked. That we are but children with wooden swords." He clutched the crenelations, ignorant of his bleeding fingertips. "Soon, he will be blinded by the very light he seeks to extinguish. He will learn that even dragons may bleed."

"You speak as if the legions of hell are at our gates."

"Trust me, that would be preferable."

At last, Baldwin returned to his company in the cloisters, Humbaba and Desdemona waiting among their pit-fighters and feminine rogues, just as he'd predicted.

"Well?" asked the sultana.

"Is the *Tarrasque* prepared for combat?"

"Our crew is ill-equipped, but I'm sure —"

"Very well," Baldwin said. "I believe I have a plan."

Gipi bit her lip. "Oh, this'll end well."

Baldwin forced a smile — when fatigue gripped his heart. Strange streets and familiar faces faded in and out of vision, a whirlwind of beige and brown. Breathing was a burden, and his blood ran slow and cold. Planting the Broken Blade into cracks in the cobblestones, he leaned against the shaft of steel, unable to contain a mouthful of crimson bile — spewing upon the ground. Even now, he felt no pain yet knew his ulcerated flesh was failing now more than ever. His friends closed in, words of emergent horror ringing in his ears. Slowly, the world dimmed.

Baldwin fell limp and prone against the desert wind.

Only Death seemed to touch him.

CHAPTER SIX

Baldwin dreamt of nothing—no misadventures to be had, no honor or shame to be felt, only the cessation of existence, the atrophy of the soul. Thoughts numb as his flesh, he drifted as a corpse in a tideless sea; breathless, devoid of purpose. It was liberating to feel so little after a lifetime of struggle and adversity. He had no legacy to yearn for, nothing save the certainty that he would return to the Sea of Souls. Not as a champion to be immortalized in constellations, but to be fed the cosmic depths from which all life rose and returned to. If he had the will, Baldwin would've smiled.

Strangely, Death was not to greet him.

Despite his submission, Baldwin woke to blurred glimpses of the lazaretto, of physicians who tended to his wounds, readying a saw-toothed blade for amputation.

"Don't," he squatted the surgeon aside, "touch me. It is not time."

"My lord, your sword arm is septic. If we don't sever it now, you'll surely—"

"Enough!" Baldwin roared past his delirium—haunted, ashamed by what he'd almost crossed willingly. "The enemy is upon us. What time is it?"

"Evensong, my lord."

In a fit of desperation, Baldwin shambled out of bed and cried out for a squire, desperate to don his arms and armor. Cradling his deformities, bad humors flowing from his face, he shambled about his deathbed, ignorant to his clammy skin and rising fever. Though all but blind to the world, the leper could've sworn he heard whispers among his attendants.

"Been like this ever since we found him."

"Still going on about that...Conqueror Worm?"

"Gone mad, the king has."

Baldwin's eyes widened in horror, his mind spiraling in a mania of doubt. Had he dreamt the entire crusade? What if he'd never left the Holy Land? Was it all a dying dream? No, it couldn't be, and yet, why was he here, where it all began? The same hall from his departure. Lost in the throes of hysteria, the leper barreled out of the hospice suite, pursued at a distance by men in raven-beaked masks, armed with syringes and sedatives. At last, he came to the balcony. The Cathedral City gleamed in the twilight. Gipi was seemingly waiting for him, and Baldwin collapsed to his knees — heaving, tears pooling against dry stone.

"Was it?" he wept. "Did it — ?"

"It's all right," Gipi dismissed the doctors, "he's not a threat."

"Gipi," he pawed at her trousers, "was it real?" He raised his head, eyes milky with knowing delusion. "Did it...really happen?"

Gipi knelt to the leper's side. "Yeah," she said, haltingly, "it did..." Upon hearing those words, Baldwin's mind began to clear. He stood, slowly, though hardly at the peak of health. Aching and shaking, the leper eyed the heavens, where spirals of locusts blotted out the sun; light fleeting as it fled west. As the skies darkened, Gipi's smile was warm and genuine, and she cupped his shoulder. "Let's not keep the enemy waiting. They'll be here by nightfall."

"Nightfall? How long was I...?" the leper paused, for he did not know the answer. "Never mind." He said, though hesitant to trust his senses. "I will be fine," he lied to himself. "It was a moment's weakness. Nothing more."

"Would a rousing speech help?"

"Yes," Baldwin said. "One worthy of a bard's recital."

Glancing over his shoulder, the physicians were nowhere to be seen. He cradled his skull, cursing his addled mind. This was no time to falter. His people needed him. Now more than ever. As he took to the narrows of the Leper Quarter, he wandered the streets he knew were rooted in reality, Gipi shadowing his every step from afar. Once more, he passed provisions from the palace, basking in a righteous echo of healthier days. The feeble and the meek took his offerings just as they had so many years ago. It was enough to anchor the leper to the present.

Regardless of its root in reality.

Word spread swiftly of Baldwin's recovery, and he met to face the entourage in full. He would not rally in the cathedrals commissioned by the Holy See, but in the Basilica of the Far Messiah — an old temple, a locus of earth and the Empyrean, the site of miracles yet to come. Clad in the regalia of younger days and golden armor, Baldwin stood at the altar and, despite a crippling cough, spoke to his subjects, to the allies he'd forged and honored.

In the shadow of worthier saints, he began. "I have seen things," he said, "in my long pilgrimage. Cities were razed to ash in an hour's time. Innocents bought and sold in shackles on distant shores. The hubris of empires, the ambitions of tyrants, and the price we all unjustly pay. The world," he shuddered, "is a dark place. A cruel place. One would be forgiven to believe it unworthy of redemption. However," his voice rose, "without this…crucible of sin, I would not stand before you now. Not as the man I am. For it is not in spite, but because of these atrocities that we stand fast. From the liberated slave to the widowed queen, the troubadour at my side to the men who've long fought for the Holy Land. Arise, now," he roared past his ailing heart, "people of the world! Ours is a city — no, a temple of all faiths. Though the forces of darkness march upon our gates, our valor and our brotherhood will weather this onslaught. We do not die as men, or as martyrs — we die standing. That alone is worthy of immortality!"

The motley armies he'd mustered raised their swords and shook their spears, cheering at his valor. Baldwin turned to his companions, a blistered smile across his lips — how long had it been since he'd delivered such hope, such aspiration? It was almost enough to ignore the shadow of Death, who seemingly shared in his pride. Though the doubt of dreams still gnawed at the back of his mind, Baldwin had little left to fear — soon, none of it would matter.

"Prepare the *Tarrasque*," he said.

"What for?" asked the banneret.

"As I said," Baldwin winked, "I have a plan."

———————

Night had crept upon the Cathedral City. Despite his tremors and atrophied sinew, Baldwin scaled the Wailing Walls on his own, joining rows of longbowmen upon the outer tiers, overlooking the legions of the Fool General. Battlement upon battlement, its aged limestone traced to the Old Imperium, though its foundations had since joined the labyrinthine buttresses commissioned by the Holy See, which offered no boon to the otherwise impenetrable bastion. No army had ever taken the city from the west, though in the face of the Fool General, Baldwin would not deny the possibility. He glanced about the front-line; naught but chainmail and visors of ceremonial ferocity, shaky grips betraying their terror. These soldiers were ill-equipped to fight slave-soldiers of Othello, let alone Imperial forces of such caliber, and yet, such faith would not surrender so easily.

Great peals of thunder rumbled in the heavens, and rain fell in torrents upon steeples and spires, rattling against shields in light percussion. He prayed the enemy gunpowder had been dampened, but knew better than to hope. Shrieks and squelches drew near, the maggot host crawled across lands turned sour by their presence alone. Iron braziers announced their arrival, filling the Gap of Golgotha like a horde of livid fireflies, illuminating the Fool General's slithering forces. They were as horrific as Baldwin had remembered.

Pale and hideous, the Vermillion army had been reduced to miserable mockeries of the modern soldier. Mutations had worsened over the long march, carbuncles and cancerous growths fusing rifles to hands, sagging skins as one with their uniforms, like snails in flimsy shells. Amidst the ranks of pike and shot, rotund fighting vehicles rolled down the hills, rimmed with small arms and domed with sheets of riveted steel, to say nothing of the scythed chariots pulled by pill-bugs of monstrous size. Men in thick leather suits, once reserved for marine expeditions, had been repurposed into shock troops with canisters of liquid fire strapped to their backs, connected to long-barreled hoses in swollen grips.

And yet, the Lindwyrm was nowhere to be seen.

The banneret nodded in silence, eyes wide upon the sheer vastness of the maggot host. "You weren't exaggerating," he said.

"I wish I did as often as people thought."

The enemy halted mere leagues before the Wailing Walls, snarls audible from atop the battlements. Moment by moment, they began to bleat in a sad mimicry of speech, as if robbed of language by morbid infection, rising in a rageful lament of their former humanity. Certain as the corruption of worms, Baldwin drew his sword and bid his defenders to take aim — until even thunder was eclipsed by earthward booms. Cast-iron mortars opened fire, erupting in clouds of cinder and smoke, cracking the age-old masonry and defacing statues of saints upon the West Doors. True to his plan, Baldwin had the first beacons lit — a wordless order for the sally ports to be opened, unleashing twin calvaries of cataphracts upon the enemy flanks.

Driving the maggot-folk to send sappers upon the wall, phalanxes were mustered on either side of the advancing army. Fighting horsemen, though well-armored, were hardly immune to Vermillion gunpowder. Sabers meant little in the face of firing squads. Despite the initial tramples, the cataphracts were soon impaled in pushes of pike or gunned down with tastes of grapeshot. Amidst the cacophony of battle, Baldwin remained resolute and ushered a volley of his own, as battalions of archers fired from the courtyard and over the wall.

Then came the ladders.

Baldwin muttered a prayer into his rosary and rose to

greet whatever horror awaited the defense. Swinging wide, he met the ladder with a diagonal cleave, slicing through the skull of a wretch, only for dozens more to prop against the walls. Troglodytic fodder flooded the battlements. As if armed in mockery of the defenders, they wielded nothing save spiked clubs and crude scimitars, and even they proved worthy opponents to the terrified men-at-arms. Spitting with ringed maws, the fluke-men latched onto prey at random, draining them of blood in seconds, only to lunge at the next. Baldwin, having yet seen worse, remained undeterred and led with violent example—cutting through any and all in his path.

This would not be another Gravesend.

Things would be different this time.

That much he swore by.

And yet, Baldwin was ignorant of the flying machines that had circumvented the bastion walls—swollen balloons and baskets from which dragoons descended with wings of wood and leather, eager to immolate any in their sights. The lesser gates began to quake. The harbors on the Black River were rushed with amphibious creatures, breaching the naval chains with monstrous jaws. The battlefield began to quake—not due to cannonfire. Something stirred under the very soil of the Holy Land, burrowing, rapidly gathering speed towards the West Doors.

"Get off the wall—!"

Colossal force burst from the shallow earth under the battlements, reducing the Wailing Walls to a hailstorm of rubble in mere seconds, knights and fodder tossed like ragdolls into the midnight air. The Cathedral City had been breached. And yet, Baldwin felt no pain. He was still standing, though in the courtyard, surrounded by soldiers on the retreat. The world seemed to slur in a blur of beige and brown, the battle raging on in stupor beyond thought and time. He tried to speak out, to give the order—no words escaped his lips.

Then his eyes fell on the first among the corpses—his own.

Though Baldwin heard the faint cackle of the Fool General, a more immediate threat stood in the fading world; scythe drawn, astride a pale horse, black robes as tattered banners of war. She who would claim his soul when the stars were right.

"It is time," Death said.

———

"We can't hold them!" the commander cried.

Gipi stood fast in the Leper Quarter, clad in a studded leather jerkin and armed with a rudimentary crossbow — hardly fit for military action. She ushered the last of the refugees into the lazaretto and helped bar the third doors. Not far away, the iron-banded gates to the district began to crackle and burn. Vermillion legions battered and bashed against its heavy wooden paneling. The Knights Hospitaller stood fast and at the ready, every soul an aspirant to the king's prestige, a phalanx of shaky shields and spears, while squires and pages propped beams and barrels against the doors. Such efforts were for naught.

In a barrage of splinters and stone debris, the enemy had entry.

Humbaba and his pit-fighters stood fast by the troubadour's side, only to rush in and greet the swarming tide head-on, side by side with the ailing knights. Firing squads took potshots from behind the initial waves of vermin, content to open fire indiscriminately upon soldiers and civilians alike, gradually marching through rubble and ruin, mouths agape and oozing.

"Kill them," Humbaba roared as he caved in a musketeer's skull, discarding the corpse like a side of worm-ridden beef. "Kill them in the name of our freedom!"

The gladiators roared and held them at the gate — until jets of liquid flame erupted from the flank, immolating the martyrs in a conflagration of screams and burnt flesh. Humbaba lunged behind a heap of rubble, narrowly avoiding the aim of shock troops, eyes burning with hate upon the Imperial Guard. Stifling her horror, Gipi opened fire upon the enemy, cranking and winding her crossbow with every bolt fire — some better aimed than others.

The legions of the Fool General were seemingly endless.

Her thoughts spiraled with sights along the aimless course that brought them all here. Pit-fighters and assassins, aspirants and partisans, and she, a minstrel who sought only a tale worth telling—which she had certainly found. Only in the end was she confronted with the price of epics: screams, blood, and the horror of battle. Was it really worth it? To see the world for what it truly was? Had she made the right choice to follow Baldwin? Perhaps not. And yet, as carnage unfolded around her in torrential fire and flashes of steel, she did not regret her decision. Nor would she have chosen differently, knowing her fate.

Regardless, one thing was clear.

Short of a miracle, the Holy Land would fall.

———

Baldwin reached for the Broken Blade but did not brandish it, not yet—nor did he come hither. It was the reaper who'd challenged him in dreams at his lowest, not the wizened mentor who'd goaded him to this premature end. For a moment, he almost believed her. The Cathedral City seemed but a windswept sprawl of ash and smoke, its basilicas, baptistries, and scenes of battle fleeting in the wake of lives lost. In truth, Baldwin felt a moment's solace, the last temptation of the leper errant. His spirit was resolute as ever. How bright it burned.

The Music of the Spheres welled in his heart.

"There is much to be said in death," she raised a smooth hand, before he could even speak, still aloft her ghoulish steed, "but you must not fear me. Come with grace," she raised her hood, revealing the face of a striking young woman, "you've done all that you can."

He neither moved nor obeyed.

Death's smile faded with a sigh. "Baldwin—"

"This is not how my journey ends. It is not written. Not ordained."

"Tread carefully. And do not speak to me of what it

ordained." Death pointed a wan finger. "You know nothing of the will of the Grand Conductor."

Baldwin uttered a broken laugh. After everything he'd seen, all he'd witnessed, he would not go gently into whatever awaited beyond. Though constellations of souls spiraled from the mangled dead, willingly rising to meet their fate, the leper remained where he stood. He was not as them. He was meant for a darker destiny — if one could call it such.

The Fool General would be the one to destroy him, that much he knew.

"I know more than you'd admit," Baldwin said. "You once mentioned that there may be a purpose. That perhaps God's judgment was not misplaced. Mad or not, I am loath to believe this is the fate I've earned." Slowly, he raised his sword. "You will not take me. If this all be a madman's dream, it will be mine to make as I will it."

"You deny your own time?" she hissed, the flesh of her face dissolving to reveal a skeletal visage. "You would question me?"

Baldwin tuned his gaze to the destination of these souls, past the dark clouds, and caught a glimpse of the Empyrean at the firmament's end — to the Great Seal which held back the darkness between the stars, where the Far Messiah was bound and impaled, staring back upon this potential champion, this saint in the making. God himself gave a nod and a smile.

"I do not question your authority," Baldwin said. "I deny its very existence."

Death reared her steed and swung her scythe wide.

"Mortal," she rasped, "you are mine."

In the limbo of heaven and earth, Baldwin felt the foundations of stone tremble under his boots — the courtyard a colosseum without audience, surrounded by rings of rubble and ruin, adrift in the threadbare currents of mortality. Death, astride her pale horse, rushed to greet him with steel of her own, eager to reap his soul as a worthy prize. Baldwin rolled to the side and swung upward, slicing the ribs of her spectral steed. With a ghastly whine, the pale horse bucked and reared, yet Death still clutched the reins and swung once more.

"You will not defy me," she said.

Baldwin parried her earthward strike, listening to the *danse macabre* performed by bone trumpeters circling above. Dueling atop a disc of failing stone, the leper took a stance against the reaper who charged once more—this time for the kill, only for Baldwin to swing with all the strength of the soul he could summon, decapitating the horse altogether.

"You are not my executioner," Baldwin said. "You are a daemon to be conquered."

Death rose to examine her fallen steed, eyes wide in awe, if only for a moment. With a snap of her slender fingers, she traded her long scythe for twin sickles of warped sharpness, glowering upon this upstart mortal—the man who would slay Death.

"Come at me," Baldwin said.

"Your efforts mean nothing," Death said. "Once and future kings will look upon your works and despair—knowing your shallow pride. Do you think yourself the only soul to challenge me?" She glanced at the Great Seal, if only for a moment, a lover's gleam in her eyes. "Do you think yourself so precious to the world?"

Baldwin did not reply, nor would Death relent—blades locked in a devil's embrace.

"You are not the first king I've taken," she said.

"Then why do you fear me?"

Breaking his guard, Death racked a sickle through the leper's cuirass and lesioned flesh, inches from claiming his soul. A chill ran through him, enough to drive him back, yet Baldwin would not surrender easily. Regaining his wits, he charged at the reaper and, with a tremendous blow, nearly shattered her own God-given blades, quaking her stance.

She turned to the Empyrean with a grimace.

"Is this one you'd put your faith in? A royal brat? Is he

worthy of blessing as your saint?" Baldwin did not understand at the time, nor did he care. "I suppose you would see yourself in him." She sneered at no one in particular. "Like the young man you were at your highest—and lowest." In a moment's lapse, Death let the Broken Blade slice through her chest, much to Baldwin's surprise. It was not a strike earned. Death vanished in a wisp of smoke, only to reappear by the leper's side. Brandishing her twin sickles. "Well," she jeered. "Don't just stand there." Hers was a cold wrath, one not born of hate. "Earn your righteous end,"

The next thing Baldwin knew, he had impaled the reaper through the stomach, hilt pressed against pale flesh. Death took him by the hands, letting her own blades clatter to the floor and dissipate on a whim, embracing his terrible deed. Silence wafted through the stagnant air. Her lips were close to his own, smirking at his morbid discomfort.

"You're right," she said. "Yours is not a death ordained, but you do not have a life to call your own. Not as you'd see it. It is a cursed fate." Her breath caressed his scarred ear, sending a shiver down his spine. "Condemned to walk the earth as a corpse among men. As a revenant. May you find the 'purpose' you so crave. To whatever end that leads you. Only then will you know peace. The gift you so reject—for now."

With a spiteful kiss, she parted ways, the mists of time ushering him to a terrible fate.

"Farewell, O' Saint of the Far Messiah."

Baldwin woke with a gasp to the world he'd nearly left behind. In any other circumstance, he would've been wracked with despair, yet as he forced his bloodied body upright, popping limbs back into place, ignorant of agony, the deathless king uttered a deranged laugh, the Broken Blade still at his side. With the Wailing Walls broken and breached, its defenders had fallen back to districts ablaze, and the rancid breath of the Lindwyrm wafted to greet him. Step by step, Baldwin approached what the Fool General had become.

CHAPTER SEVEN

The Cathedral City was burning, its high naves stark against rising flame. Screams of the innocent carried from churchly districts. Morale lay in shambles. The Wailing Walls were reduced to rubble and ruin, shattered by the evil that had erupted from far below — the Lindwyrm grinned behind a rippling haze of smoke where the West Doors once stood. Its lips were wide, painted with the blood of soldiers, reminiscent of a murderous clown, its serpentine form coiled about the apartments, wide and scaleless, long arms dragging a loathsome body. Yellow eyes gleamed with insatiable hunger, for as the dragon inched towards Baldwin, it sniffed the smoldering air in search of what it undoubtedly wished was fear.

"So," he hissed, "you're still alive."

Baldwin did not grant the Fool General the privilege of a response.

"I commend your durability," it said, bowing its eel-like head, "but it seems you'll only live to see your kingdom destroyed just as I have so many others." It grinned, revealing rows of jagged fangs. "How does it feel, Good King Baldwin? To see your dynasty end before your very eyes? To know you will be remembered only for your failures."

Baldwin readied the Broken Blade, relishing the chance to slay a dragon of his own. It was the epitome of the epics he so admired, the ultimate honor, and he would do it justice.

"Your taunts are as vapid as your soul, Pierrot," he said, naming the thing out of spite. "What a wicked form you've taken. Is this the Conqueror Worm's plan? To twist and torment you so needlessly? You'll be hard pressed to find a throne for your fattened body." His eyes narrowed. "Make no mistake. There is no more injury you can deal me. God wills it."

With a maddened laugh, the Lindwyrm snapped its jaws inches from the leper's face. "Bold words for a coward of a king," his breath reeked of a thousand rotting corpses. "I wonder how you will cope with your tarnished legacy. This is what you fear, is it not?"

"If you need to question what I fear, then you make a poor nemesis."

The Lindwyrm rose as a cobra, salivating a sickly bile which sizzled upon the charred cobbles, flaunting its might in a lunatic flex against the moon. "Well? What are you waiting for?"

Upon the bitter implication of permission, Baldwin dove and raked the Broken Blade along the jagged street, shredding sparks in his wake—only to be met with a swat of the Lindwyrm's tail. It cackled maniacally as the leper collided with the nearest apartment, cracking through crumbling walls by the weight of his armor alone, and yet, he was unbroken. Baldwin emerged from the wreckage within moments, cracking his neck and spine into formation, arms akimbo in a taunt. Slowly, the Lindwyrm's laughter ceased.

"Color me impressed," it said. "That's not—"

Baldwin sprinted again and carved into its serpentine flesh, not in hope of wounding, rather, to remind the Fool General that even dragons could bleed. Digging the Broken Blade deep into its scaleless sinew, he grimaced with hateful ferocity, only to be swatted aside like a gnat again by the Lindwyrm's strength, clattering and skidding across the courtyard, prone yet unfazed. The dragon exhaled, letting a rot-green miasma leak from its jaws, reanimating the dead beyond count in a breath of false life—to rally the fallen as a grinning vanguard.

Baldwin scoffed at these toy soldiers and retaliated in kind.

He did not recall the savage dismemberment or skulls crushed. With every wight put to rest, he inched ever closer to his true quarry—one already wounded. Troubled by its own mortality, the Lindwyrm struck a belfry with its tail. The great bronze bell fell to earth, ringing along a towering heap of rubble, missing its mark by meters in a deafening clatter. Baldwin scoffed at these futile attempts, basking in a glimmer of fear in the Fool General's eyes.

"For doom the bell tolls," he jeered, "but I hear nothing."

The Lindwyrm uttered only a hiss.

Baldwin smirked, knowingly, and raised his hand—a wordless order for the second beckon to be lit. At first, the Lindwyrm chuckled and yawned its python jaws once more, only to catch a scent in the skies above—sulfur and gunpowder. Waves of parachuted crewmen fell from the heavens, fleeing to safety from a heavenward light. Suddenly, the clouds burst in a barrage of flame, and a weapon of Baldwin's own radical design descended upon the courtyard.

The flaming husk of the *Tarrasque*, carrying a solid ton of explosives.

Before the Lindwyrm could so much as recoil, Baldwin raised his arms wide in blissful vengeance, letting the Imperial flagship collide with them both.

He had nothing left to fear. He was deathless.

Both were blinded by a holocaust of divine and chemical flame. Ears ringing and eyes white, Baldwin endured the disintegration of his clothes and cast off his hood and cloak— still standing. The Lindwyrm writhed, its mucus-slick skin most flammable, thrashing about the courtyard as liquid fire scorched its flesh and planks of shrapnel pierced its hide, desperate to extinguish the all-consuming blaze. In an agonized babble, the Fool General's eyes watered and widened in shock, reflecting the leper errant marching through the fire.

Baldwin let the molten bronze of his cuirass wash off his nude body, little more than a brutalized corpse animated by willpower alone—only the steel of the Broken Blade kept shape. He gathered speed, his voice rising to a bloodthirsty howl, and stabbed upward, through the roof of the Lindwyrm's maw. Baptized in flame, he endured the stench of its poisonous breath, digging his sword into the dragon's brain, blood cooling his burns.

"You will not stop me," said a weakened voice. "This isn't over."

To his alarm, the wyrm's tongue had taken the form of Pierrot, though a slime-coated simulacrum—half-formed, cased in a membrane. Even his ruff and wig were seemingly fused to the rear gullet, and with a fistful of claws, he shredded his umbilical bonds and slipped out of the dying wyrm's mouth, stumbling and fleeing past his would-be executioner.

In a parody of rebirth, Pierrot had gone.

No taunt or quip escaped his lips, no declaration of vengeance, only the gleam of yellow eyes that vanished into darkness. Regardless, the Lindwyrm had been slain. The maggot host began to falter. As if in response to the death of their commander, confusion swept their ranks. Most fell prone in fits of violent spasms, only to be slain by the defenders.

Within the hour, the Vermillion Empire faced its first defeat.

Baldwin wandered about the smoldering debris, the implications of the fate he'd been spared beginning to dawn on him. Staring at the blackened musculature of his hands, he pondered his new existence—once a leper, now something other than human. Skin had been stripped from his body, flayed by fire, though he felt no pain or anything at all. His path was indeed a violent one. Though his deeds tonight would be recited by minstrels across the Holy Land, the world he'd helped birth had no place for monsters, regardless of intentions. He'd forsaken his humanity for the chance to achieve greatness.

He was a living saint.

No one could see what he'd become. It was the nature of this gift. If Baldwin were to accomplish the deeds he had sworn by, then there would be no place for companionship or royalty. He uttered a broken laugh. Had he learned nothing since his departure? It was the selfish page in him speaking. Something he wished had been burned along with his humility.

Firstly, he needed a proper set of clothes.

In the Royal Palace and Lazaretto, Baldwin mummified himself in layers of fresh bandages and kingly garments, content to peruse for masks when a familiar presence drew near.

"Gipi," he said. "I am grateful you are safe."

"Ditto," she kept her distance, "where've you been?"

Baldwin turned to face her, solemnly. "Dead, to be frank."

"Dead?"

"Yes, and I suspect it'll be the last time for a while."

"Wait—what? What do you mean?"

"Death and I came to agreeable terms," Baldwin said. "I am not to die so long as my purpose remains unfulfilled." He unsheathed a jeweled dagger and stabbed himself in the heart, a minor discomfort, only to sheath the blade as if nothing had happened. "See?"

"Goddamnit, Baldwin," she gasped. "You can't just do that!"

"Suppose it does upset the notion of succession."

"That's not what I mean!"

"Although I wish I could taste again…."

"What happened to Pierrot?"

"He escaped," the leper said, "but the Lindwyrm is slain."

"But aren't they—the same, what're you…?"

Baldwin sat her aside and began to explain what had transpired. The color had drained from the troubadour's face, who was clearly about to faint. "So," she reached for the smelling salts, "using the *Tarrasque* as a bomb. That was your bright idea? And you really can't die?"

"Yes, and I'm quite proud of it."

"You're insane," she scoffed.

"You seem surprised."

"What about the Holy See?" she asked. "I don't think Cardinal Milan will tolerate being under house arrest. Unless," she paused, "you're content with offing him."

"There's no need," Baldwin said. "Although I'm hesitant to lay claim to the throne in any way. Considering that I cannot die. In truth, I am considering another lord-regent. To act in my stead and to improve ties with Othello and her sister cities. Perhaps this will be a new beginning for the Holy Land," he mused, "the Second Gothic Imperium...."

"What about Pierrot?"

"Oh," Baldwin said, "make no mistake, I will kill him."

"You're taking this whole 'deathless' thing pretty well."

Baldwin shrugged. "It does reduce the leprosy to an inconvenience."

"Just...I wouldn't go flaunting it around. Besides, I imagine you can still be dismembered and break your bones," Gipi shuddered, "and, I mean, who knows what'll happen if you're imprisoned and the Inquisition finds out."

"True," he admitted, "I have not made friends with the Holy See as of late."

"An understatement."

Baldwin turned out the window, watching the dead being piled and lit ablaze. He was sure to tell the Knights Hospitaller to keep watch for fleeing larva—the most insidious of worms with a tendency to parasitize the unsuspecting, likely near the sewers. Slowly, the fires were doused, and the world seemed a brighter place. Humbaba was seated on a makeshift throne of shakos and morion helmets, content to massage his raw knuckles in smug satisfaction.

"Good King Baldwin," said the thrall. "Hate to say I told you so, but...."

"Indeed, we are both," he paused, "alive, yes."

Humbaba gave a quizzical look. "Yeah, I should hope so."

"No matter," Baldwin said, dismissively. "There is much that must be done. Preparations for merriment and compensation for the widowed and orphaned." He looked at the wounded and shaken survivors. "These men have earned it. Yes, we all have."

"Enough lampreys for a pie," Humbaba smirked, "I can

tell you that much."

Baldwin smiled in turn. "I would not think them edible."

Along the lanes flanked by ruined homes, Baldwin searched for Sir Reynald—only to see his battle-scarred face among the fallen. In truth, few of the men he knew were standing. Having fought gallantly against the enemy, most perished in a last stand before the Leper Quarter. Slowly, the joy of his own survival began to fade. He saw the civilians mangled in the street. The people, his people, had suffered for Pierrot's crimes a thousand times over.

And yet, in a sick sense of irony, he'd been allowed to live.

Come dawn, guilt sank its teeth deeper than the Lindwyrm's fangs. Passing on the decree to burn the dead without exception, Baldwin returned to the Royal Palace and Lazaretto.

To spend time alone with his thoughts.

Baldwin slouched upon the vanity cabinet, staring at himself in the mirror, wondering who he was beneath the mask. If there was anyone left to find. He had no expression to give, no visible humanity left, none save for his eyes—eyes all but blind to the world as it most saw it. Pale and blue, milky with tears, surrounded by blackened flesh, addled by delusion and fantasy. Staring into his own soul, Baldwin saw inner worlds of his own making, happier years that would never be his—not as a Saint of the Far Messiah. And yet, in his own eyes, brilliant yet opaque, he saw the same wry conviction as the Great Seal's. Tears were ensnared in painless fissures of burnt tissue. He took a deep, shuddering breath and slowly began to understand. Upon the Duel with Death, he'd taken upon a far greater mantle than he'd ever fathomed.

God had plans for him.

Whether true gospel or symptoms of a martyr's madness, Baldwin did know. Regardless, deeper thoughts spoke within him—thoughts that were not his own, but those of a spiritual warmth that resonated from the soul. In that moment, he knew that he'd made the right choice. This was his ordained purpose—

to serve the Far Messiah as his champion of the age.

"If God wills it," he turned away, "then I will bear this burden to whatever end."

CHAPTER EIGHT

Within the Imperial Citadel, so named in more prosperous times, the population of the Holy Land had gathered in candlelit vigil in honor of the fallen. The Great Hall had been assembled with long tables and seating for all faiths. At the hall's end, Baldwin cupped a chalice and led communion in thanks to the Far Messiah. His speech was but a swift requiem, much to his people's relief. Aged casks were opened and roast beasts were carved, and the mood soon shifted to bittersweet merriment with a noticeable absence of lamprey pies.

Baldwin had no appetite to speak of.

His entourage by his side, Baldwin quietly observed the widowed and orphaned, wishing there was more he could've done. And yet, he knew there was no use dwelling on hypotheticals and what could have been. The Cathedral City had survived the Vermillion onslaught, and the Lindwyrm was slain—miracles both. As the wine was poured and the night wore on, Gipi strummed her lute and sang the ballad she'd written over the course of their long journey. A mere dramatization, then again, all good stories deserve a little embellishment. Her passages on the Battle on the Tower Bridge could've used some elaboration, but Baldwin was humored by the satirical account of his deeds.

Great as these accomplishments were, his wanderlust was not so easily sated.

Eventually, he stood and took an ornate box, departing to the vestibule among the lower naves, where Desdemona watched the myriad stars in the night sky.

"You've achieved much," she said. "More than you'd claim."

"Not enough, I fear."

The sultana eyed him, unsurprised. "Pierrot lives?"

"Indeed, he does."

"That is…unfortunate."

Baldwin did not reply for a long while. "You know I cannot stay here," he said. "The Fool General will return. How or when, I do not know, but it is my God-given duty to end him."

"You seem of better humors," she said.

"That I am," Baldwin paused, "yet there is something I must ask of you." He opened the delicate chest, revealing the crown he'd worn during the campaigns against her. "Our peoples cannot afford to waste in wars of faith. We share an enemy — a true evil. God willing, let our kingdoms be united in opposition to this evil. I would make you Queen of Othello and Golgotha, the Empress of the Second Gothic Imperium, should you wish it."

Desdemona's eyes widened in shock. "Is this your manner of proposal?"

"A union that will never be consummated — for obvious reasons."

She laughed, more than a bit embarrassed. "You know, for all your talk of chivalry, you are a pitiable flirt, Baldwin." She caressed the rings on her slender fingers. "Yes. I will rule our lands in your stead. I will honor our friendship — the friendship of our nations."

"I am glad," Baldwin said. "Thank you, Empress Desdemona."

"And so," Gipi slurred within the Great Hall, "that's how Baldwin became a saint."

The leper's heart sank into his chest; he barreled past the feasting tables to the troubadour strumming her lute among dancing peasants. Thankfully, the drunken crowd would doubtfully remember her slip of the tongue.

"Ah," she looked away, "it's, well…poetic license."

"Did you mention the Duel with Death?"

"Also poetic license."

Baldwin muttered in disapproval. Much to his mortification, that autumnal night would henceforth be known as the Feast of Saint Baldwin, regardless of his or the Holy See's say on the matter. Cardinal Milan would never emerge from his quarters, having died of "cardiac arrest" during the siege, his body quietly disposed of by the Sisters Dervish.

Truth be told, Baldwin gave the matter little thought.

In the following week, Desdemona's ascension was a private affair, so as not to provoke Vermillion and its sycophantic allies. Red petals rained from the upper parapets of the Basilica of the Far Messiah, and the high priestess of her choosing led the ceremony, braziers lit with burning incense and a pyre in honor of the Eternal Flame of Sarukhand. The Sisters Dervish, clad in robes and beaded burqas, raised their long knives in an arch on the opposing side of the aisle, under which the queen crossed the threshold of livid smoke. Hers was a passing of the sword, once reserved for the Sultan Khan, now bestowed upon her — the last living member of the old dynasty. She and the leper locked eyes, if only for a moment.

Baldwin turned away in silence. In truth, he was relieved that the Cathedral City would be protected by a worthy liege — that he needn't burden the kingdom with his fevered will. Girding that bejeweled blade, the Sword of Sarukhand, to her side, Desdemona stood before her subjects, old and new, as the Sultana of Othello. Then she knelt before Baldwin and his loyalist priests for her coronation. With trembling hands, the leper laid the Crown of Golgotha upon her brow and let the implications of the passing of his throne seep into a holy unction. Applause erupted from rows of those who bore witness, albeit tepidly, from Baldwin's court.

"Hail," he said, "Empress Desdemona of Othello and Golgotha."

"Hail," the crowd echoed and knelt.

Later that night, Baldwin absconded into the armories, though no masterwork weapon could replace the Broken Blade in his heart. His would be a flight to track Pierrot to lands unknown, whether on foot or horseback, regardless of who would follow.

"So you thought you could escape without a proper farewell?" Desdemona emerged from the shadows. "Content to settle me with your royal obligation and be off?" Those words stung deeper than she likely intended. "The least you could've done was stay for the festivities."

"I grow weary of this long carnival," Baldwin said with a sigh. "It will serve no purpose once Vermillion regroups. We must not become idle in celebration."

"True," Desdemona said. "Though so long as the Malachite Pyramid is safe, the Empire cannot regain its former strength."

An insidious breeze wafted from the curtained windows, threatening to snuff the candlelight on the artifact's very mention.

"Where is it?" he asked.

"Safe," Desdemona said, "beneath the basilica. I took the liberty of placing it there an hour before the siege." She looked away, as if slightly troubled. "Do you wish to see it?"

"That I do."

With lantern and copper key at hand, they crossed the empty cloisters and descended into the undercroft. The air was thick with moldering dust, though Baldwin's eyes were fixed upon the flickering torches and ossuaries cradling the bones of long-dead centurions. Halfway into the crypt, broken clay shifted under his boots. Dread washed over him. He sprinted among the pillars only to find shattered reliquaries — perhaps defiled by grave robbers, or worse.

"Where is it?" he repeated.

"It," Desdemona gasped, "should be here!"

Despite his search, there was no trace of the Malachite Pyramid.

"What manner of sacrilegious cur could've...."

Baldwin already knew the truth. Pierrot, or perhaps one of his slithering agents, had slinked into the undercroft and stolen the thing. He could almost hear the Fool General's laughter, mocking his efforts to halt the End Times. Clenching his bandaged fists, Baldwin paced about the tombs of antiquity, rage welling in his chest.

"I will send the sisterhood to track his whereabouts," Desdemona said.

The leper gripped his sword's hilt. "See to it. I have much to prepare for."

Perhaps it was his own wrath, and yet, Baldwin swore the moon bled between the darkening clouds—the Eclipse so revered by midwives and wise women of the Grünewald. Upon the passing of that crimson portent, the leper knew his course, though he did not understand it. He would return to the Old Road where it all began. Upon leaving the basilica, he watched the pit-fighters train among wooden dummies and straw targets, Humbaba instructing them as a veteran militiaman. He nodded with respect upon the leper's approach.

"What's wrong?" asked the thrall.

Baldwin hesitated to reply in earnest but divulged what had transpired. "No oath binds you to me, Humbaba, but I must be off once more."

"Pity," he said. "You've done a greater service than you know, Baldwin. You brought us home. For that, we are eternally grateful." He turned to the steeples and statues of saints in pious veneration. "I'd be lying to say I want to leave this place so soon."

"Nor should you."

"That said," Humbaba added, "if you call upon us, we will answer."

It was without fanfare that Baldwin departed what remained of the West Doors in an urgent stride. Silence filled the fields, and he felt a dry chill waft from the north, ushering with it the first frost upon blighted crops. Autumn had reached a swift end, its leaves falling to earth with trees left bare, skeletal branches in the gloaming. At the crossroads, however, he met with his minstrel once more, much to his happy resignation.

Gipi shot him a wink. "Figured you'd sneak off this way."

"And I assumed you'd be here."

Despite his will to carry on, Baldwin remained rooted in his tracks. Many thoughts stung his mind until he thought it fit to speak at last. "Gipi," he said, "I wish to make an addendum to our chronicles, if you please." He took a deep breath. "Let it be known that I died upon the Breach of the Wailing Walls, defending all I held dear, that I died a man of valor. The world does not need to know what became of me in full. My deathless state."

"Doesn't that defeat the purpose of this whole...thing?"

"No," Baldwin said. "History favors worse men for greater embellishments." He turned to his troubadour. "Let me 'die' a saint. 'Poetic license,' if you will."

Gipi scribbled a line on her log and smiled. "Well, you're not a king anymore, are you? Besides, without the pressure of legacy, maybe you'll find your end after all?"

"That I do not doubt."

With one last glance, Baldwin looked upon the Cathedral City and smiled, knowing its future was secure with the Second Gothic Imperium. Snowflakes fluttered from swollen clouds. Baldwin knew the battles ahead would be all the harsher come the winter of his rebirth. However, if this terrible quarry was to be slain, if his crusade was to be worthy of remembrance, then he had little choice. Though fractured by the greed of generals, the Empire was not yet defeated, and with the Malachite Pyramid missing, there was nothing left to ponder.

So marked the beginning of the Vermillion War.

EPILOGUE

Pierrot had since fled to the hinterlands, many a day's march from the Cathedral City, trudging through the frost-bitten fields. With the maggot host slain and his own command shattered, the Fool General was hardly a harlequin caked in mud, filth, and rain—a parody of the peerage, reduced to soiled finery and scraps. Beggars and wayfarers alike looked upon him in disgust. Even the blind could sense the malice wafting from his very soul. It was not until Pierrot came to a coaching inn that a smile crossed his face—the scent of hunter's stew and overpoured whiskey enticing even his refined palette. The swaying sign was worn and illegible. Crossing the threshold, he crept to the bar and raised a pair of fingers—a double was in order. Downing a shot of whatever swill the nameless inn had to offer, he glanced at the other patrons with venomous disdain. In the chiaroscuro of candlelight, he mustered a semblance of tolerance.

To think Pierrot was forced to mingle with the poor and the pauper, to share the same roof as they. Barely to stomach their pathetic excuse for liquor, Pierrot wrung his coattails onto the floorboards, desperate to warm himself at the hearth.

He watched the working girls bat their eyelashes over potential customers, shuddering in disgust, imagining how many godless children they'd spewed upon the unforgiving world, let alone survived their first winter. He always had a disdain for procreation—the instinct to make one's mark upon the world, a messier means than murder by and large.

"Thieves and whores," he muttered.

His eyes locked with a striking yet malnourished young woman, perhaps addicted to purgatives or host to a tapeworm, who pulled a seat beside him.

"Look for a—?"

"No," he snapped.

She left with a bitter scoff. Entranced by flickering flames, Pierrot contemplated his miserable existence. He was a man without a past — at least, not one that he could recall. Waking on an operating table did the mind no favors, for no midwife ushered him into the world — only tight leather straps and syringes deep in his veins. He never knew life before the "gift" of magic, infused into his bloodstream with the eggs of eels. With his irritable disposition and penchant for violence, it was a miracle he'd graduated from the academy, let alone first of his class, albeit under the pretense of prisoner reform. Swiftly, he rose through the ranks of the Imperial Armed Forces and led many a penal legion to decisive victories — casualties notwithstanding.

"Barkeep," he barked. "Another…if you please."

Muttering under his breath, the proprietor slid Pierrot a half pour at full price — a sign that his coin was best spent elsewhere, though the lowbrow sentiment was lost on the Fool General. Keeping to his swill, Pierrot remembered the height of his pride, the medals that once adorned his breast, and the fear he commanded in military minds. Nothing if not an eccentric, Pierrot thought himself ahead of his time, a cut above the common cloth, and, now more than ever, greater than human. He did not regret his hasty coup.

"What?" he snapped at a couple of onlookers. "Never seen an Imperial officer before? Bloody ingrates," his tone degenerated into quiet snarls, "we've defended these parts for decades from brigands and kingsmen alike. Show some gratitude, why don't you?"

Pierrot muttered into his cup, his thoughts haunted by the deathless king, the one who he could not kill, Baldwin IV of Golgotha. What the hell was with the freak anyway? Nigh invulnerable. Molten bronze melted off his flesh like it was nothing. Fighting without regard for pain or injury, assuming he felt anything at all. Perhaps there was something to be said about providence, justice, and the will to smite the wicked. And yet, there was more to it.

In truth, Baldwin was the one thing he feared.

Pierrot brushed the notion aside with a shudder. Generals lesser than he had recovered from worse. Though the short-term was humiliating, he needed only to reach an Imperial outpost, to use what clearance he had, and slowly rebuild his battalions. Perhaps he'd been too hasty with the worms, and yet, the relic was still in his keeping—his ultimate purpose was unchanged. The Malachite Pyramid was warm in his robe's pocket. Given power and time, he'd wipe this shoddy place off the face of the earth.

"Did you hear?" someone spoke up, a tad too loudly for his own good.

"Yes, Vermillion suffered its first defeat. And a crippling one from what I hear."

Pierrot clenched his fists, seconds from seizing his rapier's hilt. His eyes darted to the throng of poachers at the far table, wild and manic enough to silence the entire lot.

"You should be careful what you say," Pierrot said. "There're many...deserters in these parts. They wouldn't take kindly to such gossip—"

"Don't suppose you have any coin on you," the barkeep cut him short.

"Eh?" Pierrot spun around, eyes wide. "What kind of guttersnipe do you take me for?" He reached into his purse, only to find the seams cut. "Son of a bitch."

"Something wrong?"

"Oh, no," Pierrot gritted his teeth. "Not at all. I'm sure," he glowered, "we can come to an arrangement." He shoved his hands deep into his pockets, searching for coppers—only for the relic to nearly fall from his robes. A gleam of avarice shone in the barkeep's eyes and, despite a moment's indignation, Pierrot chuckled and thought to play along. "Oh, this? Hardly worth the trouble, I assure you. It's a trinket. A bauble, really."

"It'll do."

Pierrot pretended not to follow. "Oh?"

A crew of bouncers kept wary hands over their cudgels.

"Have to pay your tab somehow," said the barkeep.

The Fool General smirked to himself — this was going to be interesting. "Allow me to show you how it works," he sauntered to the bar, "it's a puzzle box, you see," he spoke to the entire crowd, whose attention he'd earned in full, a thespian at heart, "and quite the divination device, might I add. Easily misused in the wrong hands, if you take my meaning."

The barkeep shrank back, as if beginning to doubt the weird guest's intentions. "We have no need for black magic here...."

Pierrot's smirk only widened. "Oh, don't be such a baby. Here, let me show you." He fidgeted with its sliding pieces and mechanisms to trick the barkeep into a false sense of security. "See? It's like a zodiac. No different than a clock tower. And then," with a flick of the wrist, he tossed it in the air — only for it to float upon the palm of its hand, "oops...."

It was partly intentional.

Inch by inch, the five pieces, miniature pyramids that composed the eldritch whole, broke away and began to orbit one another in a cyclone of black wind. One by one, the candles were extinguished, and the hearth had died. Trampling each other in sudden darkness, the patrons' shouts turned to screams as lurking things emerged to feed. And yet, amidst the unseen slaughter, Pierrot's senses were elsewhere upon activating the device.

Something spoke to him, though it had no need of language.

"Oh," Pierrot thought, "hello there...."

He knew what it was, and it recognized him in kind. He had the Conqueror Worm's undivided attention. Stranger still, his surroundings warped into a facsimile of flaming ruin, the likes of which he'd yearned to witness. The floorboards seemed but an illusion to him, the heavens were devoid of starlight, the anchors of reality—food, drink, and "pleasure" company, mere ash before the truth of things. This was a meaningless house. A house that would not be missed, unworthy of thought or anger. Pierrot hesitated in the presence of the Conqueror Worm. The entity had hardly noticed the violence he so passionately dealt, though it shared in his misanthropy in a manner as placid as the moonless tide. If Pierrot were to earn his aspiring role, he would cease this wanton destruction and seek out bigger, better game—ages, saints, the flow of time itself. And yet, as he stood on the precipice of epiphany, he was siphoned back to the massacre's aftermath in a surge of cosmic suction. Reeling and nauseous, a rarity for him, Pierrot grasped at the bar and gagged, hardly primed to stomach the rotgut so common in these parts. The lingering image in his mind's eye was a castle aloft a wooded hill—one of which he'd read of in almanacs of mongrel provinces.

Schloss Fleischberg, in the Barony of Grünewald.

Pierrot lingered upon the threshold of dreams and reality. The Malachite Pyramid in his hands was more than a key; it was a relic of abominable truths. With it, he would find where the Conqueror Worm slept and stirred it in its age-long slumber. Treading over the dead, he emerged onto the Old Road and eyed the tattered spires of a nearby keep. Within the bleak hold, the Thing in the Pit lured him with unspoken promises of ruin, should the Fool General surrender his will to a scheme millennia in the making. His lips curled into a devious smile.

"Sir," a beggar broke the silence, "are you....?"

"Am I what?" Pierrot snapped. "Speak quickly, fool."

"Are you," he slurred, lips drooping, "God?"

Pierrot looked upon the ragged old man—dead eyes and bleeding gums, he could barely grasp his own staff, a vagrant who sought charity from passersby. Insane as he was, the waste of air would surely die regardless of Pierrot's answer. In the wake of this massacre, few would dare stop at the inn, thinking it cursed or worse. Stifling a wicked laugh, Pierrot tossed a token copper into the beggar's cup and followed the worn signage towards the village of Altstadt, where he caught wind of vile darkness. It was not until an armored caravan emerged from these mists that Pierrot's fortunes began to change, recognizing its Vermillion heraldry. Thorough as he'd been with the coup, for all the soldiers knew the Sun King yet lived. A lie he'd be inclined to let them believe — for now. Flashing a lantern in faux urgency, he watched the caravan come to a halt. Little introduction was needed, for the Fool General's letters and demeanor did the talking, nor did they question him. And so, Pierrot schemed once more, having a wagon full of cannon fodder. Only a limerick lingered in his thoughts, looping in an endless spiral.

That play is the tragedy, 'Man,' and its hero, the Conqueror Worm.

THE END

Diagnosed with Asperger's Syndrome at a young age, Fallon O'Neill has been writing since his sophomore year of high school. These scribblings and vignettes would eventually become the earliest drafts of his debut novel, *Geist: Prelude*. Dedicated and passionate, Fallon has worked his novels with the Blue Moon Writers' Group for over seven years, culminating in winning second place at the *Will Albrecht Young Writers Competition* of 2012, and publication in the eighth issue of the *Blue Moon Art and Literary Review*. His favorite pastimes include grabbing a beer (or four) at the local bar, blasting soundtracks into his skull, and watching German movies from the '20s to keep the existential dread at bay.